ALSO BY SAM BAKER

Fashion Victim

deadly
beautiful

deadly beautiful

A NOVEL

SAM BAKER

BALLANTINE BOOKS. NEW YORK

Copyright © 2008 by Sam Baker

All rights reserved.

Published in the United States by Ballantine Books, an imprint of The Random House Publishing Group, a division of Random House, Inc., New York.

BALLANTINE and colophon are registered trademarks of Random House, Inc.

Published in the United Kingdom as *This Year's Model* by Orion Books, London.

Baker, Sam.
  Deadly beautiful : a novel / Sam Baker
     p. cm.
  ISBN 978-0-345-47590-9 (acid-free paper)
1. Women journalists—Fiction. 2. Models (Persons)—Fiction. 3. Serial murderers—Fiction. 4. Americans—Japan—Fiction. 5. Tokyo (Japan)—Fiction. I. Title.

  PR6102.A574D43 2008
  823'.92—dc22

                              2008005254

Printed in the United States of America on acid-free paper

www.ballantinebooks.com

9 8 7 6 5 4 3 2 1

First U.S. Edition

Book design by Liz Cosgrove

For my boys, Jon and Jamie

acknowledgments

There was a moment writing *Deadly Beautiful* that brought new meaning to the phrase *difficult second novel,* and there are two people without whom this show would have been "standing tickets only" for me. My agent, Jonny Geller, whose tolerance, stamina, and ability to say, "For crying out loud, get on with it" to all concerned kept this show on the road. And my husband (and editor-indoors), Jon Courtenay Grimwood. Jon—both Annie and I would be a lot worse off without you.

Thanks to Team America, my U.S. agent Emma Parry, and editor Signe Pike, who inherited the project from her predecessor and never once made it feel like last season's It Bag.

Hannah Vere and Jonathan Whitelocke for much-needed illustration inspiration for the UK cover. Oonagh Brennan, Shelly Vella, and Nicola Rose, whose sense of humor, stupid shoes, and exaggerated hand gestures (Nicola!) got me through many eighteen-hour days at the New York, Milan, and Paris shows. Karen at Caffè Nero in Winchester who turned a blind eye to our setting up permanent camp with our laptops at the table in the corner every weekend.

The staff at Hotel Cala Sant Vicenç in Majorca, for their patience, endless refreshments, and not complaining when they tripped over laptop wires. All the models, fashion directors, and photographers who shared their Milan and Tokyo stories with me; with particular thanks to those who trusted me with their experiences hostessing in Shinjuku, Akasaka, and Roppongi. Last, but not least, thanks to my mum and dad who manage to take the news of every outlandish new idea/job change/project with—if not a smile—good-natured tolerance!

deadly
beautiful

prologue

The limousine slid to a halt under a patch of bluish light. All the street-lights in Tokyo were the same cold blue. At least they were in this part of the city.

As the young woman waited, the limo's front window slid down.

"Konbanwa," said a voice.

Good evening.

The man was well dressed and his suit obviously expensive. He had that slightly strange orange hair some Japanese men go for. *Chapatsu,* she thought. That was the term for it.

"Konbanwa," she replied.

Leaning forward, he clicked a button on the dash and one of the car's rear doors swung open to show her black leather seats inside. A bunch of orchids lay on the backseat. He had music playing. Something she vaguely recognized.

"Harajuku Girls"—Gwen Stefani.

Maybe it was a joke.

As the blond girl began walking, the car started up again. The puddles of light faded to darkness and back, marking her progress along the alley. She could hear other music from a pachinko parlor. The arcades were sup-posed to close at midnight. Somehow, the ones around here always found a way to stay open.

"Come on," he said.

The blond girl hesitated.

Glancing around, she saw she was alone.

Tourists thronged a street running parallel. She could see their faces through a gap between a garage and the side of a restaurant. The gap was blocked with plastic sacks of garbage waiting for the morning collection. She could see their faces, but that did not mean they could see her.

As she walked, the limousine kept pace. The man inside was leaning over now, looking worried. He clearly felt she should have accepted his invitation.

"Please," he said. "Get in."

Should I?

Problem was she already knew the answer to that.

Soba noodles, thought the girl, as she passed the back window of a kitchen, her heels clicking on the lid of a drain. There were no sidewalks in this alley, only doors that fed directly onto the street, a couple of old motorcycles, and a truck piled high with orange cans of butane.

She knew this area well, its sounds and its smells. A clutch of narrow streets selling overpriced street food to executives and politicians searching for memories of a Tokyo that vanished when they were still boys.

As well as hole-in-the-wall taverns and noodle bars, there were expensive restaurants, an all-night pharmacy, a pizza joint run by a Korean, and a Vietnamese tattoo parlor that hadn't been open in all the months she'd been working here. Then there were the clubs.

At least twenty of them, usually on a third, fourth, or fifth floor. One was walled entirely with mirrors, another had red leather banquettes, and one featured a special room exclusively for VIPs. None really catered to tourists, but then few foreigners had the courage to brave the elevators that led into an older Japan altogether. She wasn't the only Western woman to work the clubs. Although she was one of the youngest.

Ahead of her stood a T-junction. One direction fed back to the little ladder of streets that made up this area; the other led to one of Tokyo's famous raised expressways. That was where they'd be heading.

"So," he said. "Are you getting in?"

She nodded, and reached for the already open door.

one

When Lou woke, Scarlett was sitting on the end of her bed, staring straight at her. Tangled blond hair spread like a halo, lit by a ray of light from the window outside. For a second, Lou thought she was looking at the cover of an album.

The album.

She knew the one. It had been everywhere, topping the charts on both sides of the Atlantic—and just about everywhere else—for months and months. Back in the 1980s, when that was still possible.

Winter Skies went from silver to gold to platinum, and then triple platinum, it was so successful. The defining album of the decade. An album no self-respecting member of the dinner-party-throwing classes could live without. The one with the face of a cherub on the cover. Eyes so blue they looked retouched, although they weren't. Lou's half sister, staring from the shelves of every supermarket and record store that had ever stocked a CD.

But it wasn't the album she saw, it was Scarlett herself. Except, of course, it wasn't anything of the sort. Scarlett had long since grown up and Lou was dreaming. A dream so real it stayed with Lou for the few seconds it took her to realize she was awake.

"Shit," she said.

And then said it again.

The last time Lou saw Scarlett in the flesh the child had been six, sitting on the end of a bed in Casa de la Torre, staring silently as Lou struggled awake. The only sounds had been the swish of a fan and a whirring beep from Scarlett's weird tin toy, a present from a Japanese photographer.

Tempers rose and tolerance plummeted in everyone who came within a hundred paces of the annoying toy robot. Only Scarlett loved it. She loved it so much she refused to be parted from the damn thing, even when sleepwalking.

As Lou rolled over, it sank into her jet-lagged brain that the beeping couldn't be coming from Scarlett's robot, because Scarlett wasn't there. It was Lou's mobile, vibrating frantically on the table by her bed. With her four A.M. head on, that could mean only one thing. Somebody had died.

Then Lou remembered she was in New York. In the Hotel Gansevoort, in Manhattan's Meatpacking District, holed up for the ready-to-wear fashion shows. No one was dead; it was just some idiot sub-editor forgetting that East Coast time was five hours behind London.

What for him was "nine A.M., and Lou McCartney didn't file her copy overnight. . . ," was for her "four A.M., and thanks to jet lag I've only just got to sleep."

Catching her mobile before it toppled from the table, Lou hit keys at random and watched the screen announce it was 3:52 A.M. Putting the phone to her ear, she snarled her name, before realizing the number on the screen didn't belong to her paper, her mother, a lover, or any one of a hundred acquaintances logged in its memory.

"Took your time answering . . ."

"Who is this?"

Male, not young, sure of himself.

"It's me," he said. "I've had the Tokyo embassy on the phone. Have you heard from Lettie? She's vanished."

It wasn't the words that made little blond hairs rise on Lou's arms, or the fact she'd snapped awake thinking of her half sister and now someone was talking about her. It was realizing who was on the other end of the phone.

Her father.

Rufus bloody Ulrich, industrialist.

A man who'd felt no need to contact her in twelve years. Then called out of the blue to see if she'd heard from someone she hadn't seen for the same length of time. Frankly, it was a shock he even knew her number.

"Why would I have heard from her?" she demanded. Even her inner brat knew that was ill advised. Unfortunately, Rufus brought out the worst in her.

He always had.

You'd think, she thought, *wouldn't you? That I might have tamed my childish resentment at being dumped, along with my mother, for newer and prettier models?*

But no.

I still hate the bastard.

"You're right, Luella," said Rufus, his tone implying anything but. "Your sister's missing, God knows where. Clearly, I should have known better than to assume you could be of use to anyone."

two

"Annie, it's Mother. I was thinking, what are you doing the weekend after next?" No *How was the flight? How's New York? Have you settled into your hotel? Are you still enjoying your job at the magazine?*

None of that.

Running her hand through her short dark hair, Annie Anderson, fashion features editor for *Handbag* magazine, wiped her fingers on the leg of her Topshop jeans, and then glanced around to check no one had noticed. They hadn't; she pretty much had the tent to herself.

It was September Fashion Week and the tents at Bryant Park were back up. The grass had been boarded over, the boards carpeted, and sets designed around a central catwalk, so that Annie had two rows of benches in front of her and half a dozen rows behind. The inside of the tent smelled of plastic and PVC. An industrial air-conditioning unit was fighting the heat somewhere in the background. It wasn't winning.

Get there early, Lou McCartney's text message had said.

So Annie was here, and her best friend wasn't. That was friends for you. Meanwhile, Annie had her mother to deal with.

"Mum," she said. "Sorry, what was that?"

"Your sister's coming over with the boys that Sunday, and your dad was saying how nice it was last time you came. Now you and Jane are getting on again."

That wasn't how Annie would put it. She'd reached an uneasy truce with her elder sister, brought about by need and her mother's nagging. Eventually, a quiet life became preferable to all other options.

"And you know how much Chris loves those boys . . . ," Annie's mother was saying. "It's such a pleasure to watch. . . ."

Isn't it about time you and Chris settled down and had babies?

The message wasn't even subtle.

Feeling her stomach knot, Annie glanced around, trying to square the familiar sound of her mother's voice with the fashion scene around her. A stuffy but sparsely populated tent, bank after bank of mostly vacant benches staring down at a PVC-covered catwalk, it was a million miles from her parents' small Hampshire town house.

"Didn't you say you'd be back from the shows in Milan that Saturday? So I was thinking that would work. Chris does eat lamb, doesn't he?"

"Yes, Mum," Annie sighed. "Chris eats everything." *He's such a boy.*

"Oh," added the voice, suddenly louder.

Here it comes, thought Annie.

"I almost forgot. . . . How could I forget?"

No, you didn't.

"Guess who I ran into on Saturday?"

"No idea," said Annie, softening it to, "Tell me."

"Tony Panton and his mum. They were coming out of the bank. He was down for the weekend and . . ."

Annie had stopped listening.

In her teens Annie had gone out with Tony Panton for five months. This was how long it took him to take her virginity, reveal the thug behind the smile, call her hysterical, sleep with one of her friends, send her roses, and rape her. She'd been seventeen and three days, the evening it happened.

She failed her A levels; he moved on to another girlfriend. All of it left Annie's parents wondering why their daughter wouldn't return his calls, answer his letters, or let him through the door.

The general consensus was that she'd treated Tony Panton rather badly.

Annie let everyone think what they wanted to think, because explaining what really happened would have been far worse. Anyway, she had applied for, and got, a place on a journalism course. It turned out to be the best thing that ever happened to her.

So much easier to look at life from the outside.

"Annie . . . Did you hear me?"

"Yes, Mother."

"And that's all right?"

"Sure . . ."

"Good," said Annie's mother. "I'm so pleased. Jane said you might not be grown up about it."

About what?

"Must go. Let me know about that weekend."

A click stopped Annie asking her question aloud.

It was 90 degrees in the shade, with a grumbling threat of a hurricane off the Florida coast, according to that morning's news. Outside in Midtown's Bryant Park, the sun was behind the skyline, but its heat persisted. Cloying, suffocating, and intense. The type to sap all sense of urgency. *Must see you,* said Lou's text. *Call me now,* said a voice mail from Ken Greenhouse, her ex-boss.

Annie and Lou had yet to meet. And she still had no idea what Ken wanted, because she hadn't bothered to return his call. *Ex.* Why did men have such trouble understanding that one little word?

Clutching the collar of her chiffon shirt, Annie flapped its edges to let cool air reach her skin. It was pointless. The air in the tent was sauna hot, and Annie's shirt stuck to a white-cotton camisole, which stuck to her skin.

On the plus side, unlike most of the fashion pack, she hadn't blown a month's salary on first deliveries from the Autumn/Winter collections, only to watch her investment turn rank with sweat.

Although June Chung's show should have started half an hour earlier, the tent was still barely half-full. Like a movie before the trailers, the lights were up, revealing row on row of empty benches, a long line of paper place cards resting on each. With a few exceptions, only the economy-class crowd had shown, too lacking in confidence to be really late.

Annie dreaded to think how hot it would get when security finally relented and lifted the red rope, letting in a pack of Standing Onlies who thronged the entrance on Sixth Avenue. That was without adding the front-row elite, almost all of whom had yet to appear.

Most were still propping up nearby hotel bars, clutching chilled glasses of champagne, safe in the knowledge that no designer would dare start without them. Well, not one who needed their approval as much as June Chung did.

Glancing around to check no one was watching, Annie tugged at the waistband of her sticky jeans. "Yuck." Sweat-drenched denim.

At least Rebecca Brooks, Annie's boss and editor in chief of *Handbag* magazine, wasn't there to see her screwing with *the rules.* Rebecca attended every A-list show, with a carefully selected number of B-list ones. Occasionally she even turned out for a newcomer not yet allocated a place in the alphabet. June Chung wasn't on any list, well, not as far as Rebecca Brooks was concerned.

Just hours into her new job Annie had received an e-mail laying the rules out. In the time she'd been with Rebecca they'd gained a weird logic. Annie knew what that meant. It meant fashion was infecting her with its strange laws and even stranger conventions.

- Never be early, but never, ever be show-stoppingly late.
- Never sit in a seat that's beneath your station or beneath that of your magazine—missing the show is better than back-row humiliation.
- Never be too kind to a fashion PR, they'll only take advantage.
- Never pay for dinner with a PR; always pay with a designer.
- Always wear the right designer to the right show, but never wear the "piece of the season," you're a fashion *editor,* not a fashion victim.
- Never, ever examine the contents of a goodie bag in public.

On and on went the list, for two pages, but Annie never could get more than a handful of them to stick. Perhaps the part of her brain set aside to obey random rules never developed. When Annie was six, her grandmother had posted an equally ridiculous set on the kitchen wall.

- Always wash your hands before eating.
- No pudding if you don't finish your main course.
- No seconds if you haven't eaten your vegetables.
- No leaving the table before everyone else has finished.

Annie had been no better at obeying those.

Sighing, she pushed damp tendrils of hair from her eyes. The tent was beginning to fill now, people showing their tickets to security at the door. Security during Fashion Week came well dressed, but overmuscled, and wired into Bluetooth headsets. Someone backstage fired up the music and Annie nodded. It was something middle of the road, safe. This was June Chung after all.

So where was Lou?

Even running on fashion time, Lou was late. And Lou was never late for anything; that was Annie's game. Usually Lou would have sent a text to apologize, but this obviously wasn't usual.

"Any chance of grabbing coffee?" Lou had asked on the phone that morning, her casual words offset by strangeness in her voice.

"'Fraid not until later," Annie replied. "I'm back-to-back with shows and appointments. But I'm off the hook straight after June Chung . . ."

"I've got ten minutes now," she added. "If you want to talk?"

"It's okay," said Lou. "I'm going to June Chung too. See you there."

Annie's best friend and ex-colleague from *The Post* hung up, leaving Annie with the feeling she'd just failed to keep her side of some unknown bargain.

Friendships.

Annie shrugged, feeling sweat run down her side. She was as bad at those as she was at long-term relationships, which was why she tried to avoid both. Somehow Lou and Chris, Lou's oldest friend (and Annie's new lover), had slipped under the wire.

Which reminded her, she'd promised to call him.

But it would be late in London and she didn't want to disturb him. An image of Chris's tousled brown head gave Annie a pang, whether of conscience or longing was hard to say.

"Oh, come on," someone shouted as the tent began to fill. "Show us the rock."

A TV reporter, her hair a patchwork of highlights and lowlights, was mike-out in front of a blond reality TV star who'd just come in. Cameras flashed and the blonde obligingly held up her left hand for the viewing public.

It's dog-eat-dog down there, thought Annie, as a photographer clambered over a seated woman to get a better angle on the engagement ring everyone was so keen to see. His arm swung back, but the seated woman's outraged shriek as his elbow connected with her temple vanished in the noise around them.

"Over here," he shouted, and the reality TV star turned on cue.

That was another good point about the third row, Annie decided. You didn't need life insurance to sit in it.

As Annie's watch hit 5:50 P.M., the rest of the front row began to arrive, fashion nobility fighting their way past the paparazzi. In among the "girls of the moment" Annie spotted a Hearst heiress and a couple of Lauders. The old *Sex and the City* cast were long gone, but there was space enough for a Desperate Housewife or an Ugly Betty.

It was not a TV star who emerged next, but one of the British fashion pack. She looked cool, calm, and collected, like a woman who'd just made the seamless transition from air-conditioned lobby to air-conditioned limo and had yet to feel the heat. Maybe that cool, calm, sweat-free confidence came automatically with a front-row ticket, Annie thought.

But where the hell was Lou?

Not for the first time, Annie flicked through the running order, fingers leaving damp prints on a dog-eared sheet of paper.

Bree O'Shaughnessey was closing the show.

Getting Bree to close was a coup for June Chung. It was also a surprise. The model was making only a handful of catwalk appearances, and word had it that Bree's basic turnout fee now topped $20,000. Though everyone knew the right designer could get any girl he or she wanted for a few well-chosen frocks, this didn't apply to Ms. Chung. Money had undoubtedly talked, because June Chung's frocks weren't top of anyone's lust list, let alone Bree's.

As lights dimmed, photographers scattered, and stagehands dragged a PVC covering from the runway, a slightly built blond woman, clutching a huge Mulberry bag, sprinted across the empty catwalk, leaving a trail of dusty prints in her wake.

It was Lou. Slim, what Annie would have called posh-looking, and effortlessly elegant—everything, in fact, that Annie was not.

"I'm sorry," said Lou. "I believe you're sitting in my place."

She was talking to a man who only seconds earlier had slid onto the bench next to Annie, despite Annie's protests. When the man ignored the invitation Lou waved in his face, Lou simply wedged herself next to Annie, pushing the impostor into a woman who sat on his far side. A Mexican wave of irritation rippled along Annie's bench, to be lost under the opening chords of an old Cowboy Junkies track.

"Gosh," Lou hissed. "Surely not prairie kitsch with an urban hippy twist?"

Annie raised her eyebrows and stared pointedly at the catwalk.

"And I'd put a tenner on florals," added Lou. "Sprigs probably. If I hadn't just spent twice that gridlocked in a cab on Sixth."

That was as close to an apology as Lou would get. So Annie nodded, watching as Lou pulled a crumpled notepad from her bag, flipped to a clean page, and began to sketch. Almost as rapidly as each model appeared on the catwalk, in a procession of printed ra-ra skirts and Stetsons, their images appeared on Lou's page. Her simple line drawings a sure sign of a seasoned fashion critic. It had to be something they taught you at fashion school, Annie decided. How to draw an outfit, any outfit, in five easy strokes—colors, prints, and texture reduced to simple notes.

Annie grinned as the words *Yee-ha!* appeared beside a sketch of a tiered chambray dress and suede, fringed vest.

The Cowboy Junkies segued into mid-period Elvis Costello, a track that Annie vaguely recognized but couldn't name.

"She's channeling *Little House on the Prairie*," Lou muttered. "It's enough to put you off cowboy boots for life."

Annie, who'd never been on them, would have said she couldn't agree more. Until Bree finally set one flawless foot on the catwalk. Then, suddenly,

Annie needed a pair of battered, brick-red cowboy boots more than anything else in the world. Glitter, auto-suggestion, good lights, and a carefully selected backing track, Annie told herself. That was all. And yet . . .

From the second Bree O'Shaughnessey appeared, the nineteen-year-old redhead owned that runway, stalking its length like a hunter, making the gangling, childlike stance of other newcomers, who wobbled on coltish legs, look like baby giraffes.

Bree's mere presence transformed June Chung's show from a drab me-too, in a season riddled with dull, prairie-inspired clothes with a hint of Navajo, into something that would dominate the next day's front page.

As Bree strode toward the paparazzi at the end of the catwalk, a dozen top fashion editors rewrote their conclusions about June Chung's latest collection, if not her entire career. Having done a flirtatious 360-degree turn for the paparazzi, Bree winked for the cameras, before holding it for five.

"Fuss about nothing," hissed Lou. "Models are like buses. There will be three more along in a minute."

To Annie this was just common sense. Coming from Lou, it was akin to blasphemy. Lou was the good cop in their friendship. Sarcasm was Annie's specialty.

Then it dawned on Annie how thrown together Lou's outfit appeared. This didn't mean much, because Lou had turned *thrown together* into an art form. But this evening's look was unintentional. In addition, the badly hidden shadows under Lou's eyes were more than just jet lag.

The models had barely done a lap of honor and the designer vanished backstage, before Lou was pushing her way along the row. "Come on," she said, not bothering to see if Annie was following. "I need a drink."

"I thought you needed to talk," said Annie, looking pointedly at her watch. "Ooh, an hour and a half ago."

"Ten and a half hours ago, actually," Lou said. "So another half hour won't . . . hurt. You're staying at 60 Thompson, aren't you? Let's go sit on their roof and chain-smoke." So briefly did Lou falter, that her unhappiness would have passed most people by.

"Okay," said Annie. "Let's do that."

three

Midtown was thick with people, its air a cloying mix of dust, humidity, and gasoline fumes. Inside, their cab was little better.

"Can you turn up the air-conditioning?" asked Annie, as she slumped against a ripped seat and felt the small of her back cling to its plastic through her shirt.

The look the driver threw in his rearview mirror displayed scorn for everything Annie might be: tourist, English, rich, uptown . . . you could delete as applicable. Those rich white women who swarmed over Manhattan, they were all the same.

"Lady," he said. "I already did."

"You all right?" Annie asked Lou, after they'd crawled twenty blocks in silence.

"Fine."

Annie tried again. "What have you been doing today?"

Lou shrugged. "Stuff for Ken, remember him?"

It was a rebuke and Annie knew it. Ken Greenhouse, news editor at *The Post* had been Annie's boss until six months ago. It was thanks to Ken that Annie got an undercover job on *Handbag,* part of an investigation into Mafia connections in the fashion industry. The trouble was nobody expected Annie to like working in magazines so much she'd decide to stay.

Like wasn't the word Annie would use, but it was preferable to examining her real reasons for taking up Rebecca Brooks's offer of a permanent position. Reasons Annie had trouble admitting, even to herself. The killing of fashion designer Mark Mailer and his girlfriend, model Patty Lang, had left her reluctant to trust herself undercover. She felt partially responsible

for their deaths, that was one reason. Plus, she wasn't thrilled about returning to a job that would take her away from the man who'd just moved
from Milan to take up residence in her bed, Chris Mahoney.

The silence that hovered above Lou and Annie was as suffocating as
the heat.

"How *is* Ken?" Annie asked finally.

Glancing across, Lou opened her mouth and then shut it again. Only
to answer anyway. "He's fine," she said. "In the circumstances. Still se-
verely pissed off with you, but who can blame him?"

That was no surprise. Annie's ex-boss made it clear what he thought of
Annie's decision to file the Mark Mailer and Patty Lang story, then take up
the fashion features editor job at *Handbag* magazine for real.

"Ken got his story," said Annie. "His global exclusive. Which I notice
the syndication department didn't waste any time cashing in on."

"Yeah," said Lou. "He got his story. And lost his best investigative reporter. Strangely, he's not too thrilled about that."

"Anyway," Annie said. "Why were you dealing with Ken? He's not your
boss."

This was true. Lou's department at *The London Post* was unaffection-
ately known to the rest of the paper as "women's interest." The stuff not
worth taking seriously.

"Well?"

Staring out of the cab as it passed the Barnes & Noble on Union Square
and headed south for Washington Square, Annie's friend didn't answer.

When Lou turned, Annie could see why.

Layers of Touché Éclat blended with smudged kohl to give Lou's eyes
a punched look, but what caught Annie's attention was the single tear
trickling down her friend's face.

"What is it?" asked Annie.

Reaching out, she felt goose bumps. It had to be 80 degrees in that cab
but her friend's arm was icy.

"Tell you later," said Lou.

She began to rummage in the large leather bag that rarely left her side.
It wasn't much of a diversionary tactic, but Annie let her get away with it
because the cab was finally drawing to a halt outside 60 Thompson.

As Annie was fumbling in her purse for dollars, Lou produced a carefully folded piece of white paper from the bottom of her bag. At first Annie
thought it had something to do with paying for the cab.

"Here's why I was talking to Ken," said Lou, as if fifteen minutes hadn't
gone by since Annie first asked her question.

Shoving a ten-dollar bill through the driver's window and forgetting to ask for a receipt, Annie glanced at the sheet Lou was holding. It was a black-and-white rough of the next morning's front page. *The London Post,* read the top. It was a Ken classic. The kind of page he loved and Annie had excelled in providing. A young woman stared from under two words in bold black type:

SUPERMODEL MISSING

For a second Annie's only thought was, no one still uses *supermodel*. Then she caught herself, appalled at how quickly her brain had embraced fashion speak.

"Lettie," announced Lou, as if that explained everything.

"Who?"

"My half sister."

Your what . . . ?

Annie could see it now. The face staring from the page bore a striking likeness to that of the woman standing next to her. It showed a younger, more classically attractive version of Lou.

"Bet it's a stunt," Lou said furiously. "Publicity-seeking little cow."

Then she burst into tears.

four

"My father was a modelizer before modelizers were invented."

These were the first words Lou spoke after ordering a large Jack Daniel's and Coke, and settling herself on a banquette ten minutes earlier. It was all Annie could do not to grab Lou by her shoulders and shake her.

How come, Annie wanted to yell, *you never said you had a sister?*

But recognizing the set of Lou's jaw, Annie knew better.

So she watched Lou fold and unfold the printout, eroding its picture and whatever text might still be legible.

The arrival of a waiter with drinks—large vodka for Annie, the larger Jack Daniel's for Lou—was enough to save what remained of the *Post's* front page. If Lou had a drink in her left hand, she needed a cigarette in her right; it was the social smoker in her.

Momentarily abandoning the fax, Lou rummaged in her bag for a pack of Marlboro Lights and a red plastic lighter. "Want one?"

Annie shook her head.

The tasteful rooftop ambience of 60 Thompson made it possible to hide without appearing to. But the flare of Lou's lighter emphasized the shadows that concealer could not hide. Lou was exhausted. Worse than that, she was . . . Annie struggled to put her finger on it.

Lou looked desolate.

A modelizer, thought Annie.

Someone who books models? Or maybe spots them and makes them famous? Annie waited for Lou to pick up where she left off, and waited some more. When she didn't, Annie decided to give her a nudge.

"Modelizer?"

Lou laughed. A laugh devoid of humor.

"*Annie!*" she said, loud enough for the cluster of the thin and beautiful at a nearby table to throw glances in her direction. "Really!"

"*Really, what?*"

"You've got to be the only woman in the Western Hemisphere who doesn't know what a modelizer is! What planet have you been on?"

"Lou . . ."

"Oh, of course," said Lou, forcing a smile. "I forgot . . . *planet Loooove.*"

Truth was, Lou was wrong on both counts. Annie had just remembered what a modelizer was, and she was finding planet Love a little claustrophobic. Not enough oxygen up there.

"You know," said Lou. "A *modelizer.* Also known as a sad bastard who only shags models. Although I'm not sure that's the *Oxford English Dictionary* definition. And, to be fair, at least my father marries them. Well, the fertile ones."

"Your father?"

"Rufus," said Lou. "Rufus Ulrich."

"Fucking hell!" Annie hadn't made the connection. "As in Ulrich Enterprises?"

In the five years they'd been friends Lou had never once mentioned her father. There had been no trace of his existence, no photographs in Lou's apartment, not a whiff of birthday presents bought or received. Lou talked about her mother and grandmother, sometimes more than was necessary, but never her father.

Only once had Annie asked. Lou had simply cut her off, saying her parents didn't get along. Annie let it go, because plenty of people had families whose existence they preferred to forget.

Take Annie's own, for a start.

Perfect, 2.4-kids. Sister, anxious mother, silent father.

As Lou told it, she was an only child, brought up by a single mother. Well, single if you discounted her grandmother, whose Wiltshire rectory both Lou and Lou's mother still called home. And if Rufus Ulrich married only . . .

"I didn't know your mother was a model," said Annie, realizing, as she spoke, that it was glaringly obvious. She'd seen photographs, even seen Lou's mother once, from a distance, when she came to drop something off at her friend's flat. With those looks, that wardrobe, the woman had to be.

"I'm sure you did . . . ," said Lou, lighting up a third Marlboro and inhaling deeply. "She was huge in the late sixties, early seventies. Then she met my fa— Met Rufus, got herself pregnant, and chucked it all in.

Babies weren't an it-accessory back then, you know. After a couple of years, he chucked her."

"Rough."

"Nina Mac. You must have heard the name."

Lou's mother was Nina Mac?

"Yeah," said Lou. "Sex, drugs, and the Rolling Stones. Parties with Mick and Brian and holidays in Marrakech. *That* Nina Mac."

"What happened?"

"Along came Rufus and hello nappies, good-bye multimillion-dollar career. She'd made a bit by then, of course. But once Nina lost her contracts, Rufus lost interest. That's how he works. Only ever interested in this year's top model. Same for Arabella."

Lou didn't give Annie time to ask who Arabella was.

"Not until later, of course. Arabella was number four. Not that I feel sorry for *her*. It was obvious to everyone what Rufus was like by then. She probably thought she could change him. They always do."

Draining her Jack Daniel's, Lou caught the eye of a waiter and signaled for the same again.

"Rufus left Arabella, just as he'd abandoned my mum. He didn't leave until Lettie was twelve, though. At least Scarlett *had* a dad."

Lettie = Scarlett?

Oh, God, thought Annie. *That* Scarlett.

"Yeah," said Lou, watching the pieces fall into place.

Annie could see the likeness. Lou had muddy blond hair and a posh girl's bone structure, both inherited from her mother. In place of Nina Mac's wide mouth, however, Lou had lips that thinned when she was angry. Instead of rich hazel, Lou's eyes were a striking blue, with lashes so fair she dyed them religiously every four weeks, never missing an appointment.

It was the eyes and mouth that tied Lou to *Supermodel Missing*.

Scarlett Ulrich had been huge when Annie was in her late teens. When Scarlett was six years old her face sold fifteen million albums, and for years, there had scarcely been a product that hadn't had her angelic gaze to thank for tripling its sales.

But in the last five years or so?

Annie realized she hadn't heard much about Scarlett for a while, not so much as a Z-list boyfriend, drug habit, or sudden interest in kabala. The halo of blond curls, the cherubic but enigmatic smile that had gazed from a thousand shop windows had disappeared from view. Leaving behind, if tomorrow's front page was to be believed, an averagely attractive young woman in her late teens.

Attractive, but not exceptional.

"My God," said Annie. "You and Scarlett Ulrich are sisters."

"Half sisters," Lou said. "She's the half that a good lawyer made sure wanted for nothing."

Annie was taken aback by the anger in Lou's voice, and by her own denseness. How could she have not known this about her best friend? Her best friend whose golden life had always made Annie's own childhood look so . . . so ordinary.

"I didn't even know you had a sister," said Annie.

"Half sister," insisted Lou. "And, according to tomorrow's *Post*, I might not even have that. Here," she said, thrusting the folded piece of paper at Annie. "Read it. The rest of the world will in six hours, when it hits the newsstands."

The words were stark, the style punchy, the important facts given first. *Layer it from the top*, Ken Greenhouse always said. *Because less than half your readers are going to get past that first paragraph, and of those that do, few will get beyond the second.*

The core of the story was simple. Scarlett Ulrich, whose face had been one of the defining images of the nineties, had disappeared in Tokyo. Her father was offering a $1,000,000 reward for information leading to her return.

"I haven't seen Scarlett in years," said Lou. "Ten, no, twelve. Why would I? Haven't seen Rufus either. I didn't even know he had my bloody mobile number, until he phoned in at four o'clock this morning, like we only spoke yesterday! For all he knew I'm married with three kids, a dog, and two gerbils. And he expects me to drop everything and use my contacts to find out what's happened. 'Cause I work on a paper, so obviously I'll know how to do that."

"What did you say?"

"I told him to hire a bloody detective."

Annie and Lou had gotten tipsy together a hundred times before. But Annie knew this time Lou was drinking to bolster her courage. How else could she force herself to ask the questions that must be haunting her?

Why would someone pick Scarlett? Shouldn't there be a ransom note by now? What chance do you think there is of her still being alive?

"What happened to the name?" Annie asked, as much to keep Lou talking as anything else. "If Rufus Ulrich is your father, why not use his name?"

Anger lit Lou's eyes.

"Why would I want it?" she demanded, louder than necessary. "Nina ditched it when he ditched her, and she was right. I've used McCartney since my first day at school and that's the way it's going to stay."

"So you're saying being Nina Mac's kid made life easier than it would have been as an Ulrich?"

"Yeah." Lou nodded. "Nina's led a quiet life for years. Occasionally some hack comes knocking at the rectory, wanting to know about her wild teenage years, but she's been minding her own business for so long, no one's interested anymore. Rufus, on the other hand, thinks he's Donald Trump. Nina was his first model and there've been so many since, you have to dig deep to come up with me."

Narrowing her eyes, Lou focused on Annie through a smoky haze. "I wouldn't want the link to become public knowledge."

Annie gave a you-can-count-on-me nod.

A gesture usually reserved for case studies, not friends. But Annie wasn't being told as a friend. Well, only partially.

She was also here because Lou needed someone she could ask those difficult questions.

five

The next day passed in a blur of shows, and Annie saw her friend mostly from a distance, across crowded tents. And once, in passing, when Annie was leaving the bar at the Gramercy Park Hotel and Lou was arriving.

Lou didn't look much better.

It might be a hangover from the night before, although Annie doubted that. The redness around Lou's eyes looked more like tears to her. Pretty weird, for someone who claimed not even to like the missing model.

"You get Chris's message?"

"No," said Annie.

"Probably at your hotel." Lou hesitated, as if about to say more. In the end, all she added was "Still all right for tomorrow?"

"Of course," said Annie, and then remembered what Lou had in mind. "If you're sure it's a good idea . . ."

"Of course I'm not fucking sure."

"Lou . . ."

"See you then."

"Yeah," said Annie. "See you then."

Apparently, Rebecca Brooks's continuing fight with her Manhattanite ex-husband over custody of their four-year-old son was entering a new and dangerous phase. That was why Rebecca had missed the afternoon shows, leaving Annie to attend them with Iona Miller, *Handbag*'s fashion director. But Rebecca was still attending a supper with Mariolina Mantolini, who was opening her first shop in New York on Madison.

The Rupert Wars, Iona called them. Rebecca's fashion director made it obvious she couldn't quite work out why her boss would employ an ex-tabloid journalist on a magazine like *Handbag*.

Iona was also invited to the supper with Mariolina. That left Annie to amuse herself. Iona's words.

"There's always that event at Parsons," she said, mentioning New York's equivalent of London's College of Fashion. "*Someone* should cover it."

"So there is," Annie said.

They both knew that someone wouldn't be Annie.

It was eight o'clock before Annie got back to 60 Thompson, and over-spill from Kittichai, the ground-floor restaurant, filled the entrance. A man looked around, and then looked away. Annie wasn't blond, she wasn't size zero, and she wasn't sixteen.

Therefore, he wasn't interested.

Pushing her way between two women discussing that day's shows, Annie avoided the elevators and took the stairs to the reception area. The lobby bar was heaving, but not as bad as the bar through the swinging doors ahead. That was so busy the noise came in waves everytime some-one opened a door.

Three receptionists waited behind the desk.

"Any messages?" asked Annie.

And you are . . . ? The question might as well have been tattooed across the nearest woman's face.

"Annie Anderson," said Annie. She gave her room number, and then her magazine when the woman said nothing.

"Don't think so."

"Perhaps you could check?"

The receptionist was right; Annie Anderson had no messages.

Stepping into the elevator, Annie traveled up with two young women who kept glancing at her jeans. Both were young, both thin enough to bring out Annie's inner mother. All right, Annie might be size 8, maybe 6 if she had the flu, and the jeans were Topshop, but Topshop, Oxford Cir-cus, was the most fashionable store in the world. Hadn't anyone told them?

The message was in her room.

Sitting on a small table in a hideous glass vase. Annie just didn't know how to read it. Chris knew she hated roses, red ones worst of all. And where was his note? Surely the U.S. equivalent of Interflora sent little cards when it delivered flowers.

No note hung from the roses.

And no note rested on the table beside them.

It was only as Annie turned away from the table that she saw a business card tucked under the vase. Okay, that made more sense. A designer, maybe. Someone who hadn't given her good enough seats . . .

Except designers would send the flowers to Rebecca, and nothing this cliché. Anyway, no one would dare give Annie bad seats. *Handbag* magazine had an entire department, headed up by the executive fashion editor, to ensure that just wouldn't happen.

Any PRs reckless enough to try to put one past the executive fashion editor would find themselves dealing with Rebecca Brooks herself.

Picking up the card, Annie was preparing to trash it when she saw the name.

Anthony Panton
CEO Aprilez-Houston

Tiny hairs rose on her forearms and sweat beaded the back of her neck. She couldn't breathe, except that was ridiculous. Annie felt as if someone had punched her. No, she felt as if someone was *about* to punch her and that was worse. Her whole body was tensing around a knot in her stomach.

She wanted to call Lou, say get yourself over here. Only Lou had her own problems. Anyway, Annie had never told Lou about Tony Panton. Until the night she drank her defenses down far enough to tell Chris, she'd never told anyone. So how could Annie complain that Lou hadn't told her about Rufus, or the fact that her sister was Scarlett Ulrich?

Sorry, *half* sister.

The bit of Annie that didn't want to call Lou wanted to crawl to the bathroom and throw up every meal she'd eaten in the ten years since she last saw Tony. Only she was over that. Really, she was. She was strong enough to face down her demons. Chris said so.

"Reception?"

A blast of noise from the lobby bar drowned out the answer.

"There are flowers in my room."

"Ma'am?"

"Get someone up here to remove them."

A different voice came on the phone. A man. "Ms. Anderson," he said. "The flowers were delivered in person. Seemingly, your friend was insistent. . . ."

"I'm allergic to roses," Annie said.

Of course you are, said his brief silence. *This is Fashion Week. We have guests who are allergic to daylight, the wrong mineral water, rooms with windows that don't point east, and pillows that aren't stuffed with goose down. Of course you're allergic to roses.*

"I'll have them removed immediately."

"Thank you," Annie said, replacing the hotel phone in its cradle.

Half an hour later, the phone rang. Annie felt inclined to let the desk take a message, but it might be Rebecca, although why her editor would be . . .

"Annie Anderson," she said.

"Long time no speak."

She put the receiver down so fast it almost broke.

A second later, it buzzed again and the knot in her stomach tied itself tighter. *Ignore it,* she told herself. Only the phone kept going. The more it rang, the angrier she got. Not with him, but with herself.

"Yes?" she said.

"Annie," said the voice. "Thought I'd lost you."

You never had me. At least, not in any way that mattered.

Except he did. A month of being besotted with Tony Panton turned into a couple of months of thinking he didn't mean it, and four months of knowing he meant every insult and put-down. Just as he'd meant every second of a parting fuck that left her bruised, in tears, and bleeding.

He was her first, for Christ's sake.

"What do you want?"

"Hey," he said, sounding hurt. Tony Panton was good at that. Sounding hurt, sounding charming, sounding rational. "Didn't you get my message?"

"The roses?"

"The text. I left it on your mobile."

He didn't have her number. . . . Except he did. Annie's mother had given it to him six months earlier. Another cause for a family argument.

Flipping open her mobile, Annie checked.

Supper? Somewhere nice. Just for old time's sake? T Like she would know who *T* was, even if she'd read his message, which she hadn't.

"I'm busy."

"Annie," he said. "The table's booked. I'm in the lobby. I've got a car waiting outside."

"A limousine?"

"Yes," said Tony. "How did you know?"

As if he'd use anything sensible like a yellow cab, or even a Lincoln town car. Then Annie registered the bit that mattered. In the lobby . . . ?

"You came to my hotel?"

Annie could barely contain the fury that propelled her down seven flights of stairs and into the night. Fury, desire for revenge, ten years of pent-up hatred and resentment . . . Whatever she wanted to call it, her emotions had a funny way of making her do the exact opposite of what was sensible.

Even as she slid into the car beside him, she knew the best thing she could do was slap him hard and walk away. But she didn't. Because Tony Panton wouldn't be here if he didn't want something and Annie wanted to know what that something was. Besides, she'd never done what was sensible where he was concerned.

"Limousine?" she said, voice mocking.

"Annie," said Tony. "I was picking you up for supper. Of course I hired a limousine." His own voice was reasonable. So reasonable Annie wanted to slap him anyway. Annie could see his driver glance in the mirror, checking this madwoman out.

Around them Manhattan slid past as the limousine headed northwest toward Pastis. As Pastis was opposite Lou's hotel, Annie figured she could always bail out of the restaurant and take refuge with Lou if worst came to worst.

Grow up, she told herself. The worst had come and gone. She was older now, in control. She was Annie Anderson, award-winning journalist, on staff at one of the world's most famous magazines. She wanted him to see what she'd become. Wanted to prove Chris right when he told her she could face down her demons.

"So," she said. "You married?"

"Why? You offering?"

"Hardly. Just wondered."

Whose life you're making a misery these days.

"Five years," said Tony. "Two kids, both lovely." He sighed. "We're wrapping it up, though. Still good friends, but it's just not working. You know how it is. . . ."

Actually, she didn't.

"All this travel," he said. "I dread to think what my carbon footprint looks like."

Tony Panton, worrying about global warming? The last time they met, he'd been wondering if he could trade his Golf GTI for a Lotus Élan.

"Sorry," she said, "to hear that." Mostly she said it for something to say.

"It happens," he said, and shrugged.

The harassed woman at the door of Pastis nodded, glanced at a notebook, and began heading for a table. She'd almost reached it when she realized the man in the lightweight silk suit wasn't following. He was standing by the entrance and shaking his head, only not quite enough to disturb his expensively cut hair.

Money and Tony Panton obviously agreed with each other.

"A corner table," he said, when she returned.

"We haven't . . ."

"I specified a corner table."

"It looks fine to me," Annie said hastily.

Tony looked at her, something amused in his eyes. "If the lady likes it," he said, pushing past the woman from the door.

They had champagne. French, rather than Californian, because Tony insisted. Then he ordered steak, medium rare, with dauphinoise potatoes. While Annie ordered a tuna salad to push around her plate.

"You like it here?"

"It'll do."

Tony Panton smiled. "Annie Anderson, the never impressed. You must fit in well. . . ."

"Where?" asked Annie.

"At *Handbag* magazine. Isn't being cool what it's all about?"

Annie didn't bother to say that some days being needlessly impressed seemed to be what half the people around her did best. Mostly by themselves.

"So," she said. "Tell me why we're here." For one horrible moment Annie thought her ex-boyfriend was about to lean across the table and try to take her hand. Maybe something showed in her eyes, because instead he leaned back.

"I just thought . . . "

"You thought what?"

"We should meet." Tony took a deep breath. "I wanted to apologize."

"For what?"

"You know," he said.

"No," said Annie. "I don't. Tell me."

"For the way we ended. For the fact we parted enemies. I never meant to hurt you."

"You raped me, remember?"

At the next table, two bridge and tunnelers stopped trying to impress a blond English fashion journalist and glanced over. The woman was famously vegetarian. So offering to share their lobster was never going to get them far anyway.

"Annie . . ."

"Didn't you?" Annie kept her voice low. But she said it. She'd waited a long time to say those words to his face.

"We'd had rough sex before."

"Not like that," said Annie. "And I hated it then, too."

"How was I to know?"

"The tears," she said. "They should have been a clue." Annie was pushing back her chair before she realized it.

"Please," said Tony.

She felt about seventeen. And stupid, for believing anything could change. When she returned from the bathroom, it was with water splashed on her face. Sitting, Annie emptied her glass in one gulp.

"Feeling better?"

"What do you think?"

Tony Panton sighed. "I ran into your mother."

"Coming out of the bank," said Annie. "She told me."

"She asked what I was doing these days. So I told her I was in New York next week."

And she said, So's Annie.

"This wasn't her idea?"

The man opposite Annie looked shocked. "Of course not. But . . ."

Annie didn't bother to listen to the rest. She was putting the pieces together. Remembering her mother's comment about Jane being worried that Annie might not be grown up about it.

"You mentioned it might be nice if we met?"

"Yes," said Tony.

Fucking families.

She could sit here and make conversation or leave. Leaving would be embarrassing. Staying would be hypocritical. And she couldn't eat the tuna that had just been put in front of her anyway. Not without throwing it back up again.

six

What was that about? Annie wondered, as she edged her way between two huge motorbikes. She moved carefully, because the bikes' owners sat outside a BBQ bar watching her. The Harleys were so big, red, and phallic, she felt like kicking them.

Unless that was just being drunk.

What was that about? Because it was about something.

Noise came from the Hotel Gansevoort, but Annie ignored it. Her backup plan of escaping to Lou's hotel remained just that. Annie didn't need to escape anywhere. She'd simply pushed back her chair and made for the street. From the look on the face of the woman at the door, one person at least didn't blame her.

Walking east, Annie cut through the Meatpacking District until she hit Bleecker, and then kept east until she reached the streets north of her own hotel. As Annie walked, she picked apart her evening.

Slick suit, slick haircut, same knowing smile. All the things that attracted her the first time around. All the things that should have warned her Tony Panton was dangerous. Her first thought was obvious.

He'd wanted to get her into bed, and dinner was his less than subtle way of leading up to that. Tony Panton was twisted enough to think she'd agree. Annie didn't doubt that for a second. He'd never been a man to underestimate his own attraction.

Only why now? And why here in New York? And why . . . ? Any of the hundred other questions that fed off the first one. Old time's sake indeed . . . Pulling her mobile from her pocket, she dialed a number from memory.

"Eddie Silver?"

"Who else?" It was a snippy voice that went well with the man it belonged to.

"It's Annie," she said. "Annie Anderson."

"Thought you'd gone posh on us, love . . ."

"Get that from Ken?"

"Might have done."

So, Ken was still using private detectives. Annie was glad to discover her ex-boss hadn't let the fact that another editor nearly went to jail for using PIs stand in his way. "I need a favor," said Annie.

"This for your posh magazine?"

"No," said Annie.

"For Ken, then?" asked Eddie, sounding more interested.

"Not him either," she said. "It's for me."

"My . . ." Eddie laughed. "We are living dangerously." He obviously didn't believe it was for her at all. "So, what can I do you for?"

"Anthony Panton. CEO of something called Aprilez-Houston. Think they're management consultants. He's getting divorced."

"Annie," said Eddie, sounding hurt. "I don't do divorce work. You know that. Too much competition and not enough pay. I can give you some numbers. . . ."

"Just hear me out," Annie said.

Eddie Silver did.

"What you're saying," said Eddie, "is you want to know what's in the papers his wife's solicitor has filed? And you want to know if the solicitor has back up allegations in reserve?"

"Yes."

"That's illegal."

"Eddie," said Annie. "Why do you think I'm calling you?"

The price Eddie named was twice what she expected to pay. Although he assured her it was a special rate. This made Annie wonder what he usually charged. She'd never paid the bill herself before.

"Where are you, anyway?" he asked. "It sounds like on TV."

"I'm in New York."

"And this Mr. Panton. Is he in New York also?"

"Yes," said Annie, and could almost hear Eddie wish he'd doubled his price.

"Call you tomorrow," he said. "Maybe the day after."

"Eddie."

"Yeah," he said. "I know, love. . . . It's urgent. It always is."

. . .

Perhaps Annie only imagined the man at the door of 60 Thompson glanced at her strangely. It had been a long night. And from the crowd spilling out onto his sidewalk, it was going to be a longer night for him than it was for her.

As Annie made for the elevator, the two models who'd checked her jeans so closely the time before overtook her and positioned themselves on either side of an elevator door. No way was she taking a ride with them again.

"Vodka tonic," said Annie, when she reached the lobby bar.

A waiter nodded.

Behind the reception desk, the man who'd arranged to have the roses removed from Annie's room looked across and then slid his gaze over Annie's shoulder to someone behind.

Englishwoman, said his gaze. *Not even that attractive. What gives?* Unless she imagined that too.

Turning, Annie found herself staring at a tousle-headed man wearing a suit that looked as if he'd slept in it, which he probably had. "What are you doing here?"

It wasn't the most tactful thing she could have said.

"Bad day?" asked Chris.

"Something like that . . ."

He smiled sympathetically. "Saw Rebecca," he said. "And Iona, at the Mariolina opening. Shame you didn't come. Iona said you were going to Parsons. Was it that terrible?"

"Didn't go," said Annie. "What are you doing here?"

"Annie."

"You're meant to be in London."

Something flicked across his face. "Thought I'd surprise you," said Chris, his voice neutral. "Mariolina Mantolini's asked me to handle her British press. She suggested I attend the opening of her first New York store. As you were here . . ."

"You jumped on a plane?"

He nodded. "It's only for one night."

Annie took a deep breath. "So," she said, "have you taken your stuff up to the room?"

"No," he said. "They wouldn't let me."

She'd missed the part where she congratulated him on winning the Mantolini account. That was the problem with Chris. He couldn't play poker to save his life, everything showed in his eyes.

"Good about Mariolina."

"Yeah," he said. "I thought so."

Oh, God, now he was sulking. "We'd better get you a key card," said Annie, reaching over to take a glass from the waiter she'd seen when she first came in. "Here, have this."

At the desk, the man gave Annie a second card. He didn't say, *How were we to know this one was your boyfriend?* He didn't need to. Annie was saying it for him inside her head.

"So," said Chris, picking up his suitcase. "Where have you been?"

"Walking."

"Just that?"

"Yes," Annie said.

He scowled at her. Chris hadn't done that before, but then she hadn't lied to him before either. Well, maybe about the price of a pair of shoes. Not something like this. They had a rule against lying. She'd known it was a stupid idea when he suggested it.

"I went out."

"Yeah," said Chris. "You've done that bit."

Annie shut her eyes. *Come on*, she told herself. Get into an elevator before this explodes in front of most of London's fashion crowd.

"Annie?"

"Not here," she said.

"Not here what?"

"I'm not having a fight here."

"Is that what we're going to have?"

"I don't know," said Annie. "You tell me."

The elevator arrived before he could answer. A jumble of the self-consciously hip spilled into the lobby bar. Two models, a journalist, and a man in a black silk suit who couldn't keep his eyes off one of the models, the youngest obviously.

"Going down," said the only person remaining.

"We'll take it anyway," said Annie, stepping inside.

At the lower lobby, the remaining woman got out and Annie fumbled her own room card, fed it into a slot, and hit the button for her floor.

"All right," said Chris. "Tell me."

"It's no big deal," Annie said. "I ran into someone I knew."

"Really?"

Yeah, really.

That was what she should have said. Only she and Chris had that stupid agreement about honesty, and if she lied about this, what would she lie about in the years to come? Anyway, she'd hesitated too long.

"Tony turned up."

Opening his mouth to ask, *Tony who?* Chris shut it again. "You went out with *Tony Panton?*"

"Yes," said Annie.

Chris punched the elevator wall.

"Don't," Annie said.

"Why not?"

Because Tony used to behave like that.

"Just don't," she said.

A group of people Annie vaguely recognized parted to let Chris and her through when the elevator door opened at her floor. If one of them glanced at his hand, that was because his knuckles were bleeding.

Here it comes, thought Annie, as Chris opened the door with his card and coldly motioned her into her own room. But he just walked into the bathroom and thrust his hand under the cold tap. Although Annie caught the moment his gaze fastened on her bed. It was rumpled, just not enough for what he was imagining.

"Let me get this straight," said Chris, drying his fist on a towel. "You went out for a cozy supper with the man you told me you hated more than anyone else in the world. A man you said you never wanted to see again. A man who raped you?"

"It wasn't like that."

"Wasn't it?"

"No," said Annie furiously. "He wanted something from me."

"Yeah. I bet he did."

"Look," Annie said. "He just turned up."

"How did he know your hotel address? Come to that, how did he know you were in New York at all?"

"My mother told him."

"He told you that?"

"Yes," Annie said. "Well, she did too. When we talked yesterday."

"So he didn't just turn up after all."

"Believe what you like," said Annie. "Tony sent a text message, only I didn't read it and—if I had—I wouldn't have known it was from him. Then he had roses delivered, and turned up with a limo. . . ."

"Tony Panton sent roses to this room?"

"Yes," said Annie.

"Well," Chris said coldly. "I'm not surprised the desk clerk wouldn't let me bring my luggage up here."

"Listen to me, will you . . . ?"

Only he'd picked up his suitcase by then. Pulling the key card that reception had finally given him from his wallet, Chris placed it carefully on the tiny dressing table next to the minibar. "We can talk in London." His voice was clipped. More English than she remembered.

"No you don't," Annie said. "You can't just walk out of here."

"Watch me."

When Chris shifted Annie out of the way, he might as well have been moving a piece of furniture. That was what really hurt. If Chris minded Annie slamming the door behind him it wasn't enough to turn around and call her on it.

The room was small. Chic, probably covered it. A closet, chest of drawers, television, CD player, walk-in shower done out in fake brown marble. An air-conditioning unit that spent the day fighting New York's heat and now sounded as if it was trying to recover.

As for her bed, it was big enough. But she couldn't forget the way Chris had glanced at it on his way into her room. She'd gone through anger into a cold fury that she didn't recognize. Tears were more her style, tears and shouting. It was one reason she kept herself on such a tight leash. She didn't like it when her inner teenager appeared.

This was different.

She hated Tony, that was a given. She'd wasted a good ten years of her life doing that. But Chris was meant to understand. Annie wasn't stupid. She knew Chris had taken on the anger she felt for Tony Panton.

All the same . . . She'd trusted him. He was supposed to understand.

Local news on New York One. A couple of films she'd seen before, more than once. A drama in Spanish that looked cabled in from Mexico, unless it was Miami. A couple of cartoons. A local access channel, broadcasting the cable program for the evening.

Annie fell asleep to *The Simpsons* and awoke in an eerie glow that lit her room and cast shadows on the wall above her bed. Either she'd escaped a hangover, or it had yet to kick in.

Phone. Then she thought, *He's alone at the airport, waiting for his plane. Glad he cracked first* . . . It was only as she flipped open her mobile that the warm feeling vanished. She'd remembered why they quarreled in the first place.

"Chris . . . ?"

"No," said a voice. "It's Eddie."

Ah yes, Ken's private detective.

"Eddie," she said. "It's . . ."

"Ten in the morning at this end, love . . . And I've been busy on your behalf. Very busy." He was waiting for something.

After a second, Annie remembered to thank him.

"So," he said. "How did you know it was going to be messy?"

"Eddie . . ."

"I'm just interested."

"Sources." Annie said it from instinct.

He laughed. "Okay," said Eddie. "First off, we've got mental cruelty. Unreasonable behavior. Infidelity . . . The usual."

"This is the stuff that's been filed with the court?"

"Yeah. So far."

"And what's held in reserve?"

"Assault, rape, sodomy, sexual violence . . . " He paused. "Is that what you were expecting?"

Yeah, exactly what she expected. She'd known he hadn't looked her up for the pleasure of her company. "Thought it might be something like that. When's the case going before a judge?"

"About six weeks."

"Eddie," she said. "Thank you."

"We aim to please," he said, then became more serious. "Annie, love . . . are you okay?"

"Sure," she said. "Why?"

"You sound . . . I don't know . . . strange."

"It's five in the morning, Eddie. I'd have a hangover if I wasn't still drunk, and I got to bed about two hours ago."

"All right for some," he said.

seven

"Look," said Lou. "This is a terrible idea. I've changed my mind."

Annie's cab was turning north onto Ninth Avenue, when Lou called to say her alcohol-inspired master plan of two nights earlier was beginning to look like the dumbest idea she'd ever had. Why would Rufus want to meet Annie anyway? "You have no idea what he's like," she said.

Annie sighed.

Her taxi had just drawn to a halt on cobblestone streets outside the Hotel Gansevoort. Manhattan's old Meatpacking District no longer came with rivulets of blood and lard these days, but you could see how the cobblestones might have helped.

"Obviously not," said Annie. "But since I'm already sitting outside your hotel, do you want me to come in and drag you out?"

A groan let Annie know she'd won.

It was just after ten A.M. and a late-summer sun glinted on the hotel's sheet glass windows. The area stank of hot streets and dog waste, and even the bums were camped in the shade of a crumbling red-brick wall, their demons beaten down by the rising heat.

Evening would see them out on the cobbles howling. Annie knew; they'd been out on the streets the night before. . . .

Chris's flight would have left by now. He hadn't called her from the airport. Annie wondered why she'd expected him to.

"Your friend coming?" the taxi driver demanded.

"Yes," said Annie. "She's on her way."

Half an hour earlier it had seemed like a good idea for Annie to dress like a New Yorker going for a job interview. Now the skinny knee-length pencil skirt, black shell top, and stilettos just felt tight, damp, and uncomfortable.

She looked a damn sight better than Lou, though.

Annie felt shocked. Lou's innate sense of style usually put fashion civilians like Annie in the shade, but not today. To say Lou looked rough was like saying Nicole Kidman had lost a few pounds. She had her trademark bag-lady look, all right, just without any saving ironic twist.

"Couldn't sleep," said Lou, "so I took some pills. And then *The Post* woke me chasing copy." She sighed. "I feel like shit."

She looked it too.

For a second Annie almost suggested she go alone. But that was absurd, as Annie was only going because Lou had asked. All the same, Lou turning up looking like this wasn't going to be the way to her father's heart after a gap of twelve years.

Then Annie realized; it was precisely because Lou was seeing Rufus that she looked so rough.

"Don't worry," she said, handing Lou a bottle of fashionably unbranded Norwegian mineral water stolen from Annie's minibar. "We'll go in, see what Rufus wants, let him tell you about the last time he talked to Scarlett, and come straight out again. Ten, fifteen minutes, max."

"It's all right for you," Lou said wearily. "You haven't got a father who files his daughters in order of importance by looks."

There was no denying that.

I haven't got a father who abandoned me either, thought Annie, and felt ashamed of all the times over the years she'd idly wished her parents had.

It didn't help that the midtown traffic was from hell.

"Why on earth didn't he just take Eleventh uptown and cut across the park at Eighty-sixth?" Lou hissed, not exactly under her breath. The driver ignored her, and Annie stayed silent. She was the one who'd told the driver just to aim for the Upper East Side.

As Lou redid her eye makeup for the second time, Annie watched city blocks edge past. The residential cross streets of Murray Hill, morphing into the jewelers and brokers of lower midtown, before the cab plunged into a labyrinthine tunnel that coiled beneath Grand Central Terminal.

Businesses became shops and shops became designer flagship stores, each more exclusive than the last, as the taxi lurched north. Every light was against them, every pedestrian in the single-minded hurry that compelled New Yorkers to fling themselves in front of moving traffic rather than lose precious seconds.

Once past the 1930s-built temple to that great retail dictator, Joseph B. Bloomingdale, the crowds and the traffic began to ease, unlike the tension in the cab. Bizarrely, it reminded Annie of a grim Christmas in her teens. Dad bought Mum the wrong present (again), Annie's sister was furious because she couldn't spend the day at her boyfriend's house, and Annie . . .

Well, she hadn't been at her best that year either.

Lou is scared, Annie realized, recognizing where that memory had been taking her. Annie knew why she'd been scared that Christmas, why she'd remained so most of her adult life, in the gaps between being angry. Being savaged by the first boy you trusted enough to . . . well, it did that to you. But Lou, afraid of Rufus? She couldn't imagine Lou being afraid of anyone.

When Annie glanced across to her friend, the makeup-remover wipes were out again.

"What are you doing now?"

"Eyeliner," said Lou. "My hand slipped at that last light."

Her eyes were a state, no doubt about it, but that had little to do with eyeliner.

"Leave it," suggested Annie.

"Rufus notices stuff like this. He slapped Nina once, because her makeup was bad." Lou's voice was matter-of-fact, as if nothing about that struck her as odd. "It was just before he left."

By the time Lou's third and final face had been applied they were approaching Eightieth Street.

"Stop it, now," Annie said, reaching across to zip shut her friend's cosmetics bag. "You look fine. Really, you do." Lou didn't; they both knew that. But no amount of foundation was going to solve the problem.

Obediently tossing makeup bag and wipes into her Mulberry, Lou shrugged. "It's Fifth Avenue at Eighty-fifth," said Lou, leaning forward to make herself heard above the gospel music now booming from the driver's radio. "Take a left at Eighty-sixth and drop down."

By way of acknowledgment, the driver yanked his wheel hard and spun the cab across two lanes of traffic, unleashing a torrent of abuse from surrounding drivers.

"You got it," he said.

The block on Fifth Avenue where Rufus lived managed to look out on the Metropolitan Museum of Art *and* the reservoir in Central Park, around which joggers ran and the rest of the city just wandered aimlessly on Sunday afternoons.

That said, the sandstone apartment building was surprisingly nondescript given its grand address. Well, it appeared grand to Annie, but Lou told her the building was a disappointment to Mr. Ulrich, who understood, at least as well as the hard-to-please Upper East Siders, that Seventy-ninth Street was the ideal cross street. And that the block between Seventy-eighth and Seventy-ninth was the only address in Manhattan worth having. One a Co-op Board had denied him time and again.

"Just a few blocks from Spence," Lou was saying. "Convenient for Scarlett to get to school. When Rufus dumped Arabella, he rather generously bought her an apartment three blocks up, so Scarlett's education wouldn't suffer. Well, not any more than it already did from afternoons and evenings spent in studios."

Annie looked surprised.

"He managed her," Lou added, as an afterthought.

Annie couldn't blame Lou's bitter tone. An Upper East Side apartment for Arabella and a big fat zero for Nina wasn't exactly evenhanded.

Spence was a school, obviously. Annie searched her mental archives and found it. Spence was Gwyneth Paltrow's alma mater, featuring a list of golden alumni as long as Annie's arm. No wonder Lou was pissed off. To Annie, Lou's only-child, eccentric-granny, green-fields-and-village-post-office childhood had always seemed idyllic, all Enid Blyton and cream teas, but compared with this . . .

Well, it didn't.

"I hope *she's* not going to be here," Lou muttered, as she pushed the buzzer.

"*She?*" Annie asked as a glass door swung open, releasing a blast of frigid air that confirmed they were entering the world of money. Only the rich or corporate could afford this level of year-round chill.

"Arabella."

As a uniformed concierge stood up to block their route to the elevator, Lou's face hardened. It was a mistake to try to march past the man's marble desk, but Lou did it anyway.

"I'm here to see Rufus Ulrich," she said.

"Is Mr. Ulrich expecting you?" The concierge shifted slightly, until he was directly in her way.

"Of course he is," snapped Lou. "I'm his daughter."

"His *daughter?*" The concierge raised a single eyebrow, as if to say, *If I'd had ten bucks for every time I've heard that from a journalist today.* But he didn't let her pass. "Wait right here, *ma'am.* I'll call up."

"Do that," Lou said, folding her arms impatiently. "Tell him Luella's here."

Whether it was a bluff or Lou had, in fact, called ahead, Annie couldn't tell. Surely Lou would have said if she'd already spoken to Rufus that morning? Maybe not. There was so much Annie didn't recognize about this version of her friend. Including the name, *Luella*?

The concierge was back in seconds. "If you ladies would like to go on up," he said. "The maid says Mr. Ulrich's expecting you."

The maid? Of course, Annie should have known there'd be a maid, more than one probably.

"*Is* your father expecting you?" Annie asked when they were safely inside the elevator and the doors had shut.

Lou's smile was wry. Unconsciously, she smoothed her hands across the floral dress she was wearing over skinny jeans, with a pair of spiky cream boots that looked new, and checked her hair in the mirror.

"This is Rufus Ulrich we're talking about," Lou said. "Do you believe he'd deign to see me if I hadn't made an appointment?"

Annie couldn't think of a suitable response.

The mahogany and brass elevator opened into the anteroom of the largest penthouse Annie had ever seen, not that she'd seen many. Right in front of the doors was a huge white canvas blocking the view ahead. It was about six feet square and on either side there was nothing but empty space. *White on White 3*, said a brass plaque on the floor, Kazimir Malevich 1919. Beyond the painting, glass walls gave an uninterrupted view of Central Park. That view alone had to add several million dollars to the apartment's price. Annie gasped.

"Yeah," said Lou. "Queen's Park, it ain't."

"You have appointment Mr. Ulrich," said a voice from the side. It was half statement, half question. The woman who asked was a short Latina, wearing a housekeeper's uniform. "He ask you wait in living area while he take call."

The living area appeared to be the only area there was. A huge expanse of marble floor, broken into separate spaces by clusters of impeccably tasteful furniture and the occasional *objet*. The penthouse reeked of eau-de-interior-designer and something else . . . Diptyque room fragrance. Annie recognized it instantly because Rebecca used Diptyque in her office at *Handbag*. The most expensive air freshener money could buy. Annie always thought she'd rather spend the money on something else, like a pair of shoes.

Low-level muzak issued from Bose speakers, so low as to be almost subliminal. Something classical that Annie couldn't immediately place, which was hardly surprising given that what Annie knew about symphonies could be written on the back of a postage stamp.

Pachelbel, said a memory.

Having tossed her bag onto a spotless ivory rug, Lou had chosen a pristine cream leather sofa for herself, one that, surreally, almost exactly matched her boots. At first glance the sofa looked bigger than Annie's own living room. And from the way Lou slouched across its surface you would think she had been here more recently than the single visit sixteen years ago she'd mentioned. If Lou was even remotely impressed by the splendor around her, she was doing a good job of hiding it.

Read the room, Annie told herself. That was what any competent journalist would do. She'd been one of those once, remember? But the room wasn't giving up any clues. There were no battered paperbacks lying spine broken on the floor, no copies of *Vanity Fair* or *The New Yorker,* not even a *New York Times* folded and left unfinished. The only books she could see were defiantly coffee table; Annie Liebovitz this, Robert Mapplethorpe that . . . All arranged neatly on a display shelf beneath a glass table. From the pristine gloss of their covers, Annie doubted they'd ever been opened.

And there were no pictures except for a huge Jackson Pollock back-to-back with the Kazimir Malevich canvas she'd already seen. If Annie was hoping for a collection of family snaps to put Lou's life into context she was out of luck.

"Changed a bit since I was last here," said Lou, to no one in particular. "I suppose his current shag must have better taste than Arabella. Or else employ better interior designers."

"Now, Luella," a voice said. "There's no need to be impolite."

Both Lou and Annie jumped, though Lou remained seated while Annie scrambled to her feet.

The voice was younger than Annie had expected, more English too. Although there was little reason to assume Rufus Ulrich's accent would be anything other, since he'd spent the first thirty years of his life in Britain. Not everyone changed voices when they changed cities.

"Hello, Rufus," said Lou, her voice too empty for the lack of emotion to be convincing. Shifting awkwardly, Annie waited for Lou to introduce her.

And waited.

While she waited, Annie drew her own mental equivalent of Lou's fashion sketches, noting in her head the points that made Rufus Ulrich memorable. Taller than average, well-dressed, swept-back hair, worn longer than Annie would have expected. It had been blond once; now it was an expensive shade of ash.

He had a heavy nose, very slight jowls.

A gold watch circled his left wrist, something expensive, obviously. An understated and elegant wedding ring. He had Lou's pale blue eyes and shared his daughter's thin smile.

The man standing in front of her couldn't have been further from Annie's idea of a father. In Annie's world, fathers wore cords, chinos, or well-loved sweaters, especially fathers who were somewhere around sixty.

She wondered if Rufus Ulrich ever wore casual clothes. His suits appeared to occupy a niche between armor and second skin. Here was a man who would never be seen in dad-clothes—not even if they *were* designed by Ralph Lauren.

"You didn't say you were bringing a friend." The man's smile was wry, as if he suspected Lou of having come armed and didn't think much of her choice of weapon. They hadn't air-kissed or even shaken hands. The question of a hug, however awkward, could not have been further from their minds. There was not even the pretense of affection.

Annie still waited for Lou to introduce her.

Screw this, she thought. At the least, Lou should have let Rufus know she was coming.

"Luella?"

"Didn't I?" said Lou. "Must have slipped my mind."

At this rate they were going to be there all day.

"Mr. Ulrich," Annie said, stepping forward. "I'm Annie Anderson, I work with Lou, or used to . . . " She put out her hand.

Rufus Ulrich's hands remained firmly at his side.

All that happened was his expression darkened, his pale blue eyes narrowed, and his lips tightened to nothing. He was imposing, no doubt about it, but not handsome, and the facial features he shared with his eldest daughter were what stood between her and real beauty.

"You're a *journalist*? What kind, exactly?"

"Mr. Ulrich." Annie had an overwhelming urge to call the man "sir," and she didn't like that one bit. Standing a bit straighter, she held his gaze. "I used to work on *The Post*'s news desk."

Rufus cut her off before she could finish.

"Keep it in the family, I said . . . Interesting decision," he added, staring at his daughter. "Even for you, Luella."

It was, Annie guessed, unavoidable that Lou be saddled with a Fifi Trixibelle kind of name. With parents like hers she was lucky it wasn't worse.

"Well?" Rufus asked, waiting for Lou's answer. His voice was as icy as his eyes, his English accent even more clipped than it had been minutes earlier.

Come on, Lou, say something, Annie willed her. *You're blowing it here.*

The silence lengthened as father and daughter each waited for the other to crack.

Mind games, thought Annie. She'd never been good at them. This one was clearly an Ulrich family pastime.

"Lou said you're concerned about Scarlett's whereabouts," said Annie, feeling Lou tense on the sofa beside her.

Mistake, Annie realized the second she opened her mouth. *Big mistake. Huge.* She should have left them to their power struggle, used the time to appreciate the view. But she kept talking, the damage already done. "She said you wanted help finding her. We thought, well, finding people used to be my job . . ."

Annie's voice finally faltered.

Rufus Ulrich was watching her with something that might have passed for amusement, were it not for the cold anger in his eyes.

"Speak Japanese, do you?" he said. "Have good contacts with the Tokyo police?"

It was too much for Lou. "You said the Japanese were useless!" she burst out, outrage replacing recalcitrance. "You told me to do something useful. Well, I did. . . . Meet Annie Anderson, famous investigative reporter."

Lou's fury blew out as quickly as it ignited. Her shoulders slumped as she pushed one hand through her hair, a large art deco ring she wore catching as she did so. It took a second or two for Lou to untangle herself.

When Rufus Ulrich smiled, it felt as though someone had turned the temperature down. Annie shivered, fine, downy hairs standing on her arms. It wasn't the air-conditioning, chilly though it was.

"She might be a bitch," said Rufus. "But at least your mother had *some* style."

Lou stared at him.

As Annie looked between them and Lou picked up her bag, Rufus threw out one final barb. "Another thing," he said. "I would have thought, in your job, you could find a hairdresser who knows how to cut hair."

eight

1980—WILTSHIRE, ENGLAND

Daddy was the one who put her in front of the television. Mummy was the one who came in and turned it up.

On TV, Evil Edna was cackling nastily, but Lou could still hear the sound of grown-ups quarreling in the hall. It didn't matter, not really, it had happened before. Still, the voices made her feel cross and Lou wanted them to stop. It was all right while Edna was talking, except Edna didn't talk, she just cackled. Loudly.

But when Mavis the fat fairy came on, like now, Evil Edna stopped cackling and Lou could hear Mummy shouting. That was why Lou decided to sit right next to the television, something that usually made Mummy cross. Lou didn't like Granny's sofa anyway; it was scratchy. If Mummy came back Lou would just say the sofa had made her legs itchy.

Dragging a cushion off a chair, Lou scooted across the parquet on her bottom to get closer to the white plastic box in the rumpus room, which Daddy called the pigpen.

"Lou, don't sit so close to the box." That's what Mummy would say, if she came in. "Not so close, you'll hurt your eyes."

But Lou was close, so close she could touch the pictures. Staring rapt at the cartoon world of Doyley Woods, she watched Mavis talk to Moog. Lou didn't like Moog, because Moog was a dog and Granny said dogs were stupid. That was why Daddy's dogs had to live outside. Cats, however, lived in front of the Aga, which was why Debbo and Decca were the only ones in Granny's rattly old rectory who were never cold.

Edna was Lou's favorite character on *Willo the Wisp*. That was a se-cret. She knew she shouldn't have liked Edna, because Mummy said Edna was bad. And you weren't supposed to like bad people. Lou liked the way Edna was shaped like a TV, and she especially liked it when lightning bolts shot out of Edna's antennae and scared everybody.

Just then, a lightning bolt flicked across the screen and landed on Moog, turning him into a toad. As Moog croaked and hopped away, Lou shrieked with laughter and bounced on her cushion, clapping her hands.

Lou liked the box. She liked it a lot, she liked the noise, the colors, and the pictures, but especially she liked it because the box was like sweets; it was one of those things that grown-ups said were bad for you.

Willo was talking now. Lou wasn't sure about Willo the Wisp, he had a pointy face and was sneaky, like Robin, a boy at nursery who stole her crayons. Lou couldn't understand why Robin had cried when she slapped him, Robin should have just hit her back. That's what Lou would have done if she'd been him.

She decided to ignore Willo, just like she ignored Robin. But if Lou ig-nored Willo she had to listen to the other noise. It wasn't shouting any-more. It was gasps, like Mummy was being hurt. And the table in Granny's hall was creaking. Granny would have been cross, only Granny wasn't here. She'd gone out earlier, before Daddy came back.

Mummy and Daddy were silent now. Just the creak of the table in the hall and Willo's voice filling the rumpus room.

"Call this my good-bye," said Daddy. He sounded like someone else.

Maybe the creaking was better than the shouting? Lou decided it wasn't when Mummy began to cry.

Usually the shouting happened at night when Lou's attic room was all dark, except for a little pink night-light left on so the bad things wouldn't get her. When Lou had gone up to bed, when they thought Lou was asleep, that was the time for shouting. Well, for Mummy shouting. Daddy's voice was usually low and hard, cross-sounding like a hiss.

Now he wasn't talking at all. And, for once, nor was Willo. Stupid, sneaky Willo.

A door opened and then shut. Mummy was still crying. Although the table in the hall had stopped creaking.

Then another door opened and Mummy started shouting again.

Lou didn't think Mummy had ever shouted at Daddy outside the house before, so she decided to look.

She climbed up so she could stand on a seat and see over the back of the chair and out of the window. Now Lou could see but she couldn't hear anything. She was standing by Daddy's new car, waving her arms, and her mouth was open, but Lou couldn't hear any shouting because the window was shut, like someone had turned the sound right down.

Willo the wisp.

Robin the sneak.

Mummy the shout.

Daddy the hiss.

Only Daddy wasn't hissing now, he was ignoring Mummy. Hauling herself up some more, Lou sat on the back of the chair, so she could see better, and steadied herself by putting her feet on the windowsill. The open trunk of Daddy's big white car looked like a mouth. Daddy was feeding it suitcase after suitcase and the car was swallowing them up.

Mummy was still waving her arms, like Evil Edna's antennae, but Daddy just ignored her. Now the trunk had swallowed all Daddy's cases; he shut it and walked to the driver's door. Lou watched Mummy grab his wrist.

It was a mistake.

Anything was a mistake when Daddy was cross, even Lou knew that and she was only four. With his free hand, Daddy threw Mummy's fingers off his arm and stepped around her. He wasn't shouting, he wasn't saying anything, he was choosing a car key.

When Mummy tried to grab the keys, that was when Daddy's face exploded and he pushed her, hard.

Lou had never seen this happen before.

As Mummy stumbled, Daddy ducked inside his new car and Lou saw that Daddy's two black Labs were already sitting on the backseat, staring out of the window, and opening and shutting their mouths. If the dogs were barking, Lou couldn't hear them.

The car started to roll forward, crunching over gravel, and Mummy stopped shouting, her shoulders slumped. When she turned back to the house, she was crying.

Big, gulping sobs.

"Mummy!" Lou yelled.

But Mummy couldn't hear her through the window, just as Lou couldn't hear anything but Willo's voice behind her. His silly whiny voice, going sneak, sneak, sneak . . .

nine

"Lou," said Annie. "Are you all right?" It was one of those pointless questions, because her friend was anything but all right. People who were all right didn't stand on a sidewalk, staring blankly at the trees of Central Park, their eyes brimming with tears.

Lou didn't reply and she didn't move.

Reaching into her bag for the tissues she habitually kept for overwrought case studies, Annie remembered she'd changed jobs. The packet of Kleenex was no longer there. She offered Lou a Starbucks napkin instead.

The action popped Lou's bubble of misery. Taking the napkin, she gave Annie a weak smile and dabbed at her eyes.

"Sorry," Lou said. "I'll be okay. . . ."

"Yes," said Annie. "I know."

They were both lying.

"Let's get you a cab," said Annie. "The shows . . ."

Lou shrugged. "Nah," she said. "It's okay, there's nothing much until later. We might as well try Arabella, since we're here."

Annie did a double take.

Arabella?

"But you . . ."

"Hate her?" said Lou. "Yeah," she shrugged again. "I know, I hate her guts, but talking to her will get up that fuck's nose."

That fuck being Rufus.

"And if I ever decide to go near him again," said Lou. "Remind me not to."

"Will do."

Pulling a makeup mirror from her own bag, Lou flipped it open and groaned. "You know," she said darkly, "I particularly hate Arabella when I look like shit. There's nothing like an ex–Calvin Klein model with silicone extras for finishing off your already-crippled 32A self-esteem."

This was more like the Lou that Annie knew and half-admired. Breathing into her cupped palm, Lou grimaced. "Got any mints?" she said.

Annie shook her head.

"Also . . ." Lou hesitated.

"What?"

"Scarlett's still a kid . . ."

"No," said Annie. "She's not. She's eighteen, nineteen almost. Everyone fucks up when they're that age."

"Well, she was a kid," said Lou.

So was everyone, thought Annie, but didn't bother to say it.

After cutting north, Lou and Annie turned right, hit Madison, and headed north again for a couple of blocks, only to turn right and head toward Park Avenue. The children walking with their parents had stripped to shorts, T-shirts, and, no doubt, SPF60. Even the men, mostly gray-haired and elegant, had discarded their jackets and were carrying them folded over their arms.

New York in September was not Annie's favorite place. Too hot, too steamy, and just too exhausting to be out for long. "You want to fill me in on Arabella?" she asked.

"What's there to tell?" said Lou, but not irritably. "Tall, blond, thin, gorgeous, not even that stupid . . ." She shrugged. "Your basic teenage nightmare."

Annie was impressed by Lou's resilience. She'd gone from meltdown to something close to her old self in three or four blocks. Or she was doing a good impression of someone who had.·

"And she was number . . . ?"

"Four," said Lou, as they passed a weird rusting sculpture in the middle of the road. Annie suppressed the urge to ask where they were headed, and how Lou knew her way if she'd never been there.

Instead she said, "God, Rufus packed them in, didn't he?"

Lou threw her a quizzical look. "Only five *wives*," she said. "The rest were casual."

"Five?"

"He left Nina for . . . *Laura.*" Lou's mouth twisted, but it was mostly for effect. "She didn't last five minutes and he dumped her once Arabella came on the scene. He's a serial overlapper, Rufus. Never knowingly un-attached."

"That makes her . . ." By now, Annie was confused. The math for Rufus's wives just didn't add up. "Then surely Arabella was number three?" said Annie. "If there was only one marriage between your mother and Arabella?"

Lou stopped, suddenly deciding to examine a brass plaque that announced SYNOD OF THE RUSSIAN ORTHODOX CHURCH OUTSIDE RUSSIA.

"Nina wasn't number one," she said finally.

"She wasn't?"

"Before you ask," said Lou. "I know nothing about her. Not even her name. They were both young and she was nobody." Lou caught herself. "I mean, nobody whose name you'd recognize. His PM years."

"Pre-model?" Annie guessed.

Lou called up a weak smile. "Pre-millionaire."

The area was changing now. It was still obviously expensive, still undeniably uptown, but there was a shift away from the 1930s elegance and unabashed wealth of the area they'd left. Rufus might have set Arabella up around the corner, or perhaps she'd had a good prenup, but the area north of Ninetieth Street and east of Park was second row, while Rufus's apartment was front row and center.

Having stopped outside a 1960s glass and faux marble building, Lou was scouring a list of names. "Here we go," said Lou. "Ulrich, five-oh-seven . . . Notice *she* didn't change her name," added Lou. "I'll say that for Arabella, she's nobody's fool."

"How did you know where to find her?"

"I didn't, Ken did."

"Ken?"

"I've been calling in favors."

Yeah, Annie had noticed.

"You told him Ulrich was your father?"

"Ken knows," said Lou. "He's always known. He knew Nina back in the day. Interviewed her once."

As the double doors swung inward, cool air rushed out to meet them. The foyer of this block was altogether less ostentatious, its front desk more a plinth, its porter more a security guard. Although obviously not that secure, since he barely bothered to drag his eyes from that morning's *New York Post* as Lou and Annie walked by.

Yet the upper edge of the Upper East Side was hardly slumming it. Arabella had, after all, a several-million-dollar address, which was more than Annie could say for Lou's mother, who still shared space with Lou's grandmother at an old rectory in Wiltshire.

The elevator opened onto a cool fifth-floor corridor and silence, the interior of the building hermetically sealed from the roar of traffic and the heavy heat outside. For the first time since she'd stormed out of her father's apartment, Lou hesitated.

"What?" Annie asked.

"This is a crap idea. And I can't remember her flat number, anyway."

"Five-oh-seven," said Annie. "It's that way." She pointed to a sign showing apartments 505–510 to the left and then left again.

"You go," said Lou, leaning back against the wall.

"And say what?"

Lou shrugged.

"Come on," said Annie. "It'll be fine." She said this more from loyalty than any genuine belief. She'd seen Lou go to pieces with Rufus and could do without a repeat performance.

"Look," said Lou. "Say I sent you."

When she showed no sign of budging, Annie sighed.

But Lou just shrugged and dropped to a crouch beside her bag. "Someone's got to find Scarlett," she said, "and I can't do it."

Annie wondered if Lou had any idea what she was asking.

The carpet lining the corridor was beige and vacuumed so its nap ran in the same direction in smooth straight lines like a neatly mown lawn; semicircular uplighters lined white walls, one either side of each apartment door.

A vase of orchids rested on a triangular table in the corner, each time the corridor changed direction. And a series of tiny ceiling-mounted cameras recorded Annie's movements as she made her way to Arabella's apartment.

Checking her reflection in the polished steel plate for apartment 507, Annie reapplied a single coat of bright red lipstick. Instinct told her that appearances were going to count. Having licked her fingers and rubbed the scuffs of a Manhattan sidewalk from the toes of her black stilettos, she smoothed her skirt. Annie wasn't exactly head-to-toe Calvin Klein, but the overall impression was at least professional.

Neat, vaguely anonymous, unthreatening. She'd dressed as if chasing a case study without even intending to. As Annie rang the buzzer, she took a silent bet with herself about whether she could get over the threshold.

"Yes?"

Annie didn't know what she'd been expecting, but it wasn't this. Arabella Ulrich was blond, tall, slender, beautiful. And young. Well, youngish. The right side of forty anyway. Searching the woman's face for signs of surgery, Annie found what she was looking for when Arabella raised her eyebrows and nothing moved. Botox, maybe an eye job too, and definitely fillers.

"Well?" said Arabella, the slightest trace of West Coast obvious in her accent. *Let me guess,* said her immovable eyebrows, *another freaking reporter.*

Smiling, Annie offered Arabella her *Handbag* magazine business card. A better bet, by far, than mentioning her career at *The London Post.* Annie's exclusive on the secret marriage and sudden death of Mark Mailer a few months ago had earned *Handbag* a grudging respect from more than just the fashion industry. Plus, the woman probably read it.

"I'm a friend of your stepdaughter," said Annie. "She thought we should talk. About Scarlett."

"Why?"

"Because," Annie said, "I used to specialize in finding people."

Now was not a good time to admit that finding them wasn't the problem, it was finding them alive.

For a moment, the fourth Mrs. Ulrich looked as if she'd rather have her fingernails removed with pliers than trust an English journalist. Then she seemed to reconsider. It was the business card that made the difference. White vellum, printed to Rebecca Brooks's exacting standards by Smythson of Bond Street. An outrageous indulgence, Annie had thought, when she first saw one.

"I'm assuming," said Arabella, having examined both the card and Annie for several seconds, "you mean my *eldest* stepdaughter. There is more than one, you know."

"Really?" said Annie. "I'm afraid I know little about Lou's family." It was both a lie and the truth.

"Why didn't Luella come with you then?" Arabella asked. "If you're her friend."

"She did," Annie said simply.

Arabella tried to twitch a Botoxed eyebrow. "I don't see her."

"She's waiting by the lift."

Without a word the woman padded past Annie and along the corridor. Annie followed, praying Arabella wouldn't return dragging a recalcitrant Lou behind her, but the woman just peered around the final corner and turned back.

"Rufus?" she asked, as if no other words were necessary.

Annie nodded.

"Interesting. I didn't think they were in contact."

"They weren't, until Scarlett vanished."

Giving no indication that Annie should follow, Arabella turned for her apartment and Annie trudged after her, shutting the door behind them.

What looked from the corridor like a pleasantly roomy hotel suite proved to be merely the entrance to an altogether more interesting space. Although, to reach that, Annie first had to walk down a picture-lined passageway.

Chagall, Miró, Rothko, and de Kooning, they were prints, lithographs, and woodblocks, but good examples of each artists' work. As they went, Annie appraised the woman walking ahead and tried not to feel insecure. Not only was she far younger than Annie had expected, Arabella also had far better taste than Lou had led her to believe.

The way Lou told it, Arabella made Ivana Trump look restrained, but this woman was more Ralph Lauren than Versace. Her well-cut beige trousers hugged enviably narrow hips; admittedly one button too many had been left open on her white shirt, revealing a hint of tanned cleavage, but that was splitting hairs.

Shoulder-length tresses were pulled back at the nape of her neck, her hair color a complex mix of blonds that probably cost a month of Annie's wages. It took Annie a second or two to realize that Arabella's tanned feet were bare, her toenails a faultless French polish.

Even in her bare feet she was taller than Rufus Ulrich.

It might have taken a lifetime's work to change, but Arabella didn't look remotely like the social-climbing gold-digging father-stealer Lou described. But then Lou had last seen Arabella twelve years ago, through the eyes of a gangly, self-conscious, hormonal sixteen-year-old.

Although far smaller than the designed-to-be-looked-at display of Rufus's penthouse, the illusion of space in Arabella's apartment was helped by three large mirrors. An Art Deco fireplace dominated one end of the room, and a large picture window dominated the other, while the comfortable furniture could have come straight out of *Martha Stewart Living*, and probably had. A sofa was covered in striped poplin and the floor was scattered with colorful rag rugs. In sharp contrast to Rufus's place, almost every flat surface featured some knickknack or other.

Cluttered was the only word to describe Arabella's living space and Annie was grateful for it. The clues into Scarlett's childhood she'd hoped to see earlier were plentiful here. Pictures of Scarlett adorned every surface. One, in particular, dominated the wall above the fireplace. It was the original print for *Winter Skies*. Not so much black and white as washed out color, though Scarlett's eyes still shone a sharp pure blue.

"Mapplethorpe," said Arabella, naming the photographer.

Everywhere Annie looked she found more photographs of Scarlett, each one a striking image of the same beautiful child. No doubt about it, the room was a shrine.

She scanned the pictures again to make sure she'd read the room correctly. Not one of them was a family snap, the kind that weighed down Annie's own mother's mantelpiece. Every last shot showed Scarlett on assignment.

The Scarlett this room worshipped had vanished by the age of twelve.

ten

"So, how *was* Rufus?" Arabella asked in a tone that implied she already knew the answer. "Charm personified, I imagine?"

Annie shrugged as she worked out how to play it. There was clearly no love lost between this woman and her ex-husband, but it wouldn't do to be too critical. "I wouldn't put it like that."

"Really?" Arabella frowned, or at least Annie thought she did. She looked at Annie with interest, almost as if reconsidering. Everything from Arabella's elegant hair and makeup to her faultless clothes suggested composure, but pinkness around the eyes betrayed her as a mother whose only daughter had vanished from the face of the earth forty-eight hours earlier.

"How unlike him."

A thought crossed Arabella's face and she smiled grimly. "Oh, of course. Luella was there?"

Annie nodded.

"So you met Rufus Ulrich, the fond father, how nice for you."

This woman could match Lou for bitterness against Rufus, Annie decided. The man was good-looking, well dressed, and rich. Obviously Annie hadn't had the benefit of the full force of his intellect and charm. But what was it that left a succession of spectacular catches unable to get over him?

What kind of man could walk away, time and again, leaving a string of lives in tatters? Lou's own mother was gorgeous, intelligent, and stylish. Yet from what Lou had been saying, Nina still hadn't moved on, weighed down by a twenty-four-year hatred of her ex-husband.

Arabella seemed no different. There was no evidence she shared this apartment with a man, and no sign of any other child. Annie wondered if wives number one and three also lived in a Rufus-induced limbo.

This feels familiar, thought Annie. *The same charisma that attracted me to Tony?*

"You think you can help?" Arabella asked.

"I can try," said Annie. "No guarantees."

"At least you're honest."

Annie outlined her CV. Her life as an investigative journalist pre-*Handbag,* and the Mark Mailer scoop, neatly bypassing the fact she'd been unable to prevent Patty's murder. She touched on going undercover in Glasgow, befriending a well-known gangster.

She didn't mention her part in breaking a gang that smuggled teenagers into Britain from Eastern Europe and sold them as sex slaves to brothels in the Kings Cross area of London. Annie didn't want Arabella drawing any parallels with what might have happened to Scarlett.

"What I don't understand is why Luella is involved at all?"

Annie looked at her.

"Luella's always disliked Lettie. I mean, it's a big age gap. And Lettie was prettier. But Luella just seemed jealous from the get go."

"Of course she . . ." Annie shut her mouth in time.

"Okay," said Arabella. "I believe it. You're friends." Her smile was sad.

"Rufus asked Lou if she knew where Scarlett was," said Annie. "When she said no, he said she was useless."

"Sounds like Rufus."

"So now . . . ," said Annie.

"She wants to prove Rufus wrong?"

Annie nodded.

"And what's your reason?" asked Arabella.

When Annie slid her tape recorder onto a coffee table, she thought for a second that her host might protest. All Arabella did was fetch a small leather mat and place it underneath the machine. Arabella was a model and interviews had been a part of her life. She started with *After Rufus.*

"Rufus and I were together for fourteen years," said Arabella. "And he didn't leave until Scarlett was twelve. So you could even argue she was lucky. I also had a good stretch, no one had lasted that long before. . . ."

Arabella paused, probably realizing that Annie, as Lou's friend, was not an ally where *before* was concerned, then shrugged. "Or since."

"Can I ask why he left?"

"Oh, God, the usual reason. Another woman, of course. It always is with Rufus. Another model, as it happens, but a cynic might also note that he left just as Scarlett's career started to slide." She took a sip of mineral water and looked at Annie, although she could see that Arabella was looking inward, not out.

"It had started to slide?" Annie prompted.

"Oh yes . . . Lettie was at the top of her game until she hit eleven, twelve. . . . She launched a whole new generation of child models, was the first to make as much money as . . . Well, she was the first child supermodel, if you like."

"Was that his plan? I mean, did you and Rufus mastermind her career?"

Arabella Ulrich shook her head. "God, no," she said. "Nothing like that. Well, not on my part. Modeling can be soul-destroying, and I was relieved to get out when Scarlett was born. I wouldn't have wished the life on her. I mean, it wasn't as if we needed the money."

"So, what happened?"

"Rufus saw matters differently. Said it was an opportunity to set Scarlett up for life. We didn't know that, obviously, when we let her do the album. I mean, Kenny Pfizer . . ."

She caught Annie's blank expression.

"Kenny was the band Driver's lead guitarist," said Arabella. "He was a friend. I'd met him while I was modeling—he was dating one of the other girls big at the time—and when I married Rufus we stayed in touch with Kenny. Anyway, Rufus and I were holding a dinner one night—Rufus liked to entertain back then, put interesting people together, collecting them, if you like, he's a big *collector*—and Kenny was there. I think with Liv, his wife at the time."

Annie mentioned the surname of a well-known actress and Arabella nodded.

"Scarlett was five, nearly six, and she came wandering in, wanting a drink of water." Arabella smiled. "Wanting attention probably. Lettie knew she wasn't allowed to interrupt the grown-ups. Anyway, after I'd put her back to bed, Liv started talking about the idea for Ken's new album and how Lettie had the look Driver wanted, innocent, angelic even. Rufus and I talked about it afterward . . ."

"And?"

"We figured it would be harmless, just a nice thing for Lettie to be able to look back on when she was grown up. But the minute Robert Mapplethorpe put her in front of a camera I knew we'd made a mistake."

Arabella stopped suddenly.

"A mistake, how?" Annie prompted, expecting some terrible catastrophe. "What went wrong?"

"Nothing," said Arabella sadly. "Everything went incredibly right. From the first Polaroid we knew we had an iconic image."

She wasn't kidding, thought Annie.

Even though the music had long been consigned to everyone's most embarrassing record collections, the image still made it unfailingly onto the top ten album covers of all time.

"You could have left it at that," Annie said.

"True," said Arabella. "After all, the Driver album didn't make her much money. Although the record label did pay her the going rate, one thousand dollars. It was everything that came after. When the album took off, we had all the top agents beating down the door. Rufus interviewed about fifty before he chose one and, God knows, Rufus can drive a hard bargain."

Annie thought of the room in which she sat. Maybe Rufus Ulrich had met his match with his fourth wife. "And then?" Annie said.

"The big commercial deals snowballed, Lettie started to appear on billboards, and there was no going back. She became the face of the decade."

Poor Lou, thought Annie. Bad enough to be abandoned by your dad. Bad enough he had a new family, not just a new wife but a new daughter as well. Bad enough to be a spotty, skinny, hormonal teenager. But when that perfect family stared out at you from every magazine and billboard, every TV screen, not to mention all your friends' CD collections . . .

"What about Scarlett?" asked Annie. "Did she enjoy it?"

"Of course she did! She had a ball."

"And Rufus?"

"Ah, well, you know Rufus. Of course he liked it. He enjoyed the idea of us both being successful models. Lettie and I even did a few campaigns together. Rufus's idea obviously."

Annie already knew about the joint projects. She could see the results over Arabella's shoulder. A beautiful blonde, not yet thirty, with a mini-me daughter. They were a living Calvin Klein ad. Rufus must have thought he'd died and gone to heaven. For a while.

"So," said Annie, pressing the point. "Scarlett was happy?"

"Of course," said Arabella. "Who wouldn't be at that age? All those parties and famous friends. Having her picture in magazines. What's not to like? You've seen Rufus's place . . . Not the best part of Central Park, of course. The co-op board at Seventy-ninth Street rejected him, you know. More than once." The satisfaction was evident in Arabella's voice. "But his apartment's still stunning."

Yes, thought Annie, that was one way of putting it.

"Scarlett became ill around that time, right?"

Arabella sighed. "We . . . well . . . I enrolled her at Spence. Not that Lettie spent much time there for the first few years. Look, does this matter?"

"It might," Annie said. "It's hard to know what matters at this stage. That's why you shouldn't leave anything out." The words rolled off her tongue, repeated countless times before to scared fathers and grieving mothers, to anxious partners and mournful grandparents. Anyone, in fact, who might have had a sliver of story to tell.

"We had a limit to the number of jobs Lettie could do each term. There were laws about that even then. But, still, Lettie was always traveling, invited to every party, and all the big agencies wanted her for their campaigns. You know how it is."

"No," Annie said, "I don't. Tell me."

"Rufus invented an illness. Nothing nasty. Just something vague and undefined. And that became part of the story. It was his excuse to keep Scarlett with us."

"He invented . . . ?"

"I'll be honest," said Arabella. "I liked having her with me."

As Arabella painted a picture of premieres and parties, first-class flights and Hollywood friends, Annie decided Scarlett's parents had got far more out of the deal than the child herself. And staring at the portraits of Scarlett the model, Annie tried to fathom the unfathomable: Where was the child inside the mini adult? What was Scarlett thinking as she stared hypnotically into the camera. The tiny girl wasn't counting dollars, that was for sure. She had parents and an agent to do that.

"Modeling's not a long-term career," said Arabella. "It's finite. My career was almost over by then." She nodded at one of the later photographs. "And I was quite happy with that. But working with Lettie gave it a little boost. Also, we didn't know whether Scarlett had another ten years or twenty. You don't get long to bank the check as a model, even a top one. Child modeling is even more precarious. As it turned out, Lettie didn't have even that."

"Remind me," said Annie, "how old was Scarlett when Rufus left?"

Arabella's eyes narrowed. "Twelve. She was twelve years old. Everything was great, then Rufus met that . . . that slut."

"So it came out of the blue?"

"You could say that," said Arabella, taking a gulp of mineral water like she wished it was a vodka martini. As she did so, the rings on her fingers clinked against the glass, a slim yellow-, red-, and white-gold bangle on her wrist chiming in unison.

"Scarlett and I had just got back from Paris. I mean literally just gotten off the plane. I'd accompanied her on a job, and we'd decided to stay on a few days, do some educational things, like go to the Louvre, visit Notre Dame."

Annie nodded, wondering if those educational activities had also included film premieres and fashion parties.

"The shoot hadn't been a great success," said Arabella. "Both of us were tired, a little fed up. I remember it clearly. . . ." She paused and Annie waited, knowing better than to break Arabella's train of thought.

"We'd just walked through the door, the concierge hadn't even sent up our cases, and Rufus barely had the decency to let Scarlett go to bed before telling me. *I want a divorce*, just like that. He didn't even give me a chance to relax, didn't mix me a drink. Just said it . . . " She paused.

"What he didn't tell me, of course, was that he intended to move us out, and I didn't find out about my replacement for a few weeks—from the *New York Post*. Secrecy is one of Rufus's great strengths, so I have no doubt the paper found out exactly when he wanted them to."

"That must have been a terrible shock," said Annie.

"It was. I mean, I always knew it was a possibility. That he'd move on to a younger model at some point, but I suppose . . . "

Arabella paused, and Annie saw her eyes well up. Even now, seven years later, it looked more like sorrow than fury.

"I'm not proud of it," said Arabella. "But I guess I always thought Scarlett was my security."

Annie had suspected that was in there somewhere.

"Why?" she asked. "The money?"

"No!" Arabella looked shocked. "God no! Rufus is too rich in his own right to be interested in his daughter's money."

Annie didn't believe that for a second. Men like Rufus were always interested in money, but she let it pass.

"It was Scarlett's success. It can't have passed you by that Rufus has a liking for models."

"Hmm." Annie nodded. "Lou mentioned something of the sort."

Arabella gave a loud, decidedly ungenteel laugh. "I'm sure she did. I figured that even if I wasn't a model anymore, I was safe while Scarlett was. Safer than Nina and Laura at any rate. Unfortunately, Rufus could see what I couldn't."

"Which was?"

"That Scarlett was growing. That a massively successful *child model*—the biggest of all time—was all Scarlett would ever be. I assumed she'd go on to do catwalk and fragrance campaigns, become the new Kate . . ." Arabella's voice trailed off.

"But I thought she was still working?"

Even as she said it, Annie realized that *working* was precisely what Scarlett Ulrich did. The basic slog of a second-, even third-tier model. Annie couldn't recall having seen Scarlett's face on a billboard for several years. And then she thought about the catwalk show she'd seen last night, the shows she'd attended last season, the ads which adorned the pages of *Handbag* back in her hotel room.

All the faces that stared out at her—the Lilys and Gemmas and Devons and Brees—belonged to young women roughly the same age as Scarlett. Only Scarlett Ulrich had gone from icon to jobbing model in the time it took to spell puberty.

The same went for the gossip mags. In among Lindsay and Nicole and assorted Hiltons, there was no Ulrich. All those premieres and parties she'd been famous for attending on a school night had dried up.

"But she had a job in Tokyo?"

Arabella gave a sharp nod. "She did Milan this time last year. Then, after Christmas, her agency sent her to Tokyo. She's been gone about eight months now. I haven't seen her since."

"And you say you spoke on Sunday?"

"Sunday before last," Arabella corrected. "She seemed fine. Well, as fine as can be expected. Scarlett didn't even mind it out there that much, quite liked the place once she got used to it. She has an American boyfriend, nothing serious." The way Arabella said this implied she'd know if it was. "I'm not sure she ever mentioned his name."

"What *did* she say about him?" Annie asked, spotting a chink of light. This was the first thing that even vaguely resembled a lead.

"Said he was a photographer in Shinjuku. So I presume Lettie met him on a job." Arabella paused, her eyes misting. Annie waited for the tears, but they didn't come. She couldn't help feeling it might have been a relief for both of them if they had.

"Mobi—I mean cell phone or landline?" asked Annie.

"Cell, but it's dead. I've tried it a million times, believe me. Scarlett didn't have a landline in her apartment. If I couldn't get a connection on her cell phone I used to leave a message with the model agency. I trained myself not to worry. That's why I didn't panic this time, when I didn't hear."

"What about the agency?"

"They haven't heard either. Not since they called her about the knit-wear casting."

"Knitwear?"

"The Japanese are tiny," said Arabella. "No breasts or butts, so it's al-most impossible for a Westerner to fit their samples. Knitwear's the worst. She'd just finished a catalog job that lasted all week. It was well paid. Let-tie said she'd have walked but for the money."

"What about Scarlett and her father?" Annie ventured. "Were they in touch?"

"Oh yes. Rufus likes to give advice."

"Advice?"

Arabella said nothing.

"I don't suppose you know when they last spoke?"

"You'd have to ask Rufus about that." Her lips drew into a tight line. "It's not something I'd know."

"Not sure Rufus will be taking my calls," said Annie. "If this morning was anything to go by."

"Catch him at Cipriani." Arabella's smile was sour. "He eats there most days."

"What about you? Did you ever work Tokyo?"

Arabella blinked. *"Me?"* she said. For the first time her accent was ob-vious. *"Do the Tokyo run?* You gotta be joking. Lettie wouldn't have done it either. Not if I'd had my way."

"It was her decision?"

"Uh-uh. Rufus sent her."

"If she didn't want to . . . Why didn't she say so?"

Annie wasn't aware that she'd spoken the thought aloud, until the woman opposite laughed. "I thought you said you'd met my ex-husband."

Good point, thought Annie. "What about the agency? Are they worried about her?"

"So they say," Arabella said. "But in the long run I doubt they'd be sorry to end her contract. As I told you, Scarlett isn't what she was. Have you seen her lately?"

She paused, waiting for Annie to shake her head.

"I thought not. Oh, she's pretty by anyone's standards. But she's not model material anymore. As for catwalk . . ." Arabella shook her head, though nothing on her face moved. "She hasn't got it. She's too . . . ordi-nary. In every way. The poor kid got too many of his genes."

It was a last twist of the knife, a hint that Annie's interview was over.

Reaching across the coffee table, Annie turned off her tape recorder to show she understood and got to her feet. "Thank you for your time," she said. "I don't suppose I could have a quick look at Scarlett's room before I leave?"

A teenage life in toys and photographs, posters and junk from ethnic stalls, plastic bangles and the kind of cheap earrings that gave you a lifetime of dermatitis.

She'd been in a dozen similar rooms, looking at lives abandoned or already finished. *Why,* Annie asked herself, *are you doing this?*

It was a big question. So big, that she decided she wasn't even going to try to answer it. This was the life, the sheer driven need Annie had meant to leave behind. The reason she walked away from newspapers.

And now here she was again.

Pink and pink, with added pink. And a pink fluffy rug covering what little was visible of the white carpet.

The room in which Annie now stood was the opposite of the one she'd just left. For a start, it was small and looked it. There were no mirrors to give an illusion of space. It was the bedroom of a teenage girl, with all the detritus of a teenage life. Scarlett's bed was barely visible beneath a mound of cuddly toys, everything from teddies to My Little Ponies and a Disneyfied Pooh Bear, all jostling for space under the watchful eyes of Justin Timberlake, Leonardo DiCaprio, and Josh Hartnett.

"Awful, isn't it?" said Arabella, her faultless taste clearly offended by the fluorescent paint job and Blu Tak stains, where boy bands had once reigned supreme, only to fall out of favor. "Not my choice," she added unnecessarily.

Annie smiled. "D'you mind if I sit for a minute, take a look around?"

"Why?"

Annie shrugged. "I just want to get to know her."

It was answer enough. Obviously deciding, like a million mothers before her, there could be nothing in her daughter's bedroom that she didn't already know about, Arabella padded back to the sitting room, leaving both bedroom and sitting room doors ajar.

Shifting a fluffy red lobster to make space on the bed, Annie sat on the flowery duvet and stared around. The differences between Scarlett's room and the sitting room were stark, but so were the likenesses. Both rooms were a homage to Scarlett's childhood—except that Scarlett's homage, Annie suspected, was to a childhood she'd never had. A childhood of cheap toys and pages torn from teen magazines.

Annie recognized it. That childhood had been her own.

This room was no bigger than the one Annie shared with Chris in West London, though it looked far smaller because it was crammed with memories of childhood, the contradictions of adolescence. Not just cuddly toys beside posters of young male stars, but children's books from Roald Dahl to Judy Blume piled alongside a dog-eared Henry James, so long overdue from a school library the fine could probably buy a first edition.

Annie shifted uncomfortably, remembering the summer she'd ditched her cuddly toys, stuffing them into a black garbage bag and dumping them in the attic. She was three days away from her eighteenth birthday, half her proper weight, and had stopped keeping a diary because she could no longer bear to read her own words.

It was the summer Annie painted her room a deep, dark gray, the closest she could find to black at her local hardware store. She hadn't been sure about it, until her elder sister said it made Annie's bedroom look like the inside of a filing cabinet. Then it suddenly became Annie's favorite color.

In the other room Arabella had put on a CD and Annie took it as a cue that her time was almost up. Arabella would probably give her five more minutes, ten max, before coming back. If Annie wanted to do some digging, now was the time. Scanning the room for hiding places, Annie found plenty, but most too obvious to be worth the search. But she searched all the same.

A dressing table groaned under a mountain of cheap perfume bottles, and offered only junk-filled drawers. A pink padded jewelry box looked frail enough to have its little gold lock broken with a pencil, but Annie didn't want to leave any visible damage.

In less than five minutes, Annie had searched most of Scarlett's room. The only place left unsearched was a drawer under the bed. A few hard tugs and the drawer crept open. It was crammed to bursting with notebooks.

Annie smiled, here were the diaries.

But no, they were just abandoned school notebooks, adorned with the graffiti of any young girl in her early teens. Hearts and flowers and Leo 4 me. He loves me, he loves me not. Annie caught sight of a scrawled *Mrs. Scarlett DiCaprio* and smiled, remembering her own embarrassing teenage crushes. Stacking the books on the floor in reverse order, Annie flicked through each one. When that yielded nothing more than algebra, French vocab, and essays on the work of Nathaniel Hawthorne (adorned with yet more lovelorn teenage fantasies), Annie held each by the spine and shook.

She had to upend seven or eight before a three-by-four rectangle card dropped out. On the reverse, a girl of about fifteen grinned into the camera, gauche and embarrassed, and nothing at all like a model who'd spent her entire life having her picture taken.

To Scarlett's left, half in and half out of the picture, as if the photographer couldn't decide whether to include her, was a skinny, freckled redhead grinning awkwardly. Her arm was linked through Scarlett's own. To Scarlett's right, a familiar-looking boy-man clad in black tie and tuxedo smiled professionally.

The picture was signed, *To Scarlett, enjoy the film, Leo.*

Annie stared hard at the image. At a guess, the picture was taken about four years earlier. When Scarlett had still, just about, been someone. Already the Scarlett of *the album* was gone. The girl here was recognizable as an adolescent version of the young woman whose face stared from yesterday's papers.

She looked like an ordinary teenager, a girl who couldn't believe her luck at having her photo taken with her favorite star. And Leonardo DiCaprio was just that: a teen heartthrob having his picture taken with a couple of enamored, starstruck fans.

eleven

The air-conditioning in Rebecca's chauffeur-driven Lincoln was a relief after the soaring temperatures at that evening's Zac Posen show. Annie knew hurricanes were no joke, and they were deep in the heart of the hurricane season, but what New York badly needed was a breeze.

Rebecca, of course, looked as cool as ever, perfectly dressed for Zac's aftershow party at Soho House. Although Brit-born and bred, years of Manhattan living (before returning to London to launch *Handbag*) had *Handbag*'s editor in chief behaving like a native, right down to the weekly manicure and daily blow-out. And she'd never kicked the city's bare legs, skinny heels, and knee-length pencil skirt look that Annie was appalled to realize she'd also donned that morning. It was small comfort that Annie's outfit had at least been black.

Oh, God, thought Annie. *I've adopted my boss's office uniform.*

According to an article she'd read a couple of months earlier, it was a well-known phenomenon. She wondered idly if it would be possible to train Rebecca to wear jeans on every occasion.

Like that was ever going to happen.

"So, let's get this straight." Rebecca had obviously not yet decided whether to be angry. "You skipped three shows so you could talk to Rufus and Arabella Ulrich, both notoriously secretive, about their missing daughter? And just *forgot* to mention it?"

Annie nodded.

"And somehow you got in to see both of them?" Rebecca's voice was dangerously quiet.

"Yes," said Annie. "That's right."

"You want to tell me how?"

So Annie told her about Lou. She knew Rebecca would be impressed. *My fashion features editor is friends with Rufus Ulrich's eldest daughter.*

Rebecca might be more subtle in her approval, but eventually she'd use it. She used everything. Her brain was a solid gold rolodex of webs and connections.

Of course, Annie had promised Lou not to tell anyone, but Rebecca wasn't anyone. She was Annie's boss and if Annie was to find Scarlett—assuming, of course, she was even going to try—she'd need Rebecca's permission. No one did anything at *Handbag* without Rebecca's permission.

Having weighed up how little she could get away with saying, Annie had reluctantly decided that Lou's connection to Scarlett had to be the bait. After all, Rebecca didn't have her old news editor's dogged belief in Annie's talent.

"You're close friends?"

"Yes."

Rebecca thought about it, while her town car purred through the side streets and a thousand squat air-conditioning units jutted from the walls around them, all overheating as they tried to cope with the tropical temperature.

"I didn't know Rufus had an elder daughter," she said finally.

"Most people don't," said Annie. Of course, her boss would not consider herself *most people*. Rebecca raised an expertly threaded eyebrow.

"Whatever happened to Scarlett?" she asked. "Haven't seen her for three . . . four years? She was never going to be catwalk, but I'd have thought a beauty campaign. Some of the more mass brands anyway . . ."

Rebecca was thinking out loud so Annie let her. The woman had been uncharacteristically cheerful all afternoon, which meant the legal stuff that had kept her from the shows the previous day must have passed off amicably. It was also a sign that Annie was now accepted. In fact, she'd found herself a part of Rebecca's inner circle since she delivered the Mailer-Lang scoop.

Far from being furious at Annie's double-dealing, when Rebecca discovered Annie had signed a contract with *Handbag* magazine while working undercover for *The Post,* she seemed to have a newfound respect for Annie. Except when it came to her taste in men. "You're *Handbag*'s fashion features editor," she announced the Monday after she'd heard that Chris moved in. "You could do better."

She'd called Annie into her office at *Handbag* for the express purpose of telling her this. But Annie had just smiled and thought of Rebecca's ex-husband. She'd never done city types herself, and she wasn't about to start now.

Seven months Annie had been with Chris, something of a record for her. He'd become familiar, solid, and *permanent*. And that was the part that scared Annie, the prospect of permanence. Even her parents liked him. He'd done everything right, and not in the cynical way she'd seen before. *But permanence?* And how permanent was anything after last night?

"Annie," said Rebecca. "You all right?"

"Yes," Annie lied. Glancing at her watch, she realized Chris would be home by now, at least she hoped so. Flipping open her Nokia, she typed, *Talk later. A. XO* It was more to ease her conscience than anything else.

"So," said Rebecca, not bothering to hide her amazement. "This means Arabella Ulrich is Lou McCartney's stepmother, right?"

It had never occurred to Annie that Rebecca might regard Arabella as the more significant half of that partnership.

"And if Rufus Ulrich is Lou McCartney's father, then it's obviously pre-Scarlett, but that's not possible. Arabella was . . ." Rebecca paused. "How many times has Rufus Ulrich been married?"

Annie grinned; she couldn't help it. Rebecca prided herself on knowing everything about everyone. "Three times, officially," said Annie. "I think it's probably four, but I might be wrong." Annie knew it was five, but there was no need to tell Rebecca about the first Mrs. Ulrich.

Annie watched Rebecca consider this. "Okay," said Rebecca. "Work something up for the news section and let me see it."

"So I can carry on with this?" Annie asked, as the car turned onto Ninth Avenue, passed Pastis, and pulled up outside Soho House, almost opposite the Hotel Gansevoort. She made a mental note to check on Lou later if she didn't appear at the Zac Posen party.

"But of course," said Rebecca, looking at her quizzically. "Why ever not? It shouldn't interrupt your other work."

"It might," Annie ventured. "You see, Scarlett's already been gone"—she checked her watch—"almost seventy-two hours. I should speak to Rufus again, but then I think I need to go to Tokyo, even if just for a couple of days."

"No." Rebecca shook her head. "I can't spare you."

Annie opened her mouth to speak, but Rebecca got there first, her voice slightly clipped. "I'm keen on this story, but we're in the middle of the shows." She paused for effect. "This is our business. Fashion. The shows come first. You need to do London, Milan, and Paris, and do them properly. This is where the ideas for the next six issues come from. Then, and only then, will we discuss Tokyo."

Something in her tone told Annie that this was not a battle she would win.

Waiting as her chauffeur rounded the car to her door, Rebecca turned toward Annie. "Set up a meeting with Ulrich for the morning," she said, her tone signaling the conversation was over. "After that, I want you on the red-eye back to London with the rest of the team."

An unholy trinity of celebrities, models, and fashion journalists crowded the roof terrace at Soho House, an area that featured decking, tables, and chairs and a decent-sized roof pool that was full of petals.

This was no surprise, since the roof was one of the few places left in New York City where nicotine-addicts could acquire alcohol while simultaneously feeding their need to be seen.

"Rebecca . . ."

"Darling . . ."

"You know Zac, don't you?"

Of course she did. Rebecca was one of the editors who had championed him straight out of fashion school. She knew everyone. At least everyone she considered anyone, which was more or less everyone here. Looking around, Annie saw that one person was missing. There was no sign of Lou.

Seven floors above sidewalks so hot they were still sticky underfoot, the breeze off the Hudson combined with the scent of jasmine candles and low-level music to make the atmosphere almost chill. A hundred people thronged the roof, drinking champagne or cocktails, air kissing, and comparing notes from that day's shows.

A crowd of admirers flocked around the designer like moths around an elegant candle. Even Rebecca paid her respects. Only Annie was having a bad time, and that was self-inflicted.

She'd got the timing wrong with Rebecca, something she would never have done while working at *The Post*. Annie seethed, tossing an empty champagne glass from one hand to the other, while scanning the deck for a waiter. *Forbid her to go?* Ken would have bollocked her for not having already booked tickets.

You can always ask for your old job back, whispered a voice in Annie's head. *He'd make you grovel, but he'll take you.* She'd be doing the tea run for the entire newsroom for weeks. Ken would probably even put her back on women's interest for a month or two, on the pretext of making sure she hadn't lost her edge.

Plus, he'd only get to do that, after Rebecca had made Annie work every last minute of her three-months' notice. By then the story would be long dead. One way or another, Scarlett would be found or forgotten. That was the way the news worked. That was why it was called news.

And what would Lou do in the meantime?

Annie needed to rethink, find a way of making the decision to send Annie to Tokyo all Rebecca's own. But how?

Then Lou emerged from the elevator and Annie forgot about Tokyo. You had to hand it to her, thought Annie, as she watched her friend skirt the pool and join the outer fringe of a group of English fashion editors, all busy being unimpressed by the presence of Claire Danes and her latest costar.

She looked great.

Only hours earlier Annie had watched Lou unravel, emotional threads fraying as she tried and failed to hide behind adolescent anger and layers of Touché Éclat. Now Annie's friend looked like she'd just stepped off a catwalk herself, shiny, newly washed blond hair brushing the cotton shoulders of a vintage Ossie Clark dress, with red and white patterned bodice and black skirt.

On Lou's feet were dizzying strappy heels that a flash of red sole as Lou walked revealed as Louboutin. You either had it or you didn't, thought Annie, safe but uninspiring in her party fallback of jeans, Jimmy Choo heels, and "interesting" top.

By the time she'd emerged from Arabella's apartment that afternoon, Lou was gone, for which Annie had been grateful. She felt like a burglar in her best friend's life, and didn't like it. There were incidents in her own past about which Lou knew nothing; Annie had forced herself to admit that. How could Annie be upset not to know about Rufus, when Lou knew next to nothing about Annie pre-*Post*?

Only Chris knew all there was to know and that was turning out to be one person too many. Just knowing he *knew* made Annie feel vulnerable. A feeling she'd been fighting her entire life. Well, since Tony, if she was being honest.

Annie needed to work out who she was following this story *for*.

Lou, because she wanted Scarlett back?

Her own career, because the story had Annie Anderson written all over it?

For the ghosts of Irina Krodt and Patty Lang, a teenage hooker and a junkie modeling megastar, who died on Annie's last two stories for Ken, because both still needed someone to lay them to rest? Annie had be-friended Irina while working undercover for *The Post*'s exposé on people smuggling. The teenage prostitute had wanted to kill herself. Only the Croatian thug who'd smuggled Irina into the UK and sold her into sexual slavery had saved her the trouble.

Or, and this thought shocked Annie, did she want to follow the story for herself? For the girl she used to be before everything changed?

She shook the thought from her head. Working that out would have to wait. Right now she must talk to Lou. She needed inside information on the Tokyo run and she needed it before trying to set up a second meeting with Rufus.

When Annie looked around the roof, there was no sign of her friend. *Shit,* she thought, hoping Lou hadn't given up and gone back to her hotel.

A procession of elegant waiters navigated the crowd, wielding trays of canapés that were almost as elegant. The same guy offered Annie smoked salmon blini four times in five minutes before finally getting the hint. Had no one told him that eating was cheating?

And since when had Manhattan been dry? She'd heard there was an area of the city that was rumored to be alcohol-free, but Annie couldn't believe that Soho House would have set up shop there.

At last, Annie spotted a waiter bearing a tray of what looked promisingly like martinis and made straight for her. It seemed she wasn't alone in her thirst. Several dehydrated fashionistas descended on the waiter faster than vultures on carrion. When they scattered, there were only two cocktails left. To be safe, Annie took both. Only to have one of them lifted straight from her fingers.

"Cheers," announced Lou, downing the drink in one. "Just what I needed."

Depositing her own empty glass before the waiter could retreat to the bar, Annie asked, "Any chance of another?"

Lou flashed a grin at the waiter, who cracked a smile and headed for the bar.

"No news about Scarlett, I suppose?" Annie asked.

The grin disappeared. "No," said Lou. "Not a word. I called Ken about four times this afternoon to see what was on the wire. It got to the point where his secretary just said, 'Hi, Lou, Ken says to tell you no change.' And put the phone down."

"Rebecca wants me to fix a meeting with Rufus."

"Not going to happen," said Lou. "As far as he's concerned you're tainted by association. You'll have to come up with another plan." She smiled sourly at Annie. "How was Mrs. Ulrich the fourth, or whatever she calls herself these days?"

"All right," said Annie, pitching her reply carefully. "But not, you know . . . well, let's just say she was quite composed for someone whose daughter has vanished."

That was a good word. So much better than the others used to describe Scarlett's potential state. Annie thought of all the words that hadn't been said about Scarlett in the forty-eight hours since the news broke: words like *missing* or *murdered, abducted, kidnapped,* or *dead.*

She shivered, despite the day's dying heat. How long would those words remain unspoken and unwritten? Not much longer if Annie knew anything about anything.

"I guess you could say Arabella seemed resigned."

"Surprise me," Lou said, her eyes casting around for the missing waiter.

God, thought Annie. *And I always believed I was the one playing happy families.* "Perhaps," she said, "Arabella was just holding it together. She'd obviously been fending off journalists for most of the day . . . and she was wearing her Ralph Lauren like armor."

Lou raised her eyebrows. "Ralph Lauren? You sure? Not Versace? Cavalli? She was always more Eurotrash than Hamptons."

Annie almost pointed out that it was more than ten years since Lou had seen her stepmother. It was hardly surprising if Arabella's wardrobe had kept pace with the years. But she didn't, there was just too much back history between Lou and Mrs. Ulrich the fourth.

"You know," Annie said, "she struck me as too poised to lose it in front of a journalist. She's not the kind to wash her dirty laundry in public. I mean, if Arabella wants a therapist, she'll pay for it."

"Or Rufus will."

She could see Lou's point, really she could. How did Arabella fund her lavish Upper East Side lifestyle? Was it, as Lou claimed, alimony from her ex-husband? Of course, Annie reminded herself, Arabella had been a successful model herself, and she was nobody's fool; she might have banked the money. And Rufus made every Rich List going. While Scarlett had trust funds worth millions.

Welcome to the world of high-net-worth individuals, where fathers ran credit checks on their daughters' new boyfriends, security came ahead of comfort, and shops opened at one A.M., if that was what you wanted.

"What I mean," Lou was saying, "is that Arabella is as bad as Rufus. Who do you think gets the cash if Scarlett never comes home? I don't know anything about anything, but my money would be on Arabella, wouldn't yours?"

It was the first law of any investigation, follow the money. And Lou was right; the money trail probably led to Arabella. But in this case Annie wasn't so sure. "Arabella says she'd rather Scarlett had just chucked it all in, but Rufus wouldn't let her."

"Well," said Lou. "She would say that, wouldn't she?"

"Come on," said Annie. "I'm not saying I believed her, let alone liked her. I'm just saying let's suspend disbelief for a minute."

Relieving the waiter of another martini, Lou nodded slowly. "At last," she said. She took another deep gulp, emptying half the glass. "All right," she said. "Let's suspend it if we must. . . ."

"Arabella says the agency sent Scarlett to Tokyo. She didn't want Scarlett to go. According to her, Rufus insisted. And Scarlett was too afraid to say no."

Lou shrugged. "You met the man. Wouldn't you be?"

"Look," said Annie, ignoring the question. "Why would Rufus insist on his daughter doing the Tokyo run? And what is it anyway? The way Arabella told it made it sound like the modeling equivalent of purgatory."

"Tokyo's worse than purgatory. It doesn't have to be, but it mostly is. Several of the agencies send new faces there to see if they can hack it. If they can, Tokyo can make them loads of money. If not, they burn up out of sight."

"That's harsh," said Annie.

"Yeah. I remember one girl, a couple of years back. Usual thing . . . she was the next Kate Moss, everybody agreed she had it. So her agency sent her to cut her teeth in Tokyo and that was it. Last seen in Littlewood's catalog. She's not the only one, either. Plenty of them never recover from the shock."

"Shock?"

"Culture shock," Lou said carefully. "You can't get more different, more lonely than Japan, can you? Different language, different alphabet, probably living away from home for the first time. Not to mention different food and entirely different etiquette. You can't make yourself understood, and most of the time you don't know anyone except your local agent. At least in Milan you're a two-hour plane journey from home."

"Only if home is London."

"Psychologically," Lou added, "anywhere is closer to home than Japan. One model once told me she hated every second of her time there. Hated the food, hated the culture, couldn't speak the language, hated being bigger than everyone else—felt like Gulliver in Lilliput, she said—but she refused to come home until she'd earned enough to buy herself a new VW Beetle. And that's what she did. The minute she'd banked sixteen grand, she got the first plane out of Narita."

"And did she make it big after that?"

Lou drained her glass. "Chucked it in the moment she got back. Last time I saw her was on *Pop Idol*. These days she probably gets her VW Beetles free!"

"Okay," said Annie. "I get it. The run is hideous, but well paid. But what I don't understand is why *Scarlett* would do it? And, more importantly, why Rufus would make her. Surely for Scarlett it's . . . well, an insult?"

Better to bow out gracefully, in Annie's books, than go on as someone who used to be iconic. Surely Rufus Ulrich, of all people, would not have wanted that for his daughter?

"Maybe she'd just outlived her usefulness," said Lou, grabbing two more martinis. "Not all new girls do Japan, of course," she continued. "I mean, hello, can you see them sending Lily Cole? Or Bree O'Shaughnessey?" Lou waved her hand toward a couple of post-pubescent redheads with legs that appeared to come up to Annie's shoulders.

"So," said Annie. "You're saying it's only a certain sort of girl who gets sent to Tokyo?"

"Commercial, rather than catwalk. At the beginning or end of their careers. It's pretty obvious where Scarlett fits on that scale."

"You're saying her career's over?"

Lou nodded, her mouth twisting sourly. "Look," she said. "This is the moment I longed for when I first met Scarlett, Rufus's perfect offspring, and her trashy *gold digger* of a mother. Okay? I prayed daily for Arabella's life to fall to pieces, for Scarlett to get herself in trouble, and Rufus to turn to me for help."

"And?" said Annie.

"I'm not enjoying it nearly as much as I thought I would."

twelve

Lou had never been on a plane before. All the other children at school had, even Teresa Waring—and everyone knew her mum and dad couldn't even afford to buy their own council house! So how come *they* could afford to go to Spain for their holidays?

But when Lou suggested Spain, her mother, Nina, had just shrugged, hugged her daughter's skinny shoulders, and said, "Sorry, Lou, no can do."

Biting her tongue, Lou had swallowed her complaints. It wasn't fair. She hated being the only one who couldn't have anything, but she didn't say anything because she didn't want to upset her mother.

In the eight years since Rufus left, Nina had scarcely let Lou out of her sight, except to go to school or visit a friend's house for tea. And then Lou was only allowed to go if Nina was sure she could afford to invite them back a week or so later.

Proud, Gram said.

Broke, Lou called it.

Lou hadn't been allowed to go to London ever, not even for a school trip to the Natural History Museum. And as for the year-six skiing trip, she hadn't bothered to bring that letter home.

Nina had been to London, Lou was sure of it. That's where Nina went when she had to "go away for a few days." Up to London, to see friends and have fun, but she never took Lou with her.

"It's a school night," she'd say, and Lou would have to stay behind.

Tea, homework, bed, in that order. And no television.

Now, though, Lou was by herself on a plane. Just Lou, a copy of that fortnight's *Smash Hits,* and her walkman. A walkman Nina and Gram had bought Lou the day after her twelfth birthday a week ago.

A "late birthday present" they'd called it. Lou knew why she'd got such a big present. It was because of this plane, 37,000 feet above the ocean, because Lou was on her own and because of Daddy. Although, obviously, Lou wasn't meant to know that. Just as she wasn't meant to notice that Gram's box of silver teaspoons had gone from the sideboard.

The thought of seeing her father again gave Lou a sick feeling in her stomach, so she put on her earphones and turned up "I Should Be So Lucky." Somehow it seemed right.

(Gram hadn't thought to buy Lou any tapes, so Lou had spent her pocket money on a blank C90 in Smiths, and recorded songs she liked off the radio.)

She wasn't scared of the plane. Of course not. Nor of the enormous gap between her and the ocean, but she was scared, a little bit, of meeting Daddy. *Rufus,* she said under her breath. Not Daddy, *Rufus.*

Nina had been insistent about that.

"Are you okay?" It was the flight attendant again. Nina had handed Lou over at Heathrow Terminal 4, and then burst into tears.

"Mu-um," Lou had said. "It's only a week."

She never called Nina "Mum," but she'd been so embarrassed. Nina was normally cool, everyone said so—*You're so lucky, your mum's cool.* The flight attendant told a sobbing Nina that she'd make Lou her special responsibility, and she'd been stalking Lou since.

"Absolutely, thank you," said Lou.

"Always mind your manners," Gram had said. "You can be as rude as you like, as long as you do it politely." Gram had a hundred rules like that. No hats indoors, no elbows on the table, decant red wine before drinking it.

Adults had rules they had to follow too. The most important of which was no alcohol before midday or six P.M., although it was fine to be drinking at five if you were still going from lunchtime.

She wasn't sure why she'd said yes when Daddy asked her to come and stay; Nina hadn't wanted her to. . . . Lou guessed it was good she'd been the one to answer the phone. If Gram or Nina had answered, Lou might never have known she was invited.

Come to think of it, Lou still didn't know why he'd called after all these years of forgetting her birthday and Christmas. But this year, just as Lou was about to sit down at the dining room table with Gram and Nina, the phone had rung, and Lou found herself with the biggest birthday present she'd ever had. A return ticket to New York.

"Not so much as a sodding birthday card since she was four. Eight bloody years!" she'd heard Nina hiss at Gram in the kitchen, when they both thought Lou was busy clearing the table. "What the hell is he playing at?"

Gram's voice was quiet, sensible and calm.

"He is her father, dear," she said. "He's legally entitled to see her. But only if Lou agrees." Heavy emphasis had been placed on that final sentence.

"I'll talk to her," Nina said, sounding more relaxed.

Lou knew she was meant to say, *I don't want to go.* The trouble had been she did. She wanted it badly. She didn't want to upset Gram or watch her mother's face crumple, but she did want to see her new sister.

Somehow, Lou was expecting Rufus, Arabella, and her new sister to be waiting at the airport. Gram had given her a picture of Rufus cut from a magazine, to make sure Lou would know him. She'd pictured the scene a thousand times in the past week. Her dad would be waiting when she came off the plane, with his new wife, and their baby girl, and he would hug her until her bones cracked and say how much he'd missed her.

And Lou wouldn't think, *Well, why did you never come to see me then?* She wouldn't think it even once, not even at the back of her head where Lou put all the things it was better not to think.

But when Lou dragged Nina's battered blue suitcase out of Customs at JFK in New York she was greeted by a sea of unfamiliar adult faces. Black people, brown people, Chinese people. It was different from Wiltshire, where her school had one Indian boy and a girl who was half Chinese, whose dad ran the takeout restaurant in the village.

And there were families, lots of them. Noisy and not polite. Brothers, sisters, mothers, and fathers. All waiting to meet new arrivals coming through the sliding glass door. Only there was nobody for Lou. No one whose face had been cut from the pages of a glossy magazine.

She saw a group of men standing in a gaggle, some wearing suits, others in shirtsleeves, all holding cards with people's names on them, mostly written in felt pen. None of the cards said Lou McCartney.

It's fine, Lou told herself. *Dad's probably just late.* Nina was always late, always getting stuck in traffic. He'd be here soon. As people pushed past or around her, and sometimes tried to walk right through her, Lou decided she'd better drag her suitcase to one side, out of everyone's way.

And then, putting on her headphones, she rewound her favorite track and waited, letting Kylie fill her ears. After that she skimmed her copy of *Smash Hits* for the hundredth time, then rewound the tape again. Lou didn't know what else to do. She didn't have a phone number so she couldn't call Rufus.

I should be so lucky.

Lou wanted to call home, but she couldn't do that either, because then Nina would know she and Gram had been right all along, Lou should have been happy with the family she had.

I should be so lucky . . .

The suitcase was hard and Lou's bottom was numb. She shifted from one buttock to the other, but that just meant both now ached. When the song finished, Lou rewound it and played it all over again.

"Miss?"

A black-haired man with a bushy mustache was tapping her shoulder and standing close. One of the men from the group wearing suits and carrying pieces of card.

Lou yanked off her headphones.

"Miss Ulrich?"

"No," said Lou, turning away.

"Miss?" the man repeated. "Are you sure?"

She scowled. Of course she was sure. She was twelve, not some stupid baby. Standing up, she planted her feet apart and put her hands on her hips. She was five feet five inches already, tall for her age, so everyone said, the way her mother had been. Just maybe she was going to be model material; everyone said that too.

Over my dead body, Nina usually replied.

"Miss Ulrich," the man said patiently. "Luella? Your father sent me."

Then Lou realized he did mean her. "My name's not Luella," she said. Then remembering Gram's rule about manners, she put out one hand.

"It's Lou . . . Lou McCartney. How do you do?"

Driving across a bridge should have been fun, especially in the back of a huge black limousine, where Lou could stretch out full-length on cream leather seats and not even touch the sides. But when you were on your own behind a sheet of glass, nothing was as much fun as it should be.

The driver was nice ("Call me Raul," he said), although Lou was trying hard not to like him. As hard as she could while still being polite.

"This is the Brooklyn Bridge, Miss Luella."

"Lou."

Unperturbed, the driver glanced in his mirror and winked. Like he thought it was a joke. "Best view of the Big Apple you can get," he said. "Stays with everyone. Their first drive into the city."

For Lou it was like being inside her own film. The driver pointed out the Twin Towers and the Empire State Building, the shiny silver top of the

Chrysler Building and the looming mass of Grand Central Terminal. He showed her the Plaza and Bloomingdale's and the painted carriages and blinkered ponies along the edge of Central Park. She didn't appreciate until years later that Call-me-Raul had taken the scenic route to end all scenic routes to show her Manhattan's best in one trip.

Her new family wasn't waiting when he pulled into the basement of an enormous apartment block right opposite Central Park. Opening her door, Raul took Lou's hand to help her out and lifted her suitcase from the boot, which he called the "trunk." When the lift, which he called the "elevator," opened, he held the doors back for her and put her suitcase on the floor.

"You'll be met at the top," he said. "Nice meeting you, Miss Luella. See you again, soon."

Lou smiled, and swallowed hard.

Raul had been nice and she had a nasty feeling he felt sorry for her, which only made the sick sensation in her stomach worse.

When the lift doors opened Raul had been replaced by a small scowling Spanish-looking woman. So Lou scowled back, standing aside so the woman could get in, but the housekeeper just grabbed Lou's suitcase and dragged it out, inclining her head to show Lou that she should follow.

The room through which they walked was enormous, but empty. A black leather sofa had black leather cushions. The huge white furry rugs looked big enough to have been stolen from a polar bear. Lou found it hard to believe anyone really lived here. There was no mess, no toys, and no signs of a baby sister. Lou wanted to ask where her father was, but didn't dare.

Hauling Lou's suitcase behind her, the housekeeper led Lou to a door in the far wall. Another door, at the end of a tiny corridor, opened into a double bedroom, with twin beds, matching bedside cabinets, a wardrobe, and a cupboard with a basin sunk into the top. Lou thought it looked smart but rather stiff and unwelcoming. A bit like a hotel.

"This is where you'll be sleeping, Miss Luella."

Lou was sure the woman placed unnecessary emphasis on the last two words.

"Shall I unpack you now?"

"No," said Lou. "Thank you." She didn't want this strange woman going through her suitcase, and then telling everyone how crappy her stuff was.

The housekeeper shrugged. "Your father says change, and then he'll see you on the terrace." She jerked her head back the way they'd come, and then vanished in that direction herself.

Shoving the suitcase onto its side where it thudded softly on the thick cream carpet, Lou slumped against the nearest bed. *Magnolia,* she heard Nina's voice rise scornfully in her head, as Lou eyed the paintwork.

Nina hated magnolia, cream, barley, and all those other colors that tried so hard not to be white. Her mother's taste was for the eclectic and obscure. A taste that had rubbed off on Lou, almost unnoticed. She looked at magnolia walls, cream carpet, nasty pale bedspreads, and matching curtains.

Lou rolled her eyes. It was a million miles from the dark-stained floorboards and battered old Turkish rugs that littered Gram's rectory. Which is where she should have stayed. No one to meet her at the airport, no one to meet her downstairs, and no one even cared now she was here.

"*Stupid cow,*" said Lou, talking about herself. And she pinched herself hard.

When the tears had passed and Lou's anger burned out, she splashed water on her face and sat back on the floor, pretending it had never happened. Taking a deep breath, she tried to think matters through. "He doesn't want you, you know," she said finally, as if talking to someone else. "So why are you here?"

There was no answer to that.

Well, there was. Only not one Lou could bear to say aloud. Lou was in New York because she'd bullied Nina into letting her come. Nina always went to London, so Lou had wanted to go one better.

She didn't have a dad, she never had . . . What had she expected?

Opening her suitcase, Lou stared at the clothes folded inside. Gram and Nina had bought Lou new clothes with the money they got from selling the spoons. A couple of T-shirts, a sweatshirt, and a denim skirt that Lou secretly hated, but didn't have the heart to say, plus a new pair of Levi's 501s. It was more than they could afford, but Lou already knew nothing in the suitcase was suitable for where she now found herself.

Eventually Lou settled on a white vest top and her old jeans. "Better to be comfortable," her mother always said. Sliding bare feet into sneakers, Lou wrapped an embroidered shawl she'd taken from Nina's wardrobe around her thin shoulders. She took the elastic band from her ragged topknot and combed out her hair. When it lay shiny across her shoulders, she applied eyeliner and a layer of the lip gloss her friend Karen had shoplifted from the local drugstore and sold to Lou half price.

Eyeing her reflection in a mirror over the basin, Lou nodded. She looked okay. No one was going to call her beautiful, her mouth was a little too thin, her nose too distinctive . . . But she was tall and thin without being skinny and her breasts had finally begun to grow. Older boys noticed her in the street, and her height made most of them think she was more grown up than she was.

Back in the living area, Lou noticed what she had missed earlier. The glass wall at one end was a huge sliding door, which stood open onto an enormous roof terrace with umbrellas and people.

Drifting through a gap in the door was a murmur of voices, accompanied by the kind of music you heard in shops. Not just one voice or two, but several, some raised louder than others to make themselves heard. It wasn't only Rufus and his new wife out there. A whole crowd appeared to be waiting.

She was about to turn back when the housekeeper appeared. "There you are," said the woman. "Mr. Ulrich is waiting. Come on."

Lou had no choice but to follow.

Outside, Lou was hit by a blast of light and heat and noise. It was hot and blue-skied and sticky in a way she hadn't experienced so far, going from air-conditioned airport to car to apartment. Daddy's garden was a swimming pool, complete with a bar at one end. Lou could almost have forgotten they were thirteen stories above Central Park if not for the surrounding rooftops and the whir of a helicopter in the distance.

"Sir," said the housekeeper. "Miss Luella is here."

And the voices faded.

"It's Lou," said Lou into the silence.

"Luella," said a man, who looked like he belonged in the pages of an expensive magazine. Lou didn't know whether this comment was a correction or greeting so she didn't reply.

She waited. . . . This was not the family reunion she'd imagined. *Rufus,* she decided, looking at him. Not *Daddy,* not even *Dad.*

When Lou didn't move, Rufus got out of his seat and walked toward her. Despite the heat, he was wearing black trousers, polished black shoes, and a white cotton shirt, open at the neck, with the sleeves rolled to just below his elbow.

And glancing about, Lou realized she'd got it wrong. Her father hadn't stepped out of a magazine; she'd stepped into one. All around were small metal tables interspersed with white chaise longues. Draped across the loungers and slouched at the tables were the most elegant people Lou had ever seen. More elegant even than in Nina's old copies of *Vogue.*

In the pool, small children played under the eye of a foreign-looking nanny, who had her hair tied back in a ponytail and wore a white T-shirt to cover the upper part of her body.

What had Lou expected? She didn't know, but it wasn't this.

"How was the flight?" asked Rufus, looking at her as if she was something he might buy, not the daughter he hadn't seen in years. "You seem a little"—Rufus sought the right word—"jaded?"

"No," Lou said. "I mean, thank you, my flight was fine."

Sun ricocheted off the water's surface, and Lou put up one hand to shield her eyes, painfully conscious that she was the only person on the roof not wearing dark glasses.

"Come and meet your stepmother," said Rufus.

Obediently Lou trotted across the hot pavement, feeling sweat prickle under her arms and hair cling to her forehead. As she passed, small groups of strangers eyed her without bothering to disguise their amusement. Some smiled, some whispered, a few laughed or simply looked away. She knew what they were thinking. *So this is Rufus's other daughter. What terrible clothes.*

When Rufus stopped near a slender blonde on a lounger, Lou gasped. She'd never seen anyone so pretty in real life. Arabella looked like a poster for a sophisticated film.

The woman was all body, long thin legs, taut brown stomach, and firm breasts barely contained by two tiny triangles of black fabric joined by a gold chain. Her knickers were even smaller and Lou looked away.

Jealousy flooded her.

At the woman's outfit, at her catlike body, at the way she looked up and gave a warm, confident smile. Lou wanted proper boobs, not her own silly little bumps just threatening to grow. She also knew, if Nina was anything to go by, she was unlikely to get them.

She'd wanted them so much Gram bought her a training bra, a humiliating 30AA, as if further proof were needed that Lou had no need for one. It had been her prized possession until she wore it to school.

"If you didn't have feet, would you buy shoes?" Colin Felps demanded, and Lou had shaken her head, leaving herself wide open for his punch line.

"So, why are you wearing a bra?"

The whole class had collapsed into laughter. Lou had stood her ground, but the Marks & Spencer bra had gone back in her dressing table drawer and stayed there since.

"Bella, darling . . ." Rufus bent to kiss the woman's forehead, his eyes lingering on her body long enough to make Lou feel distinctly uncomfortable. "This is Luella. . . . Luella, this is your stepmother."

Languidly, Arabella Ulrich swung her legs from the lounger, slid narrow feet into the highest pair of gold heels Lou had ever seen, and pushed sunglasses emblazoned with the word Dior to the top of her head. Arabella looked bored, more bored than anyone Lou had ever seen, even in double maths.

Opening her mouth, Lou shut it again. Arabella was beautiful, but she didn't look much older than some of the sixth-form girls at school.

"Hey," Arabella said. She didn't look like a mother, or even a step-mother. Like most of the other women draped across Rufus's roof terrace, she looked like someone from a magazine.

Rediscovering her voice, Lou offered her hand.

The woman gave a barely perceptible nod, her fingers only just grazing Lou's own. As Lou nodded back, Arabella's face shut down. Then her attention flicked to something behind Lou, something that made her frown deepen.

"Darling!" she shouted. "Lettie! Don't do that! Please!"

Lou followed the woman's gaze across the pool to where a blond toddler sat on the far edge, shrieking with excitement. White curls cascaded wildly as the child frantically kicked her feet, like an outboard motor, soaking a small boy who sat on a float a few feet away.

Scarlett wasn't a baby at all, Lou realized. She looked like a little doll. An expensive little doll, as did all the other small girls around the pool, with their frilly bikini tops, matching hair bands, and tie-waist skirts. Everything matched, right down to their toddler sunglasses. Lou had no idea what it cost to dress each child, but she bet it was lots.

For the first time in her life, Lou was able to put words to the feeling that had lurked at the edge of her mind since Rufus had left them. She was *not good enough*. She didn't belong with these people. In fact, Lou was beginning to think she didn't belong anywhere at all.

"Maria!" Arabella shrieked.

The skinny dark-haired girl in a baggy white T-shirt looked up from where she was flicking through a magazine. She couldn't have been more than three or four years older than Lou. Irritably, she glanced at Scarlett and clambered to her feet.

Arabella sighed.

"Fire her," said Rufus. "Find someone else."

She had to be Scarlett's nanny, Lou realized. And then she noticed there were several such girls, in the pool or clustered on the far side. Most of them looked Spanish.

"Scarlett," Maria called. "Don't splash Leif."

Tiny legs still working up a whirlpool of foam to drench her own designer outfit as well as those of the children around her, Scarlett shrieked with laughter and ignored the lot of them.

Lou couldn't help it; she was impressed.

"Luella," said Rufus, steering Lou away from Arabella. "You'll want to see your grandmother." It was more an order than a question.

Grandmother? Lou frowned. What was Rufus talking about? Gram was in Wiltshire, and judging by most of the things Lou had overheard Gram say about Rufus, she wouldn't come here if it was the last place on earth.

Smiling indulgently, Rufus put his hands on Lou's shoulders and propelled her toward the far end of the pool. An elderly woman sat alone, drinking from a champagne flute. A fat paperback lay open, spine broken, facedown on the tiles, getting splashed as she gazed indulgently at the cherub causing such mayhem in the water.

"Mother," said Rufus. "You remember Luella? Nina's daughter," he added.

As if dissatisfied by what she saw, the woman swapped her dark glasses for gold-rimmed spectacles and held them to her eyes, trying to find out exactly who this girl might be.

Lou scowled.

"Oh yes . . . Of course." The woman's Austrian accent made her words even more cutting than they might have been. "Good height," she added, glancing at Rufus. "You were right about that. Pity about the rest."

What a horrible woman! So far as Lou knew she'd never seen this old bat before in her life. From a distance, the woman's age was hard to place. Up close, however, this woman had to be even older than Gram. Though Gram would never dress in a cut-away black swimsuit and leopard-print sarong.

A gold and pearl brooch adorned the costume's halter-neck, and the woman's wrists were heavy with bangles that served only to highlight the thick veins beneath her papery skin. As for her hair . . . Dyed a harsh auburn that made her face look even more like parchment, this had been teased until its curls stood inches above her skull, and through its fine brittleness Lou could see pink scalp.

This looked like no grandmother Lou had ever seen.

Beady eyes watched Lou.

"Sullen too . . . She gets that from her mother."

Lou felt fresh fury rise inside her, mixing with the exhaustion, fear, and anger. She'd upset Nina, worried Gram, and traveled halfway around the world to meet people who didn't even bother to come to the airport. Even worse, she'd let Gram sell her silver teaspoons to buy Lou clothes she didn't need.

And for what? So some old bitch could be spiteful about her mother. It was more than she could bear. Lou's latest defense mechanism came to her aid, her favorite new phrase from school.

The one she should have used on Colin Felps.

"Why don't you just piss off."

For several long seconds Lou thought Rufus might explode, but his fury was not like Nina's, red and swift. It was white and cold and far more scary. Nina would have sent Lou to her room and left her there until she apologized, or grounded her for a fortnight, maybe even a month. If she was really cross, Nina might even have snapped and given Lou a slap.

Rufus was different. Recovering quickly, he regained his smile, though his eyes remained hard, and his request that Lou apologize to her grandmother was a direct order.

Too terrified to defy him, Lou did, almost gagging on the words.

Apology made, Rufus sent her to her room, to change into "something more suitable."

Lou avoided pointing out she didn't have anything suitable, since she lived in a freezing cold rectory in Wiltshire and had never been to an Upper East Side Manhattan pool party before.

As she stomped back into the guest room and pulled her only swimsuit costume from the bottom of her suitcase, Lou decided she would not unpack, because she wasn't going to stay. Of course, she knew that wasn't true, but the pretense made her feel stronger.

Her school swimsuit was navy, with round legs and a round neck. To make matters worse it was baggy across her bee-sting boobs. If that wasn't enough, Nina had bought it nine months earlier in the summer sales, before the start of a new school year, and the vile thing was too short for her body.

How could Lou possibly return to the pool wearing this?

The answer was she couldn't . . .

Slumping to the floor, Lou sat with her back to a cupboard and banged her head against its white doors. Then, pulling her knees tight to her chest, she let the sobs break again through her defenses.

She should never have come. What did she think she was going to find here that she couldn't find at home? And more importantly, why, since she was clearly such an embarrassment, had Rufus Ulrich bothered to invite her at all?

When the crying fit was done, Lou fought her way into her swimsuit and dragged a T-shirt over it, the way she'd seen one of the nannies do. Then she stomped her way outside, scowled at the old bat, smiled blandly at Rufus, and began to swim endless lengths of his pool.

It was only several days later, when she was on the plane home, that Lou realized she was always introduced as "Nina's daughter." Rufus never once referred to her as his.

thirteen

It had been after three in the morning when Annie finally got to bed. Admittedly not her own bed, although that wasn't nearly as exciting as it sounded. She'd finally crashed, fully clothed, on Lou's king-sized at the Hotel Gansevoort.

Why go to all the hassle of getting herself back to Soho, when she could walk half a block and sleep where she dropped? It had seemed like a good idea at the time. But like all things that have the warm glow of divine inspiration at three A.M., it hadn't looked so clever an hour or three after dawn.

Mind you, Annie told herself, as she whirled around Lou's room, vacuuming up scattered belongings before throwing herself into a cab on Ninth Avenue, *it could have been worse.* Although, if memory served, she and Lou had been politely requested to leave Soho House . . .

Not classy, not classy at all, and definitely not in Rebecca Brooks's Fashion Week guidelines. But at least there was no waking in a strange bed with an even stranger man, no drugs, no credit card receipts for inexplicably large bills, and no drink-and-dial shame.

Opening her bag, Annie found her mobile and rapidly ran through sent messages and calls dialed. Nope, no drink-and-dial shame. No calls to Ken, Chris, or worse still, to Tony Panton.

Annie gave herself a mental pat on the back. *See, things could be so much worse.* It was easy to ignore the fact there was also no, "Yes, we must talk" from Chris. One day of silence on his part had turned into two. All the same, Annie couldn't face thinking about that right now.

She had more pressing matters, like getting back to 60 Thompson and morphing into *Handbag*'s fashion features editor, grabbing a bar of Dean and Deluca chocolate, and washing down two Tylenol with a bottle of mineral water from the minibar. After that, all she had to do was reach Bryant Park in time for Ralph Lauren at ten A.M.

God knew when she'd find time to process Lou's childhood memories or even how much of them Annie could remember. The plan had been to get Lou hammered and let her talk. How was Annie to know someone could get that upset about a baggy school swimsuit?

Rummaging for her room card, Annie's fingers closed on something large, hard, and square. She frowned, pulled the object from her bag, and groaned. A glass ashtray, stolen from the roof bar of Soho House. Also not on Rebecca Brooks's list of guidelines.

She'd take the ashtray back later, Annie promised herself, provided she and Lou hadn't done anything last night to get themselves blacklisted. Apart from drink the bar dry and outstay their welcome. She'd have to do it after she'd done all the other things she needed to do today. And at the top of that list was pay Rufus Ulrich another visit.

Unfortunately, when Annie reached Bryant Park, *Handbag*'s editor in chief had other ideas.

"But you said . . ."

It was pointless, Rebecca had made her decision. Despite her promise that Annie could use her last morning in New York to chase down Rufus Ulrich, Annie's boss had drawn up an agenda so full it barely left Annie time to pack. Being Rebecca Brooks, and not having drunk too much the night before, Rebecca's own packing was done.

"She got a call," Iona said at the door to the first show, while Rebecca dipped to air-kiss a rival she'd happily see dead.

"Who did?"

"Rebecca."

For once, Iona's gossip hunger was useful. Annie waited, because Iona could be relied on to say more, probably much more, given a long enough silence to fill. "It was before breakfast, from London."

"Who called?"

Iona glanced around, as if afraid of being overheard. "Sir Ivan Carlyle," she said, naming the notoriously reclusive owner of *Handbag*'s holding company.

"Don't tell me," said Annie. "He'd had a call?"

Iona nodded. "Guess who from."

"Rufus Ulrich?"

Iona nodded.

It turned out Rufus knew Sir Ivan, or maybe it was Sir Ivan's wife, Iona wasn't too clear on the details. Anyway, the upshot was Rufus called Sir Ivan, who then phoned Rebecca.

"You know what about?" Annie asked.

"Obviously," said Iona, who'd probably just been eavesdropping. "He wants you off the Scarlett story."

"Shit," said Annie, before she could stop herself.

Iona immediately glanced around, checking that Rebecca wasn't near enough to hear. "You're not coming to the lunch, are you?" she said, her tone suggesting she found the idea of Annie being invited unlikely.

"Of course I am," Annie said, thinking, *What lunch?*

"Then," said Iona smugly, "perhaps I can leave you to confirm the table?" Annie smiled. "If I could trouble you for the number?"

As Iona slipped into the show, Annie took a turn around Bryant Park, threading her way between old men playing chess and beggars pretending to be war vets.

A table had been booked for four: Rebecca, Iona, and two guests. If Annie intended to crash the party she needed to make it five. The maître d' came to the phone himself to regret this was impossible, even for Rebecca Brooks.

Annie didn't bother to say that was what she'd been counting on.

Promising to call back, Annie took a turn around the park as she worked out how to handle this. Rebecca's choice of restaurant was ten blocks away. Her guest, as revealed by the maître d', was impressive. Alfonso de Soto, the new CEO of Amberlich Inc, newly anointed Most Powerful Man in the Beauty Industry and one of *Handbag*'s major advertisers. He was bringing his number two, the company's marketing director William Moray.

Only, Rufus Ulrich ate at Cipriani on Forty-second Street. At least he did according to Arabella. So it followed that Rebecca also needed to eat at Cipriani . . . Because Annie was going to get her meeting with Rufus one way or another.

Calling Cipriani, Annie asked for a table. When even Rebecca's name was not sufficient, Annie tossed in Alfonso de Soto's, and mentioned she was a friend of the Ulriches, as in Rufus and his ex-wife Arabella.

It was enough.

A table was promised for five people, at the time Rebecca had named. Canceling the previous booking without a second's thought, Annie cited the muddle over numbers as her reason and hung up.

"Done it," she told Iona, when the show was over and everyone tumbled out of the marquee onto Sixth Avenue.

"Done what?" Rebecca demanded, appearing behind her fashion director.

"Confirmed the table," said Annie, adding, "Actually, I had to switch restaurants."

Ice-cold eyes examined her. And at Rebecca's side, Iona went white with shock.

"You did what?"

"Alfonso de Soto hates . . ." Annie named the owner of the first restaurant. "It's well known. They argued a few months back."

Rebecca's gaze flicked to Iona, as if this was something Iona should have known.

Her fashion director stayed silent.

"You'll need to let Alfonso's PA know," Rebecca said finally.

Annie smiled. "I already have."

Three hours, two shows, one press appointment, and half a business lunch later, Annie still felt like shit but she was where she needed to be.

Opposite Grand Central on Forty-second Street, Cipriani was heaving with a lunchtime crowd that looked more business than fashion. Advertisers rubbed shoulders with the sort of lawyer who watched the backs of big corporations, and Annie supposed this was just one of many reasons it was Rufus Ulrich's chosen lunchtime haunt. He would never miss an opportunity to show that he meant business.

A chic midtown sister of its downtown namesake, Cipriani also featured the most flattering lighting north of The Mercer, and boasted someone who was someone at every table. From Ron Perelman to Donald Trump to John Dempsey, there was not a table in Cipriani that wasn't moving and shaking.

If Annie had ever been in any doubt that Rebecca was a player of epic proportions, that doubt was long gone, but the woman's chutzpah also impressed her. She rejected the table on offer with an easy shrug, selected the table she wanted, and made it clear that her busy schedule meant she wanted one course only and would need to be out of here at two P.M. And, to all this, the maître d' just nodded.

"Good choice," said de Soto, arriving a second after Rebecca, Iona, and Annie took their table. Rebecca shot Annie something that could have passed for a smile.

The room was noisy, the air rich with spices, grilled duck, and expensive cologne. Only the cigarette smoke was missing.

Tired of listening to Rebecca selling the merits of *Handbag*'s select readership to her lunch guest, Annie scanned the cavernous restaurant in a poor pretense that she was not:

a) bored to death,

b) rubbernecking,

c) frantically looking for Rufus Ulrich.

The ceiling had to be three stories high at least, Annie decided. A sure sign of money. Those two extra floors made up serious real estate in the heart of Midtown. So filling them with nothing but air was impressively spendthrift. Having exhausted the room, Annie turned her attention back to her own table.

Could Iona make that carpaccio last a second longer? Watching *Handbag's* fashion director chase a scrap of raw tuna around the middle of a large white plate, Annie sighed. If only Iona would pretend to be interested in eating it, Annie might have been able to muster a little respect. Iona still hadn't developed Rebecca's skill at appearing to eat while simply rearranging the plate.

Annie, on the other hand, demolished her chicken Caesar (hold the dressing, hold the croutons, light on the chicken), while fighting off her hangover's demands for an egg and french fries.

The second de Soto's deputy, William, placed his knife and fork parallel on his plate, Annie excused herself and headed for the ladies', still marveling at the man's manners, which were perfect enough to make him almost invisible.

Alfonso de Soto and William Moray, one Spanish, one blond WASP, both perfectly dressed, and between them, controllers of a press advertising budget of ten million pounds in the UK alone. Include the United States and you could add a nought to that figure. If Annie had been Rebecca, she'd have been listening politely too.

As always, there was a line for the bathroom. Even in Manhattan there were too many women and not enough stalls. So Annie passed the time watching a tall blonde precision-apply lip liner. Twenty-four, twenty-five at most, masterfully highlighted hair, legs up to here, the woman reminded Annie of a younger Arabella Ulrich, although something was missing. *Class,* she thought, imagining Lou's mocking snort. This woman was no Arabella Ulrich. . . .

She was head to toe *Sports Illustrated.*

Instinctively, Annie did a surgery audit. Boobs, nose, plus collagen (unless she was born with a trout pout). Botox? Right on cue, the woman arched an eyebrow to shade in her neatly threaded brows.

Nope, not Botox. Yet.

When Annie finally made it to the front of the queue, and found herself standing in front of the mirror as she waited for her turn, the woman was still there, brushing hair that had been blow-dried only hours earlier.

Dark curls, pale white skin, a body several inches too short and too wide to be any sort of model but plus size, the only features Annie had going for her were good skin and her cheekbones.

Don't undersell yourself, Chris always told her. *Yeah, right,* thought Annie, remembering his claims to find her body perfect. Part of her problem was she couldn't believe she was with him. Not a problem the blonde would ever have.

Sighing, Annie gave up on her own hair and began to apply her default makeup of black eyeliner and red lipstick, before watching the blonde push open the restroom door and head outside. As the door swung slowly shut, Annie's eyes followed her across the foyer to where a tall man chatted idly with the maître d'.

Glancing down at his gold Rolex, Rufus Ulrich scowled at the woman who'd been keeping him waiting. A second later he noticed the scruffy Englishwoman trailing his date like a shadow and Annie watched his scowl deepen. Perversely, she felt flattered that she'd registered highly enough on the radar for Rufus to clock her at all, let alone so quickly. But, ego aside, her advantage was lost. It would take Rufus less than a minute to cross the foyer, exit the door, and reach his car.

Still, she'd got front page exclusives in less than that.

"*Mr.* Ulrich," said Annie, stepping out of the blonde's shadow and into his path.

Glancing again at his watch, Rufus gripped the blonde by the elbow and steered her around Annie.

"I'm sorry," said Rufus. "Do I know you?"

It was always a good sign when someone was rattled. "You might not remember." Two could play that game. "I'm a friend of your daughter's. . . . We met the day before yesterday." Keeping pace, Annie could see the maître d' watching her, wondering whether to alert security.

Rufus halted. "I believe I said all I had to say then."

Which was more than you intended, thought Annie.

"Just one question," she replied, leaning forward to push open the door ahead of them. Ha! One-up. The man was thrown, but had no choice but to step through. The blonde followed, eyeing Annie nervously.

Annie struggled to stop herself smiling. *Don't worry,* she wanted to say. *Your clothing allowance is safe.*

Cajoling, coaxing, and trying to convince him that talking to her was all his own idea was pointless when dealing with a guy like Rufus Ulrich. The chances of Rufus answering anything honestly were less than zero. The best Annie could hope for was to get behind that snake-eye stare.

Screw subtle, Annie went straight for the jugular. "What exactly did you say when you last spoke to your daughter, Scarlett?"

The man turned, looming over Annie, his lips thin enough to be almost invisible.

"Why?"

"Just curious. And when exactly was that conversation?"

Anger flared behind his eyes, his face closing down as he fought to control his fury. "I hadn't spoken to her in weeks."

That was interesting in itself. Rufus had been trying to get ahold of Scarlett, Arabella had told Annie. Obviously Scarlett had been less than keen to speak to her father.

"Quarreled, did you?"

"What business is it of yours?"

Annie ignored him. It was only a matter of time before his driver arrived. That telltale hand in the man's jacket pocket was pressing redial, summoning his twenty-first century servant. Annie had seen Rebecca do it. No words were necessary, just one ring would do. *Come NOW.*

"Why did you make Scarlett go to Tokyo?" demanded Annie. "It seems odd. I mean . . . Scarlett's so much bigger than that. Don't you think?"

Rufus narrowed his eyes and a vein in his forehead began to throb. The great Rufus Ulrich was seconds away from losing it in public.

The blond woman was openly staring now, eyes flicking from Annie to Rufus and back. It occurred to Annie that the woman had never seen Rufus rattled before and, for a second, Annie felt the smallest twinge of guilt. She'd been inside one of these relationships. There was no question which cat Rufus would be kicking when he got home.

Out of the corner of her eye, Annie saw a black Lincoln slide discreetly to the front of the restaurant. Rufus saw it too and turned, gripping the woman's elbow.

"Just a minute," said Annie. "You haven't answered my question."

"And I told you . . ." Rufus spun around. "I've said all I'm going to say. I don't know what Luella was thinking, letting you near my family."

Family?

A dozen retorts rose in Annie's throat, but she swallowed them, gritting her teeth and forcing one final smile. "Scarlett's boyfriend. Did she ever tell you his name?"

Rufus stopped as he was about to get into the Lincoln and turned. "Scarlett," he said, "does not have boyfriends."

"Honey, what was . . . ?" the voice was anxious, southern, and abruptly cut off as Rufus's chauffeur slammed the car door behind them.

Interesting, thought Annie. *Very, very interesting.*

"What on earth do you think you're doing?"

Satisfaction fled as Annie turned to find herself face-to-face with Rebecca, who was wearing her new-season Prada like armor. As usual Annie felt small, scruffy, and one hundred percent in the wrong.

"This kept ringing . . ." Rebecca thrust Annie's mobile in her face. "During coffee."

The lie was transparent. Not about Annie's mobile going off, since the screen showed six missed calls. But about the fact Rebecca might schlep around Cipriani after her staff for any reason other than to scold them.

With nothing but a look, Rebecca ordered Annie back inside. "Don't ever . . . ," said Rebecca, her smile belying the threat in her words as they headed back to the table, "get up and walk away in the middle of a business lunch again."

"I . . ." Annie started to explain, to defend herself and her tactics, then thought better of it. She needed Rebecca on her side. "I'm sorry," said Annie. "I forgot myself."

"Quite."

As Annie filed back through the restaurant like an errant child, she could see their table was now occupied only by Iona and an empty espresso cup. The cow didn't even bother to disguise the triumph in her gaze.

"Bitch," muttered Annie under her breath.

Rebecca glanced over her shoulder.

Damn . . . Annie hoped her boss hadn't heard that. Or if she had, she didn't think Annie was talking about her.

"Annie," said Rebecca. "A word to the wise." Her tone was almost pleasant, maternal even. Annie held her breath, it could go either way; either she was off the hook or there was a bloody big ax over her head right now.

"Think carefully before you cross Rufus Ulrich. He makes a very dangerous enemy."

"Bu—"

Raising her hand, Rebecca said, "That wasn't a question, Annie. It doesn't require an answer."

Annie held her tongue. It had been a long time since she'd obeyed someone who told her not to speak.

fourteen

The calls were from Lou. Who else? Six calls in all, but no voice mail and no *where-the-hell-are-you?* texts. Very un-Lou. Very worrying.

"Do you mind . . . ?" Annie waved her Nokia at Rebecca as they walked the two blocks back to Bryant Park for the Vera Wang show.

"Who is it?"

"Lou McCartney."

"If you must," said Rebecca, nodding sharply. All the same, she quickened her pace along Forty-second Street, a resentful Iona trailing behind her.

Annie was surprised. Not because Rebecca broke one of her own guidelines and walked the two blocks to Bryant Park in her Prada slingbacks, but because it seemed her boss couldn't resist a good story any more than she could.

Lou picked up on the first ring. The silence in the background told Annie that wherever Lou was, it wasn't in the second row of any fashion show.

The voice was scarcely recognizable as Lou's. It was thick and hoarse, as though she'd been crying.

"They've found Lettie's body."

Oh, fuck.

Traffic roared down Fifth and across Forty-second, past New York City's public library. Horns honked and drivers swore at pedestrians. Rubber burned in heat and in fury, and the air was sticky with humidity. All Annie could feel was her stomach plummeting beneath her.

Scarlett, whom she'd never even met.

"When?" asked Annie.

"An hour ago. Ken called. . . ."

"Who found her?"

"A tourist. The Japanese police are identifying the body now."

"Lou," said Annie. "Slow down. Has anyone identified the body or not?"

Static crackled down the phone.

"What does that matter?" said Lou. "It's bound to be her." The weariness in her voice was at odds with the implied frenzy of six calls in the space of half an hour. *Shock,* thought Annie, easily identifying the early symptoms.

"Think carefully," she said, falling back on case study tactics. Stay calm, ask only simple questions, and state the obvious. "What did Ken say? Exactly?"

"They'd found . . ."

"What?" said Annie. "Scarlett or a body? It matters."

In truth, Annie knew neither choice was good. A dead Western girl was a dead Western girl, but Annie was trying to be logical.

Silence stretched down the line, heat rose off the pavement, and denim stuck to Annie's legs. Early-afternoon sunlight flashed off chrome bumpers; fumes bit her eyes. Today was going to be as bad as yesterday.

Come on, Lou, it's me, Annie. I know you're in there.

"A body."

Yes! There Lou was, beginning to sound like she might just risk sticking her head above the emotional parapet.

"You sure?"

"Yes," said Lou. "I'm sure."

"Good," Annie said, releasing a deep breath. "Hang on, let me get off the sidewalk."

Cutting around the side of the library, Annie slipped into the back of Bryant Park, behind the hulking marquees that formed the main setting for New York's Fashion Week. The thud of bass boomed from the back of a tent, gently rocking the ground beneath Annie's feet.

"You still there?" asked Lou.

"Yup. I'm back. What else did Ken say?" She wondered how her old boss had handled this. Would he treat Lou as a colleague or place her in the box labeled VICTIM'S FAMILY and keep her in the dark?

Annie knew Ken and would—and once actually did—trust him with her life. But not with a story.

"Did he tell you anything at all?"

"No. He said he wanted me to hear it from him before I saw it on the news."

"What about the others, do they know?"

"Others? What others?"

"Oh, you know, parents . . . stepparents . . . Rufus? Arabella? Nina?"

Annie could almost feel Lou shaking her head. "Fuck Rufus. Like I'd call him after yesterday. And I'm not exactly gonna bust a gut getting this particular piece of news to Arabella . . ."

Lou caught herself. "I mean," she said, "I don't think I'm the person she'd want to hear it from."

"Call Nina, then."

"Nina doesn't even know Scarlett. Never met her to my knowledge. Never wanted to."

"I know, but . . ." Lou and her mother had always seemed so close, best friends, sisters, mother and daughter, all rolled into one.

"Anyway," said Lou. "I'll be on the red-eye. I'm going home to see Nina this weekend. Sod London Fashion Week. My deputy can cover Saturday and Sunday. I'll pick it up again on Monday. I need a break."

Home, where Rufus wasn't.

"Say hi for me to . . ." Annie was about to say Nina, when she realized how absurd that sounded. "Say hi to Ken."

Lou snorted, which could only be a good sign. "Come to think of it," she said. "Ken did say something else. He asked if I thought you were going . . ."

"London Fashion Week? Not if I have anything to do with it."

"To Tokyo."

"Why would he be interested in that?" asked Annie, trying and failing to disguise a surge of interest. "I don't work for Ken. . . ."

"He reckons if . . ." And then Lou faltered. Annie could hear the deep breath taken on the other end of the phone. "He reckons if Scarlett's still alive, you're the one to find her."

Bastard.

"Look," said Annie. "My track record's not that impressive at . . ." She stopped. "I'm better at finding people dead," she finished lamely.

Ouch. Bad choice of words, very bad.

When Lou spoke she sounded surprisingly calm. "If it's not Scarlett, I want you to find her for me, before it is . . . If you know what I mean. Although, obviously, you've got other people to consider. So I'll understand if . . ."

"Rebecca? She's not keen, as you can imagine."

"I didn't mean her," said Lou.

"Who then?"

"I meant Chris."

"Ah . . ." Annie felt a small but undeniable surge of shame. Lou didn't know about her argument with Chris, obviously. "He'll understand," she said.

The silence that swirled across Manhattan told Annie that Lou didn't buy this any more than Annie did. He would mind. If she was honest, he already did. "We had a fight," she admitted.

"About what?"

"I did something stupid."

"*Annie . . .*"

"No," said Annie. "Not that."

"A serious fight?"

"Yes," said Annie. "At least, I think so. Chris turned up here un-announced, when we had already agreed we'd see each other again next week."

"Why agree that?"

"He's busy," said Annie. "And I'm working." *And I don't share my work space with anyone. My bed, yes. Bits of my life. Even the mess inside my head . . . But work? No, that's never going to happen.*

"How serious was it?"

Annie shrugged, watched only by a couple of sparrows and a half-dozing bum. "Not sure," she said. "I'll find out when I get back."

It was past seven P.M. in London but Annie knew Ken would still be at the office. He always was.

Annie didn't recognize the voice of the woman who answered the phone. This was hardly surprising. Her old boss went through secretaries like he went through cups of coffee. There was a slight flicker of recogni-tion when Annie gave her name, almost imperceptible, but it was there all the same.

"Think he's in a meeting." The woman made no effort to sound con-vincing. Annie knew as well as she did that unless a big story had just bro-ken, the only meeting taking place would be in The Swan, the news desk's local. "I'll check."

Annie glanced at her watch. It was 2:20 P.M. New York time. Rebecca would be seething at her lateness, but there was little point in Annie going into battle without every available bit of ammunition, and there was only one place Annie could get what she needed.

"So, the fucking prodigal daughter returns. . . . " Ken's limitless supply of clichés was obviously still in place. "To what do I owe this unexpected pleasure?"

It's entirely expected, thought Annie. *You've probably been taking bets on how long it was going to take me to call.*

"Hi, Ken," she said, all sweetness and light, though she'd happily have kneed him in the balls. "Lou said you wanted to speak to me."

"Can't think where she got that idea." Annie listened for the grin in his voice, but couldn't detect it.

"Is it Scarlett?" Annie asked.

"Who?"

Annie gritted her teeth. As if it wasn't enough that she'd picked up the phone, now Ken wanted her to beg. "The body in Tokyo," she said. "Do they think it's Scarlett Ulrich?"

"Not sure I can disclose that, love." The old bastard was enjoying this a bit too much.

"Come on, Ken, give me a break here."

"Ha!" Annie's ex-boss burst out laughing. "Fucking got you! Knew you couldn't keep away from a story like this."

About to protest that she was only doing it for Lou, Annie changed her mind. She didn't have a winning hand here, at least not yet. And Ken had something she wanted, information not yet released to the public, so better to play by his rules.

"Just tell me."

"Why? What about that stuck-up cow you work for now? What's she got to say about all this?"

Annie hesitated a beat too long.

"You haven't told her, have you?" Something in Ken's tone told Annie he was playing to an audience. She had visions of the entire news desk dying of laughter at her expense.

Wait, she told herself, as her fingers flexed over the off button. *You dumped him for Rebecca; this is the price you pay for wanting his friendship back.*

"Don't tell me," said Ken, "the famous Annie Anderson is scared of some fucking mag hag. I reckon I ought to be offended."

"I'm no more scared of her," said Annie, "than I was of you. Which is not at all."

The comment earned her a second's silence and then Ken was back. "Yeah," he said. "I guess that might just be the truth."

"Believe it," said Annie. "You've had your fun. Do I get your help or not?"

"Depends. You heading for Tokyo or not?"

"Could be," Annie said, crossing her fingers and praying to the God she didn't believe in that she wouldn't be flying out there as a freelancer.

"You'll give us the exclusive?"

"News exclusive. You'll have to share it with *Handbag.*" Annie knew Rebecca going for that was about as likely as Jennifer Aniston lending Angelina Jolie her best pick-up outfit, but Annie could face that later. "That's my best offer."

There was a bark of laughter. She had a deal, Annie knew it. Now all she had to do was convince Rebecca to fund the trip and come up with the goods herself.

"So," said Annie. "What are the Japanese police saying off the record?"

Ken's hesitation was Annie's first clue that she might not like what she was about to hear. "It seems," said Ken, "that it's not the first body . . ."

"*What?*"

"The Tokyo police have been trying to keep a lid on it," he said. "Word is the victims are all Western, all female, all blond, and all around the same age."

Annie felt sick.

"What's the MO?" she asked.

Ken's voice was somber. "Nasty . . . Let me give you what I've got first. And," he added, "don't tell Lou any more than necessary, all right?"

"Of course." Like she'd do that.

"A tourist found a body early evening. So, this morning UK time. Came in on the wire, five feet nine inches, blond, female, Caucasian. That's all the Japanese will say right now. Lying under some motorway bridge. Hang on, let me pull tomorrow's page up. It's the lead on five."

Annie clocked that. Relegated to page five already? That had to mean Ken didn't think it was Scarlett.

"Nah," said Ken. "Not a motorway. Something called the Shuto Expressway number three. Means fuck all to me, but it seems that's like the M1, only right in the middle of the city. One of the guys on the sports desk went there to cover the World Cup, you know the one . . ."

Yes she did, and he happened to be a stupid one-night stand she'd been trying to live down ever since. "Get on with it."

"Well, he says imagine the Westway, make it six lanes, and stick it above Oxford Street. It's in the area where the Westerners live." Ken paused for effect. "Place called Roppongi."

Oh, shit. Annie could write the headline herself.

"Don't tell me," she said. "You're calling him . . ."

"The Roppongi Ripper."

Why did she even like this man? Annie wondered, hearing the glee in Ken's voice. Because he was a bloody good journalist, and because sick humor was Ken's way of staying sane after forty years in the business.

"What do we know about the others?" Annie asked.

"Only one body so far, bar this one. Claudine Mitchell. Australian, twenty-three, had been working in Tokyo for six months, teaching English with a sideline hostessing, so I hear. She was the first to vanish, although the police found her only about ten days ago. In a shallow grave near Narita, not far from the airport. So this is different. . . ."

Again, that hesitation.

"Tell me," said Annie.

"Mitchell had been kept alive. Probably for weeks. The body was far less decayed than anyone had been expecting. It didn't get much pickup here. A half column, page ten or twelve. She wasn't a Brit. None of them are, so far. But Scarlett Ulrich's different. She got front-page treatment. Obviously none of us had connected her vanishing with the Australian girl then."

"And this one?"

"Could be an abduction gone wrong. Or . . ."

"We have more than one friendly neighborhood psycho," Annie said, finishing the sentence for him.

"Alternately, it could be a copycat. From what I hear, Tokyo has some weird people. Never been there," he added. "Never want to . . ."

Despite herself, Annie smiled. It was a miracle the guy had left his northern hometown long enough to find himself in London, let alone make a career there.

fifteen

Elbowing her way through a crowd of Standing Onlies, who were penned at the entrance to the Bryant Park tents, Annie discovered the Vera Wang show was running forty minutes late.

Perfect. So was she.

Waving her ticket at a security gorilla, Anne stepped past the red rope he flipped to let her pass and watched him glare at a fashion student who tried and failed to slip through on Annie's tail.

Strange how life changed. Last season, even with a decent seat allocation, Annie was regarded with suspicion—contempt, even—now the guards just waved her in. She didn't feel any different, didn't look different either. Her clothes were mostly crap, her hair still overdue for a trim. Maybe appearance didn't matter so much as behaving like you belonged. And, in a way, she did belong now.

Somehow, she'd managed to wind up as part of an industry that was even tardier than she was. Everywhere else, Annie's problems with punctuality had landed her in hot water. School, parents, boyfriends . . . all had regarded her flexible approach to timekeeping as lazy or just plain rude. Here, it was a positive asset. In fashion, she just looked nonchalant.

A familiar rush hit Annie as she pushed her way through the crowds still thronging the catwalk. Excitement and anticipation, tinged with disbelief and a dash of horror at the sheer extravagance and excess of the entire spectacle.

Although Annie still tried to view the whole charade with an outsider's eyes, she couldn't deny a macabre fascination with fashion's excesses. Sure it was big business . . . but it was also the closest the twenty-first century got to a traveling circus. Fashion was the modern equivalent of the old carnivals with their bearded ladies, fat women, and dwarves. It was like a living hall of mirrors.

Milan was altogether more flamboyant than New York, but still flagrantly commercial. It was Paris, the city of fashion and light, which held the undisputed artistic crown. Paris was where the talent flocked. From Galliano to McQueen to Lagerfeld, Paris was the city of fashion spectaculars.

Traumatized, exhausted, and up against two unforgiving deadlines, Annie had missed Paris last season. At the time it had felt like no hardship, but now she was intrigued by the prospect of her first Dior show the week after next, her first McQueen. Fashion could do that to an otherwise sane person. So secure was it in its own worldview that it crept under your defenses. While logic said there were more important things than shows and tickets, next season's key pieces or this season's model, the fashion world waved its front-row seat allocation, its A-list guest goodie bag and begged to differ.

Not yet wearied by years of shows running late, or jaded enough to regard a third-row seat as beneath her, Annie had at least learned not to laugh aloud. Not to stare at other editors pretending they couldn't care that camera crews surrounded Anna Wintour and not them.

People-watching was Annie's favorite part of the whole affair. The clothes came a poor second. All the same, she was learning to recognize vision, talent, and cut, and could spot a trend at a hundred yards.

Elbows out, conscience in, Annie pushed her way to where the British press were banked, too far along the catwalk, too close to backstage for a good view. Typical New York PR positioning. Only two empty seats remained, in rows two and three. Since Annie's seat was in row two, behind Rebecca and next to Iona, Annie guessed the other belonged to Lou.

No need to cover for her though. Lou had no one in New York to check up on her. And there was no point in Annie even trying to hide her own clumsy entrance. Rebecca might appear to be chatting amicably to Colin McDowell of the *Sunday Times,* but she missed nothing. Though Rebecca did not even move her eyes, Annie knew that her watch had been checked and Annie found wanting.

Ignoring Iona's pointed sigh, Annie leaned forward and rested one hand lightly on Rebecca's Prada-clad shoulder. She knew it was childish, but the familiarity of the gesture would enrage Iona.

Darkness fell and the auditorium echoed to the rustle of PVC being lifted and notebooks being opened, all eyes settled on the gap where backstage became front. *Handbag's* editor in chief was no exception. Rebecca didn't turn or show the slightest awareness of Annie's presence, but a tensing of her shoulder told Annie that for the next few seconds at least she had her boss's attention and should make good use of it.

"They've found a body," she whispered, as close to Rebecca's ear as she dared to get. "It's being identified now."

After the show, backstage formalities dispensed with, Rebecca Brooks was standing on Sixth Avenue, impatiently dialing her driver before most other editors had even gathered their belongings.

"What do you mean?" she demanded, waving her hand at a procession of shiny black Lincoln town cars, one of which would have her name on it. "They've found a body?"

"It will be in tomorrow's papers," said Annie. "Four missing girls. And this is the second body."

She caught Rebecca's look. It showed appalled fascination.

"Four?"

Annie nodded. "There's every chance this body won't be Scarlett. . . ."

"But the next one might be?"

Annie let the silence hang as Rebecca identified her driver, slid herself into the back of the car, and motioned for Annie to join her. Iona was back at the tents, filling in for Rebecca. For Annie this was just a happy side effect.

"Come on," said Rebecca, so briskly Annie thought she was speaking to the driver. "Give this to me straight."

So Annie did, saving the best for last.

"I was thinking . . . ," said Annie, winding up. "I'm not saying our cover exclusives haven't been great."

Careful Annie.

"Drew Barrymore, Scarlett Johansson, Hilary Swank, Jennifer Connelly . . . all classic *Handbag* covers, women with rather more to say than your standard-issue Hollywood airhead, but we've had nothing *newsworthy* since . . ."

Annie let the word hang, waiting for Rebecca to catch up, but not to overtake her. She wanted to stay in control of this story for as long as she could.

"I don't mean to sound callous," Annie went on, knowing she did, "but whichever way it goes . . ."

She meant, *If it's not Scarlett.*

Annie needn't have worried. Rebecca Brooks had magazines to sell, advertisers to impress, the competition to whip, press coverage to garner, and awards to win, the latter almost more important than the former where a magazine with *Handbag*'s turnover was concerned. And Rebecca would do what it took to achieve that. In fact, within reason she would do anything.

"And if it is?" Calculating brown eyes regarded Annie.

Picking up her Hermès Birkin bag, Rebecca extracted her BlackBerry, manicured nails clicking against keys. The machine flashed to life and Rebecca hunched over it. Annie recognized the signs. Her boss was checking deadlines, working out the longest possible extension on the current issue, checking who was on the next cover and whether that star's publicist would tolerate her being tossed back an issue.

All the while, her impressive photographic memory would be rearranging the magazine's flatplan, shuffling features like tiles on a board.

"And if it *is* Scarlett's body?" said Rebecca.

Lou will be devastated, Annie wanted to say, *and I'll probably be the one who has to tell her.* But that wasn't what Rebecca wanted to hear; and it wasn't going to pay for a return ticket to Tokyo.

"Tragic, obviously," said Annie. "But practically speaking, not a problem."

"When will we know?"

Annie considered the question. "Depends on the Japanese police," she said.

"Would you use the same approach as the Patty Lang piece?"

"Use Lou to get access to Arabella and maybe Rufus?"

Rebecca nodded.

"Yes," said Annie.

"And if you can't?"

"Then . . ." Annie paused, wondering if she was really going to do it. She was. "Lou McCartney becomes the story." For a second she couldn't believe the line she'd just crossed. She wasn't sure why she was shocked at herself. After all, it wasn't as if she hadn't used people a million times before. Just not a friend. Her best friend.

It's what Lou wants, Annie told herself. *Lou asked you to do this.*

The hypocrisy wasn't lost on her. Because hanging the story around Lou would expose a secret her friend had spent her whole life hiding. The fact she was Rufus Ulrich's daughter. It was a truth that would change everything.

Lou McCartney would cease to be. She would become someone else. She would be Luella Ulrich. The living memory of an unhappy union between a financier who was now one of America's 100 richest men and Nina Mac, one of the seventies' biggest supermodels.

Rebecca was eyeing her with open interest, and for a split second Annie got the uncomfortable feeling her boss knew what she was thinking.

"Go on," said Rebecca. It was an instruction.

"Cover-wise," said Annie, forcing Lou to the back of her mind and preparing to say the unsayable, having just thought the unthinkable. "I was wondering . . . I mean, I know it's a departure. But who owns the rights on the Mapplethorpe image—the *Winter Skies* cover?"

Rebecca's smile looked like nothing so much as that of a cat. In this case, a cat that had cornered a mouse and now intended to extract its intestines, slowly. In Annie's experience, that smile was not a good sign. Although, if her guess was right, the victim Rebecca intended to torture was the competition.

"Call the office," said Rebecca briskly. "Get Alicia to change your ticket and find you a hotel."

Annie tried to contain her glee.

"One week," Rebecca said. "And I mean it. I want you in Milan a week from Saturday, as planned. And you stay in touch, every day. This time keep me in the loop."

sixteen

After two hours, Annie had packed, called Rebecca's latest personal assistant at home, confirmed the details with Ken, and even put in a call to Arabella, who finally gave Annie the name of Scarlett's agency in Tokyo. Everything that could be organized had been. The plane tickets were reserved and the Tokyo hotel booked—some excessively flash place in a district called Akasaka, miles from Roppongi and not what she'd had in mind at all.

It was now five P.M., her car was booked for nine A.M., she needed to be at JFK by ten-thirty and her JAL flight to Narita left on the dot of noon. Although she'd believe that when she saw it. Mind you, they were Japanese, so maybe her plane would take off on time.

Rebecca, she thought, *I love you.* New York/Tokyo/Milan, it was going to be one hell of a week. So why didn't she feel better about it? The fight with Chris. If she was honest, she'd known all along that that was what troubled her.

She hadn't called him. He hadn't called her. No phone calls, no texts since her tentative white flag yesterday morning, not even an e-mail. All she felt was a tight knot of fury that he hadn't understood, hadn't given her a chance to explain. A tight knot of fury, and a fear that things might have gone too far to be mended.

The love of her life . . . the stupid thing was, she meant it on the days she wasn't wondering what the hell she'd got herself into.

Oh, fuck it, thought Annie.

She called her place first, knowing Chris wouldn't be there. He'd be at his office, working late on seating plans for the London shows, wondering which fashion editors and celebs he had to indulge and which he could afford to offend.

As the phone rang and rang, fourteen, fifteen, sixteen times, Annie realized she felt sick. Whether it was dread at how Chris might react, or her own alarm that she minded so much, Annie didn't know. Either way she didn't like it.

When, after twenty rings, the machine hadn't picked up, Annie punched the cancel button on the phone, saved from committing a final act of cowardice. Scrolling through her mobile's address book, Annie found CHRIS MOBILE, and pressed CALL. For several horrible seconds she thought he was going to reject her call.

She should be so lucky.

"Hello, stranger."

Annie searched for anger in his voice and found none. The guy was either a saint or past caring, and Chris wasn't the past-caring type. Early on, his capacity for tolerance, hidden beneath layers of pure lust for her, had only added to his irresistibility.

But how far could she push that tolerance? And had she already moved beyond it? She never had been good at working out boundaries for herself.

"Hi," she said. "Look, I'm . . . "

"Yeah," he said. "Me too, Annie."

Changing my plans was what she'd been about to say.

"Where are you?" he asked.

"At the hotel. Packing for tomorrow."

"Good. What time's your plane?"

"Noon."

"Hey, that's earlier than I thought. What time d'you land?"

Annie felt beyond guilty. He hadn't smelled a rat. She was surprised, too. After all, there were no flights from New York to London at that time of day. What's more, he'd clearly decided to give her a break over Tony. He'd want answers, but he'd listen. Which was more than most men would do.

She was tempted to let it go. Not lying exactly, but not telling the whole truth either. Chris had to be *the one*—bizarre as it sounded—because she couldn't lie. With any of her previous boyfriends she'd have prevaricated, picked a fight, or just plain lied. Or she wouldn't have bothered to call at all.

But this was different. This was Chris.

"Look," she said. "My love, I'm sorry. . . ."

"Hey, let it go. I shouldn't have been so cross."

"No, that's not what I mean." Annie sighed. "I mean, I do . . . I am sorry, but that's not what I . . . Look, I'm not coming back to London tomorrow."

There was a silence. Rather than let it develop, Annie plowed on.

"Rebecca's sending me to Tokyo instead."

"Tell her no."

"She's my boss."

"Yes, and I'm your boyfriend. We need to talk. Anyway, you're allowed the occasional Saturday off."

"Not in this job."

"Annie . . ."

"Chris, I *want* to go." There, she'd said it.

"Why?" There was anger in his voice now. It frightened her, but it didn't stop her from wanting to go.

"It's Scarlett Ulrich, she's missing."

"Yeah, I know. The whole world knows. It's all over the news, but what's that got to do with you? You chose *Handbag*, remember? You said after Milan you didn't want that life anymore."

Annie remembered.

She remembered, too, that Chris had asked her if she meant it, and Annie had insisted she'd had enough of dark, cold lives and tortured souls. She'd been lust-addled and in love, and it had been the truth. Back then.

Oh, God, thought Annie, feeling the words form in her head. *I'm going to have to do it again.*

"It's not just me," she said. "It's Lou."

Her best friend's sister was missing in Japan. Surely, it was only human to want to help? But still, words that Annie had thrown at herself a dozen times echoed in her head, *Shouldn't you deal with your own can of worms first?*

No, she thought. *That's not what this is about.*

"This is about Lou."

"What's she got to do with it?"

So she told him, using Lou's secret to buy herself time.

"Scarlett Ulrich is Lou's sister? And Lou's asked you to find her?"

"Uh-huh."

"Lou McCartney?" said Chris, his voice revealing part hurt, part disbelief. "My Lou . . . ?"

Annie got it now. Chris and Lou went back years. They'd been friends long before Annie met Chris. In fact, if it hadn't been for Lou, Annie and Chris wouldn't be together at all.

"Shit," Chris said. "I can't believe Lou wouldn't tell me something that big."

"She hasn't told anyone," said Annie. "She only told me because of Scarlett and probably wishes she hadn't. It's been under wraps all these years, and now . . ."

Annie paused. Now *what?*

Now Lou's chance of keeping herself out of the news was almost non-existent. Whatever happened next, whether Scarlett was alive or dead, Lou would become part of the bigger story. Rebecca, Ken, and Annie all knew it. Annie wondered how long it would take Lou to work it out for herself.

"Okay," Chris admitted. "So, you've *got* to go. But why not come home first? Just for the weekend. Have a break, get yourself together . . ."

She would have done it, braved Rebecca's wrath and yet another change of plane, and returned to bed, as hungry for Chris as he was for her. She would, if only he hadn't described her place as *home*.

Home is where the heart breaks.

It was probably a lyric, and if it wasn't it should be. Her flat, that scuzzy little set of rooms in Westbourne Grove, had become home. His home, their home. The word didn't have the same comfortable resonance for her that it did for him, and they'd still have to talk about Tony Panton.

"I'm sorry," said Annie. "I really am. But I've got to go tomorrow."

When Chris spoke again his voice was flat.

"No," he said. "You haven't *got* to. You *want* to. You won't find Patty Lang in Tokyo, you know, Annie. Or Irina. You won't find who you were before Tony Panton. Move on, Annie. . . . No one gets to turn back time."

Stung, Annie stared at the wall above her bed and a floor-to-ceiling leather headboard that had been the height of fashion when the hotel was designed. The last rays of sunlight through a badly drawn net curtain split into a kaleidoscope of colors behind her tears. Better by far than watching what waited behind her eyes.

A gothic choker of purple bruises around a teenage hooker's neck, the emptiness in Patty Lang's ice-blue eyes as they stared unseeing at a gray Italian sky. There was no one to blame but herself. She shouldn't have told Chris. She'd given him this power to hurt her by sharing the things that haunted her dreams.

"I'm going now," she whispered. "I've got packing to do."

No answer, but he was there, because the words CHRIS MOBILE still filled her Nokia's small screen. Chris didn't say a word; he didn't need to.

She knew what he was thinking: *Why am I sitting in your flat in London, if you're not here?*

"I'll call you as soon as I get to Tokyo, I promise."

"Yeah, you do that."

"I love you."

That was when Annie realized CHRIS MOBILE was gone. In its place she read, CALL ENDED.

seventeen

The plane stank of noodles, even in business class, unless it was miso soup. The smell was salty and vaguely sexual, but that could have been just her. Neatly dressed cabin crew crouched beside seats, so as not to look down on customers. The food had been something very dead and equally uncooked. She could have had penne arrabiatta or salt-crusted roast salmon, but she'd chosen the Japanese alternative, mostly because she felt she should.

Sleeping on planes had always given Annie problems. They could shut the blinds and turn up the temperature, pour alcohol down her throat, and force-feed her enough nibbles to induce a carbohydrate coma, but it never worked. On the screen a small white plane crept, millimeter by millimeter, across Alaska as Annie tried to order the thoughts fizzing around her head.

Height: 39,000 feet.

Temperature: -76 degrees Celsius.

Distance from destination: much too far.

Another eight hours to go. It was a form of water torture, death by a thousand useless facts.

Tapping a button to lower her seat, Annie pulled a blanket up to her chin and closed her eyes. All she got were thoughts of Chris. . . . Chris angry with her, Chris feeling upset, Chris looking sulky, Chris's tousled head on her pillow, Chris naked.

A familiar ache started up again. Without even thinking about it, Annie trapped her hand between the thighs of her jeans and locked her muscles so hard they made her fingers hurt.

Sex had been something Annie barely bothered with after Tony. Unless she was drunk, and even then she hated the following mornings for more than just their hangovers. And then she met Lou . . .

With her easy come, easy go, flatter-them-and-dump-them procession of young blond surfer boys, beautiful idlers with chiseled bodies and easy lives. The kind of pretty boys that only a woman born to self-confidence, self-belief, and a private income can afford. Or so Annie had always thought. Although she'd been wrong about the private income. All those vintage clothes came from Nina and Nina's mother. The place Annie had dubbed Granny's attic.

Annie's own post-Tony routine had been simpler, its rules primitive:

1) Never fall in love.
2) Never let anyone get close enough to hurt you.
3) Never sleep with anyone you really like.

Bad plan, sleeping with men you really like. It was breaking rule 2. And look at her now—she'd fallen for Chris.

And yes, there was one other rule, rule 4. The one about using condoms. Annie wasn't stupid. Often.

For the first eighteen months after Tony she'd chosen celibacy, kept single and safe by an aura of simmering anger she wore like cheap perfume. And then a drunken one-night stand with that sports journalist tipped her into a different phase of her life. Not that Annie could remember why she began having sex again, because she never felt much better for it, just picked herself up, showered thoroughly, and moved on. And, unlike Lou, she'd been terrible at picking up men.

If there was one man in a bar not afraid of the C-word, Annie would find him. The one man among the hundreds wanting *commitment*. Finally she met Chris, whose messy brown hair never looked brushed, even when it was, whose warm blue eyes made her insides wobble when he looked at her, whose smile made his face collapse and her with it.

It wasn't lust; it was love.

Annie just hadn't bargained on it finding her. And not expecting it, she'd forgotten to dodge. For the last six months she'd barely been able to be in the same room as Chris without touching him, and the feeling was mutual. When they weren't at work, they were in bed, making love and talking, eating and drinking only when they remembered.

She got used to seeing her own body naked, she got used to seeing his. Chris had wanted to come to New York for the whole week. All she had to do was say yes. Annie still wasn't sure why she hadn't.

Actually, she did know.

Chris knew too much about her. He'd peeled layers from her memory the way other men might strip off your clothes. And in return he'd given her confidence. A confidence every other man who met her assumed she already had.

And somewhere down the line she got scared that Chris knew too much. Scared and careless . . . Careless enough to believe she could face down Tony Panton.

Taking a deep breath of recycled air, Annie tried to steady herself. An addict in withdrawal was how she felt about Chris, as if a drug on which she'd become dependent over the past six months was being removed.

Not wanting him to come to New York and being angry when he did, being *busy, busy, busy.* All that burying herself in work. She'd been seeing if she could survive without him. If she could go cold turkey on Chris and remove him from her life as smoothly as he'd slipped into it.

But she couldn't.

Worse, she didn't want to. A week away from him and she was hungry for his voice and touch. The miles between them only made her need greater. Now, perversely, she was heading in the opposite direction. Not to London but to Tokyo, flying backward into tomorrow.

Undoing the buttons of her jeans, Annie slid her hand over her belly, thoughts of Chris leading her fingers into her panties, finding herself already hot and wet with longing. Chris's head between her legs, his tongue inside her, images came rushing as her fingers curled inside. His hands on her breasts, fingers kneading her nipples, as he ignored her plea to just fuck her.

Annie let her fingers trace the path of his tongue, over and over, until she finally came, in silence, grinding against her own hand, trying to free herself, but only leaving herself in tears.

How did I let this happen? she asked, as her body shuddered beneath the red airline blanket. *What was I thinking?* But soon she stopped thinking, her brain empty, her body finding sleep in the remembered arms of the man she was running away from.

eighteen

"I think this one's mine," said Lou McCartney, reaching into the overhead locker for her Mulberry. The girl next to her just nodded. Almost everyone on the flight was carrying the same tan leather bag, heavy with pockets and buckles.

As the fashion bus from JFK landed at Heathrow, Lou and pretty much everyone else on the plane ignored the pilot's instruction not to turn on their phones until they were at the gate. At once, Lou felt her Motorola go ballistic, almost vibrating itself to bits under the weight of incoming voice mail.

Rufus, she thought, feeling the cloud that had settled over her life grow a little darker. *Why can't he leave me alone?*

Her phone continued vibrating all the way from the arrival gate to passport control, from passport control to baggage reclaim, and from baggage reclaim through customs to the arrivals hall, where Lou scanned the crowd for her driver, still conscious of an unwelcome buzz against her hip.

"Lou . . ." A tousle-headed man in a black T-shirt, jeans, and striped suit jacket held up a card that read MCCARTNEY. He had the look of someone who'd worked all night and spent the last hour dozing in a car park.

"Chris! What are you doing here?"

"Picking you up from the airport. Didn't you get my texts? I paid off your taxi and gave the man another twenty. He seemed happy enough."

"You could have been anyone!"

He shrugged. "Needed to talk," he said, taking her suitcase. "And I wanted to do it face-to-face. I have to be back in London by two. That still gives me time to get you down to Wiltshire."

"What are you driving?"

"Bought one of the new Mini Coopers. The S model."

Lou smiled. He might be one of the least macho men she'd met, but he was still a boy. "We'd better move then," she said.

As his Mini headed for the M4 and Wiltshire, where Nina and Gram waited at the rectory, Lou checked the messages on her mobile, giving Chris time to collect his thoughts.

One text announcing that the man beside her was at the airport. Plus nine missed calls, two from call back, and seven from him. He'd sent the first at 5:45 A.M.

Lou didn't know whether to be relieved or worried. On the plus side, the calls weren't from the man who suddenly seemed to consider himself her father, but this might be worse. Lou hadn't had so much as an e-mail from Chris for months. Not since he and Annie vanished into bed.

She didn't mind, not really. Lust happened, though this time it had taken her two closest friends AWOL at the same time. Besides, it was her own fault for introducing them.

Recognizing Annie and Chris as kindred spirits who had too much in common not to get along—both suspicious, both hurt by love—Lou had been sure she'd created the perfect couple. Now she was beginning to wonder.

The slip road gave way to the M25 London orbital and then the M4 motorway itself. Still Chris said nothing, merely dodged traffic and kept his eyes out for the speed cameras. Just one of dozens of vehicles to slam on their brakes every time a camera appeared.

"Hey," she said finally. "Talk to me."

"I thought Annie might be with you." He hesitated. "That wasn't why I came. I mean, I knew she wouldn't. But I thought she might, you know . . . ?"

Lou didn't.

Surely, Annie hadn't gone to Tokyo without telling the poor bastard? His next question answered that for her.

"So she went?" he said.

She sighed, part relief that she didn't have to tell Chris where Annie was, part sorrow at the hurt in her friend's voice.

You did this, she told herself. *You are to blame.*

What the hell had she been thinking, imposing Annie on the nicest man in the world? "Didn't she explain?" asked Lou.

"Uh, I just didn't think, you know, she'd really . . . go. We were meant to be spending the weekend together."

"Chris, London Fashion Week starts tomorrow! You're insanely busy."

"Yeah. That's what Annie said."

"Did she say why she'd gone?"

"That's the other thing," said Chris, sounding hurt. "I'm really glad the body's not Scarlett and I hope the Japanese police find your half sister quickly. But I can't believe you didn't tell me about Rufus Ulrich being your father."

Bloody Annie. It was obvious she'd tell Chris, but who else had she told? If Rebecca Brooks knew about Scarlett, then she knew about Rufus, and if Rebecca knew then it was only a matter of time before the world did. Years of carefully crafted disguise out the window.

"When would I have told you?" asked Lou. "We haven't seen each other in months."

"You could have told me any time in the last seven or eight years," Chris said. "I thought we were friends."

"We are. If it's any comfort I haven't told anyone."

"Annie said that as well."

"Well, she was right. And I wouldn't have told her if I'd had any choice."

"So why did you?"

"You know Annie," said Lou. It was meant to be soothing, one of those passing comments used to fill silence. But it was the wrong thing to say.

"I'm not sure I do. I mean, I thought I did. But then I thought a lot of things. I flew all the way to New York to see her and she didn't even pretend to be pleased to see me. So I turned around and came straight back."

"Chris . . ."

"She didn't even call until last night. And now . . . Well, we need to talk and she's on her way to Japan . . . Look," he added before Lou could speak. "You can tell me. Has Annie got someone else?"

Lou laughed; she couldn't help it.

Men . . . even the good ones were all the same. If you weren't with them you had to be with someone else.

"Annie said you had a fight?"

"She told you that?"

"Yes, something about an old boyfriend."

"Did Annie tell you he turned up at her hotel in New York? That he sent her roses and she went to supper with him? This is a man who . . ."

"What?"

"Doesn't matter. *She went to supper with him,*" said Chris, pale with anger. *"He sent her roses."*

"Annie hates roses," Lou said.

"Yeah."

"She's going to Tokyo for me," Lou said firmly. "I want Scarlett found and Annie can do it. I know she can. But I should have thought . . ."

"It's okay," he said, suddenly abashed. "And I'm sorry about Scarlett. All the same I bet she didn't take much persuading." His anger had blown over as quickly as it blew in.

"True," said Lou. "But I'm still sorry it's fucked up between you. It's my fault for asking her. She's doing this for me."

"I'm sorry, too, but I don't think she is." Chris sounded sad. "She's doing it for herself. She thinks she can find Patty and Irina. That somehow finding Scarlett alive will bring them back. That's the truth, isn't it?"

"Chris . . ."

"Well? Isn't it?"

"No," she said finally. "Annie knows Patty and Irina are dead. She might not like that fact, but she knows it. If you want to know the truth, I think Annie is trying to find a part of herself."

For a moment Chris was silent. "I'm not sure that's any better," he said.

nineteen

Another year, another airport. Another limo driver bearing a card with someone else's surname where Lou's own should be. Another limo driver standing where her father should be, and never was. The difference, this time, was she knew the card was meant for her. It didn't make it any better.

"*You* are Scarlett's sister?" the man asked.

The holiday at Casa de la Torre went downhill from there.

"Did you sleep well?"

Rufus sat at a large rectangular table, crowded with coffee pots and milk jugs, bowls of jam and butter pats, when Lou walked into the villa's dining room at precisely nine A.M. as directed.

"Yes, thank you," Lou lied.

(Have you done your homework? Did you stay at Monique's last night? Have you been smoking? Yes/Yes/No. Stick to it and repeat.)

Taking one of two vacant seats, Lou sat next to Scarlett, rather than go anywhere near Rufus's mother. It was no contest. Precocious or not, Scarlett won. *Look at the parents to discover the infant,* Lou heard Gram's voice say.

She eyed the croissant, butter, and Danish pastries with alarm. At sixteen, Lou didn't eat breakfast at the best of times. One Weetabix with skimmed milk and black coffee if forced by her mother, but Nina had long since stopped fighting that battle. Lou just knew Rufus wouldn't be so accommodating. And even if Rufus was, there was no chance that his mother, now eyeing Lou's outfit of band T-shirt with the sleeves hacked off and cut-off denim shorts, would be.

Lou stretched across the table for a cup.

"Luella!" Rufus said sharply. "Where are your table manners?"

Meekly Lou withdrew her hand and waited for Rufus to pass her a cup. He didn't.

"The girl has no manners," said Inge, the woman Rufus seriously expected Lou to call Grandmother. Lou glared at her, daring Inge to say, *I blame the mother.*

The only missing element of the Ulrich family triumvirate was Arabella. Lou couldn't imagine Arabella was a breakfast woman. Black coffee and half a grapefruit, if pushed, much like Lou herself probably. However, Rufus wasn't a man to tolerate objects being out of place, and with Arabella missing, the breakfast table felt strangely awry.

"*Scarlett,* don't eat that," said Inge. "It's bad for you. Have some fruit."

"Hullo, Loulou," the small girl said, as if her grandmother simply hadn't spoken, and stuffed a piece of bread dripping with jam into her mouth. Lou was sure she could detect a hint of *screw you* in the six-year-old's action. As if to prove it, Scarlett placed her small jammy hand on top of Lou's own and squeezed.

Lou grinned, despite herself.

"Lettie, you'll make a mess." Arabella's voice made them all jump.

"Mama," said Scarlett, her face breaking into a smile as she held out sticky hands, wanting a kiss. She looked a million miles from the knowing cherub splashed across the Driver album and half the posters Lou had seen on her way to the airport.

Arabella sighed. Her blond hair was slicked into a chignon, her gaze hidden behind the blackest of glasses. She bent to kiss the top of her daughter's head, keeping her own white swimsuit and sarong as far away as possible from the jam.

"Look at her," said Arabella, her anger finally settling on Rufus.

This was new, thought Lou. Four years ago, which was the only other time Lou had seen the woman, Arabella wouldn't have dared.

"What is Lettie doing even eating jam?" she asked Rufus. "You *know* how hyper she gets. . . . And how did she get so messy?" She switched her attention back to Scarlett. The answer was obvious. In brushing one of many errant strands of hair out of her eyes, Scarlett had left a sticky raspberry trail across half of her face.

"Come on," said Arabella. "We'd better let Pia clean you up."

"Arabella! What about breakfast?" demanded Inge, before Scarlett could clamber down from her chair. "You must eat something."

"I'm not hungry."

Lou watched the exchange, wondering if that line would work for her.

"Of course you're hungry," the woman persisted. "You hardly touched dinner last night. You must have breakfast. Breakfast is the most important meal of the day."

Arabella's teeth set in the least convincing smile Lou had ever seen. Taking advantage of the standoff, Lou stretched across the table, grabbed a cup, and sloshed coffee into it as Scarlett busied herself wiping jammy hands on a pink frilly skirt. Obviously, the skirt matched two triangles of gingham that passed for a bikini top. What was it with dressing small girls like adults?

The coffee was so dark and chewy it was a miracle the liquid sloshed at all. Still, Lou took another slug, pretending it wasn't too strong for her taste. Here she was spending the summer at a private villa near the citrus- and fig-covered mountains north of Deja, Majorca's most sophisticated part. Blue skies and blinding sun reflected off a glittering sea. There were yachts in the bay, an old Moorish castle on the headland, noisy crickets providing a backdrop to the high-pitched whine of bare-topped Spanish boys on tiny motorbikes. It was near perfect, apart from the present company.

All that was missing was a Gauloise hanging from her lower lip, but there was no way Rufus would let her get away with anything like that, not even a Silk Cut from the packet bought at duty free and hidden in her suitcase.

Worse, he'd probably tell Nina and Nina would go mad. Lou had been chain smoking behind her school since she was thirteen, so God only knew how she was going to get through these two weeks without a cigarette.

"Arabella," said Inge. "What can I pass you?"

Pushing the thought of nicotine from her mind, Lou reveled in Arabella's obvious discomfort. Although she understood enough to spot it when Arabella neatly deflected the attention onto someone else.

"Lettie!" she said. "Your skirt!"

Arabella had found her victim, and Lou surprised herself by feeling sorry for the child.

"Now we must change you!"

Scarlett began to wail. Rufus winced, nursing an expensive hangover behind even more expensive sunglasses.

"Get. Her. Out. Of. Here."

But Arabella was already gone, yanking Scarlett from her seat and dragging her away, bare toes scraping across rough tiles.

"So, Luella," the elderly German woman said, as if nothing had happened. "What are you having for breakfast?"

"I'm not hungry either," said Lou, trying to brazen it out. "I had an enormous meal on the plane yesterday." It wasn't technically true, but Lou was willing to bet she'd eaten more last night than Arabella had.

"Nonsense! Rufus! What is this? They must eat! Tell Luella she must eat!"

Annoyance flashed across Rufus's face. "Luella, for crying out loud, get yourself some breakfast."

"I'm not hungry." Lou could feel her back teeth clench. "I don't *eat* breakfast. *Nina* doesn't make me."

"Your mother," Lou wasn't sure whether his venom was aimed at her or her mother, "should know better."

"Ah, Rufus," his mother said. "She doesn't. Never has. You know that."

Lou dug sharp nails into her palms. She wanted to hiss and cry or throw her coffee in the old hag's face. She wanted to use every blasphemous word she'd taught herself for good measure. But she had another two weeks of this. And Lou had learned early that there were better ways to fight a war than head-on.

The last time she'd met Inge, their total conversation had contained two fine blasphemous words. Lou wouldn't fall for it again; she was better than that. She was Lou McCartney. Inge Ulrich was nothing to her. None of the Ulriches were.

"Luella." Rufus shot her a warning glance, and for the first time Lou saw fatigue in his face. But she saw no affection either. No *Come on, give me a break* in his glance, just irritation.

"Cereal," said Lou, scraping back her chair. "That's my best offer." When she returned, it was with a thin layer of Special K covering the base of her bowl and the merest splash of milk. Fifteen grams of Special K were fifty calories. Lou knew that, a friend's mother kept a calorie book, and Lou had memorized the whole thing while sitting on the counter, drinking endless cups of Red Mountain.

The second Lou emptied the bowl; she pushed back her chair again, its metal legs scraping across terra-cotta like nails down a blackboard.

Rufus winced. "We'll be by the pool at ten," he said. "I'll see you there." It wasn't an offer.

Lou turned on her heel, ready to stalk to her room. Then she remembered what she'd wanted to ask him.

"Rufus," she said, deciding not to pussyfoot around. "There's a strange door in my room. It's locked. Do you know where it goes?"

Her father looked at her, his expression a mixture of curiosity and amusement. "To Scarlett's room," he said. "Pia is allowed the occasional night off, you know."

Something woke Lou. Somewhere in the distance a wild dog barked, the noise echoing off limestone cliffs and becoming a howl before dropping into the tarlike sea.

Listening to waves crash against rocks yards from her window, Lou lay still. She'd been awake only a few seconds, but she was wide-eyed already. Just a slither of early-morning light crept under the curtains, barely enough to make out the huge Spanish wardrobe next to her balcony doors.

Only one more day of this and she could go home. Her father and the others were staying a full month at Casa de la Torre, but Lou had only ever been invited for the middle two weeks of that. A full fourteen days too long if you asked Lou. Another day, and then she was out of this hellhole.

Except it wasn't a hellhole. It was a lovely old villa, with peeling stucco walls, wild goats in the garden, and an olive tree so old it had split in two and each half had taken on a life of its own.

Lying awake, listening to the sea, Lou heard another sound. It was so faint that at first Lou thought she must have imagined it, but the harder she listened, straining over the sudden hammering of her heart, the more certain she was that it was there. The sound of someone breathing.

Someone close. Someone who wasn't her.

As Lou stared hard into the half-light, her eyes slowly adjusting to the dimness of her room, she caught the faintest silhouette at the foot of her bed. Sitting bolt upright, she stared at the figure and realized it was smaller than she'd thought. The shape hadn't moved, hadn't made a sound but for breathing. And then, as the first light of dawn cleared a hilltop outside, the silhouette gained a sudden halo of fine blond hair.

"*Scarlett!* Fucking hell!" Suppressed fear came out as a string of four-letter words.

The child barely blinked.

"What the fu—" Remembering she was talking to a six-year-old, Lou reined in her anger. "How did you get in here? You scared the sh—You scared me."

Scarlett said nothing, didn't move or cry as Lou had expected, didn't call for her mother. Just sat there. And for a split second, Lou thought she was looking at the cover of an album.

The album.

The one that was everywhere, top of the charts both sides of the Atlantic and just about everywhere else. From silver to gold to platinum, and then triple-platinum, *Winter Skies* was a classic, everyone said so.

Even Nina.

The defining album of the decade. An album no self-respecting member of the dinner-party-throwing classes could live without. The one with the face of a cherub on the cover. Eyes so blue they looked retouched, although they weren't.

"For Christ's sake, Scarlett," snapped Lou. "Say something, you're freaking me out." All she got in reply were waves, dawn birdsong, and silence. Flicking on her bedside light, Lou blinked. For a second Scarlett looked so beautiful it almost hurt.

But Scarlett wasn't a photograph, she was real.

How long had she been there? Lou had no idea. The kid had taken to trailing Lou like a shadow for the past two weeks, sometimes just sitting across the table and staring like a character out of *Children of the Corn*. And she was still holding that damn tin robot some Japanese photographer had given her, clutching it tightly to her chest.

"*Lettie?*" said Lou, clambering out of bed and forgetting to yank down her too short T-shirt. The child didn't move, just stared with the piercing blue eyes Lou had seen a million times before on posters.

"*Lettie?*"

Lou reached out to shake her half sister, panic clouding her brain. What if Scarlett was ill? Then it dawned on her.

She wasn't ill, or anything like it. The kid was asleep.

Lou had never met anyone who walked in their sleep before, but one of the girls in her class had a cousin who did, and had announced with some authority that it was bad to wake her. You could kill a sleepwalker if you woke them badly, the same girl said. Lou wasn't sure she believed her.

Moving slowly, she crouched beside Scarlett and waved her hand in front of the cherubic face. Not even a blink. What was she supposed to do now? Gram would know. But Gram wasn't here, and Lou didn't want to wake her with an early-morning phone call. She'd have to deal with this on her own. Or find Rufus, and Lou certainly wasn't going to do that.

Casting around for inspiration, Lou's gaze fell on the mystery door. Ajar now, it had been shut and locked when Lou turned out her light. This was obviously how Scarlett had got in, but who had unlocked it? Had Pia done so before she finished for the evening?

Or did Scarlett have a key? Surely they wouldn't give a six-year-old the key to her own bedroom door? No, Lou thought, the truth was more pro-saic. Rufus or Arabella had probably done it.

Play with Lettie.

Take Lettie for a walk.

Pia's busy, see what Lettie wants.

Two weeks of being at everyone's beck and call. That was why she was here. That was why Rufus invited her, she should have known. She wasn't here as his daughter, she was the substitute childminder. Some sort of un-paid nanny. Well, she wouldn't fall for it again. And who was going to know if she woke the child with a shake?

"Scarlett," said Lou sharply.

It was so tempting. . . .

But she didn't. It wasn't Lettie's fault, it was *his.* "Come on," said Lou. "We'd better get you back to bed."

Scarlett took the hand Lou thrust at her, the small fingers warm and soft in Lou's own, holding tight.

"This way," Lou said, leading her through the unlocked door into a mir-ror image of her own room, with everything from bed to basin reversed. *Through the looking glass,* thought Lou.

The smell hit her immediately. And Lou realized she'd half-noticed it already, but now it was unavoidable. Scarlett had wet the bed.

Leaving Scarlett by the door, Lou followed the smell to the twin beds. One was undisturbed, the other a soggy mess of soaking sheets. The am-monia wasn't overpowering, just obvious, like school loos but without the pungent chemicals that were meant to mask the smell but never did.

Picking up a plastic cup on the bedside cabinet, Lou found a sticky residue of orange still evident in the bottom. Someone had given Scarlett juice before bedtime. Not a great idea, if the child was inclined to wet the bed. Well, replacing the sheets wasn't her job, and Lou was damned if she was going to clean up. It was bad enough she had to sort the kid out. There was no way she was going to change her . . .

Lou sighed. Scarlett was six. Was it her fault if Rufus was a shit?

Pulling Scarlett's bedspread up over the soggy mess, Lou drew back the covers on the other bed, plumped the pillows up for Scarlett, and opened and shut drawers until she found a clean nightie.

"Here we go," she said.

Scarlett just stood there.

"Some family," Lou muttered, coaxing the toy from the child's fingers and easing the sodden nightie over her blond curls. "She's not even my real sister."

Lou tossed the garment into the basin and then rinsed it through as an afterthought. She wet a flannel and wiped Scarlett down. Then smoothed the new nightie over her head, picked her up, and put her carefully in the bed, pulling the covers up around her.

"Bloody child," she said.

But when Scarlett was tucked under the sheets, the tin robot resting beside her on a freshly plumped pillow, spooky blue eyes firmly shut and thumb in her mouth, Lou remained there, watching, to make sure Scarlett was safely asleep. Once the child whimpered and Lou quietly stroked her cheek until she settled again.

Scarlett Ulrich, six-year-old superstar.

How could any child be that beautiful? wondered Lou, as she chewed her lip. Well, Nina might call Arabella "trailer trash," but Scarlett's mother still looked gorgeous. So did Nina, most of the time. Scarlett got her mother's looks. Lou got her father's. What kind of justice was that, when she couldn't stand the man and he evidently couldn't care less about her?

As Scarlett rolled over, taking her weird little robot with her, Lou winced, reaching out to snatch up the toy before it started up, but the alien didn't wake and neither did the child. So Lou remained there, perched on the side of Scarlett's bed watching and waiting, babysitting the most famous child in the Western Hemisphere as she slept.

When Lou was sure Scarlett wasn't going to wake, she crept back to her own room. Although she left the connecting door open, just in case.

twenty

Flight JAL005 from JFK to Narita offered full Internet access, something Annie still thought of as a novelty, although plenty of airlines were offering it these days.

Huddled in a pool of light, Annie skimmed the news sites, checked her e-mail, and learned the same fact from five different sources. Ken had been right: the body found in Roppongi was not Scarlett Ulrich.

So she typed "photographers Roppongi" into Google, in case it gave her a lead on Scarlett's boyfriend. But there were dozens of studios in the area, and most of them featured at least one person with a Western name.

She'd have to persuade Lou to ask Arabella for more details.

Lou wasn't going to like that one little bit. Still, Lou was talking to her, which obviously meant she hadn't talked to Chris yet. And her last e-mail with the Spanish holiday memories of Scarlett had been interesting. Lou didn't strike Annie as the type to be good with children, and yet she'd obviously been fond of Scarlett, in spite of herself.

As an afterthought, Annie downloaded a couple of maps of the Akasaka and Roppongi districts onto her laptop, checked the instructions for catching the limousine bus from Narita Airport to Akasaka, where her hotel was based, and skimmed her way down a list of useful Japanese phrases.

A search for English-language Japanese newspapers produced seven. Most of these had websites with copy taken from that day's editions. None of them seemed to include staff lists.

Annie finally stopped wanting to shoot herself about thirteen hours into the flight. Eight hours in was worst, around the time she looked at her watch and discovered she still had six hours and ten minutes to go before her four-star metal prison landed in Japan. This was shortly before today became yesterday and then segued into tomorrow all in the width of a dateline. By the time her plane finally landed she'd passed through the exhaustion barrier and emerged briefly on the other side.

What struck Annie most as she joined a line that shuffled from one form of confinement into another—the first of a succession of gray corridors at Narita Airport—was the smell, or lack of it. Each airport had its own scent, of heat wafting off runway, of damp permeating the fabric of buildings, of spices mingling with chemicals in the air . . .

But Narita, well, Narita didn't. It smelled of nothing, and somehow that felt even more alien.

The line waited quietly, nobody breaking rank. The Westerners on Annie's flight made instantly obedient by the first touch of Japanese soil. Or maybe their jet-lagged brains were incapable of independent thought, let alone mutiny.

Annie checked her watch to make sure it had been reset from East Coast time, to which she'd barely adjusted, to her new time in Tokyo. She decided she really didn't want to know what the clocks said back home.

Konichi-wa, sayonara, domo arigato . . .

She practiced her few rudimentary words, hello, good-bye, thank you. But saying those words and understanding the answer was likely to be a different matter. As for identifying them in *hiragana, katakana,* or *kanji,* forget it. People could study written Japanese for years and still struggle.

Annie needn't have worried. Beneath every sign in Japanese script was the meaning translated into English. *Immigration. Customs. Baggage.* Thoughtful and polite, but strangely sterile. She'd been expecting her senses to be assailed as they had been in North Africa and India, even North America, where the assault came from the chaos and gruffly issued instructions. Narita Airport was quieter than a hospital.

Nowhere was the silence more deafening than in Immigration. Noiseless queues snaked back and forth. No officious uniform-clad immigration officers shouted "Step down" as kiosks became free, or lost patience when you didn't realize they were talking to you.

No children cried from confusion, lack of sleep, or boredom. Sounds were muffled by miles and miles of pale gray carpet where usually there was hard cold tile. Clean, quiet, ordered. All the clichés she'd ever heard about Japan appeared to be true.

"Ec-scuse me, Miss." The voice was so quiet Annie scarcely heard it, let alone registered the man was talking to her. "Ec-scuse me?"

Annie turned and a small middle-aged passenger with the flattened features of a South Korean nodded at the space in front of her. The queue had moved on but Annie, lost in thought, had not.

Quickly nodding her thanks, Annie moved forward. The man smiled and closed the gap, the line behind him following. Not so much Mexican wave as Narita shuffle, decided Annie. To make sure she didn't repeat her mistake, Annie focused on the bright yellow windbreaker of a teenage boy several places ahead of her, and moved whenever he did.

Getting into Japan turned out to be easy. Unlike New York, where immigration officers gave the distinct impression they might chuck you out for the hell of it, the Japanese stamp on Annie's passport came with a nod and smile. Annie waited for the catch, but it didn't come.

Exiting the airport was a whole other matter.

It had taken all of Annie's willpower to turn down an offer from Rebecca's PA that she prebook a car. Her reasoning was that if she was going to find Scarlett she had to become Scarlett, get inside her head. That was how she'd always worked as an investigative journalist. Kind of method journalism.

If Annie was honest, she knew she'd spent too long inside other people's heads already. It was one reason she gave up her job at *The Post*. And here she was, doing it again, trying to channel an eighteen-year-old girl who'd been used to having everything done for her.

Well, been used to it once.

Lou's e-mails, her early memories of Scarlett helped, but Annie still needed to choose a beginning. And that beginning was here at Narita, where Annie had just got off the same flight Scarlett had taken eight months earlier, landing bemused, jet-lagged, and alone. Scarlett would have had no driver to meet her, no all-expenses paid limousine to drive the two hours into central Tokyo, where a cheap apartment waited, arranged by her agency. How did it feel to have no one to carry her suitcases and pay her bills, no one to do her bidding?

Yes, Miss Ulrich. Of course, Miss Ulrich. Will there be anything else, Miss Ulrich? All that was in the past. Instead, she'd been sent to modeling Coventry, and like any other student, tourist, or returning midlevel Japanese executive, she would have had to take the limousine bus into town.

Whoever came up with that name had clearly never been anywhere near a limousine. And by the time Annie worked out which of a dozen round trips to the city stopped at her hotel, the bus was already pulling away without her.

"When's the next hotel bus to Akasaka?" asked Annie, paying three thousand yen for a ticket. Roughly twelve pounds she worked out, doing a quick calculation in her head.

"Akasaka Prince or Akasaka Tokyu?" asked the young woman behind the counter, handing Annie a ticket held carefully between both hands.

"The Prince . . ."

"Fifty-five minutes to the hour." The young woman smiled, as if the news she was giving wasn't the most depressing news Annie could have heard.

"What about to Hotel Tokyu?"

The young woman looked puzzled. "Ec-scuse me?"

"Can I get a bus to the Akasaka Tokyu and walk to the Prince?"

"Yes." The young woman smiled. "Number fifteen, fifty-five minutes to the hour."

Annie groaned. There was obviously a system and that system could not be tampered with, especially not by someone who didn't speak the language or even know where either hotel was.

There was no coffee shop in the arrivals area, and nowhere to sit, so Annie wheeled her luggage to a small kiosk hung with magazines. It was an oasis of color in an otherwise beige landscape. The Japanese editions of *Elle* and *Vogue* fought for space with homegrown-style magazines, their English-language logos looking out of place in the burst of Japanese text. Picking up *Vogue*, she began to flick through, remembering to start from the rear. Unfortunately, even then, Annie couldn't tell the ads from the editorial. The whole magazine gave her a headache.

Dropping *Vogue* back onto its pile, Annie pulled her suitcase around to the other side of the kiosk in search of a *Herald Tribune*.

She couldn't have missed the picture of the blond girl if she'd been blind, the smiling face standing out among all those politicians and serious business leaders. Annie couldn't read a word, but she understood it was the girl they'd found, the girl who wasn't Scarlett. Lou's sister alive meant someone else dead.

Assuming Scarlett was still alive.

A small Japanese woman half-bowed and half-nodded and Annie nod-bowed back. "Do you . . ." said Annie. "I mean, have you . . ." She stumbled, uncertain how to ask for an English-language paper.

The woman said something unintelligible. There was little Annie could do but shrug, only to get a horrible feeling that shrugging was one of the many Western habits that were the equivalent of sticking up two fingers in Japan. Rummaging through a pile of newspapers, the woman re-emerged seconds later with a copy of the *Tokyo Herald*, which bore the same photograph but with an altogether more familiar language.

"*Domo arigato,*" said Annie, handing over a ten-thousand yen note and smiling apologetically. The woman smiled back, every muscle in her flawless face screaming *irritating tourist,* in the politest possible way, as she emptied her money apron in search of change.

Paper bought, Annie pulled her mobile from her bag and switched it on, wondering who to phone first. The screen lit, the battery for once was full and Annie's phone began searching for a network.

And searching.

"Come on," Annie muttered, skimming the front page of the *Tokyo Herald* while she waited. The dead girl was Donna Newton, twenty years old, a Texan who modeled part-time and waitressed at a club in Roppongi.

Annie held her breath, eyes racing down the page. Surely it bore all the hallmarks of the Roppongi Ripper . . . ? But no, it didn't. According to Phil Townend, the *Tokyo Herald*'s chief crime reporter, the victim had fallen twenty-five stories, from a building above Shuto Expressway number 3. Her boyfriend was being questioned about a *crime passionnel,* and the police weren't looking for anyone else in connection with their inquiries.

"*Crime passionnel?*" muttered Annie.

She thought that phrase had gone out with the ark, except in France, obviously. Annie didn't know whether to be relieved or appalled. Relieved it wasn't the Roppongi Ripper, or appalled by the fact this girl's murder no longer warranted police time now it had been redefined as domestic.

Searching, said Annie's mobile.

Five minutes went by, then ten, and Annie went to find her bus, but even with her luggage stowed and the limousine bus about to leave, Annie's Nokia hadn't found a compatible network. Rebecca was going to love this.

All right, Annie told herself, first stop the Akasaka Prince, and pray it has a decent Internet connection. Second stop, call the offices of the *Tokyo Herald* and see if Phil Townend, its chief crime reporter, might favor a quick drink. Third stop, find herself a damned cell phone that worked.

The journey from Narita to the center of Tokyo was no more or less surreal than the journey from SFO into San Francisco, JFK to Manhattan, or Charles de Gaulle to central Paris. Roads, houses, and road signs, meandering urban sprawl—it was all there, where it should be, but something was off. It looked the same but felt different, and Annie wasn't sure why.

Maybe it was not being able to understand the advertising slogans? Perhaps it was the neatness of everything around her? Then again, maybe it was just jet lag. She felt as if she'd left her brain in New York, her body somewhere above the Pacific, and her heart . . . who knew where she'd left that?

Annie was lolling sleepily, with her head to one side like a drunken commuter on the last train home. Shaking herself awake, she tried to concentrate in spite of the heat. It was hot in Japan and raining as well now, and the inside of the coach was steamy despite the air-conditioning.

The city began to defeat the countryside long before Tokyo proper began. Neat shrubs along the side of the motorway were being repaired by men in orange uniforms, who grubbed up sick-looking bushes and swapped them for lush green plants of the same size. As if the endless replacement could keep nature looking natural.

She had to be at least twenty miles outside the city, Annie guessed, when what looked like small paddy fields and isolated industrial units gave way to state housing. Squat tower blocks, almost indistinguishable from those lining the approach to Waterloo or Kings Cross in London, appeared to the right of the motorway. Despite the traffic, smog hadn't stained them, and no windows were boarded or broken.

Clothes dried on the balconies like colored flags, not slung across hastily erected washing lines but arranged in neat rows, with mats also hanging over the sides to air. And below the blocks, nestling in their shadow, small houses stood higgledy-piggledy, their tiled roofs—not exactly Western, but not obviously Asian—a patchwork of green and black and red and brown. It was all so . . . normal, and yet so not.

Project housing gave way to commerce as factories soared above the roadside. Annie noticed familiar names written in neon and plasma across their roofs. BMW, Seiko, Mitsubishi, and Toyota fought with less well-known brands. Annie might never have heard of Homey Roomy Depot, but she could hazard a guess that it sold furniture.

Had Scarlett sat on this side of the bus? Did it matter which side she sat? Shaking her head, Annie tried to dislodge the jet lag and only succeeded in making her headache worse. The coach was stifling, and all she wanted was to be somewhere safe in bed. Maybe Scarlett had felt that way too? Annie was willing to bet she had.

Sometime over the previous ten minutes the motorway had begun to rise, inching upward until Annie could see into the tenth- or twelfth-floor windows of a tower block that loomed alongside. At first all she saw were deserted offices and rows of empty desks.

As she stared, a Japanese woman standing near the window of an otherwise-empty office turned and their eyes met. The shock Annie felt was reflected in the woman's face, then she was gone.

As the bus pulled up outside her hotel, Annie suddenly realized she'd seen it before. It was that huge fanlike building at the end of *Lost in Translation,* the one Bill Murray was driven past while The Jesus and Mary Chain sound-tracked into the closing credits and his character was carried away from Tokyo.

The Prince Hotel loomed at the junction of two of Tokyo's four expressways, traffic streaming in every conceivable direction on raised roads twenty feet above people's heads. The giant white forty-story fan loomed over Akasaka, a district where narrow lanes hid expensive restaurants, mostly used by the civil servants and bureaucrats who worked in the area. Or so Annie's hastily purchased guidebook had told her.

It was the same guidebook that told her the Akasaka Prince was one of Tokyo's grandest hotels and an instantly recognizable architectural landmark. This must have been why it was featured in the film.

Once inside, the logic that made Rebecca's PA book the hotel became obvious. It might not be the Park Hyatt or Tokyo's equivalent of the Mercer, the kind of place judged fashionable enough for *Handbag*'s editor in chief, but it was very, very *proper.*

At the desk, Annie handed over her passport. As he opened it, the skinny assistant manager's face lit up in delighted surprise and he bowed again, a beaming smile splitting his face.

Annie nodded back and tried not to let her confusion show. What did he have to be so elated about? Obviously she didn't know him from Adam, so maybe he had mistaken her for someone famous. . . . Did he think she was Kate Winslet or someone? Not likely. Maggie Gyllenhaal? Slightly more plausible, but equally unlikely.

Annie grinned as the man handed her a form to sign.

"Thank you, Miss Anderson," he said in faultless English.

Obviously he had the wrong person, Annie decided, wondering who the famous Miss Anderson might be. Mind you, who cared if she got service like this?

Her room on the thirty-second floor looked down over cherry trees and what looked like a lost piece of castle moat, complete with small wooden boats and a man fishing with a long pole. Annie walked over to the window to take a closer look and wished she hadn't. The ground dropped away beneath her, adding vertigo to her growing list of phobias. She gave the window a tug and was irrationally grateful that it refused to open.

The room was huge, with a white sofa, a desk, two bathrooms, and the second largest television she'd ever seen, after the one in Rufus Ulrich's living room. It also had three beds, a couple of singles at one end, and a double bed behind a screen at the other.

All three beds were calling to her.

It was only seven P.M. and Annie knew she shouldn't. She would regret it bitterly at three A.M., when she woke eager to get going just as the city began to shut down around her, but her body was betraying her. Without bothering to unpack or even finish exploring the huge room, Annie unzipped her laptop case and logged on. There was little about the dead girl on the BBC, Sky, *New York Times,* or CNN websites, so either the fuss had come and gone, or it was thought inconsequential.

Annie suspected it was the latter.

There was, however, a piece on the *Tokyo Herald* site. It was short, mostly catch-up on what had gone before, with a couple of paragraphs of what-if at the end, and an intro and sell to drag the reader in.

Phil Townend, read the byline.

It was only after she wrote the name in her notebook that Annie noticed she already had it. He'd written the piece she'd read earlier. *Serious jet lag,* Annie told herself, putting a star next to the name so she'd remember to fix that drink.

And then she settled down to her e-mail.

Have arrived, she wrote, as if, like with text, she was restricted for space, when all that was restricted was her brain. *E-mail okay, but no mobile phone connection. Going to sleep now, but will collect e-mail in the morning. Annie. OX*

She sent it three times, once to Lou, then again, removing the kiss, to Rebecca and Ken. She shut down her laptop, closed the curtains, shucked off her jeans, and climbed into the nearest bed. At the point she was about to crash into sleep, Annie reminded herself there was someone else she should have e-mailed, and then had the honesty to admit she'd known that all along.

The light that seeped through the gap in Annie's carelessly pulled curtains was not proper daylight. And the sound that woke her was not one she recognized. She couldn't place it and couldn't find her alarm clock, let alone stop it. She fumbled across the bedside cabinet and over the wall above her bed, yet failed to find a light switch either.

It took another thirty seconds for it to dawn on Annie that the flashing red dot at the side of the bed belonged to a hotel phone.

"There you are. What kept you? I've been ringing and ringing."

She knew that.

"Rebecca, it's . . ." Annie fumbled on the bedside table for her watch, found she was still wearing it and realized it was too dark to read. "Late," she managed feebly. "Or early."

"Is it? Did I wake you? Oh, sorry."

It was the kind of apology Annie had met within a week of starting work at *Handbag* and had encountered a dozen times since. The kind of apology that told you firmly that if there was any fault it was yours.

"It's all right," said Annie, as if there was any other reply. "I was more or less awake anyway."

"I got your e-mail. What are we going to do about this mobile?"

Annie rolled herself out of bed in the hope that standing upright might kick-start her brain. It didn't. An ad in *Tokyo Today* had offered cell phones for tourists, delivered to your hotel reception, precharged with credit and ready to go.

"I'll rent a Japanese one in the morning," she promised, adding, "What's the time there?" It was her best hope of finding out what time it was in Tokyo.

"Seven," Rebecca said. "In the evening. You know I don't check my BlackBerry often on the weekend."

Annie could think of a thousand replies to that but didn't bother. Rebecca's weekends (known by the *Handbag* staff as "Rupert time") were sacrosanct, dedicated to her four-year-old son from her now ex-marriage. Everyone who'd ever worked for Rebecca knew better than to intrude on them. It was one of the few things about Rebecca that impressed Annie. Actually, that was unfair, there were plenty of others, but it had been the first.

Counting back on her fingers, Annie arrived at the time.

"It's four in the morning," she said. "I'll get the phone sorted first thing and track down Scarlett's roommate, and you'll have an e-mail update waiting for you when you get up, I promise."

"Part-time model?" said Rebecca.

What? Annie tried to kick her brain into gear.

"That's what it said on the news. The dead girl was a part-time model."

She could almost hear the doubt in Rebecca's voice. *What kind of modeling? Part-time where?*

"Hang on a sec." Finding a light switch, Annie blinked as her room revealed itself. The paper was where she'd left it, folded in half and shoved into her bag. "Texan, doing a gap-year by the look of it. Been here four months. Waitressing, read hostessing," Annie added as an aside.

"Is that a given?"

"Mostly," said Annie, who'd skim-read a couple of cultural sites on the web. "Are they talking at your end about the Ripper?"

"Yes," said Rebecca. "Seems this has been going on for a few months." Annie nodded.

"She bore all the characteristics of a Ripper victim. Only, the police claim not. They say she fell from a building."

"Suicide?"

"They're questioning her boyfriend."

For a second Rebecca was silent. "What about the Ulrich girl?" she said finally. "Do you think she's alive?"

It was the million-dollar question. Either way, an inside track would give *Handbag* hundreds of column-inches and thousands of pounds in global syndication deals. But it was about more than this for Annie. More even than just getting the story.

"I don't know, Rebecca," said Annie. "What's the feeling at your end?"

"Not good. Rufus Ulrich has upped his offer to three million dollars for information leading to her safe return."

"Oh, God . . ."

"It gets worse," said Rebecca. "He's threatening to visit Tokyo himself."

"Do you think he will?"

"Doubt it," Rebecca said. "I'll ask around. See what's being said."

Annie couldn't help wondering if her boss was getting off on this Nancy Drew stuff. Rebecca's next comment answered the question. "Kenton knows Rufus a little. We went out to dinner once. I might give him a call."

Having mentioned her ex, Rebecca clearly regretted it. Her voice trailed off.

"That would be good," said Annie, keeping her tone neutral.

"Leave it with me," Rebecca said, firm once more, that part of the conversation closed.

When they stopped talking at four thirty, Annie was wide-awake and the sun was rising behind the hotel, lighting the hotel gardens and the narrow streets beyond.

"Lou?"

"Annie . . . You're so in the doghouse."

She'd called Lou and the phone had been answered first ring.

"Hi, how are you? Lovely to hear from you," said Annie. "How was your flight? You must be knackered."

"You have to sort it out, you know," Lou continued, oblivious. "Chris met me at the airport. He's really upset about the fight. He wanted to know . . ."

"If I fucked Tony?"

"Annie!"

"Well, you can tell him I didn't. And I'm horrified he'd think I might."

"You tell him," Lou said.

"Why should I? Anyway, I've tried to sort this out already . . ."

"Your call from New York? Chris says you hung up on him."

Outrage flooded Annie. She was at fault, she knew it, Chris knew it, Lou knew it, doubtless Annie's mother knew it too, but she hadn't hung up, he had.

"I did not." She heard her own voice and stopped. "And I've been on a plane ever since, remember?"

Sarcasm, thought Annie, *lowest form of wit.*

"Look, you probably think it's none of my business . . . Only Chris mentioned roses and you going to dinner in New York with this ex-boyfriend."

"Tony Panton."

"Who?"

"My first . . . you know. And I hate roses."

"Yeah, I told him."

"You don't get it," said Annie. *"Why do you think I hate roses?"* She took a deep breath. "Believe me," she said. "It's not like that. I screwed up, all right. I shouldn't have gone to supper with him but I did. He turned up at my hotel, wanting to talk."

"About what?"

"Us," said Annie. "As in Annie and Tony."

"Annie."

"*Listen* . . . He's getting divorced. The bastard wanted to make sure I'm not going to pop out of the woodwork and give him problems."

"What kind of problems?"

"Like appearing as a witness for his wife if it all gets messy." It was the only version of the evening that made sense to Annie. Tony Panton would have screwed her if he could have got away with it, but that wasn't why he was there.

"Why would you do that?"

"Because . . ." Annie hesitated. "He's a thug, okay?"

"Chris knows?" It was Lou's turn to hesitate. "About him being a thug?"

"Yes. I told him right at the start. It was only fair." Annie's laugh was sad. "Chris deserved to know what he was taking on."

"And you told Chris why he took you to supper?"

"I only discovered the reason later."

"Dare I ask how?"

"I made a few calls to a man who does stuff for Ken."

Lou laughed. "You put a private investigator onto your first boyfriend?" She sounded impressed. "So tell Chris, he'll understand."

Will he? Annie wondered. "I'm glad," she said, changing the subject. "You know . . . about it not being Scarlett."

"Yeah . . . Rufus called. That was a joy."

Rufus.

"How *is* Rufus?"

"Delightful as ever. Hired his own PI. Says the Japanese police are worse than useless. I pointed out they had a reputation for being one of the most efficient forces in the world. . . ."

But Annie wasn't listening, she was thinking about Rufus.

Damn it, of course, he had. With his bank balance, a PI was the obvious route to go, but it was also the last thing Annie needed. Staying under the radar was much easier if there was only one person on Scarlett's trail. Two would definitely be a crowd.

"The thing that gets me is the way he keeps phoning," said Lou. "Like it's normal or something. As if he's shown the remotest interest for the last—"

"Japanese?" Annie interrupted.

"What?"

"The investigator. Is he Japanese?"

"American, I imagine. Or Australian? Mind you, I can't see Rufus trusting a stranger. To be honest, I don't know. But, being Rufus, he's probably already got a whole team of PIs on retainer and it'll just be one of those. He asked after you, by the way."

"Who? The PI?"

"*No!* Rufus. Wanted to know if you were visiting Japan."

"What did you say?"

"Told him you were in London. It seemed like the right answer."

"Thanks." It was the right answer. It was also pointless. If Rufus had his own man over here, it would take him all of five minutes to discover Annie was here too.

"Look," said Annie. "Can you do me a favor?"

"Not if it's Chris-sitting."

"Lou . . ."

"I mean it," said Lou. "You're the one who got into bed with him. And now he wants me to hold his hand because you climbed out again." Lou sounded as if she wanted to say more, but after a second or two, it became clear that she wasn't going to.

"I'll sort it out, I promise," said Annie. "Meanwhile . . . can you call Arabella and get me numbers and addresses for Scarlett's contacts in Tokyo, if Arabella has them?"

"That's some favor. We haven't spoken in years."

"Look," said Annie. "She doesn't hate you as much as you think. Not as much as you hate her. Anyway, you're not in a position to talk about favors!"

"What d'you need?" asked Lou, ignoring the comment.

Annie reeled off a list that included the model agency, other friends, the boyfriend in Shinjuku, plus anyone else Scarlett might have mentioned. "Oh, and ask Arabella whether Scarlett had a laptop, and if so, whether she brought it to Tokyo with her."

When she'd been sitting among the pastel debris of Scarlett's adolescence Annie had been conscious that something was missing from the room. This was the twenty-first century, for God's sake! Teenagers spent their lives IMing or on MySpace. But apart from an archaic fourteen-inch television, Scarlett's room had been technology-free.

twenty · one

Harsh sunlight woke her, a startling brightness that Annie did not associate with dawn. Her face was squashed against the window ledge, the grooves of an air-conditioning grill digging into her cheek. Light was pouring into her huge hotel room, and a digital clock spread across two floors of an office block to the left of the Suntory Tower read 10:38.

"*Shit!*"

Dragging herself onto cramp-crippled legs, Annie headed for the nearest bathroom. So much for her plan to go out early and be waiting on Scarlett's doorstep the minute her roommate awoke.

Even less forgiving than the sunlight outside, the lightbulbs in the cubicle that passed for a bathroom were bright enough to make Annie grimace. She'd never woken to semipermanent creases like tribal scars in her skin before. Equally, she tended not to use air-conditioning ventilation as a pillow.

When did that happen? When had her face begun looking like it needed a good iron first thing in the morning?

"Old age," muttered Annie, scowling at herself in the mirror and seeing the creases double. The idea of hitting the big three-oh filled her with horror. *Would thirty,* Annie wondered as she examined a succession of plastic packets containing miniature versions of everything a wealthy tourist might need, *be too young to start lying about my age?*

Of course, she could ease up on the cigarettes and booze, both of which were doing her skin no favors, but she needed those to keep her both focused and sane. Only she wasn't either of those, right now, because . . .

Shit, thought Annie, *I promised Lou I'd sort things out with Chris.*

The toilet and tub were in two separate cubicles, both within the bathroom. Tiny self-contained units that slotted together like Legos—toilet and bidet in one, tub and basin in the other. A Russian doll of a bathroom. Its door opening to reveal smaller, more compact rooms inside.

As Annie squatted on the low-level toilet, she felt its seat sink slightly and the cistern began to flush. Alarmed, she stood up and the noise stopped. Sitting made it flush again, only this time Annie realized there was no water, just a recording of water emptying and refilling.

What the hell? she thought.

The first button Annie pushed to get the toilet to flush for real activated a spray, which hit her bottom. The second sprayed her at the front. The third caused the toilet to flush, and the fourth simply twisted like a radio dial. It took Annie a second to get that this one adjusted the warmth of the seat.

Breakfast was even more bemusing. Jet-lagged and starving, a headache nagging behind her eyes, Annie took one look at the Japanese choices on her room service menu and ordered the Western breakfast, which translated as fruit salad and tiny bread rolls. Still, after the flight, anything without raw fish and miso soup was fine by her.

Fruit salad, it turned out, was precisely that: fruit and salad. Slices of apple, orange, pineapple, and melon lay across a bed of shredded lettuce leaves. Annie had never seen anything so literal in her life.

Picking up a small jug filled to the brim with milk, Annie peeled back its cling-film lid and sniffed. Something told her whatever it was, was not going to be what it seemed. The slightly acidic scent proved her right. Not milk or even yogurt but salad dressing.

Of course, she thought, smiling despite herself. *What else would I expect with fruit salad?*

At least the cell phone was waiting for her when she checked at the executive desk. A flip-top Nokia in a padded bag, with her name written neatly on the front. A compliment slip announced she had a hundred U.S. dollars credit, but her card would only be charged for what she used. Should she need more, she could . . .

Annie skipped that part. If needed, she'd read it later.

On her way out, Annie clocked a row of umbrellas for hotel guests to borrow, one for each room. So she guessed the guidebook had been right; this was monsoon season.

That morning was warm and bright. The weather much like a hot summer's day in London, but just as at home, there was a threat of less temperate weather on the horizon. Never forget, warned a low rumble so distant as to be almost not there, things can change.

Cherry trees lined the path from the hotel to the road, their branches shimmering in the breeze and their blossoms long gone. Children walked quietly behind neatly dressed adults, and a family of five waited at the edge of a deserted crossing for the lights to change. She'd been wrong about the city not smelling, Annie decided.

The little lake she'd seen from her window stank of stale water and sewage. Not fiercely, but enough to be noticeable as Annie walked down a slight slope, toward a four-way pedestrian bridge, which would take her over a busy intersection and deposit her where she wanted to go.

Provided Annie could work out where that was.

All the big signs seemed to be in kanji. She tried matching the characters against a map in the back of her guidebook but gave up. A few of the road signs had English translations underneath. These also didn't want to match. Although it seemed likely that the *Aoyamidori* in her book was Boulevard Aoyami.

In Annie's pocket, hastily scribbled on expensive hotel paper, were all the numbers and addresses contained in Lou's e-mail. The one she'd signed, *Don't forget Chris, Lou. XX*

Annie hadn't forgotten. Far from it, the need to mend things tugged at her mind like homework undone, birthdays missed, or promises broken. *It's the middle of the night in England. I'm trying to concentrate on the job. We would only end up having another fight. He'd say I had to call Tony's wife. . . .*

She had a dozen more excuses for putting it off where those came from. All equally convincing, or not. Annie wasn't prepared to discuss it right now, not even in the privacy of her own head.

Lou had done a good job. Or Arabella's memory had improved since she and Annie last spoke, because Lou's e-mail contained names and numbers that Scarlett's mother had claimed to have no knowledge of only days earlier.

Whether Arabella had a guilty conscience, had fallen prey to some perverse notion of family, or simply wanted to annoy her ex-husband, Annie wasn't sure. But at least she had the previously forgotten name of Scarlett's booker at her agency, and, most precious of all, an address for Scarlett's apartment.

That was what Annie really wanted. After all, what mother, even an ex-model of Arabella's epic self-absorption, didn't have her daughter's address? When Annie had seen it in Lou's e-mail, she had almost whooped aloud. But once it was scribbled down the address looked somehow unfinished.

Minato-ku, Roppongi, and then a sequence of numbers.

Minato-ku, Roppongi, that much she could cope with. Just like Upper

East Side, Manhattan, but back to front. She looked for a bench to sit and check her guidebook. If she got really lost, she'd ask the nearest Western tourist, especially if they were Australian. Seemingly, all Australians ended up in Roppongi. But what did the numbers mean, and where was the street name?

Annie longed for the low-maintenance navigation of New York where, apart from the West Village, where the streets rebelled from the city's matrix, even the most dyslexic tourist would struggle to get lost.

Spotting a bench, Annie pulled the guidebook from her bag, too irritated by the address to worry about looking like a tourist. After a second, she noticed the bench was one of five, fixed under a row of cherry trees so their blossoming could be watched in tranquillity each spring.

The guidebook said the numbers stood for district, block, and building. Which would be fine, if she knew where each district began and how to tackle the numbering, since many buildings were numbered, not by their position on the street, but in the order they had originally been built.

At a pedestrian crossing beyond the intersection Annie hit a crowd. From her window, she'd already noticed how Tokyo's inhabitants moved in flocks, surging so some sections of pavement were empty and others busy. When a group going in one direction met another coming the other way, an intricate dance followed, as people weaved politely around one other, careful not to touch. Then both groups were gone and the pavement empty once more.

Now, trapped at the back of a silent group, Annie began to push her way through, earning herself strange glances. Not irritated ones, as people might have given back home, more . . . Annie couldn't place it, almost shocked. The expressions made her wonder what she'd find when she reached the front: a pedestrian struck by a truck, someone taken ill surrounded by a circle of concerned but useless onlookers?

All she found was an empty dual carriageway. Double-checking for traffic, Annie stepped out into the empty road and heard a small child shout.

Instinctively, she jumped back, out of the way of what she imagined was an unseen car hurtling toward her and felt her heel catch something soft. She turned to see a young Japanese woman with a child. The woman bowed apologetically, giving no sign that her sneakered foot had just been crushed by Annie's heel. Then the crowd surged forward, carrying Annie with it, toward a light that had now turned green.

It was not safety in numbers that produced the waves of pedestrians, nor coach parties or groups of tourists, just obedience and police officers. Traffic or no traffic, if the lights in Tokyo said *Don't Walk,* you didn't walk.

After half an hour of heading in what Annie assumed to be the general direction of Roppongi, she realized she knew even less about Tokyo than she imagined. There were wide and elegant avenues, expensive shops, and endless side streets that looked more Shanghai than Tokyo to Annie.

Shops and restaurants dominated at ground level, with hostess clubs and bars piled almost randomly, layer on layer above. And in among the shops were pachinko arcades, where middle-aged men gambled away their boredom on pinball machines, even at midday on a Sunday.

Annie guessed they started at ground level, and if their tastes ran that way, moved on up through drinks or karaoke, to drown their sorrows, or lavish their winnings on the company of young girls. Western girls, quite possibly, like Donna Newton, whose body had been found in Roppongi.

And like Scarlett? Annie wondered.

Had Scarlett moonlighted as a hostess too? Unlikely. It wasn't as if she needed the cash. Most of the papers had mentioned the amount Scarlett had stacked up in offshore trusts. And yet . . .

The Japanese press seemed to assume Scarlett was a victim of the Roppongi Ripper, whose other victims had all worked clubs. But, so far, there was no evidence that Scarlett had ever been a hostess. Annie's priority was to discover as much about Scarlett's life in Tokyo as she could, and she had only a handful of days in which to do it.

Annie stopped for a moment and stepped into a doorway, out of the flow of human traffic. On the other side of a window belonging to a restaurant, a huge ugly fish floated idly in its tank, waiting to become someone's lunch or supper. The black coffee in Annie's stomach lurched and she turned away.

Why hadn't she seen it straightaway? Surrounding her was Soho, Tokyo style, less plastic and less tourist-riddled, but Soho all the same. It was only a stone's throw from the heart of the Japanese government. Restaurants, bars, hostess clubs, and upscale strip clubs for Japanese civil servants were all parked conveniently on their doorstep.

How . . . civilized.

Japanese society was notorious for its orderly distinction between public and private.

It was a world where visiting a hostess club straight from work was acceptable, but it was impolite to hold hands with your wife or kiss your boyfriend in public. Where, to judge from the shops she'd seen so far, you could buy a vibrator key ring at your local chemist but tampons were damn near impossible to find.

Emerging from a maze of narrow streets, Annie realized that many of the signs for restaurants she had thought were at pavement level related to establishments far above the ground. Life in Tokyo was obviously lived vertically, not just in business hierarchies, but outside in the streets as well.

The sensible thing for Annie to do would be to get a cab—assuming the driver could read her writing. But being delivered door to door was a last resort, almost an admission of defeat. One of the first things her original news editor taught her was to get under the skin of every story. Get her bearings and get to know the location as well as the people, because without knowing the place, how could you possibly understand its inhabitants?

Another fifteen minutes of walking and Annie, almost literally, hit a brick wall. Rough-hewn from gray stone it towered thirty or forty feet above her, and on top, if Annie's map-reading was right, was the main road to Roppongi, crossing over this road, *Blade Runner*–style, before heading south.

The intersection where Roppongi's Gaien-higashi-dori crossed Shuto Expressway number 3 formed the area's very own Leicester Square. Traffic roared overhead and alongside, while Starbucks, Subway, T.G.I. Friday's, and McDonald's competed for space with Japanese bars, clip joints, and arcades. Jingles seemed to call from every storefront.

There were more Westerners here. Not one person in two, or even one person in three, but maybe one in four, enough to be noticeable. Almost all of them were young and most were female. Most of the Japanese were also young, also mostly female.

A gaggle of dark-haired Tokyo schoolgirls crowded the door to a café, and behind them, looking taller, paler, and much blonder but also substantially broader, stood a pair of Eastern European women in their early twenties, doing their best to ignore the giggles and glances.

Annie guessed she'd arrived where she needed to be.

It was steam-room hot, the air muggy enough to glue her hair to her neck, and her cotton shirt had stuck itself to her back. As for the balls of her feet, they ached from walking farther than she had expected, but Annie hardly noticed. From a tower block high above this maelstrom of humanity, a young woman had fallen to her death.

The yellow crime scene tape Annie had expected to find was not in evidence. No flowers on the pavement marked the spot, as they would in London. If anything had marked Donna Newton's death at all, it had gone.

Somewhere in the streets behind this, in a small apartment owned by her agency, Lou's half sister had spent the previous eight months. Whether those were also the last months of Scarlett's short life, Annie was determined to find out.

twenty · two

The brown-haired woman behind the café counter turned out to be Australian. This wasn't a surprise, since nearly everybody in Happy Daze, a saccharine pink coffee shop, one street down from the Roppongi crossroads, spoke with an Australian accent, although there were Koreans visible through a door leading to the kitchen.

Annie wouldn't have bothered with Happy Daze at all, if not for her guidebook describing it as a well-known meeting place for young expatriates.

Pushing a cotton-candy-pink paper hat back from her eyes, the girl whose badge announced she was Lise, frowned at the address Annie held, then jerked her head over her shoulder.

"Roppongi Hills," said Lise, as if that in itself was an explanation.

Annie looked puzzled.

"It's a complex of shops and restaurants round the back. You can't miss the place. It's huge."

"You're certain that's where this is?" asked Annie, deciding it sounded too upscale for agency apartments.

"This bit is," said Lise. "The first number, that's back there, but the second number's like the street, and I don't reckon that's in the Hills. Maybe just outside. Hang on, I'll ask Kim."

She turned toward the kitchens where, Annie assumed, Kim worked. A few seconds later she was back.

"He says it's not the Hills itself. So don't go left outside, go right and take the first right again. Try about halfway down."

"Thanks." Annie smiled. "Can I have some of that?" She pointed at a gooey gateau behind the glass counter. Annie didn't even like chocolate cake, but she wanted to pay for something.

"Actually, make that two slices." Models didn't eat, everyone knew that. A packet of Marlboro would have been a better introductory gift. Annie should have thought of that and invested in a whole box of duty free at JFK. Still, cake was better than nothing.

Wrapping was obviously an art form in Japan, and as the Australian girl folded pink-and-white-striped paper into an elegant box, Annie asked, "Is this your main job?"

Lise stopped what she was doing. "What d'you mean?" she said, sounding defensive.

"I just wondered . . . I mean, the woman I'm meeting is a fashion model, I thought you might know her." Annie was ashamed of herself. That wasn't what she'd been implying at all, but it did the trick.

"Me?" said Lise. "A model? You've gotta be joking!" But she smiled, flattered. And she was thin enough. "I work in a club at night, most girls do. You can earn a lot that way."

"Round here?" asked Annie.

"God no." Lise laughed, handing Annie the paper box and taking the five-thousand yen note. "It's just pissed-up backpackers round here. I do shifts over in Akasaka, better class of punter."

"Really?" Annie tried not to look too interested.

"Yeah . . . salarymen . . . you know, Japanese executives. They can be weird, but at least they're not gropers like most tourists."

Annie glanced over her shoulder at the growing queue. "I know you're busy," she said, leaning forward. "But I wondered if you recognized this person." Pulling out a picture of Scarlett, she showed it to Lise.

The girl nodded. " 'Course," she said. "I mean, no, not personally. Only I know who she is. It's been all over the news. She's the missing model who used to be famous."

"Yup." Annie nodded. "Did you ever see her around here? Did she ever come to this café or meet anyone here?"

"She came," said Lise. "Maybe once or twice? Not sure about meeting anyone. I didn't know her, though, not to speak to."

Picking up her box, Annie realized Lise was watching her with open curiosity.

"You a journalist?"

"A friend . . ."

Lise allowed herself to look doubtful.

"Well," said Annie. "A friend of a friend." Turning to go, Annie stopped. "Look," she said, rummaging in her bag for a business card. "If you should hear anything, I'd appreciate it if you gave me a call. I'm staying at the Akasaka Prince. Ask for Annie Anderson."

twenty · three

Away from Roppongi's main drag, the neon glitz began to fade. Annie soon found herself wandering a tawdry Tokyo version of the backstreets of Benidorm, alive with small tourist bars and cafés, saunas and hostess joints. Handwritten signs announced TOURISTS WELCOME and CREDIT CARDS RECEIVED HERE.

Baddgirls, Wetwelcome, Leggy Lovelies. The names were trying too hard to appeal. It was all a bit red light district. But as the street wound downhill, following the curve of a slope that dropped away from the main road, the area began to change again, and Annie's surroundings became almost villagey.

She could have been in any residential district in the world. Flowers spilled from narrow window boxes, bicycles and rusting mopeds leaned against old street lamps. Small dogs stared from ground-floor windows and a tiny kitten mewled from a crack between houses.

The smell of grilled chicken filled the air and Annie could hear the sound of a radio and the whir of a washing machine on spin cycle. A man and a woman were talking in a room somewhere above.

It was reminiscent of San Francisco or Paris, a million miles, in atmosphere at least, from the self-consciously seedy onslaught of Roppongi's main tourist thoroughfare. A place where street decoration switched between posters, a huge plastic alien glued to a wall, and the neon-lit labia-shaped doors of the Venus Cabinet.

Here, the shouts of deliverymen drowned the sounds of distant traffic, while store owners clanked crates, small children shrieked, and Japanese women chatted as they wandered slowly from café to clothes shop and back.

The only vehicle Annie could see was silent, as a young Japanese boy, looking comically forlorn, pushed his broken-down Suzuki moped toward the open black cave of a machine shop. For the first time Annie began to see how someone could come to call Tokyo home.

It might have taken hours to find Scarlett's apartment, if a tall skinny girl, hip bones jutting above the waistband of boyfriend jeans, hadn't appeared through a side door near the Frangipani café. Annie had been standing and staring at two bowls of salt placed by a wall, and wondering if the little offering was Buddhist or Shinto or some other Japanese tradition, when the door opened and a girl stepped out.

Scarlett's roommate?

"Excuse me," said Annie. "*Jess?* Jess Harper?"

The girl stopped, looked at her, and shook her head. "No." Even in that one word the Australian accent was distinct.

"Oh, sorry," said Annie, knowing it would have been too good to be true. "I'm looking for her. She's English, about twenty, and a model."

The girl gave a smile. "Round here," she said, "who isn't?"

Good point, thought Annie, watching as a tall slim blonde and a lanky European-looking boy with spiky black hair loped past, oozing the effortless sex appeal of the young and gorgeous. Although Annie couldn't see how sex could be comfortable if you were that thin. All those sharp edges.

Who isn't, indeed.

Annie pulled in her stomach and straightened her shoulders, as if that would make a blind difference.

"*Jess?*" said the girl, considering. "English?"

"You know her?" Annie asked.

"I've only been here a week. But there are a couple of English models living upstairs. At least, I think they're English, you could try there."

She held the door open to let Annie in. "Top floor."

Annie smiled and slipped past. *You've just let a total stranger into your home,* she thought. *Didn't your agent tell you anything?*

Watching the girl waft away, Annie sighed. She was eighteen, nineteen at the most, the same age as Scarlett, her body that of an adolescent boy.

Annie shivered.

The world was full of them, innocents who drifted through life in the belief that nothing terrible could ever happen. No psychopathic stranger would ever stumble across them, no trusted friends betray them, and no lovers try to break or own them. And with a bit of luck they were right.

And then there are the rest of us.

Annie knew she was one of the lucky ones, not like Patty or Irina or—God forbid—Lou's sister, but there was still bitterness at the base of her throat. A pocket of darkness at the back of her mind. She carried the mental scars long after the physical ones had healed. And that had taken long enough.

She had to find Scarlett for Lou, for her best friend, who was obviously more fond of her half sister than she was prepared to admit. And she had to find Scarlett for herself, because she desperately needed to close a story where the missing girl wasn't dead.

The stairwell was clean but grubby, the white walls so overdue for a paint job that they'd become accepted as gray. Stepping over that day's flyers, Annie flicked a timer switch to stop the stairwell from plunging into darkness. A pile of mail filled a metal basket on the back of the door.

Annie reached in and lifted it out.

An English-language newspaper, a copy of *alt.Japan,* another of *Metropolis—Tokyo's No.1 English Magazine.* Beneath the papers were sample packs of dried noodles and a tiny, cellophane-wrapped packet of tissues advertising Toyota cars. Then came a couple of leaflets. *Hostesses wanted,* read one. *Buddhist massage,* read another. At the bottom were an assortment of letters and cards.

But there was nothing for Jess Harper or Scarlett Ulrich. Annie wasn't that surprised. That would have been too easy. Flicking through the letters and postcards, Annie noted three from Sydney, one from London, and two from Austin, Texas. The history of the flat in postmarks.

Standard-issue stair carpet had become worn from a thousand itinerant footsteps, the wear growing less obvious as Annie climbed upward. There was only one door on each floor, always to the left. It was painted the same dirty white as the walls, and only slightly less grubby than the area around each timer switch, which Annie flicked each time she passed, as she used to push buttons at pedestrian crossings when she was small. Whether or not she wanted to cross. It used to drive her mother mad, but then most things did.

When Annie reached the top, the silence was absolute. It was too high for sound to drift up from the street and no tinny blast of TV or radio came from behind the last door, nothing to indicate that anyone was home. And yet . . .

It was instinct, Annie told herself. An instinct in which Ken believed, and even Rebecca was beginning to accept. There were other words to describe it, such as fear, heightened awareness, and lessons learned from uncontrollable levels of adolescent stress. Annie preferred to think of it as instinct.

Air shifted a few feet away on the other side of a door Annie could kick open easily enough, given the right degree of pressure just below its lock. As if somewhere in a forest, a deer froze at the crunch of a twig underfoot.

Someone was there. Someone who had listened as Annie's footsteps climbed higher.

Closer.

She knocked again, and this time she was certain she heard a movement.

It happened a lot to journalists. People hiding inside their own homes, frozen in fear at every ring of the bell, pulling back from the windows in case someone went around the back and peered in. But there were no windows here. Just one cheap lock with—Annie guessed—a scared teenager on the other side.

"If that's Jess," said Annie softly. "My name's Annie. I'm a friend of Scarlett. Well," she added, raising her voice slightly, "a friend of Scarlett's sister, Lou. Her sister asked me to come."

"Who?"

The voice was so close, Annie jumped. The girl had been just on the other side of the door the whole time.

"Lou," Annie repeated. "Scarlett's half sister. I've also talked to Scarlett's mother. She gave me this address."

Silence.

One, two, three, Annie would give her until ten if necessary, then try again, *seven, eight . . .*

A chain rattled and Annie heard the scrape of a key, then the door opened as far as the safety chain would allow. One swift kick at the edge of the door and that chain would be history. She'd seen it happen. Only then she'd been the one hiding inside.

An eye peered through the crack. It was bloodshot and dark-rimmed, the skin above and below blotchy with tears. "Scarlett's mother?"

"Arabella knows I'm here," promised Annie. "She gave me this address."

"Not her dad?"

Annie did a double take. "No, why?"

The eye examined her, disbelieving. Annie took a chance. "I don't think Scarlett's dad is my biggest fan," she said. "He threw me out of his flat, and then tried to have me fired."

The door shut and Annie heard the chain clink before the door swung open again. She was in. At least she would be when she got past the girl in the woolly socks and too-big jeans/too-small T-shirt model uniform standing in the doorway. Jess Harper was not what Annie had expected. For a start, the girl was short by model standards, only a couple of inches taller than Annie, her nose was slightly wide and she had a large gap between her front teeth.

"You're Jess Harper?" asked Annie.

The girl frowned. "Yes," she said. "Who were you expecting?"

It was her hair, Annie decided, white blond and falling like rain around her narrow shoulders. That was what the agency's talent spotter had seen in her.

The living room reminded Annie of the place where Patty Lang had stayed in Milan. The same feeling of impermanence. It was lived in, yes, but lived in by too many fleeting lives, each person leaving a little of themselves behind in abandoned possessions as they passed through. Dog-eared paperbacks lined a windowsill, with a cactus on a saucer balanced on top of these. A teddy bear stared one-eyed from a corner. The room smelled musty and the carpet looked as if no one had remembered to vacuum it for weeks.

Jess pulled back the curtains to let the early-afternoon sunlight flood in, revealing a million dancing dust motes. A sofa and chairs crowded a steel and glass coffee table that overflowed with clutter, mostly dirty coffee cups, plus magazines, books, and an overflowing ashtray. Annie felt strangely at home.

As Annie was looking for somewhere to put her pink and white package of cakes, she noticed a copy of *Vogue* on the top of the pile, coffee rings staining its once-glossy cover. It was the British edition and a copy of *Handbag* lay beneath. Annie didn't have a big feature in that issue, just bits and pieces and a comment piece, written in a hurry when a freelancer failed to deliver on time.

"I work for *Handbag*," Annie told Jess. "I'm fashion features editor."

Flicking to the masthead, she found her own name and handed it to the girl.

Jess looked impressed. "Really?" she said. "I like *Handbag*. I like *Vogue* too, but *Handbag*'s a bit younger, more me."

Annie smiled, knowing Rebecca would be pleased.

"So," said Jess. "This sister of Scarlett's. Which one?"

Annie's mouth fell open.

Damn it, she thought. She hated to be wrong-footed. Now she dimly remembered Arabella mentioning Rufus's other daughters. Why the hell hadn't she asked Lou to fill her in?

"There are three sisters," said Jess, looking suddenly suspicious. "Half sisters and stepsisters. Didn't you know?"

"No . . . I only know one." Annie took a punt. "The oldest, and she doesn't talk about the others much." This was the understatement of the year. A week ago she'd been envying Lou her life as an only child.

Jess nodded knowledgeably, poking the tip of her tongue through her teeth, as if Annie's reply made perfect sense to her.

"What made you think Scarlett's father sent me?"

"Because he could be hiring people to check up on each other," Jess said, folding her arms across her stomach as if suddenly cold.

"What?" Annie frowned.

"A man turned up this morning," said Jess. "Australian guy, said he was a private investigator. Wanted me to tell him all about Scarlett. He was bit older than you. About my dad's age."

Annie winced. How old did she look? But then Annie realized Jess's dad could be only six or seven years older than her, if he'd started young.

"I was surprised," Jess continued, "that it was her dad and not her mother. Arabella's always calling my mobile in case Scarlett shows up. But I hadn't heard anything from her dad. Mind you, that's not a shock."

"What d'you mean?"

Jess plonked herself in a chair. "Scarlett was close to her mother, called her every Sunday, like you do. But her dad . . . They'd quarreled. He left a message on her mobile about two weeks ago, I'm not sure Scarlett even called him back."

"Really?" Maybe Scarlett's family life with Rufus wasn't as much fun as Lou seemed to imagine. It occurred to Annie that being the one with Rufus in your life might not be the best end of the bargain.

"Yeah," said Jess. "And this guy, he didn't look like a private investigator to me. He just looked like a regular bloke. You know jeans and T-shirt, cropped hair. He showed me an ID from some firm in Bangkok, told me Mr. Ulrich had sent him, and asked lots of questions I didn't understand, but now you're here I'm beginning to."

"He didn't leave a card, I suppose?" said Annie, not expecting a positive answer.

When Jess shook her head, Annie shrugged off her jacket, plucked a single packet of Marlboros from her bag, and offered one to Jess, lighting one for herself and trying not to cough as she half-inhaled.

"What did this guy want to know?"

Jess reeled off a list of questions with a shrug. "When did I last see Scarlett? Did Scarlett have a boyfriend? Was he two-timing her? Was she two-timing him? Had the Japanese police interviewed me? Could he look in her room? Then he asked if anyone else had been looking for her? Maybe an Englishwoman? He gave me two descriptions, one of them was yours."

"And the other?"

"Well," said Jess. "Now I think about it, the other one sounded like an older, smaller Scarlett. Bit taller than you, skinny, blond highlighted hair, blue eyes, pointy nose. Scruffy. Is that Lou?"

Annie nodded, knowing Lou would be furious if she heard one of Rufus's lackeys describe her carefully thrown together style as scruffy.

Jess hesitated.

"Tell me," said Annie.

"This guy, he said you didn't represent the Ulriches. I wasn't to help you."

"You didn't take to him?" Annie asked.

The girl shook her head.

It wasn't remotely surprising that Rufus had put a PI on a plane so quickly, but the fact the man was as interested in Annie's movements as finding Scarlett made Annie twitchy. Healthy competition was a fact of life, but the PI's interest felt like something more sinister. The last thing Annie needed was for this to turn into a fight between Rufus and Arabella. Or, even worse, a three-way scrap with Lou as the unwitting third party.

"What did you tell him?"

"The truth. I gave him numbers for Scarlett's friends and let him look around her room, though I watched to make sure he didn't steal anything. And I told him I hadn't seen any Englishwomen, because I hadn't."

Jess pushed her tongue through the gap in her teeth. "Was that wrong?"

Annie shook her head.

"How long before I got here did he leave?" she asked, cursing herself for oversleeping.

"Fifteen, twenty minutes."

Frantically, Annie tried to remember if a cropped-haired man had been hanging around outside when she arrived. Not that she could recall. But around here an Australian in jeans and a T-shirt wasn't going to stand out. Back in the lanes of Akasaka, she'd have spotted any Westerner a mile off.

"Is he the only one?"

"One what?"

"Person who's been around, asking questions?"

"You mean apart from the police and all the journalists?"

That was hardly a surprise. Journalists would have started flooding into Tokyo the moment the Ripper story broke. Or at least, when it gathered enough momentum to merit the airfare. Some stories were like that; they bubbled under for weeks or months until something happened to give them weight. Something significant, like Scarlett.

"These journalists," said Annie casually. "Any Brits? Americans?"

"Mainly Japanese," said Jess. "But there have been a few foreigners,

Australian mostly, and usually on the phone. If they persist, I tell them the police said I shouldn't talk and that makes them go away."

Annie could hardly hide her relief.

"Except this one guy," said Jess, thinking about it.

"Uh-huh?"

"Yeah, there's this guy from the *Tokyo Herald*. You know, the English-language paper? He won't leave me alone. He calls my mobile and shoves notes under the door. He's come round here three times. That's who I thought you were when I heard your feet on the stairs."

"What did you say his name was?" asked Annie, feeling certain she knew the answer already.

"I didn't," said Jess, pulling herself to her feet and sorting through a purse full of jumbled items near the door. "But it's Phil Townend. You can have *his* card."

She knew it. The *Tokyo Herald*'s chief crime reporter. Grinning, Annie said, "You want me to see if I can make him go away?"

"Would you?" Jess's pallor lifted for a second, as her face lit at the prospect. "That'd be great. Want a coffee?"

"Sure," said Annie. "Let me make a call."

Townend-san was out, so a rather breathless Japanese girl told Annie. She could leave a message with the girl or use Mr. Townend's voice mail.

Annie chose voice mail.

"Hi," she said. "My name's Annie Anderson. I'm a journalist at *Handbag* magazine. But you might know me from such papers as *The Post* in London."

He'd get *The Simpsons'* reference or he wouldn't.

"I'm investigating the disappearance of Scarlett Ulrich. I've already interviewed her mother and father and one of her sisters. I think we should talk. . . ." If that didn't snare him, then nothing would.

Jess's cigarette had burned to its filter when Annie returned. She wasn't sure the girl had taken even a single drag, other than the one needed to light it. Unlike Patty Lang, who had chained Camels as if her life depended on it, Jess clearly got her comfort from holding the cigarette. Mind you, Jess and Patty, how different could two models be? A gap-toothed model with genuine breasts. It was weird.

"Want another cig?" asked Annie, when Jess returned with two black coffees, milk and sugar not an option.

Jess shook her head. "No thanks. Don't really smoke."

Annie frowned at the ashtray. "Whose are those?"

"Oh, mine. I started smoking when I began modeling. It stops you eating, gives you something to do with your hands. It used to make Scarlett laugh the way we'd both sit here, pretending to smoke, when what we both wanted was a Big Mac."

"Cake then?" Annie held up her package. "I haven't eaten breakfast," she lied. "You could keep me company."

"No thanks. I'm trying to give up food. Not doing very well, though."

Annie smiled, accepting defeat. "About Scarlett," she said. "I know you've probably been through this a million times, but when did you last see her?"

"A week now. I only discovered Scarlett was missing when the agency called to find out why she hadn't shown for a casting."

"Was that a surprise?"

"Yes and no . . . If Scarlett said she was going to do something, then she did it. But she hated castings. We all do, you feel like a piece of meat. It's bad enough in London. Go into a magazine, stand for hours, so some fashion editor can look at you like you're the ingredient on the back of a ready meal, flick through your book, and sigh. Here it's even worse because the Japanese bookers make you feel so . . . *cumbersome.*"

Annie rolled her eyes. Okay, so Jess wasn't exactly six foot and under a hundred pounds and she did have breasts . . . well, almost. But she couldn't have been more than a size eight, at most.

"By most people's standards you're tiny," Annie said pointlessly.

"Thanks," said Jess. "Just not here. In Japan, even if you're small and you get cast, the clothes may not fit. It's a weird contradiction. The bookers demand tall, Western, and blond, but it's like every shoot is intended to bring us down."

"So why stay?"

The girl looked at Annie as if she was crazy. "How long have you got?"

Annie smiled. "All day."

twenty · four

Jess told her that Roti had been one of Scarlett's favorite restaurants. Annie wondered if Jess knew she'd begun talking about Scarlett in the past tense.

"They do a brilliant afternoon brunch," said Jess, as she locked up the apartment. "It was our dirty little secret, Sunday brunch. So for God's sake don't tell the agency if you see them."

Annie decided not to ask if either model kept the meal down afterward.

Walking to Roti took less than ten minutes and felt like crossing the front line between two, even three worlds. Roppongi Hills was a world within a world.

It was also a hotel, an art gallery, a museum, and shopping Mecca, featuring stores that stocked Gucci, Armani, and Vuitton, plus restaurants that could just as easily be on Manhattan's Madison Avenue or the Faubourg Saint-Honoré in Paris, if only those cities raised their hipness a notch.

The café to which Jess led Annie was more laid-back, if a little self-consciously so. Americans and Australians, Brits and New Zealanders jostled elbows with affluent locals. Annie didn't rate their chances of getting a table, but clearly Jess was a regular and the manager soon had them ensconced in a corner by the window with English breakfasts and Bloody Marys on their way.

Tracks changed, and suddenly "Stuck in the Middle with You" was belting out of a speaker right above Annie's head.

"Stealers Wheel," said Annie, suddenly appalled to realize she knew.

"Tarantino," she added quickly. *"Reservoir Dogs."* Tony Panton's favorite film. "You want to tell me why you're here?"

Jess glanced around, checking the brunch-time crowd in Roti.

"I mean Tokyo."

"Well," said Jess, taking a sip from a glass of iced water. "Firstly there's my agent back home. She'd freak if I blew it, or worse, sack me. Tokyo's a rite of passage. If I can make it here, I can make it anywhere. The agency has promised they'll send me to New York next."

Annie nodded. That was pretty much how Lou described the Tokyo run.

"Then there's me," said Jess. "If I copped out, I'd feel like a failure . . . and my mother would kill me."

Annie reckoned she probably wasn't meant to hear that last bit.

"And then," added Jess, "there's the money."

Annie raised an eyebrow.

"Why else would I be here? If I can stand another six months, I'm sorted. I want to save twenty grand to set myself up, and buy a Mini Cooper."

"Which?"

"Both, of course."

"How you doing so far?"

"Not bad," said Jess. "I've saved eight toward the set-up fund, but haven't started on the Mini yet. Scarlett was doing better, she had fifteen in her Japanese account last count."

"She what?" said Annie. "Fifteen thousand dollars?"

"Sterling," Jess said. "Pounds sterling. I don't work in dollars."

"You sure?"

Jess nodded. "Impressive, huh? She took every job offered and never wasted a penny, unlike me. I'm here to make my fortune, but still blow half of everything on designer clothes that would be half the price back home. Scarlett was never like that."

That wasn't what Annie had meant. Why would Scarlett Ulrich who had a trust fund and a childhood fortune be saving every penny for a measly fifteen grand?

Arabella struck Annie as clingy, but what mother wouldn't be when her daughter had gone missing? Rufus was a whole other matter. He would be quite capable of going through his daughter's account, particularly if her monthly allowance was paid through his bank.

Scarlett had to need something she didn't want him to know about. Drugs was Annie's first thought. Weren't models meant to live on cigarettes, coffee, and cocaine? Only what if Scarlett wasn't like that? Maybe she needed the money to pay someone off? But then it wouldn't be sitting in a Japanese bank account, would it? It would be already gone.

Annie sighed. "So that's why you were worried when Scarlett didn't show for the casting?"

"God, yeah. Scarlett might hate castings, but she worked like crazy. Never stopped."

Spoiled rich kid works herself into the ground for pocket money. It didn't sound right to her.

"You last saw her when she left home that morning?"

"Uh-uh." Jess shook her head, her mouth full of mushroom and fried tomato. "Nigh' befo.'"

"What time? Late?"

Jess's mouth was full again, almost as if she was loading up intentionally every time Annie asked a question.

"What time?" Annie repeated.

The fork was in motion again, this time piled with egg and a piece of toast. Annie rested her hand gently on Jess's own, firmly enough to restrain it but not enough to be threatening. "What time?" she tried for the third time.

Jess put down her fork and let egg tumble back onto the plate. "Not sure," she said. "Why does it matter?"

"Come on," said Annie. "You know why. If I'm going to find Scarlett, I need to talk to the last person who saw her, and so far as I know that person was you."

Annie looked at the girl, wanting to worry but not frighten her. It was obvious Jess was hiding something more than secret brunch sessions, only damned if Annie could work out what. "Surely you've been asked these questions before?"

Jess shook her head. "Not really," she said. "People ask once or twice and then they lose interest."

"Even her dad's guy?"

She nodded. "Especially him. He treated me like I was an idiot."

"And you let him?"

Jess nodded, shoveling more food into her mouth.

"I won't give up," Annie assured her. "I'll keep asking. I have to, Lou needs me to."

Looking at Annie, the girl scowled. "She came in about seven," she said. "Then she went out again."

"You didn't hear her after that?"

Jess shook her head sullenly.

"So she didn't come home that night?"

More head shaking.

"She had a boyfriend in Shinjuku, didn't she? A photographer. Is that where she went?"

"Wouldn't know," said Jess. "Mike hasn't returned my calls." She spoke through a mouthful of breakfast.

"When did he last see her?"

"I told you, I don't know. Ask him yourself . . . if you can find him."

Annie was on the point of losing Jess, she could hear it in the girl's voice. "You say he's called Mike? Can you give me his number and address?"

"Why not?" said Jess. "I gave it to everyone else. Won't help, though. He's on holiday."

"How do you know?"

"I called the studio," Jess said, as if she thought Annie was the one who was stupid. "When Scarlett went missing. And he's not a photographer, he's a photographer's assistant. It wasn't serious, or anything."

Any second now that fork would be in motion again and Jess would have shut down altogether, unless. . . . Annie knew she was on the edge of something, but if she pushed too hard she'd lose it. Case studies were often like that, in the early days, before Stockholm syndrome kicked in and they started wanting to please the person demanding answers.

"Look, Jess," said Annie gently. "All I want to do is find Scarlett, if she's alive . . . for the sake of her sister and mother. If you know where Scarlett is, where she might be, you must tell me."

"I don't," Jess said firmly. Then she relented, shoulders relaxing. "Honestly," she said. "Don't you think I'd say if I did? I miss Scarlett too."

Annie believed her.

"Assuming she wasn't staying over with her boyfriend, where might she have been? With another *friend* . . ."

The fork hit Jess's plate with such a clank that a Japanese woman three tables across glanced their way, and then hastily pretended she had been looking out the window.

Across the table, Jess's eyes were brimming with tears.

"Scarlett wasn't like that," she said.

"Like what?"

"You know."

"No, I don't," said Annie, though she did. "The thing is," she added, "if Scarlett wasn't with another friend, then where was she?"

"At work."

Annie flung herself back in her chair, exasperated. All this sullenness for *"at work"*? "Then her booker will know where Scarlett was," she said. "And I'll be able to find out what time she left."

"Christ," said Jess. "You don't have a clue, do you?" She looked like a stubborn thirteen-year-old, holding out on a stupid teacher.

"Try me," Annie said.

"Not her day job, the *other* one. You know, hostessing . . ."

twenty · five

"Where are you going?" asked Lou, raising her head.

The shadow noiselessly shifting in the semidarkness stopped. It was quiet, without even the distant squeal of a police siren or the predawn chorus of drunks swearing and scraping their keys against parked cars as they staggered up Chalk Farm Road. So quiet, Lou could hear Gabe swallow as he composed his answer. She knew what it would be, but she wanted to hear him say it anyway.

"Gabe, where are you going?" Another silence, another swallow, the rustle of combats being pulled up, buttoned.

"Home, Lou."

Home. How could that one harmless word hurt so much?

"What time is it?"

"About four."

"But it's so late, almost morning. Why bother leaving now? You'll still have to explain."

"You know I have to go," he said patiently. "I need to be there when the kids get up for school."

Lou winced, shutting her mind to the thoughts that came tumbling in, and rolled away from the damp patch, pulling her thin duvet around her body as she did so. She was glad it was too dark to see the hideous pink duvet cover Gram had given her for college—care of the charity that Gram now volunteered at two days a week. Lou hadn't the heart to give it straight to another branch.

The shadow that was Gabe sat on the edge of her bed, lacing his Nikes. He was not like a grown man at all, Lou decided, listening to the familiar sounds of his departure. Not as she'd thought he would be, and nothing like the only other man she knew, not that she knew Rufus at all.

No, Rufus would never be seen dead wearing the adolescent uniform her lover favored. Not now, and not even when he'd been Gabe's age. Gabe was thirty-three, but dressed younger. His life, however, was one hundred percent grown-up. His wife was a journalist, two years older, with a picture byline of her own. Lena Cosby . . . dark-haired and pretty. Suited and booted. Lou knew, she'd studied the picture obsessively.

His children were six and four, Charlie and Emma, the boy older by two years, exactly as it should be. Gabe's clothes hid his adult life. Lou wasn't sure who from, but she suspected it might be from himself.

The shadow was bending over her now, denim jacket flapping open, record bag heaved onto one shoulder.

"See you soon, Lou," he said, leaning in to kiss her. Appearing not to notice when she ducked her head, so his lips missed her mouth and grazed her forehead.

"When?" she asked, hating herself as she uttered the word.

"Tomorrow," he promised. "Well, later today."

"Where?"

Stop it, she told herself, loathing the eagerness, feeling contempt for the need that oozed from her voice.

He moved away and, as he did so, the warmth began to seep from his voice. "At college, of course."

"And after?"

More silence, more swallowing. A sure sign the man was weighing up the benefit of truth or lie. More evidence, as if Lou needed it, that she had stopped being fun and was becoming *a problem.*

"No, not tonight, Lou, I have something on. Maybe Thursday." There was the sound of lips on flesh, then his palm touched her cheek. For once, maybe the first time since they'd started, Lou's cheek was dry.

Stair treads creaked a coded message to Lou's housemates that her secret lover had been and gone, and once again, they had missed their chance to catch her mystery man in the act. Lou heard a key turn in the deadlock and the latch click, signaling Gabe's departure.

Under her pink duvet, Lou willed herself to stay put. She imagined her feet turning to lead, heavy and immovable. Any trick to kill the need to stand naked at her bedroom window, as she'd stood so many times before, tears streaming down her face as she watched her lover hurry away from her and back to someone else.

"He'll never stay," she told herself, her voice breaking the silence of the once-again still house. "You do know that, don't you?"

Did she?

Of course she did. She wasn't an idiot. She didn't need reminding. Gabe had never stayed and never would. Just as he never noticed Lou in front of his colleagues or her friends. To begin with it had been romantic, their lovers' secret, but now . . . She hated being the ghost in his life.

"It's better this way," he'd say, after that nervous swallow of his. "C'mon, Lou, you know the score."

He was right, she did. Lou would never be a real part of Gabe's life. She should have known that from the start. And what was she doing getting involved with someone almost twice her age, anyway?

"Can I get you a drink?" he had asked. The man who spoke had close-cropped hair, small round glasses with blue wire frames, and was leaning against the pub bar like he was surgically attached. He hadn't been there long, a few minutes earlier Lou had noticed him sitting at the far end of a big group of students from her art college.

His face was vaguely familiar, Lou thought. She had seen him in the refectory. He looked older than most of the others. Five, maybe even ten years older? A mature student probably, but he wasn't in any of her classes and Lou had never been interested enough to find out.

"S'okay," she said. "I've got a few to get. You'll only get stung."

"Go on." He grinned. "It's my round anyway and I can probably afford it better than you can. Tell you what, buy me one back at the beginning of next term, when you get your grant."

Lou hesitated. But for the man's blue eyes, she would have dismissed him as a flash git, a smug bastard splashing his cash. No one in their right mind went around volunteering to buy rounds, let alone for students. "I won't force you," he said, when Lou didn't answer.

As he began to turn away, Lou relented.

"All right," she said.

Flash or not, she was broke. It was only a week until term finished for Christmas and she had a fiver to get her through. And that fiver wasn't strictly hers, since it was the last five pounds of her prearranged overdraft's overdraft.

And then there were those clear blue eyes and the freckles that peppered the bridge of his nose beneath those dinky little glasses.

"Two pints of lager, half of Guinness, and a pint of snakebite." The order rushed out, as if trying to get there before she could stop it.

"*Snakebite?* Surely no one drinks that anymore." He laughed. "It's disgusting."

"Clem does," said Lou, inclining her head toward a lone punk, sitting glaring at them from under his blue hair. Every so often Clem's gaze slid along the bar to a wiry boy, all long dark hair and cheekbones, wearing a retro eighties stripy jumper that on anyone else would have looked like something their gran had knitted. On him, it just looked cool. And then Clem would drag his gaze back to Lou and the interloper.

"Of course." The man laughed. "Clem would. He'd probably drink purple bastards if he knew they even existed."

"You know Clem?" she said. Clem had never mentioned it. She wanted to ask what a purple bastard was too, but the Clem question seemed more pressing.

"Who doesn't?"

It was a fair point. It was hard not to know Clem. Lou had met him within minutes of setting foot through the door of art college, and they had been firm friends since.

"He's not your . . . ?" The man looked at her quizzically, voice trailing away. "I mean, you're not?"

Lou laughed. "Me and Clem? I don't think so! We're bound by a shared passion for Johnny Depp!"

Blue eyes crinkled. "I think you're more Johnny's type," he said, his eyes settling on hers, before turning to rummage in his pocket and handing over a twenty to the Goth behind the bar.

Lou felt her cheeks turn pink and stared hard at her shoes, gold Mary Janes with the leather flaking off, her big find from a jumble sale in Kentish Town the previous week. Her gaze drifted from her shoes to the man's battered sneakers and on up his tatty combats to a Cocteau Twins T-shirt, partially hidden by his battered denim jacket.

When her eyes had traveled the length of his body, Lou had a strange feeling in the pit of her stomach and the man was staring at her again, an amused expression in his eyes.

"Sorry," he said. "I should have introduced myself. I'm Gabe, Gabe McLennan, and you're Lou, aren't you? Lou McCartney?"

"How did you . . . ?" Lou couldn't hide her surprise.

"Ah, we lecturers have our ways." he laughed. "I confess, Clem's in my second-year art class, I've seen you waiting for him afterward."

That was when Lou started to feel like an idiot. Everyone knew Dr.

McLennan. He was deputy head of the fine arts department, and half the female students at the college had a crush on him, not to mention half the male students. And she'd just given him the double-O up and down. She felt about seventeen. No, fifteen, with rioting hormones and a pang in her groin to match.

"Come on," said Gabe, much later. "Let me give you a lift."

Closing time had come and gone and the group had scattered. Half of them, the half that included Lou and Clem, had gone on to a nearby bar that Gabe knew, under a theater just off Charing Cross Road. It claimed to be members only, but that was only so it could charge everyone a one-pound entrance fee after eleven P.M.

Gabe had paid her entrance, just as he'd bought her drinks all evening. And Clem's as well. Clem had raised an eyebrow at Lou, not disapproving so much as inquiring, and accepted the drinks in silence.

When a move was made to find a club at two A.M., Lou shook her head. She'd had enough, plus she was trashed. And she had an early history of fashion class. Not that she planned to go, but nobody needed to know that. Oxfam on Kensington Church Street put out its new stock on a Friday morning, and Lou had a regular appointment.

"You go on," she told Clem.

She knew all about his unrequited crush on the boy with the cheekbones and stripy jumper who was making his move for the door. Clem nodded gratefully. He'd been trailing after Cheekbones for weeks. Why the boy wouldn't just put Clem out of his misery Lou didn't know. Perhaps he got off on it? Who knew?

"You be okay?" asked Clem, glancing suspiciously from Lou to his fine art lecturer lingering behind her.

"Sure," Lou assured him, giving Clem a shove toward the door. "I'll get the night bus. Stops right outside my door."

And though Clem looked less than convinced, he didn't protest. The truth was he wanted Lou to be safe, but he also wanted to get laid. Even if they both knew it wasn't likely to be with the object of Clem's affections.

"Come on," said Gabe, when the others had wandered away and they were standing alone, just yards from the early hours bustle of Charing Cross Road. He smiled. "Let me give you a lift. I couldn't forgive myself if you didn't get home safely."

Looking at him through her alcohol- and lust-addled brain, Lou tried to work out whether Gabe was sincere or an old letch. It was tempting. . . .

"Nu-uh," she said. "That's my bus stop right there. I'll be safe." But her heart wasn't in it. Lou knew it and Gabe knew it and within minutes she was in the passenger seat of his old BMW as it bounced through Camden Town.

Gabe didn't come in, not that time. He didn't try to kiss her or even touch her. He didn't need to.

"Good to meet you, finally," he said, leaning over to open her door and, accidentally or not, letting his arm briefly brush hers. Every synapse in Lou's brain fired. She was sold. He had her and he knew it. Lou felt like she'd been waiting for him her entire life, all nineteen years of it. Gabe was older, intelligent, amusing, and grown up. . . .

By the end of that week Lou knew Gabe's timetable better than her own, and the next time she met Clem outside fine art, he knew and she knew it wasn't Clem she was waiting for.

"Lou," Clem said, then stopped.

"What?"

"Are you sure?"

Yes, she almost said. *Completely sure.* But Clem was looking so worried. So she shrugged instead and hoped that would do.

"It's just, Nik said . . ."

Nik fancied Lou. Lou didn't fancy him.

"What did Nik say?"

"You've got a dad complex going." Clem must have seen her face, because he stopped. "Hey. I'm just saying."

"Well, don't," said Lou, then touched his arm. She liked Clem and didn't want to lose his friendship, but she was going to have to be careful. "Look," she said. "Do you fancy having a drink with me sometime?"

"What, like us going out?"

"Why not?"

The prettiest bisexual in college looked at her. "Nik's going to be furious," he said.

Her housemates were still up the first night Gabe came back. They were sitting in the living room as they did most nights, dissecting their evening's various triumphs and failures. Having made Gabe park on a side street so her housemates wouldn't hear his car doors slam, Lou opened her own front door silently.

"Go up," she whispered, pushing Gabe toward the stairs. Any second now Kate or Clare might stick their heads around the living room door to see if she wanted a coffee. There were precious few seconds in the window that would preserve Lou's secret. And if the others heard two sets of footsteps on the stairs, they would be out like a shot.

Not romantic or even subtle, but Lou couldn't have cared less. She knew Gabe wanted her like she'd never been wanted before, and she wanted him so badly she would have done it in his car or the art supplies cupboard if he'd asked.

It wasn't Lou's first time. That had been a couple of years earlier. Bill Jackman wasn't her type, he was captain of the rugby team for a start. Too blond and brawny, too obvious. He was in the year above and already talking about turning professional.

Lou didn't even know why she'd done it, other than the fact everyone else in her year was experimenting and she felt left out, and because Bill wanted to. God, had he wanted to. Half the girls in his year fancied him and he fancied Lou, so it seemed almost rude to refuse.

They'd drifted on for a few months, and then he found someone else and Lou found she didn't care, and a year later she went to Saint Martins and he went . . . Who knew? She hadn't bothered to keep in touch, having nothing more in common than very average beginner-level sex.

After that, she'd been to bed with one or two other students, but found she wasn't that interested. Fashion was Lou's passion, nothing excited her like an old Lanvin frock from the Tooting Broadway branch of Save the Children, to augment Nina's old Ossie Clark dresses that Lou had requisitioned from Gram's attic.

She had her clothes and her friends—who were all female or gay (an occupational hazard of studying fashion)—and she had Gram and Nina. All in all Lou hardly even noticed she didn't have a boyfriend.

Until Gabe.

Once the bedroom door was locked she killed the lights and let him draw back the curtain so he could see her. Lou undressed herself, hanging her jeans carefully over the back of a rickety chair.

When she turned around he was smiling.

"What?"

"Nothing," he said, stepping toward her. They kissed once, and then he drew back the cover to her bed and she climbed in, shuffling across to let him onto the narrow mattress. He didn't grab her or roll himself on top. In fact he kept his hands to himself and simply leaned across and kissed her slowly.

Gabe tasted of red wine and pizza.

As she kissed him back she felt his hand touch her side and then set-tle itself on her stomach, just resting there as he kissed her again. Only later did she feel it rise to cup one of her breasts, his fingers finding the edge of a nipple.

She shivered and watched him smile.

Gabe dropped his hand between her legs and she pushed up to meet him, she couldn't help it. Just as she couldn't help gasping as his finger curled against her wetness and slid inside.

"Please," she said.

He made her wait until she hung on the edge of coming, and then he positioned himself over her, reached down to part her knees.

Lou was ashamed to admit it, but she cried as he entered her.

She wasn't sure, when it was all over and she was curled up against him and he was stroking her hair and telling her she was beautiful, if cry-ing like that was to-die-for romantic or hide-your-head embarrassing. She'd wanted him so badly it felt like a pressure valve released the second he slipped inside. And after he'd stroked her hair and they'd made love again, Lou knew it wasn't just lust. She was in love.

And then he left.

"I have to," he said. "I'm taking the kids swimming first thing."

She knew he was married. Gabe had never pretended otherwise. He wore the ring, and if he hadn't exactly talked to her about Lena or the kids or his big house in Highgate he'd never tried to pretend they weren't there. He didn't lie or tell her his marriage was in trouble or promise this was for-ever.

The most he'd said was she was beautiful.

The sex had been good, better than she realized sex could be. He was slow and gentle, then fast and urgent.

Loving him was enough.

Sex became a pattern. They'd go out for dinner or a drink, small restau-rants not too far from her student house, where they could be sure not to run into anyone he knew. Too divey for his friends, and way beyond the reach of Nik, Clem, and the others, who survived on value cans from Tesco.

But before long they started skipping the meals and going straight back to hers, always taking care to meet first, so Gabe never had to ring the bell. He'd bring wine, and sometimes takeout that invariably remained un-touched. And at two or three o'clock in the morning, maybe four, if Lou was lucky, he would get up to leave, and she'd watch him go from her win-dow, tears cutting grimy trails of mascara down her cheeks.

What Gabe told his wife he never said. What his wife thought, Lou couldn't bring herself to care. She told herself she felt no guilt, no sympathy for Lena, with her big house and high-powered job, new BMW and expensive holidays. Why should she? So far as Lou could see, Lena had everything she didn't. Lena was married to Gabe. He belonged to her, and whatever it was Lou had the night before, by morning her bed was empty.

twenty · six

It was exhaustion and alcohol that made Annie cave in to missing Chris, and missing Chris that made her pick up her Rentafone mobile and pull his number from memory.

Exhaustion and alcohol, longing and guilt. Guilt could always be relied on to appear somewhere down the line. It was the alcohol that made it stupid for her to call anyone, let alone a lover with whom she'd quarreled.

"It's me," she said, already wondering, as the words left her mouth why she hadn't said something else. Something more friendly.

"Lou said you'd call."

As openings went, it left as much to be desired as her own. Still, even now she could salvage things.

I'm sorry. . . . I miss you. . . . I love you. . . . Let me explain about Tony.

All the words she should say. She didn't because screwing up relationships was apparently what she did best. Why? Annie didn't know.

What she did know was she was horrible at apologies. Too selfish, Tony had said. Too self-absorbed, said her sister. Too scared inside, was her own guess. All failings Chris had never once leveled at her.

"How are you?" she asked instead.

"Busy. We've got two shows tomorrow, a third the day after."

"Busy's good."

"True. It's chaos, though. I'm still trying to get confirmation on most of the celebs. And you know how it is these days, no celebs, no publicity."

Annie could hear the sounds of office life in the background. The clatter of a printer, the noise of two PRs talking across the office. Chris must have the window open because she could hear traffic growl in the road outside.

Homesickness hit.

"Chris," she said.

"Mmm?" He was tapping a keyboard. "Sorry," he said. "Another message from Mariolina. That makes five since breakfast. Anyone would think I didn't have other clients."

"I should let you go."

"In a moment," he said. "I've got a meeting. How are things going with Scarlett?"

"Early days. I've tracked down her flatmate."

"That's good." Chris hesitated. "But every day that passes . . ."

Makes finding her alive more unlikely. Yes, Annie knew that.

"Lou's grateful," he added, "that you're searching."

And you're not, obviously. Instead of saying what she should have said, Annie took another swig at her white wine. Five days away from each other, 5,937 miles apart, and she couldn't find the words to say *I'm sorry.*

And finding the right words was meant to be what she was good at.

"Oh," said Chris, just as Annie was wondering how to get from this call to a bath and her bed, and the oblivion that sleep might bring. "Your mother telephoned. . . ."

"She called *you*?" It wasn't meant to come out like that.

"Not quite. She called the flat." Chris's voice sounded defensive. "She said you'd agreed to go down the weekend after Milan."

"What did you say?"

"In that case we'd see them then."

Annie didn't reply, it was safer not to. What was she supposed to say? *Good call, just what we need?*

After Tokyo, she had the shows in Milan, and then Paris. At the very least, she needed forty-eight hours to sort things out with Chris. Not a big family lunch, watching her father watch him play uncle to Jane's twins and hearing Jane tell her boring husband, *"Chris is so good for Annie."*

All the while she'd be wondering what Chris was thinking and if the ax was going to fall. She'd had enough of pretending everything was all right in her teens.

"You know," he said. "Your mother didn't know you were in Tokyo."

Obviously not, she thought. "You didn't tell her?"

"Yes. Of course."

"Why?"

"Annie."

"Don't," she snapped. "Look, I'm sorry about New York, all right? I'm sorry I'm a fucking mess. But they're my parents, all right? And I've spent the last twenty-nine years learning how to deal with them."

This had been Annie's position since she was seventeen, and she wasn't about to compromise it now. Chris obviously understood that, because even with him nearly ten thousand miles away she could hear a second of cold silence before he put down the phone.

twenty · seven

"*Handbag* magazine," said Annie firmly. She fixed the Japanese woman holding a clipboard with what Annie hoped was her best Rebecca stare. When this didn't work, Annie extracted a business card from her bag and offered it to the woman.

Instant confusion.

Japanese tradition demanded the woman take Annie's card with two hands, but she was already holding a clipboard in one of them. Down went the board, leaned hastily against a wall, and Annie's card was examined carefully.

"*Hai,*" said the woman, bowing and sliding Annie's card into her own pocket.

Annie was in.

Who knew it could be that difficult to get into an open casting? Obviously open only meant open if you were five feet eight inches. Plus, size zero and blond.

This had been Scarlett's life, some of these models must have been Scarlett's friends, and the girl waiting inside knew facts about Scarlett that Annie needed to know. Starting with the details of that *other job*. And when this was over, Jess had promised to take her to Scarlett's favorite place in all of Tokyo.

"You made it," said Jess, when Annie caught up. Annie nodded, taking a look around her. Young, painfully slender female bodies lined a windowless corridor. All Western, all waiting patiently.

So thin, thought Annie, her eyes catching ribs and hipbones and wrists like twigs. Much thinner than any woman you might see in the street and much thinner, it had to be said, than her.

She had no place here, a size-ten-on-a-good-day, five-feet-five-inches brunette voluntarily attending a model casting.

But, get close to your case studies was one of the basic laws of journalism. So here Annie was.

Admittedly, it was their job to be size zero, and have bodies too slight to get in the way of the clothes they were paid to wear, but all the same. There were girls here whose thighs were as thin as Annie's upper arms, maybe thinner.

All of them, including Jess, who now slouched beside Annie chewing piece after piece of gum, wore the model's universal uniform of hip-slung jeans, child-size T-shirt, biker boots or tattered Converse sneakers, with a jacket slung over the top. Every single one was blond, or at the least fair skinned and highlighted. Although none were so overtly, unnaturally white blond as Jess.

There was no doubting she stood out, but what point did Jess hope to make, with her gappy teeth and waterfall peroxide hair. What point was her agent making? Whatever it was, Annie doubted if the Tokyo bookers were getting it.

The only Japanese woman in sight was the one with the clipboard, demure in her black turtleneck and knee-length skirt, standing five foot in her flats. Every few minutes, she would reappear and pluck one of the girls from the line, with as much interest and enthusiasm as someone choosing toilet paper from a supermarket shelf.

Most of the models leaned against the corridor walls, large black-bound portfolios hooked under one arm, causing them to list sideways. A few crouched, their collection of previous work balanced between their knees, staring intently at the screens of their phones.

And one, making no pretense of her boredom, slumped on the standard-issue-for-offices carpet, her portfolio tossed aside, cards spilling out, and skinny legs splayed in front of her. That was Jess.

It wasn't that Annie hadn't seen it all before. She had, in the bags of bones stalking the catwalks of Milan, Paris, and New York. Somehow, those models managed to look imposing, in control of their destiny.

These girls were younger, more *naked,* somehow.

"It must be hard," said Annie, "doing this."

"I've done worse," said Jess, and Annie could see her thinking, *What are you, my mother?*

As the queue inched forward, Annie and Jess rounded a corner and Annie could finally see an open door at the far end of the corridor. It gaped like a maw, swallowing model after model, and spewing them back out again minutes later.

"Really," said Jess, when Annie made some comment. "It's no big deal. It's the business. As my dad would say, it is what it is."

Quite probably, thought Annie, filing it with the list of clichés her own parents used.

"I got a few jobs at home," explained Jess. "A little editorial, some teen magazines. Editorial doesn't pay so well, but it can look good. And I did the odd catalog shoot, but the fashion magazines wouldn't take a risk on me. So I'm here, 'getting the experience.'"

Annie frowned.

"Yes," said Jess. "I know. . . . I'm queuing with a hundred other also-rans for a bloody knitwear job. I know, all right? But it's still worth it. If I can make money, the agency will bump me up a league. As it is, I've been around too long to remain a 'new face' much longer. And if they decide not to move me up to the main board . . ."

Touching a finger to her throat, Jess made a slicing motion and grinned to show she was joking, sort of . . .

Had it been mean to block Jess's dash to the loos after brunch yesterday? Of course it had, out-and-out cruel. But five minutes in the loo would have been enough for Jess to lose her lunch and regain her composure. Scarlett's secrets would have been safe, which wasn't Annie's plan at all.

After Annie left her yesterday afternoon, Jess would have made herself pay, Annie knew that. She didn't like to think too hard about how.

"You come now, please."

"C'mon," said Jess, as she clambered to her feet and followed the small Japanese woman toward the open door.

"You sure?"

"'Course. Why not?"

The only thing worth noticing in the large bare room was its window, the first flash of natural daylight Annie had seen since getting out of an elevator on the twenty-third floor. Beyond the window, Shibuya-ku sprawled, in all its glass and metal glory, unrecognizable beside the city's nighttime neon persona.

Seated at a large round table, oblivious to the astonishing view behind him, sat a Japanese man in black jeans, and beside him a younger woman. So neutral was the body language between them that they could have been on a subway, never having met before or spoken. Everything about the man screamed *photographer*. He was clad head to toe in black, his long black hair tied in a ponytail that bordered on tragic given that he was the other side of forty. In his left ear was a tiny pearl stud, and a Belstaff leather jacket slung casually over the back of his chair. As Annie and Jess walked in together, he threw a cursory glance at Jess, treated Annie to a double take, and then glanced not-too-subtly at a large silver Seiko on his wrist.

The woman on the other hand was corporate from the tips of her toes to the top of her head. Her spine erect, feet tucked underneath the chair, she sat as if she'd had deportment classes. There were no prizes for guessing that she—all pin-striped skirt suit and sensible heels—was the client. She too wore pearl earrings, only hers were substantially larger.

Women like this existed in every city in every country all over the world, thought Annie. She might have been five years younger than the photographer, or she could have been fifteen; her clothes gave nothing away and she'd probably been dressing this way since she was sixteen.

The woman at least managed a smile and the most cursory of bows.

In front of her on the table was a sleek silver Sony VAIO that she tapped at idly, as if scanning e-mail so as not to waste precious time. Apart from this, and a pile of model cards, a Polaroid camera, and a pile of snaps of young girls in ugly knitwear, the table was bare.

Annie wasn't expecting introductions, so she wasn't surprised when she didn't get them.

"Here, please," said the small woman, who was clearly a runner. So Jess placed her portfolio in front of the pair, before heading for a screen in the far corner, which half-concealed a rack of pastel knitwear.

"You put this . . ." Annie heard the woman say.

The room was silent but for the rustle of Jess stripping, the hum of air-conditioning and the client's manicured nails tapping the keys of her laptop. It was obviously all the photographer could do not to drum his fingers in irritation.

"Ouch!"

"No, you put this one. Pink."

More rustling. Jess's naked arms appeared over the top of the screen and vanished again.

"It doesn't fit," Annie heard Jess hiss.

"Okay." The woman sounded flustered. "We try this."

Seconds later Jess emerged, hands smoothing a hideous lemon twinset where her T-shirt had been.

Annie did a double take.

If that did fit, Annie hated to think how small the pink outfit must have been. The loose knit cardigan strained across Jess's shoulders and didn't even begin to button over her breasts.

Jess forced a smile all the same, as she stood in front of the photographer and turned every couple of seconds to display all four sides. She already knew, because everybody in the room already knew, that it was futile. Jess would not get the job. She was kooky, she was blond, she was Western, she was everything the booker had asked for, but the teenager in front of them was still too big to fit into the samples.

twenty · eight

Lunch-hour Shibuya made Oxford Circus at rush hour two weeks before Christmas look chilled. Traffic streamed in from eight different directions, crowds swamped the pavements, and songs clashed with advertising jingles every five paces.

When Annie thought it couldn't get worse, the heavens opened, rain hit steaming tarmac, and rivulets ran together, until streams filled the gutters and cars seemed to slide over thin sheets of water.

Annie hadn't realized Jess was carrying an umbrella until she snapped it open above their heads.

"Rainy season," she said.

You don't say, Annie wanted to reply, but she was trapped in a polite stampede toward shelter, the suddenly opened umbrellas only making matters worse.

"It'll be over soon enough," said Jess, steering Annie toward the overhang of an office block that had a Mercedes showroom as its ground floor.

HMV and McDonald's, Starbucks and Gap might mix with the chilly calm of department stores, but between the global franchises found on every high street in the world were pachinko parlors, electrical goods stores, and arcades that could only be Tokyo.

No one set a single foot on the road, not even to avoid a bunch of squealing tourists who rushed for the overhang under which Annie, Jess, and fifty other people already sheltered. How anyone could live in a city where it was considered social suicide to jaywalk, Annie couldn't understand.

Despite the rain, the crowds still waited and only surged forward from both sides as the lights changed, to meet, merge, and become separate again on the other side of the road.

As quickly as the rains struck, they subsided.

"Told you," said Jess.

Annie nodded.

As they headed up Jingu-dori, the pedestrians on the sidewalk began to change, subtly at first. So when Annie and Jess finally began to dry out, the shops around them were no longer chains but vintage, the clientele more Camden than Oxford Street. There were tourists in the mix, but tourists who considered themselves *travelers*.

For the first time that day, Jess looked at ease. Now the clouds had broken and the sun was high in a blue sky, the air fresh from the rain. Jess slipped off her battered leather jacket, slinging it over one skinny shoulder.

"Scarlett hated Shibuya," she said. "Couldn't stand the crowds or the crap shops. Said it represented all that was rotten about Tokyo, almost as spoiled as Ginza, only trashier."

Tokyo, *rotten*? Ginza, *spoiled*?

Ginza was the city's designer shopping Mecca. Annie hadn't been there yet. Still, she didn't see how anywhere could possibly be worse than the over-crowded trash-onslaught of Shibuya. And Annie had thought Scarlett was spoiled. Surely Rufus Ulrich's daughter would like the overpriced clothes and ostentatious labels? Wasn't that what the Ulrich lifestyle was all about?

"Are they always like that?" Annie asked. "Castings, I mean. That jumper . . . cardigan . . . whatever the hell it was. You didn't stand a hope in hell of getting into it. They were doll's clothes."

"Japanese clothes," said Jess, and shrugged. "You should see the shoes here! Most of the Western girls look like Ugly Stepsisters trying to force their feet into Cinderella's slipper. I know one girl who's seriously thinking about having her little toe removed. Trust me; all her toes would be more like it!"

"You serious?"

Jess nodded. "Believe it or not," she said, "this is the only place where being mid-height is a positive advantage. I stand a better chance of getting footwork than most, thanks to my size-four feet. Usually they say, 'You short for a model.' As if they don't believe I am one. And I say, 'Yes, same height as Kate Moss.'"

She saw Annie's smile and grinned.

"Okay," said Jess. "Sometimes it works, sometimes it doesn't!"

"What about Scarlett?"

"What *about* her?"

Annie paused, wondering how to phrase it. "Well, you know, I'm not being funny, but I heard that she'd got a little . . . *heavier*. I don't mean by real people's standards," Annie added hastily. "I mean, for a model."

Jess put one foot in front of the other, seemingly concentrating on the road's slight incline. "Who told you that?" she asked.

"Her mother."

"Oh, God. Mothers, eh? Always know how to make you feel good about yourself."

Annie stifled a smile.

"It got her down, to be honest," said Jess. "I mean, Scarlett knew why she'd been sent here. Punishment for Milan. She was here to see if she still had what it took, and every casting confirmed she didn't."

What happened in Milan?

Annie didn't want to wreck Jess's train of thought. So she filed the question away for later. "Look. Did Scarlett talk to her Japanese agent about it?"

"Netsuko!" Jess almost spat the name. "That bitch is only interested in money-spinners. She's already on me to clear out Scarlett's stuff so she can put another girl in her room."

"You serious?"

"Oh yes," Jess said. "You'd better believe it."

Motorbikes streamed past. High overhead a plane banked before turning for Narita Airport and a cluster of Japanese students, too old and cool to be Harajuku girls, stumbled to a halt. Then split, to walk around Annie and Jess, because Annie had come to a standstill.

"That's obscene."

Jess shrugged, but still she looked close to tears. "Harsh, huh?"

"Understatement of the year."

Compared with the kid-traffickers and pimps Annie had faced in her previous job, Netsuko's behavior was nothing. But somehow, the assumption that Scarlett was dead or AWOL, and it didn't matter which so long as her room didn't go to waste, seemed equally callous.

"Modeling is a drug," said Jess fiercely.

"You're saying Scarlett was addicted to it?"

The girl rolled her eyes. "Of course not. Scarlett couldn't wait to get out. It would have been better for everyone if Arabella and Rufus had just banked her cash and let Scarlett go back to school and finish studying. No, they're the junkies, the pair of them, hooked on Scarlett's fame."

Now, for the first time, she was hearing the truth, Annie realized.

"Scarlett tried every diet going," said Jess. "She starved and starved but it didn't do any good. She was all bottom and no top, that was Scarlett's problem. Your classic English pear-shape. Scarlett said she got her body shape from her grandmother on her father's side. Obviously her mother is six feet of nothingness and silicone."

"Yep." That sounded to Annie like an accurate assessment of Arabella, and she had only met the woman once.

"And I understand why she agreed," Jess said. "But I do think Scarlett regretted her boob job."

"*Her what?*"

"That's Rufus for you," said Jess, as if Annie hadn't spoken. "Always full of good ideas. I think he thought it might miraculously turn her into Gisele."

"Not her idea?"

"No way," said Jess. "Definitely not. She hated it, kept talking about getting the implants taken out again, only she wasn't sure if she could, because she'd had one of those fancy ops where they put them under the muscle wall."

"Ouch."

"Meant to make them look real, the one stars have when they want to be able to pretend they haven't. It's the Mercedes of boob jobs."

Ahead of them was a crossroads with cars passing over and under. A spaghetti-junction of high pedestrian bridges offered their only way forward. And opposite, on the other side of a four-lane strip, stood a wall of trees.

Annie had the feeling she was being watched. But no one nearby fitted the description of Rufus's PI. "So," she said, taking the footbridge two steps at a time. "Scarlett spent all day chasing after jobs she rarely got. How come she managed to save fifteen grand? Is hostessing really that profitable?"

Halting at the top, Jess glanced at her watch. To their right lay traffic and noise, exhaust fumes from the road beneath them, and groups of pedestrians rolling in waves along the sidewalk. To their left were the trees.

"Okay," said Jess, her voice quietly determined. "Why not? I'll tell you about Scarlett's other job, but if I do that's the end of it. You leave me alone. And you make that guy from the *Herald* and all the others leave me alone as well."

She said it softly enough to be a whisper, but somehow, even over the roar of a passing subway train, Annie heard it.

"I can't speak for the others," she said honestly. "But I'll talk to Phil Townend. If that's what you want."

Jess nodded.

"It's a deal," said Annie.

"Okay," Jess said, pointing to an expanse of grass and trees. "We're here. Let's visit Yoyogi-koen."

twenty · nine

Yoyogi-koen turned out to be a big park with a smaller park inside, designed to cloak the Meiji shrine in silence. A double layer of insulation to protect the shrine from the brutality of the surrounding city.

Food stalls crowded the park's entrance, drowning out the sound of cars with their own hiss and sizzle of meat frying. Wooden spatulas clattered on metal as exhaust fumes mixed with oily smoke, griddled fish and chicken fried to just the right side of burning. Annie could smell the yakitori spices and see steam rise from individual cartons of freshly cooked noodles. She wasn't remotely hungry, but still the smell of soy and grilled spices made her mouth water.

"Hungry?" Annie asked.

Jess shook her head. "No thanks. I'll have a Diet Coke though, if you're buying."

As well as two Diet Cokes, Annie bought a tub of stir-fried buckwheat noodles and took a couple of pairs of disposable wooden chopsticks, in the unlikely event that Jess changed her mind.

God, thought Annie, as she followed Jess through the gates. *I really am turning into my mother.*

Only Annie's mother would never have let her own life get so messy. Meet nice boy, marry him, have babies. Annie had only ever got to number one on that list and she probably wasn't going to be there much longer, not after last night.

"You okay?" asked Jess.

"Sure," said Annie, wiping a hand across her eyes. She was cross with herself for letting jet lag, Chris's anger, and her own inability to apologize take her mind off the job. It had been a bad night. "Just tired," she said. "Where now?"

"How about there," said Jess, pointing to a wooden bench under the shade of a cypress, just beyond earshot of a group of American students sharing a carton of noodles and a bottle of sake.

"So," Annie said, when Jess had flipped open her Diet Coke and Annie had split the two sets of chopsticks, handing a pair to Jess who grinned and pointedly stuck them in her hair. "Tell me about Scarlett's savings."

"I've told you," said Jess. "She made her money the way we all do. She just didn't spend as much as the rest of us."

"Which way is that?" Annie already knew the answer. She just needed to hear the girl repeat it.

"She worked a club. Most of us do."

"A bar?"

Jess took a swig, shook her head. "No. A *club* . . . a hostess club," she added, when Annie refused to look away. "I know what you're thinking," she said. "But it's not like that. You're paid to turn up and look"—Jess struggled for the right word—"*nice*. It helps, of course, if you flirt with the customers, encourage them to buy more drinks. The more drinks you sell, the more commission you make, it's as simple as that."

She said this like it was nothing, but Annie knew there was more to being a hostess than that. If there weren't, she wouldn't have to crowbar the truth out of Jess.

"This club," said Annie, "is it in Roppongi?"

"You're joking," Jess said. "The clubs in Roppongi cater to tourists, and that's two reasons not to work there."

"Two?"

"Yup. Firstly, you might see someone you know. Secondly, tourists are gropers, and tight too. They don't understand the rules."

"Which are what?"

"No wandering hands," said Jess as if it was obvious.

Yes, that was pretty much what the Australian girl in the cake shop had said. About tourists being gropers anyway.

"Scarlett started out at a club in Roppongi, but it was grim, so she changed. A couple of times, I think."

Annie waited.

"Scarlett worked . . . works," Jess corrected herself, "with me, in Akasaka, at the Blue Flamingo. There are dozens of clubs in the area be-cause it's so near the parliament building. Also, it's classier, because some of the clubs run on expenses. So punters only get in if their company has an account. The Flamingo's a bit like that, but the mama-san also takes private customers, if the price is right."

"What's the job like?"

"Much better," said Jess. "You still get the occasional wandering hand, but not many, less than you'd think. Mostly salarymen are so polite it's funny." She hesitated. "Of course, what people do outside is their business."

"And what do you do?" asked Annie. *"Outside."*

"Nothing," said Jess, looking hurt. "And I'm pretty sure . . . no, I'm a hundred percent sure Scarlett didn't either. I mean, she had a few clients who took her to dinner. One guy came to the club a lot, started leaving if it wasn't Scarlett's night on. That's all it was, though, just dinner."

"And he paid her extra for that?" Annie knew she sounded naïve, but she had to ask.

Jess laughed. "Of course he did. Why would she go otherwise? It wasn't a date, it was work. Money in the bank."

"Did you? Ever go to dinner with him?"

"No, he never asked." Disappointment flickered across Jess's face. "I make most of my money from tips and commission. You wouldn't believe the drinking games I could teach you. Mama-san has a league table, you get a bonus at the end of the week if your clients have drunk the most champagne."

"This man," Annie said. "Describe him."

"In his forties, well-dressed, expensive clothes. An old samurai family, or so he told Scarlett. Polite, quite formal. Always shook hands, never tried to grope. He did read poetry to her once."

A total fruitcake, that much was clear. But dangerous?

"Did Scarlett have a dinner fixed that night? The night she vanished?"

"Not that she told me. I asked Mama-san but she just played dumb. She says Scarlett's customer came to the club but Scarlett left on her own. As if that makes a difference. Scarlett never *left* with him, no one does. He used to meet her at a restaurant, a different one every time."

Clever, thought Annie, swiftly shoveling soba noodles into her own mouth, before they had the chance to slip from the chopsticks and decorate her lap. *If you never go to the same restaurant twice, no one's ever going to be able to recognize you. Especially not in a city of twenty million people.*

"I wasn't working that night," said Jess. "We used to try to share shifts so we could travel home together, if we were both coming home, obviously. Sometimes Scarlett stayed at her boyfriend's. And occasionally sharing shifts just wasn't possible, because everyone has to split Sunday nights."

"How do you mean?

"Sundays are quietest. Most of the salarymen are home being good family men, so you don't make much in tips that night. I don't even know why Mama-san bothers to open. It was Scarlett's turn to do Sunday."

"And you're sure she turned up for work?"

"So Mama-san says. Scarlett left around midnight when Mama-san shut up shop. Earlier than usual, because it was so quiet."

Jess looked at Annie. "And yes. She left on her own, before you ask."

"And her boyfriend?" asked Annie. "What was his name again?"

"Mike. Scarlett never mentioned his surname."

"Did you meet him?"

"Only once." Jess shrugged. "American, bit of a jock."

"You didn't like him?"

"Full of himself," said Jess. "You know, some photographers think they've got a right to sleep with the models, but he wasn't even a photographer, just someone's assistant. Never understood what she saw in him."

"Describe him."

"Tall, fit, longish dark hair."

It didn't sound so bad to Annie. "Was it serious?"

Jess shook her head. "No. I think it was over. Scarlett didn't say. But she hadn't mentioned him for a while."

thirty

The mama-san at the first club, the one where Scarlett had begun her hostessing career, proved polite, even friendly, but remembered little about Scarlett and said nothing that Annie had not already heard from Jess. Annie rather expected her to point out that girls came and went, but she didn't.

After a half hour of stilted conversation, Annie bowed, offered her thanks, and let herself out into the neon bustle and chichi sleaze of the backstreets of Roppongi. She was due to meet Jess at the hotel for supper, not that she expected the girl to eat anything.

The meal with Jess was going to cost thirty thousand yen, roughly one hundred fifty pounds, plus another twenty thousand yen, about one hundred pounds, for the mama-san at the Blue Flamingo to release Jess for the evening. Not having that much cash, Annie had hit an ATM with her credit card and given a fattish bundle of notes to Jess, who promised to fix everything.

What Rebecca was going to say about her expenses when she got the bill for fifty thousand yen so Annie could have supper with a girl who worked at a hostess bar was anyone's guess.

Assuming Jess turned up, of course. It was twenty-four hours since Annie had suggested it and Jess agreed. Plenty of time for her to change her mind.

Three vodka tonics in and Annie couldn't get the girl to shut up. Drinking on an empty stomach did that to you.

"If you ask me," said Jess, "all this drama about hostessing is a fuss about nothing." She dug into a tempura parcel, pulling it apart and scattering the contents across her duck-egg-blue plate. On the other side of a slate counter, the tempura chef almost visibly flinched.

Annie and Jess were in a tiny restaurant in the basement of Annie's hotel. They were the only customers in the room, and at the last count they were outnumbered by staff three to one.

"Really?" said Annie.

Jess nodded. "Absolutely," she said, putting down her chopsticks and picking up her glass, only to discover it was already empty.

Annie signaled to a kimono-clad woman, who slid from the shadows.

"At least," said Jess, "you get paid to be bored to tears by sleazy old men. Not like in Milan. You should have seen some of the *after*-after-show parties we had to go to."

"We?" asked Annie.

Jess took a gulp of the vodka tonic that had just appeared next to her right hand, then put the glass down with a bang. Everything about her body language suggested she wished she hadn't said that.

"Everything you tell me," said Annie, "helps Scarlett."

"Me, Scarlett, and Bree," Jess said finally, adding, "You s'pose they'd mind if I smoke?"

Annie glanced around the room, with its subdued lighting and silent staff studiously avoiding eye contact. "I think," said Annie, "they'd probably mind very much."

Jess rolled her eyes.

"You and Scarlett go way back, then?" Annie said, wanting to add, *And Bree* . . . As in Bree O'Shaughnessey.

Who knew?

"Not really," said Jess, ignoring the fresh piece of tempura that had appeared on her plate. "Well, perhaps. In modeling terms, but not life terms. We're not old school friends or anything."

"We met in Milan, a couple of years ago, kept seeing each other at the same castings. To begin with, Scarlett was always with Bree, but when Bree started getting jobs and Scarlett didn't, I think Scarlett realized she had more in common with me."

Jess sounded almost proud.

"Bree and Scarlett were the ones who went back years," she added. "Their mothers are friends, and Bree and Scarlett went to the same school. That posh one Gwyneth Paltrow went to."

"Spence," Annie said, cursing her own stupidity. She'd just remembered the photograph that fluttered from Scarlett's schoolbook. The one with Scarlett, Leonardo DiCaprio, and a gawky, freckly redhead standing off to one side. *Bree and Scarlett went way back.*

Yes, indeed. Of course they did.

"Anyway," said Jess, "they were best, best friends at school. Scarlett was a superstar and, I guess, Bree probably worshipped her. Only things went wrong last year. Scarlett, well, we've talked about that already. She wasn't so much on the way down as over. And Bree . . ."

She hesitated, looking almost wistful.

"Right now," said Jess, "Bree's on her way to Milan. She'll be walking the runway for every big-name show and opening half of them. Starring in their ad campaigns by spring. And Scarlett . . . Scarlett's stuck in Tokyo." Jess paused. "I hope."

"Yes," said Annie. "Me too."

"It all came to a big head at the Mantolini casting." Jess put down the chopsticks she'd been fiddling with and hunched her shoulders. "Mantolini's a good show, all the best girls are in it. . . . Well, it was obvious Scarlett wasn't a Mantolini girl, even before she started . . ."

"Gaining weight?" asked Annie.

Jess nodded. "Their look is strictly size zero. Childlike, not womanly. You know, if you think a model's too skinny, too pale, Mariolina Mantolini will love her. Scarlett's look was more Versace, especially after the boob job."

"What happened?"

"What you'd expect." Jess inhaled deeply, let it out slowly. Annie looked at her. The girl was tired, lonely, and in a strange country, all things that applied equally to both of them. To all three of them, because those undoubtedly applied to Scarlett as well. Except that Scarlett and Jess were teenagers, and Annie was supposedly big enough and ugly enough to look after herself.

"Mantolini optioned sixty models," she continued. "And once we got over the excitement of being optioned by Mantolini, we could tell it was a total downer, because we couldn't do castings for shows scheduled either side of her, just in case we got the job. Even though, in my heart, I knew I wouldn't make the cut."

Pausing, Jess reached for her vodka.

"That's how it works?"

"It is if you're me, Scarlett, or even Bree back then. *Now* Bree's a money girl, this year's model. Back then she was just one of us."

"Out of sixty, how many got cast?"

"Twenty, twenty-five max."

"What about the rest of you?"

"*We won't be needing you this time*. Believe me, that's better than you get from most of them. Anyway, we got called to the show venue at Corso Venezia for a ten P.M. fitting, all three of us. We were feeling good, 'cause at that point we thought they might have optioned maybe twice as many models as they needed at most, so we were in with a chance."

Jess paused.

"You know Milan?"

"I'll be there on Saturday."

This wasn't a real answer, but Jess barely noticed.

"From the minute we got through the door there were girls everywhere, hanging out in the courtyard, sitting on the marble stairs, crowding the hall. And Villa Carlotta's a big place, though Mariolina Mantolini managed to make it look intimate by setting a catwalk up in the middle and only putting two rows of seats around it.

"The lights were low, show style, so we signed in, found ourselves a corner, and hung out. When nothing happened, I wandered over to a girl I knew, smaller than me and skinny, from the Ukraine, I think. Anyway, turned out she'd been called for nine and had friends who'd been called for eight.

"We weren't that fazed. Waiting's common. We just sat around, picked the bread off the panini, and drank Diet Coke. No smoking, though, Mariolina won't allow it in the auditorium. But ten o'clock came and went, and still we hadn't been called. Bree was the first, just after midnight. I don't know about Scarlett but I just wanted to go home by then.

"Bree was gone for ages, which we knew was a good sign. When she returned we couldn't tell at first, because her face was dead straight. So Scarlett got up, went to hug her, and Bree punched the air.

"I got it," she whooped. "I'm doing Mantolini."

"And Scarlett was thrilled, really she was. Bree was her best friend. Then I was called. I wasn't holding my breath, to be honest, but I'm small, slight, and quirky, there was a chance I'd be what Mantolini was looking for."

Yes, Annie could see that.

"Anyway," said Jess, "backstage there were about a dozen people, dressers, cutters, and Mariolina herself. I could hardly speak I was so in awe. They fitted me with a couple of linen shifts, did some pinning. All in all it took about twenty minutes. Then an assistant said they'd call me in the morning. I knew what it meant, it meant I wasn't a shoe-in, but I would do if someone better fell out."

Annie raised her eyebrows.

Half smiling, Jess said, "Don't hate me, but I was praying Lily Donaldson would get food poisoning."

A member of staff glided over when Annie laughed.

"Everything's fine," she said, ordering another white wine and deciding it should be her last. The tempura was still piling up, almost-raw this and recently dead that, and Annie was beyond hoping that someone would come soon and begin taking it away.

"It was two A.M. when Scarlett was called," said Jess. "There were only a handful of girls left by this point, ten at most. She'd tried to get Bree and me to go back to our hotel, but we said we'd stay. Looking back, I think she wanted us to go, not for our beauty sleep, which is what she said, but so we wouldn't witness her humiliation.

"You only had to look at the girls who'd made it to know that Scarlett didn't have the look. Why Mantolini put her through it, I don't know. . . . I guess they were just keeping their options open. Or maybe they owed her agency."

"Unless Rufus was behind it," said Annie. "I can imagine him calling up Mariolina personally." She could also imagine Mariolina knowing the value of doing Rufus Ulrich a favor.

Jess looked sick.

"What happened?"

"Ten minutes later Scarlett was back. She loped over to our corner smiling, but when she got close I could see her eyes. 'No way,' she told us, still smiling like her life depended on it. 'Thank you for your time, bullshit, bullshit, bullshit.'

"After grabbing her bag, Scarlett headed off without even looking at Bree. It wasn't Bree's fault, but after that everything changed. . . . I can't begin to know how Scarlett felt, because I've never been a face. So I don't know what it does to you when you stop being one.

"But I know about rejection because I never got their call, or anyone else's for that matter. While Bree was storming the catwalk—second out, and her picture everywhere—Scarlett and I were in a bar on Naviglio Grande, drowning our sorrows and calling up the courage to attend a party near the Duomo.

"Our minder said we had to. Scarlett didn't want to and we ended up returning to the hotel, so she could change and redo her makeup. She made the mistake of answering her mobile. . . ."

Annie waited.

"None of it was Bree's fault," Jess repeated, and stared into space as if replaying Scarlett's downfall in slo-mo. "It was Rufus, he phoned."

Annie froze, her glass halfway to her mouth.

It wasn't unusual, Jess's fugue state. Case studies often got so lost inside their own words that everything else vanished. Annie was getting close to the truth and from the hollowness in Jess's voice it was going to be ugly.

"What happened?" she prompted.

"He wanted to know about Mantolini. . . . When she told him, he just went quiet. I could hear her trying to fill the silence. It was hopeless. And when Scarlett realized it was hopeless she lost it. . . ."

Jess hesitated.

"I've never seen anyone lose it like that," she said, her eyes almost haunted by the memory. "It's not like we were even close back then. Scarlett was pleading down the phone, begging to be allowed to stop, to go home. All she wanted was for him to say something. And he did, because when Scarlett put down the phone she just curled into a ball, sobbing. So I knew he'd said no."

"And then . . . ?"

"It got worse. Scarlett started pulling at herself, yanking at the skin around her waist, pinching her arms. It was embarrassing. . . . No," said Jess. "It was more than that. It was hideous. I felt like I was watching . . . I dunno what, but it was too much. She just sat there, sobbing about how fat and ugly and useless she was."

"She wasn't any of those." Annie realized too late that she'd just used the past tense. "*Isn't* any of those," she said, correcting herself. "Really, she isn't."

Even to her own ears it sounded hollow.

"Her father told her she was. And in modeling terms she certainly wasn't thin anymore."

This, Annie had to admit, was true. For your average girl on the street Scarlett was a babe. In an industry where women dieted themselves to nothing so as not to affect the way the clothes hung, even a UK eight was pushing it. "The party," said Annie, signaling for another vodka and tonic. "Did you go?"

Jess shook her head. "Scarlett refused. Said she wouldn't do any more parties. So the next day her agent called Rufus to say they've got no choice but to take her off the books. You see, Scarlett wasn't right for catwalk, she wasn't getting the big-money beauty advertising that everyone had expected, and now she was refusing to play ball, what was the point?"

Play ball?

There was a euphemism if ever Annie heard one.

"Her father went mad. He summoned her back to New York and Scarlett went. At first, she swore she wouldn't, but then Arabella called and did some crying and off Scarlett trotted. . . ."

"And that was it." Jess shrugged, shook her head as if coming out of a trance. "I didn't hear from her for ages. I texted, e-mailed a couple of times, but she never replied. So I figured she just wanted to wipe the memory of Milan. I even thought she might have been allowed to start studying like she wanted.

"I heard from Bree O'Shaughnessey, though. One minute she was lucky to get a major show, the next she's doing *Vogue* and campaigns for Missoni, Etro, and Calvin Klein. All I could do was watch as she got bigger and bigger, and Scarlett vanished off the map. It didn't help that, wherever she was, I knew she was watching Bree too.

"Then, about four, five months ago, right out of the blue, my mobile rang and it was Scarlett. She said she was in Japan and why didn't I come? She didn't say, of course, that her dad had bullied the agency into giving her one last shot and she'd been here ever since. Why would she?

"I think she was lonely and needed some company and she knew my career wasn't exactly stellar either, so she guessed I'd jump at the chance. Netsuko called my agents in London and I was on the next plane."

"And the hostessing?"

"Scarlett was already into that when I arrived. Said a friend of Netsuko put her in touch with a club in Roppongi, but she found the Akasaka club for herself. She was making way more money from the Blue Flamingo than from modeling. It was harmless, she said. Just dressing up nice, persuading Japanese executives to have another bottle of champagne, and making them think they spoke good English."

"How far does the entertaining go?"

"I've told you," said Jess. "It's not what you think. They don't expect you to sleep with them."

"You just have to make them think they could?" said Annie.

Jess ignored her.

"In the end," she said, "it's just using your body to sell stuff. You know, like modeling."

thirty · one

The September sun hung low in the sky, cast an orange glow across Annie's hotel room, even though it was only eleven in the morning when she returned from taking her hangover for a walk. The message-waiting light, flashing red from the phone on a bedside table, was barely visible from behind her dark glasses.

What's wrong with using my mobile? Annie wondered, then realized the person had. She had a call missed and a ringback icon on its screen.

The room looked as big a mess as when she'd left. Probably because she hadn't bothered to take the DO NOT DISTURB sign off her door. Tossing her bag on the floor, Annie flung herself across the bed, lifting the receiver and hitting voice mail.

Chris, Lou, or Rebecca?

Bracing herself for Rebecca's abruptness, Annie got an unfamiliar voice instead. "Bloody machines," it said, which was much how Annie felt about voice mail too.

"Hi, this is Phil Townend at the *Tokyo Herald*. I got your message. You mentioned Jess Harper. . . . I'm interested in talking, call me back." It was somewhere between a request, an order, and a suggestion. The accent was hard to place, the voice of a nomad whose origins were hard to detect. If pushed, Annie would have said Mancunian with a slight Ozzie twang.

Here we go again, thought Annie, punching in his number.

"Mr. Townend?"

"Yes," he said. "Is that . . . ?"

"Annie Anderson," said Annie. "Thanks for getting back to me."

"No problem," he said. "I'm happy to talk to anyone who's talked to Jess. I think we should meet."

Hang on, Annie thought.

"You okay with that?"

"Mr. Townend . . ."

"Phil," he said. "Call me Phil." He was about to say something else but swallowed it. Then decided to say it anyway. "I Googled you. . . . Three press awards, two commendations for bravery from the police. You're a legend in your own lunchtime."

It was glib. That was how Annie knew he meant it. Didn't mean he liked it, of course.

"Okay," she said. "But first a question."

Silence greeted her words. Phil Townend was wondering if she intended to pull a fast one. At least, she imagined he did. It was what she'd think.

"Did you track down Scarlett's boyfriend?"

"Ex-boyfriend," said Phil.

"So you talked to him?"

"He was deported," said Phil.

"God, why?"

Annie was expecting . . . She wasn't sure what she was expecting. Something messy, maybe. Not a simple visa problem. Australians were allowed to work in Japan, most other nationalities, including American, weren't. At least, not without mountains of paperwork. Scarlett's exboyfriend thought he could get away with outstaying his visa and working illegally.

He was wrong.

"When did this happen?" Annie demanded.

"A fortnight before Scarlett vanished."

Well, thought Annie. *That puts paid to that theory.* Flipping open her notebook, she scrawled a line through the words, *Scarlett's boyfriend.* And then remembered something Arabella had said.

"You sure?"

"Yes," said Phil. "Why?"

That was the problem with talking to other journalists. They knew when there was a story behind the story.

"Thought she'd mentioned him more recently than that," said Annie.

"No," said Phil. "Believe me. I've checked with the airline. He was walked onto a United flight to New York by two officers from immigration."

Five minutes after this, Annie was headed for the door. Although she stopped to swap her sneakers for heels and wash down another two Tylenol with a glass of tap water. A slash of red lipstick was her nod to professionalism. She also, briefly, brushed her hair, because her inner mother told her she should.

Stifling a yawn, Annie got into the elevator next to an elegant if elderly Japanese man with graying hair and an expensive suit. He quickly moved across to the other side.

When Phil Townend suggested Starbucks she'd been disappointed, but now, sitting in one corner among the familiar wood and dark-green seating with a Japanese-style cookie instead of a muffin, she decided his choice had been a good one. Even in Tokyo Starbucks provided the ultimate in anonymity. So much so, that lost in her thoughts of how the conversation should go, she didn't spot the other reporter until he was standing next to her table.

"*Ms.* Anderson?"

She jumped.

The man in front of her looked nothing like his voice. If the voice was Russell Crowe channeling Liam Gallagher, the man was more John Simm on a good day. He was shortish, not much taller than Annie in her bare feet, with mousy hair in a faded Britpop style, his suit jacket looking like he'd salvaged it from wherever he'd dropped it the night before. The end of a dark red patterned tie flopped from his pocket, where he'd obviously shoved it the second he escaped the office.

"Phil Townend," he said.

Annie didn't get up. Twisting his lips in a half smile, he put his hand up in a half salute and deposited his latte on the table, pulling out the chair opposite as he did so.

"So, *Ms.* Anderson," he said, that half smile lingering. "Presumably I have something you want."

Annie grimaced. *Journalists, yuck.*

"Annie," she said.

"Phil."

"Okay, *Phil* . . . I think the point is, I have something you want, and in return you can give me a few leads." She hesitated. "I take it you're planning to sell this story onto someone else?"

"And I take it those dark glasses are your idea of a disguise?"

"No, they're my idea of a hangover cure," said Annie, and he laughed, the ice broken between them.

Either Phil Townend was good, or he really was as relaxed as he looked, because he flipped the lid from his latte and sipped it slowly, waiting for her to break the silence. Annie had thought hard about what she was prepared to say on her way to this meeting. It was anathema to give another journalist a lead, but this was different. . . .

She paused, wondering when she'd worked that out.

If Annie could find Scarlett for Lou then she would, even if it meant sacrificing all her own rules and giving this man a break. Sitting back in her chair, Annie took a sip of her own lukewarm coffee.

"You can take it from me. I've got Jess Harper."

The guy leaned forward and put his elbows on the table, so he looked Annie in the eyes. "Little Jess? How did you manage that?"

"Sheer brilliance," said Annie, brushing aside his question and hoping like hell Jess would play along, once Annie let her in on the game. "I can get Jess to talk to you, but first I need whatever you've got. I'm an outsider and the police won't talk to me."

"You tried?"

She nodded, and Phil smiled.

"Western women journalists and male Japanese police officers . . ." He shook his head. "Never going to happen."

Annie didn't bother saying she'd made one call and recognized a dead end when she met one. Obviously enough, her need to find a way around the dead end was one of the reasons she was sitting opposite Phil Townend.

"So . . ." She looked at him. "Are you going to tell me?"

"You're not the first to try this," he said, grinning. "Sources are like buses. You're the second today."

Suppressing her urge to splatter Jackson Pollock dribbles across his suit with what remained of her coffee, Annie grinned back. "Australian? About forty? Spiky hair?"

"How did you know that?"

She shrugged. "What did you tell him?"

"Fuck all," said Phil. "There's no one-way traffic on this street. He had nothing I wanted."

"That's because he's not a journalist," said Annie, finishing her coffee. "He's a PI hired by Rufus Ulrich. The man works out of an agency in Bangkok."

Phil's grin showed grudging respect.

"Before I give you anything, I want proof you've got Jess."

Pushing back her chair until it hit a wall, Annie stood up. "Lend me your mobile," she said, holding out one hand, while salvaging a scrap of paper with Jess's number from her pocket. "I'll be back in five."

The journalist looked uncomfortable, like he'd already lost too many mobile phones that way, but he gave it to her. Once outside Starbucks, Annie stood where he could see her through the window and waved, before punching Jess's number into his phone.

She could have used her rented mobile, of course. But this was an old habit, using people's own phones. Somehow they always seemed more inclined to believe what they were told.

"Just give your name," said Annie, after Jess had squealed in horror at the mere suggestion. "Say you'll only talk if I'm there."

"This will work?"

"I promise," said Annie. "He'll leave you alone after this."

"I want you both to leave me alone," Jess said.

Annie winced. "Okay," she said. "I'm going back inside now. . . ."

Handing the phone to Phil, she watched him while he listened and then silently handed the phone to Annie so she could finalize the arrangements. If he was irritated that she carefully deleted Jess's number from his records after she'd killed the call, he didn't let it show.

The brunette behind the counter at Happy Daze who'd originally sold Annie the two slices of cake had gone off shift when she arrived, at 5:56 P.M., four minutes before she'd agreed to meet Jess and Phil. About thirty seconds after that, Phil walked through the door.

"You think she'll come?" he asked, before he even said hello.

Annie nodded, and when a smallish skinny blonde with gap teeth and small, high breasts appeared at the top of the stairs, Phil glanced at Annie grudgingly.

He owed her big time.

"I'm only doing this because Annie asked me," Jess whispered, choosing a chair that put her back to the rest of the room. Annie wanted to hug her.

Like feeding candy to a baby, thought Annie, stirring Gum Syrup, the liquid sucrose that passed for the sugar she didn't take, into her black coffee. She was watching Phil scribble furiously. Jess told him about the Blue Flamingo and Scarlett's late-night dinner dates. It all went on the pad.

Annie knew exactly what he was thinking. If the Ripper had Scarlett, all Phil had to do was find Scarlett's regular and he'd have found the Ripper. It was a story that could take Phil Townend into a different league.

In any other circumstances Annie would have fought him for the story. Instead, she felt on the verge of tears, torn between explaining to Jess the meaning in her own words and letting the teenager work it out for herself, which is what Jess seemed to be doing.

If Scarlett had met someone after work and that someone was the Ripper, then there was no doubt Scarlett was dead. If.

As Phil continued to question Jess, Annie fought the blackness growing inside her. She had been hoping and praying Scarlett was alive, not only for Lou, but also for herself, because Annie wanted to write a story where the subject lived to tell the tale.

Adding Scarlett's name to a list that already featured Irina Krodt and Patty Lang had never been part of the deal. Stupidly, superstitiously Annie had been praying this would be third-time lucky.

Fifteen minutes later Annie and the man who was looking much like her newfound partner were back on the pavement, watching as Jess's skinny form receded into the human crush. Everything she'd told Phil would be anonymous, sourced as "friends of Scarlett Ulrich" and "people who know her."

And Jess would get her wish. Annie was going to leave her alone now, and Phil had given the girl his word. Whatever that was worth.

"Poor kid," said Phil, surprising Annie. "Where the hell does she go from here?"

Annie looked at him.

"I don't mean right now," said Phil. "I mean with her life after this. Home, I guess. . . . Surrey, here she comes."

"Solihull," said Annie. "And, actually, I think she'll stay." She recognized Jess's type. The girl might be pale, frightened, and alone, but she was tougher than she looked. Annie was certain Jess would be giving the West Midlands a wide berth until she could return there in a fully paid-off Mini Cooper.

Watching her earlier, Annie had seen a change creep across the girl's face as Jess reconciled herself to the fact that Scarlett was almost certainly dead. With that thought came a new resilience. It wasn't that Jess didn't care. She wasn't cold or heartless. It was just need. Life reasserting its pull on the living.

"So," said Annie, turning to Phil once Jess's white-blond head was swallowed by the crowd. "Now for your side of the bargain. What are the police saying?"

For a second it looked as if he intended to renege on the deal; then his face broke into a grin that screamed, *Got you.*

"You hungry?" he asked, waving down a taxi. Orange with a white stripe, it bore no likeness to the blue and white cab Annie had used to get here earlier. It had looked so like a police car she'd been uncertain about getting into it. She made a mental note to ask Phil what the difference was between different colored cabs.

"You don't like Tokyo much, do you?" said Phil, waiting while the taxi driver opened its door.

"Not sure yet. I've hardly been here!"

"It's easier once you understand the place," he said. "Although I'm not sure anyone Western ever understands it completely. So let's get dinner and I'll fill you in on what I know about the Roppongi Ripper. But first I want to show you what you haven't seen. The city's heart."

A moat surrounded the Imperial Palace, wide enough to be a small lake. Strutting long-beaked cranes stood among the rushes. The palace itself was not visible, though green tiled roofs showed through fir trees lining the far bank. And a stone wall lined the moat, made from massive slabs of black granite.

"Well, I can't deny it's big," Annie said.

"Huge. An island of serenity in a sea of chaos."

Annie glanced at him.

"If you don't understand why that matters, then you understand nothing about Japan." He wasn't being nasty, Annie knew, just factual.

The taxi dropped them on a main road that headed north. By then, the island of green was on their left, separated from the road by a grass verge and a vast gravel parade ground.

"This way," he said, heading in the opposite direction.

A five-minute walk took them past office buildings, and then Phil took a right and a quick left.

"This is it?" Annie said suspiciously.

Logically she knew they were within spitting distance of Ginza, the city's famous shopping district, a place where department stores had their own subway stations. And Tokyo boasted more branches of Louis Vuitton per person than anywhere else in the world, but there was no sign of luxury where he'd brought her. This was more Kings Cross than Knightsbridge.

A train rattled overhead on raised rails. Empty beer crates stood piled against a filthy brick wall. Gone were the bright lights of Roppongi's pachinko parlors and Akasaka's upmarket restaurants. Here shacks were built into arches supporting the tracks above. Name boards shook and wooden walls rattled, red and black lanterns rocked, and Annie covered her ears as another train growled overhead.

She didn't deny it looked real; she had just been hoping for something a little less demanding.

"Not up to your standards?" asked Phil.

Annie shrugged. "It's not that," she said, embarrassed. "It's just . . . jet lag, you know. I could do with something a bit more restful. And quiet enough to talk," she added pointedly, lest he be planning on getting her drunk enough to forget he still owed his side of the bargain.

"You'll love it," he said, slipping behind a street stall, nodding to a gap that gave no hint of being there, apart from a bucket of empty beer bottles standing to its right.

"Trust me."

That was just the problem. She didn't.

A black-painted passageway joined a cobwebbed path that threaded between two walls. The cafés were back-to-back, Annie saw, and she was in the gap between them, stepping over pipes, electric cables, and, she noted, a broken children's pram.

"You're doing this on purpose," said Annie, when they finally exited into another black-painted passageway.

From behind, she saw Phil nod.

The café he chose was heaving with bodies and rich with the sweet smell of chicken and yakitori spices. Annie tried not to groan; after all, it could have been worse. It might have been sushi. The mere thought of those little rolls of raw fish made her stomach roil.

Orange and yellow lanterns clustered overhead, dimly lighting the customers beneath them.

"I'm the only woman here," said Annie.

"We're foreigners. It's okay. They'll make allowances."

He said something in Japanese to a small man in a greasy apron who looked surprised, and then impressed, and then showed them to a table in the corner.

"You speak Japanese?"

He nodded. "But not too well," he said. "I never make that mistake."

"What do you mean?"

"Speak perfect Japanese," said Phil, "and the Japanese will expect perfect manners." He caught Annie's look. "No foreigner can pull that off. So it's better not to set up the expectation. They cut us plenty of slack as it is," he added. "Given how most of the tourists in Roppongi behave, it's just as well."

"What is this place?" asked Annie.

"The guidebooks have taken to calling it Yakitori Alley, the gits. Now it's only a matter of time before the tourists wreck it."

A kimono-clad waitress, white-socked toes wedged through traditional sandals, appeared beside their table.

"Beer?" Phil raised an eyebrow at her.

Annie nodded. She wasn't up for sake, not yet anyway.

"Nama birru," Phil said, holding up two fingers.

"Two beers?" Annie asked.

"Two draft beers," he corrected. "None of that Sapporo bollocks, or worse still, imported muck."

Annie grinned.

"What?" he asked.

She said nothing, just smiled and added *Nama birru* to her collection. She could now order draft beer in German, French, Italian, Spanish, and Japanese.

"Have you been to the Blue Flamingo yet?" He was obviously working out how far ahead of him she was.

"No," said Annie. "That's tomorrow's job. Let's talk about your side of the deal. You've got a contact in the Tokyo police?"

"Yup. He's called Ryu."

Annie very much doubted that was his real name.

"What's his line on Scarlett?"

"Ripper," Phil said, taking a swig of the iced Ebisu that had appeared in front of them. "Pure and simple. That Australian kid they found buried out near Narita, Scarlett, the other three, it's all down to the Ripper."

"Convenient."

Phil nodded. "Keeps it neat and tidy. Although Ryu's less happy now the story's out and people like you have started turning up!"

The beer was good, slightly sweet but icy cold, and so refreshing that half of her glass had gone already.

Pace yourself, Annie, she thought.

"So how does he account for the Texan . . . ? Donna Newton? Now that they've let her boyfriend go."

"Ryu's take is that either the girl jumped. Or the Ripper panicked and made a mistake."

"Increasingly chaotic activity?" suggested Annie, quoting something a CID officer once said to her.

"Sounds reasonable to me, I mean the Ripper's all over the place, two girls kidnapped in the last two weeks when the other three were each months apart. Increasingly risky behavior is what the police profiler predicted."

"They're using a profiler?"

Phil looked at her, as if to say, *Of course they are.*

"You know what the profile says?"

"Middle-aged," said Phil. "Polite. Mind you, that's a given around here. Quiet, removed, probably lives alone."

It sounded like Scarlett's dinner date to Annie. Maybe Jess was right, the only way to think about Scarlett was in the past tense.

Annie shivered.

"Has Ryu got any leads on Scarlett?"

"I take it you're not interested in the others?"

Her shrug was noncommittal. "Scarlett's my main interest," said Annie, wondering how far to hedge her bets. "I work on a fashion maga-zine now, remember? Scarlett used to be a megastar, an icon. Well, that's our angle, and whatever happens, Rufus Ulrich is of interest, and her—" Annie caught herself. "Other members of Scarlett's family are in the in-dustry too."

"Yes," said Phil. "So I gather."

Annie was about to ask what he meant by that, when the food arrived.

"I ordered it," he said, "when we came in. You don't mind me ordering for you, do you?"

Annie did mind; she minded a lot. She never allowed anyone to order for her. Except Rebecca, who routinely took it upon herself to recommend everyone eat Caesar salad, hold the everything. Annie was just about pre-pared to tolerate that from Rebecca, because:

a) She was a woman, and
b) She was Annie's boss.

She hadn't allowed a man to order for her since Tony Panton decided she liked Cinzano and lemonade and ordered it without bothering to ask every single time Annie went near a pub. She should have known what it said about him then, but she was young and had crossed the line between romance and obsession. It was just one in a long list of flashing road signs she'd driven straight through.

Get a grip, Annie told herself. *You've never been here before, you don't know the first thing about Japanese food, the guy isn't being controlling, he's being a tour guide.*

"It's okay," she said.

Annie had no idea how hungry she was until she started eating; then she felt like she'd never stop. The yakitori was salty, sticky with a strange sweet-sour marinade, and the more slivers of chicken she ate the more she drank, until two hours and three beers later she realized her head was spinning.

God, she thought. *What are you? Fifteen? You'll be ordering Malibu and pineapple next.*

A light touch on the back of her hand made her jump. It was Phil and he was smiling at her. "I know," he said. "Let's go check out the Blue Flamingo. Take a look at where Jess and Scarlett worked."

"Don't be ridiculous!" Annie laughed. "It's an upscale club, not a tourist dive. We'll never get in without an account. And if we do we'll stick out like sore thumbs."

"Nah, we won't. Honest, it's on the tourist trail."

"The Blue Flamingo?"

"The whole hostess thing. We're just tourists crashing a hostess bar to rubberneck. The regulars hate it, of course. But I bet you we won't be the only Westerners there."

Weighing this up, Annie nodded. As hiding in plain view went, she couldn't get much plainer than that.

thirty · two

Annie insisted on picking up the tab for supper. Power lay in paying; she had learned that early on. It was her trade-off for letting Phil get away with ordering the food.

"What you Westerners forget," said Phil, as he helped Annie into a cab and slid himself in beside her, "is that hostess clubs aren't sex clubs. They're precisely what it says on the tin."

Annie stifled a laugh.

You Westerners, indeed. So says the man from Cheadle Hulme. Via Sydney, admittedly, but still from Cheshire.

"And it says *what* on the tin?" asked Annie, partly to oblige him but mostly because she wanted to know the answer. When it came, his answer was more complicated than she expected.

"First off, Tokyo isn't Japan, the way New York isn't America. It's more sophisticated. Outwardly it feels removed from the heartland, but scratch the surface and you hit the same bedrock."

Bedrock? Annie must have said it aloud, because Phil nodded.

"It's all about the difference between face value and what's real. *Honne,* that's real value. *Tatemae* is surface value. You keep them separate. It looks screwed up to us, no PDA here, no hugging your lover in the street, no public kissing, you are not even meant to walk down the street while eating. But you can buy used knickers from a vending machine in Shinjuku, no problem. Get yourself a blow job in a sleazy bar in Kabuki-cho alongside eight other guys sitting on chrome stools, with only a tiny cardboard cubicle wall between you."

Annie fixed her flight attendant smile in place. The night wind had begun to sober her up and she was beginning to wonder what she'd got herself into. "I thought we were just going to the Blue Flamingo."

"Chill," said Phil. "We are. I'm explaining the setup. The customers, and the girls, Jess, your Scarlett, all the Japanese girls who work there . . ."

"Japanese?"

"Of course," he said, seeing Annie's surprise. "Most hostesses are Japanese. And all nationalities make a big distinction between hostessing and selling sex. Even doing what Scarlett did, having *dinner* with clients after hours . . ." Annie didn't like the way he stressed dinner, but Phil was oblivious. "That can be against the rules."

"So they don't all do that?"

"Some do. More than some maybe, given the chance. Time's money, and if you're a Western blonde . . ."

She knew the guy had a point and she'd seen far worse. Starting with the lives of immigrants back home, the illegals who spent their nights cleaning offices populated during the day by the wealthy and the white. Eastern Europeans who arrived expecting to waitress in pizza parlors and be able to send money back to their families, and found themselves sold into sexual slavery.

By comparison, Jess's and Scarlett's lives looked almost empowered. But it still made Annie squirm. She didn't doubt that Scarlett had done nothing but talk for her twenty-thousand yen, and her reasons for wanting the cash were probably good ones. All the same, Annie didn't believe you could win at that game. And it was beginning to look horribly as though Scarlett hadn't.

The brightly lit lanes behind *Sabatori-dori* were alive with people. Gripping her arm, Phil led her left and right, and then left again until they were three or four streets back from the main road, in a bustle of tourists and sharp-suited Japanese executives.

Annie wasn't sure the hand on her arm was strictly necessary.

The lanes they walked through were narrow, straight as arrows and awash with neon and a warm glow from shop windows. A smell of curry filled the air and Annie did a double take, and saw they were standing outside Ultimate Balti.

"It's new," said Phil. "Indian, Mexican, and Philippino are all popular." He laughed at Annie's expression. "Used to be Italian," he said. "Before that Korean."

Weaving past a group of Australian tourists, Phil stopped by a window filled with slices of pizza, a plate of spaghetti Bolognese, and ravioli in tomato sauce. "All plastic," he said, and Annie realized they were indeed glistening, edible, tummy-rumbling plastic. The trattoria they advertised was five floors above, next to a Vietnamese tattoo parlor and two floors below the club for which they'd been looking.

"Here we go," said Phil, tapping a neon wall sign that flashed lazily on and off.

The bar was on floor eleven, and there were several more bars, clubs, and restaurants advertised as being above and below it. In the middle of all the signs was one for Marie's Hair and Nails.

"Ready then?"

Annie nodded. "Just one thing," she said, as Phil reached for an elevator button.

He stopped. "What?"

She'd done a bit of research; Ken's use of *The Roppongi Ripper* wasn't original. The man in front of her had been the first to use the phrase. "Why the name, if he hunts his prey in Akasaka?"

"That's the clever bit," said Phil. "That's where he went right for so long. It's the girls who are Roppongi, not the killer. They're all Westerners and most Westerners live in Roppongi, so the police just assumed that was where he went hunting. I didn't get it myself, until Jess filled in the last clue by telling me about Scarlett. That's when I clocked they all had something else in common. They aren't just blonde and Western; it's not even that they're all hostesses. The key is that they all worked clubs in the same area. Akasaka."

"Surely the police must have spotted that?"

"The victims modeled, one of them danced in a disco, another had done some topless work in Shinjuku, two of them had overstayed their visas, all were foreigners, all lived in Roppongi. Until Scarlett's story broke in the international press, finding out what happened wasn't exactly a priority."

"But now . . ."

"We've nailed him, Annie. Maybe he thought by dumping that body in Roppongi, right where she lived, he'd throw everyone off his scent, but Akasaka is definitely his hunting ground. . . ."

"And he will strike again," said Annie, finishing the sentence. She felt furious and elated and half-drunk. Angry that Phil hadn't shared this sooner and irritated that she hadn't worked it out for herself, but fired up by a familiar thrill. The thrill of knowing she'd get her story.

If this was where he hunted then this is where he'd have been seen.

More than once, obviously. Because there was more than one victim. So a Japanese man who liked Western girls and drank at the upscale clubs in Akasaka.

It was still a pretty big field, but it had just narrowed significantly.

"Don't ask questions," said Phil, "when you get in there. Not at first. Let them get used to us."

Annie grinned. This was what she did, and this exhilaration why she did it. For a moment, the implications of what she might find slipped away. Annie Anderson, always ready to rip open someone else's can of worms.

"Come on." She pushed past him. "Let's take a look."

thirty · three

The elevator doors slid open onto a small dark foyer little bigger than the lift itself. A small square of cerise carpet that would not have borne the scrutiny of daylight acted as doormat to a red-lacquered door. To one side, on a black-painted wall was a large gold plaque declaring this CLUB BLUE FLAMINGO. Japanese lettering beneath presumably said the same.

"Do up your tie," hissed Annie, as Phil stepped out of the elevator. He glanced back, and they both laughed . . . Annie embarrassed at the sudden appearance of her inner mother.

A young Japanese woman in a tight silver-gray satin halter top, black miniskirt, and high-heeled sandals appeared before Phil could finish opening the door. Her job was obviously to wait on the other side to greet, intercept, or inspect new arrivals. She bowed and smiled, revealing perfect white teeth.

Tourists. Annie could almost see the thought cross her face.

"*Kombanwa,*" said the woman. Then in English, "Welcome to the Blue Flamingo. Let me find you a table."

This time, Phil kept his fluent Japanese to himself.

It was one of those rooms that gave life to the phrase "smoke and mirrors." Reflective glass lined all the walls, making it impossible to tell how big the shadowy room was, each mirror reflecting the smoke that hung below the ceiling. Cigar smoke, the indulgence of wealthy businessmen at play.

"Wait here, please," said the woman, adding hastily, "Just for a second."

She left them at the bar, having muttered something to a young blonde behind the counter. Annie was irritated to see the blonde scuttle away and a Japanese girl take her place. Was that significant? To stop Annie and Phil striking up a conversation with a Western girl . . . Had Rufus's PI somehow got here first?

Annie checked the room, trying to remember Jess's description of the guy—*cropped hair, looked like a regular bloke*—but there was no one who fit that description. Actually, Phil was wrong. Apart from him, Annie, and a handful of girls working the club, everyone else was Japanese.

Chill, she told herself.

It was just as likely the woman wanted to give the tourists a genuine Japanese experience, one that didn't come with an American accent.

A bottle of sake and two tiny glasses wouldn't have been Annie's first choice on top of three large beers and a dozen skewers of chicken yakitori. Annie didn't even like sake, but she imagined Phil ordered it because sake was what tourists would have ordered. Everyone else was drinking either whiskey or champagne. Phil chatted and smiled, asked the hostess to explain how sake was made, and Annie took advantage of this to scour the room.

Phil had been right about one thing. Despite their being the only European customers, Annie and Phil were bizarrely inconspicuous, made invisible by low lighting, cigar smoke, and the virtue of not fitting the natural order. At home, if you didn't fit, you stuck out like a sore thumb. Here everyone ignored the incongruous, as if ignoring it was enough to make it simply disappear.

Apart from a karaoke booth, which involved little more than a tiny stage, five chairs, a microphone, and soundproofed glass walls, the club stuck to a single style: mirrored walls offset by red light fittings and a red-lacquered bar.

Around the edge were horseshoe-shaped sofas in black leather, curved around smoked glass tables, as if to create a sense of intimacy. Most of these were occupied by groups of men, ranging from the young to the seriously old. Seated within each group, like the proverbial rose among thorns, was a scattering of young women, one or two to a table, mostly Japanese but some Western.

Judging by their bone structure, the shape of their eyes, and their sallow skin, the Western girls were mainly Eastern European. A blonde sat with three men in the booth closest to Annie, her accent so strong and English so poor that Annie could only assume her clients had not the faintest idea what she was saying. Presumably it didn't matter, so long as they laughed and bought whiskey, and then bought some more.

The low buzz of conversation was occasionally broken by high-pitched giggles from around the room. American voices mingled with Eastern European. So far as Annie could tell, the only English accents in the place were their own.

It only took a glance to work out that Jess wasn't there, or if she was, she was working one of the private dining rooms at the back.

As Annie turned, an elderly Japanese woman appeared from behind a curtain by the bar and called the woman who'd been talking to Phil. She did this by placing her fingers parallel with the floor, then flicking down once.

Excusing herself, the Japanese girl hurried over and the mama-san whispered in her ear, sending the girl scuttling toward the door in time to greet a vast man with a topknot wearing a tentlike suit and large gold Seiko. A dozen people stopped talking to watch as he was ushered to an empty sofa in the far corner.

"Yokozuna," said Phil. "A sumo wrestler. Grand champion."

Annie was more interested in how the mama-san had known the wrestler was on his way. Not sixth sense, she decided. A CCTV camera in the elevator more likely, linked to a screen in Mama-san's office.

"Get anything?" she asked, leaning into Phil so Mama-san couldn't hear.

Phil shook his head and took another sip of sake. *"Is it usually this busy? Are you open seven days a week? How many days do the hostesses work?* Even then, I probably pushed a bit too hard."

"With me, please." It was the original hostess, offering to take them to a sofa.

"Look at the view from up here," said Phil.

Annie glanced toward a window and then looked back, slightly dizzy. A tower of glittering lights could be seen in the distance, like the wall of a castle. It was magnificent, slightly scary, and seemed to belong to another world.

"Shinjuku," said Phil, smiling at her reaction. His gaze flickered around the room. "They were waiting to give us this table," he added.

Annie frowned, puzzled.

Nodding at the buildings in the street beyond, he signaled the gap through which Shinjuku's lights were visible. "It's the only one with this view."

Group after group of suited executives came and went, but no more hostesses appeared. The ones already working split up and switched groups at the slightest hand signal from Mama-san, who leaned against the end of her bar, bestowing nods and smiles on her preferred customers. The place was doing a roaring trade.

Annie and Phil chatted, anodyne stuff, giving little away and learning only snippets in return. But as the alcohol and a tranquil nothingness entered her blood, Annie found it comforting. It had been months since she'd been allowed to be anonymous and she'd forgotten how much she liked it. And Phil obviously liked her. Either that or his knee kept touching hers by accident.

The club was beginning to empty when a blonde with a Southern twang wandered over to their table. "We're closing soon," she said. "Can I get you anything else?" The girl was early twenties at most and, while gorgeous, her body was not that of a model. Too curvy for a start, her hips and breasts obvious beneath her tight red dress.

Annie shook her head. "Better not," she said. "Thanks. I think we've had enough."

"Speak for yourself," said Phil, and as Annie began to bristle she caught his wink. *Play along*, it said.

"How long you guys here for?" the hostess asked, sounding genuinely interested. It was an art, making small talk and sounding like you gave a damn about the answer.

"Just a few days," said Annie. "Working holiday." Which was true, for her if not for Phil.

"We're on a world tour," Phil said. "Bangkok before this. Singapore next, then Australia."

The American was called Juliette, with two Ts and an E at the end. As Annie expected, Juliette was from Alabama, doing a post-university around-the-world trip. Tokyo was just a pit stop where she hoped to make enough money to fund the next part of her trip, which involved visiting an ex-boyfriend in Australia.

"Speaking of friends," said Annie, pulling a photograph of Scarlett from her bag, "a friend of a friend works here. We were hoping she'd be on tonight."

Feeling Phil tense, Annie smiled.

She knew what she was doing, and she knew now was the time to do it. The worst thing that could happen was they'd be escorted from a club that was already closing. Worse things happened, mostly in Kings Cross, in Annie's experience.

"Here," said Annie, sliding the picture across the table.

Juliette put a hand to her mouth. "That's Scarlett," she said, paling beneath her tan. At the end of the bar, a young Japanese man turned and stared, but when Annie caught his gaze he looked away.

"Yes," Annie said. "That's right. Is she on tonight?"

The girl looked at Annie and shook her head slowly, something close to pity in her eyes. "I'm sorry," she said. "I can't believe you haven't heard."

"Heard what?" asked Phil. "We've been traveling."

"Shit," said Juliette, her glossy sophistication in tatters. "Her abduction is all over the papers. Scarlett's dead."

"Fuck me, that was a high-risk strategy," Phil hissed after Annie burst into tears and insisted on leaving immediately. "I thought we were going to ask gentle questions. Let them get used to us and come back tomorrow?"

He hesitated, obviously thrown by the sight of Annie wiping her nose on the back of her hand and then taking a shuddering breath and wiping her eyes.

"You were *faking* that?"

"Of course I was," said Annie crossly.

"Pretty good acting, then."

"It wouldn't have worked if you knew." Annie stepped out of the elevator and took another deep breath, feeling her heart steady. Phil had to know the tears had been for real, didn't he?

Poor, poor Lou.

"Anyway," muttered Annie. "You didn't run that we're-on-a-world-tour routine past me first either."

Phil shook his head. "Jeeezus," he said. "That's different. Don't you know the first thing about working with a partner . . . ?"

"Did you want to leave there with nothing?"

"What did we get?" asked Phil. "That was worth the risk?"

"Don't you see?" Annie said. "Juliette thinks Scarlett's already dead. She's convinced of it."

Phil looked at Annie, pity in his eyes. It was the second time in the last twenty minutes Annie had seen that look.

"Annie," he said, "Juliette's not the only one. Everybody does."

thirty · four

It had been pretty clear to Annie that Phil was planning his move from the moment he touched her hand at supper. She had her rebuttal all worked out, firm enough to give the guy a definite brush-off, without upsetting him enough to find herself locked out of his police informant's information loop. But that was before three bottles of local beer, two cups of sake, and a crying jag that turned out to be real.

There was Chris, of course.

Or maybe there wasn't. Annie wasn't too sure about that.

So when Phil wrapped his arm around her shoulder as they hit the still-throbbing street outside, Annie didn't remove it. Although she knew she should have. At that point there was still time to turn back.

"So, where to?"

Annie didn't miss a beat, didn't give herself a chance to think about it. She'd obviously decided. Well, her body and the alcohol had. "My hotel's near here. Fancy a coffee?"

Sex began with a shared shower. "Wash away the evening," Phil suggested, helping her out of her jacket. Neither of them mentioned the coffee Annie had originally offered. It wasn't as if her room even had a coffeemaker.

"I'll join you," he said.

Phil stripped easily, comfortable in his own skin, though his body was okay, nothing special. Which, Annie guessed, made them equal.

"Come on," he said, reaching for the buttons on her shirt. She should have found it sexy, but she was wearing a washed-to-gray bra and everything was moving a little too fast.

"You run the shower," she said. "I'll be with you in a minute."

A moment later she could hear the splash of water. He was humming. And then his humming was lost beneath water and Annie found herself alone again in front of a mirror. Not so bad, she thought, discarding her bra. Her breasts were too small, her nipples too pale, and her hips wider than she liked. But her body looked normal, and Annie guessed not liking it was normal too . . .

"Thought you'd changed your mind," said Phil. "Come on in, the water's lovely."

He washed her, he really did. His fingers didn't grip or slide toward hidden places they weren't invited, they simply lathered up and soaped her.

"You're smiling," he said.

"I'm drunk."

The hands faltered.

"Not that drunk," said Annie.

He dried her gently, dried himself, and led her to the nearest bed, lowering her onto a cotton bedspread.

No kisses, no cuddles, it was too quick. Except it wasn't. Folding her legs, Phil opened Annie's knees and lowered his head.

When she came it was hard enough to bruise his mouth, although she only discovered that when he crawled up her body and she realized his bottom lip was a bit swollen.

"Shit," she said. "I'm sorry."

He grinned, fixed his mouth over her own, and kissed her slowly.

"Okay?" he asked.

Annie nodded.

His lovemaking was slow and steady, and got harder as her hips began moving up to reach him. When the dam inside her was ready to burst, he bent his head and bit her lip gently. It was enough.

"You know," he said afterward, "if you're in Tokyo for a while . . ."

"What?" said Annie. "Do this again?"

"See each other," he said. "That's what I was going to say. Make this more than a working relationship."

Thank God, he wasn't a stayer. Well, not after she told him about Chris. He'd simply got up, found his clothes, and left, visibly shaken. Rolling over, she groaned and buried her head in the pillow.

She wasn't crying, honest.

Annie slept, woke, and slept again.

When sunlight woke her the final time she glanced at her bedside table to check the time. Nine A.M. Right now, Chris should be in her apartment and in her bed. She didn't deserve him and he didn't deserve her, not the way she was now.

Picking up the phone, she dialed her own number without thinking of it. There was no plan, no prepared speech, she was just going to do it.

The phone rang and rang, six, seven, eight times before the answering machine kicked in, her own voice telling her that Annie Anderson and Chris Mahoney were busy right now, but if the caller would like to leave a message . . .

Fresh tears pricked Annie's eyes. She knew precisely what *busy* had meant when she recorded that message. It meant, *We're too busy fucking like rabbits to talk.*

They hadn't been able to get enough of each other, had gone to bed at every available opportunity. She learned to ask for what she wanted, learned to take him to bed almost as often as he took her, learned that sometimes men needed foreplay too.

Silence hissed as the answering machine failed to record her thoughts, waiting for her to speak them aloud. But Annie couldn't bring herself to leave a message. Not *that* message, telling her own voice she wanted out, she didn't deserve him, it was over.

A message she'd probably replay endlessly in the coming weeks.

Hanging up, Annie dialed Chris's cell. Her stomach dropped away in panic. It could be the beer or the sake or the yakitori, or all three.

More likely it was panic. Panic and guilt.

Five rings later Chris's voice mail picked up.

Hi, can't speak right now, leave a message. It helped, a little, the message was so curt. No niceties, no chat, just an abrupt instruction. If she'd recorded that greeting it would have sounded downright rude, but something about his tone softened it, made the words almost endearing. That was PRs for you. Only Chris was different, the charm came naturally to him. That was why everyone . . . *loved* him.

Before Annie could stop herself she spoke.

"Chris, it's me. Uh, obviously. Look, I'm sorry about Tony. He really did just turn up and Lou can give you the reasons. You know how I've been screwing up lately? Well, I was thinking, you know. And I think, well, maybe it's . . . Shit, it's not working. You can't be happy, surely? Perhaps we moved in together too fast. Maybe I just can't do this stuff. Anyway, you deserve better. So I . . . Oh, fuck it . . . I'm sorry, but I want you to move out."

Annie killed the call.

Nice work, Annie.

As good-byes went it was right up there with her personal worst, and so much less than he deserved that she could barely contemplate what she'd done. It would have been kinder just to change the locks.

Seated on one of the three beds, the one reminiscent of a passing hurricane, Annie stared around at her vast hotel room and the trail of her own clothes leading into the bathroom.

A memory of her and Phil startled her and she closed her eyes. Only what she found inside her eyelids was no better, and her eyes snapped open again. That was how she found herself staring at a used condom lying twisted and spent on the mottled blue carpet inches from where she sat.

As the shame set in, Annie started to howl.

thirty · five

The bed was empty.

Lou knew it without opening her eyes. She knew it without reaching out to pat the crumpled, no-longer-warm sheet beside her. But she did it anyway, because habits were hard to break. And married lovers had become a habit for Lou in the five years since she left art college.

A habit she hid behind her publicly proclaimed passion for surf boys, indie guitarists, and male models. Only Clem from college had mattered. Even he had wondered at how little she'd required from their relationship.

So now her public dates were the terminally self-obsessed. Those too tied up with how they looked or their own genius to wonder what she did on the nights she wasn't hanging around the clubs with them.

Opening her eyes, Lou allowed them to adjust to daylight. The sheet was cold beside her and her flat still. Hours must have passed since Max had let himself out as she slept. The cat was evidence of that too; there was no way Ossie would have been curled asleep at the foot of the bed if Max had only just gone.

Max and Ossie didn't get on. Scratch that, they hated each other, outright jealousy on Ossie's part and a claimed allergy on Max's part. Ossie recognized cat haters and kept well away, casting dark looks in Max's direction whenever their paths did cross.

There was other evidence that things were about to change. For a start, it was Saturday morning. Max never saw Lou on a Friday evening, let alone spent the night with her. Unless, of course, they were away on a shoot together. It was family night, and Max had never so much as agreed to an after-work drink before. Not even the time it was Lou's birthday.

With hindsight, Lou realized the fact Max had suggested dinner on a Friday should have told her something was wrong. Funny how sometimes she needed the cold light of morning to make her see what had been staring her in the face all along.

Although, she had to admit, there'd been one Friday night at the beginning. She had been so distressed at the thought of being alone, while Max played happy family with Mrs. Max and three little Maxes, that he'd been scared to leave her, scared of what she might do.

That was before Lou resigned herself to weekends spent with the surf boys.

"They'll never settle, you know," said Nina. "Boys like that." Meaning, *They'll never give me grandchildren.*

Lou just smiled. That was the point, after all, the single most attractive thing about them, the Toms and Jamies and Matts and Charlies. They were only after one thing: fun. And if Lou, all of twenty-six, wanted to play the older woman, that was fine by them. Not least because she had her own place and a glamorous new job on a London paper.

It was only after Lou started at *The Post* that she began to worry that the different parts of her life might collide. Before that, nobody gave a toss about her private life. Her old art college friends barely noticed that she was always skipping out of parties early for no reason.

One minute, Lou McCartney was next to you, holding a glass of cheap white wine, the next she'd vanished. No one ever saw her sprinting for a black cab the second the clock struck nine, like the adulterous Cinderella that she was.

And then Lou met Annie.

Annie Anderson, the first person Lou had come close to calling a good friend since Clem. Annie, who never missed a trick and turned asking candid questions into an art form.

For the first time in her life, Lou felt uncomfortable about being flexible with the truth. Annie's questions gave Lou pause every time a surf-boy-shaped lie tripped off her tongue and she saw a flicker of amused indulgence in her new friend's eyes.

But it wasn't just Annie's curiosity, or even that Lou was getting serious about Max . . . No, Lou's arrival at *The Post* and her friendship with Annie coincided with Lou turning twenty-six. Not exactly geriatric, but old enough in Nina and Gram's book for her biological clock to start ticking.

In need of armor, Lou paraded ever-more openly her supposed liking for pretty boys—as far as she could get, in truth, from her true love, Max Caterham, pet photographer to fashion's upper echelons.

And, Lou had to admit, the boys could be fun. What her barely post-adolescent lovers lacked in skill, they more than made up for in energy, willingness, and enthusiasm. Occasionally, though, the hanging out at gigs, the cruddy flats where nobody washed up, and the endless babble became too much, and she longed for a quiet meal, a decent bottle of wine, and her own bed.

With Max.

It looked like that safety net had just snapped.

Climbing out of bed, Lou scooped up her dressing gown and peered through the chink in the curtain. Max was so long gone the place where he'd parked his Jag outside her flat was no longer empty.

Max was ending it.

She'd been here before. She knew the signs. She could write the book, actually. The final piece of evidence lay, as she'd known it would, on a worktop in the kitchen. A note scribbled on the back of her unopened credit card bill, carefully positioned next to an empty cat bowl so there was no way Lou could miss it.

Miss it! He might as well have put a flashing sign over it. As if she'd miss a Dear Jill letter like that. Opening a tin of Felix, Lou's stomach heaved at the smell as she dumped it into Ossie's bowl, while Ossie wound himself around her bare ankles, like he loved her more than life itself.

"Slut!" said Lou, plonking his bowl on the floor and watching the tom abandon her. "Men, you're all the same."

She didn't need to read the note to know what it said. *Love you . . . Can't go on like this . . . Hate myself for doing this . . . Blah, blah, fucking blah.* It was so predictable, as if fill-in-the-blanks letters for dumping were downloaded into men's brains from an early age. Although "letter" was an overgenerous description for this cursory note.

And then she saw it. The final nail in the coffin. *It will be better for both of us if you don't call. M.*

Not even M.X.

Lou swallowed, biting back the tears. Nice touch that. Better for whom, precisely? Better for him, the bastard.

A whole year they'd been lovers and he ended it with a note on the back of a used envelope. Was that all she was worth? Her third married man. You'd think she'd have learned by now. And it wasn't as if her expectations were even high, so why did everyone always have to live down to them?

Lou made a cup of black instant coffee (all out of real, all out of milk) and slumped at her kitchen table, pushing bills aside to make space for her mug. With luck, the cat wouldn't pick up on her sadness. Ossie was weird like that, given to bringing her presents at strategic points, as if to say, *See, there is one male you can rely on.*

That was Ossie for you. No garage forecourt bunches of flowers for Lou McCartney, where that cat was concerned, only a freshly chewed vole carcass was good enough. If she were lucky, he'd leave her a mouse head. Although, if Lou had her way, Ossie would be bringing her the head of something altogether larger . . .

The tragic thing was Lou knew this was all her own fault.

Yet wasn't it reasonable to believe that, after a year together, she might ask for a little bit more? The odd weekend maybe? Even, God forbid, a whole night in her own bed with company that wasn't furry, didn't have sharp claws, or treat you to a blast of corpse breath when he returned from a three A.M. killing spree . . .

That was all she had asked.

She and Max had spent whole nights together before, of course. When they were in South Africa on a shoot. Lou was sure, even now, that no one at *The Post* or his agency knew of their affair, because they never shared a room. Although that would have helped her meager budget.

Lou had loved Max's work since art college and couldn't believe it when he'd agreed to shoot three stories in Thailand for her previous paper's Saturday supplement. They met several times to plan the trip, each meeting a little longer than the one before.

Max was just her type. In his mid-forties, he'd shot covers for *Vogue* and worked for the *Sunday Times* Style section. He was married, of course. Before they'd even boarded the plane Lou had fallen for him like a rock from a cliff, and he hadn't exactly beaten her off. By the end of the week they were lovers and Lou was horribly afraid Max was The One. That this time, for Lou McCartney, there was no holding back.

She hadn't been looking for a ring on her finger when she raised the stay-the-night issue last week. She wasn't stupid; she knew Max would have turned pale if she so much as put a hula hoop on her ring finger. She was just asking, after a whole year of loving him and living for the times they were together, to be acknowledged by him. To know he felt the same way about her. And this, it seemed, was his answer.

It will be better for both of us if you don't call.

That would be a no, then.

Lou eyed her mobile. He was asking for it, surely. Bunny boiling was not her style. She'd always had too much pride for that. Stalking an ex-lover, making silent phone calls, threatening to expose him to his wife, destroy his family, all those things turned her stomach. They were so . . . *desperate*.

But they both knew "better for both of us" meant "better for him."

It meant, "don't phone me at home." As if she would stoop that low, if only he hadn't suggested she didn't.

Less than a second later she'd pressed MAX HOME on her Motorola and could hear the line connect. Hear his house phone begin to ring.

He deserved it.

His wife deserved to know what kind of a man she had married, what kind of ratlike genes she had bestowed on her children.

"Hello?"

It wasn't her, it was him.

Lou held her breath at the sound of his voice, her heart pounding. Static fizzed between them on the line.

"Hello?"

She could hear the fear in his voice. He knew it was her, and he was terrified at what she might do. In the palm of Lou's hand was a four-story town house in Holland Park, a ten-year marriage, and three children. . . .

All she had to do was curl her fingers and squeeze and she could rip his life away from him. All she had to do was speak, and his carefully built cunning would all come tumbling down. It wasn't Max that made her pause; it was the thought of his children.

"Hello?"

Max wanted to ask if it was her. Lou could feel, almost hear, his internal battle. His fear of being overheard, his fear of what Lou, with his home number, could do . . .

"Hello?"

"Who is it, love?" A voice in the background, a woman's voice coming closer.

"I . . . ," said Max, his voice muffled, hand now over the receiver.

And Lou hung up, not wanting to be the bunny boiler she so despised, but also unable to bear the pain of hearing him lie, of hearing herself described as a wrong number.

thirty · six

Annie wheeled her breakfast back into the corridor, untouched. A clear piece of Saran Wrap still covered the jug of salad cream that sat next to a neatly arranged bowl of strawberries and kiwi fruit on lettuce. The toast was cold on its plate under a perfectly laundered white napkin.

She'd been tempted to try the coffee, but just the smell of it made her want to throw up last night's supper, the one she'd eaten with Phil in that strange bar under the railway arches.

Instead she hid in her room and drank bottle after bottle of mineral water from the minibar as she went over her notes, writing them out on fresh sheets of paper. If it made her head hurt, so what? She deserved it. Her head hurt anyway. She might as well be doing something useful.

On the sheet of paper in front of her, lines led from Scarlett's name, which she'd circled in red, to the Happy Daze coffee shop, the Blue Flamingo, the model agency, and the address of the flat she'd shared with Jess. Another line led to the American photographer's assistant, although, for now, she'd take Phil Townend's word that he was out of the picture.

A separate sheet of paper held times and dates. The time Jess said Scarlett left the flat and the time she'd got off work that night. The time she should have presented herself for a knitwear shoot the next morning and the time the agency called Jess to ask where Scarlett was.

The whole table was covered with sheets of paper.

An open laptop, balanced on the air-conditioning grill, had half a dozen Web pages offering different versions of the same story. A photo-composite of the Ripper, new that morning, looked like every Japanese businessman of a certain age that Annie had seen in Akasaka the previous evening.

As she went through her notes Annie couldn't help feeling that something was wrong. Not in her life, because dozens of things were wrong with that, starting with more or less everything about last night. No, she had been lied to.

Somewhere back up the line she'd blinked and missed something really obvious about this story in her jet-lagged haze. Too much of what she'd been told about Scarlett's disappearance didn't add up.

Annie had never been a big believer in the wisdom of crowds. Just because the world seemed to believe Scarlett had been kidnapped and killed by the Ripper didn't make it true. So, if it wasn't true, what were the alternatives?

Midday came and went and still Annie felt hollow.

What was worse, her stomach cramped and she felt physically sick. She'd heard friends at *The Post* talk in hushed tones about the forty-eight-hour hangover, as they washed down aspirin with black coffee and turned green at the mere suggestion of a bacon sandwich. And here she was, with an irrefutable sense that this was to be her first voyage and she still had a day and a half to go. Plus she was all out of Tylenol.

Fantastic, she thought.

Just one of the many great things about hitting thirty. She had a few months yet, six to be honest, but she could feel the three-zero closing in on her. And now this . . . Alcohol, which had previously been one of her closest friends, her nearest and sometimes dearest, had become her enemy.

Mind you, give sake its due. It could probably produce the queen of hangovers whatever your age. And three bottles of God-knows-what-proof lager plus sake was nothing to the aftereffects of that spectacularly stupid phone call, mixed with liberal dashes of guilt.

"Call me," said a voice mail from Rebecca, the message obviously left at some unearthly hour London time.

"Annie, you're a fuckwit." Lou's message had been angry, accurate, and to the point. Annie guessed she'd heard from Chris, then.

"This is Ken. Give me a call."

Did no one sleep in London?

No calls from Chris, though. And nothing from Phil. Both understandable. Annie wouldn't have called her if she was either of them.

She'd been showering, checking her notes, showering again, and drinking mineral water when the various calls came through. Talking to people was not top of her Things To Do list, not today and maybe never.

Annie hadn't bothered to write separate e-mails to Rebecca and Ken, simply cut and pasted the same one. *No change, Scarlett still missing, now presumed dead.*

Time was not on Scarlett's side. It was getting to be too long since she walked out of the Blue Flamingo on her way to supper with a man yet to be identified. Annie didn't need a police profiler or a private investigator to tell her that.

There was still no e-mail from Chris. It was a relief, since watching for his name to appear every time her e-mail downloaded brought her close to vomiting and tears.

I need to get out, thought Annie. *A walk to clear my head.*

Checking that her photo of Scarlett was in her bag, Annie grabbed a jacket and her keys and headed for the elevators. A dose of sunlight and some much-needed vitamin D would do her good. There was little point glancing in the mirror before leaving the hotel. She didn't need a looking glass to tell her she had eyes like piss-holes in the sand.

And the truth was she couldn't bear to look herself in the face. This time, and not for the first time, she had gone too far. Annie Anderson was deeply ashamed of herself and she didn't like the feeling.

To compound matters, the space between her legs grew damp, wetting the crotch of Annie's jeans within ten minutes of leaving the Akasaka Prince. Her stomach had been cramping, but Annie had put that down to alcohol or food poisoning or both. Now the stickiness between her legs said otherwise. Her period had come on.

"Christ almighty," muttered Annie, raising her eyes to the heavens and looking away quickly as the late-September sun hit her dehydrated pupils. "Somebody up there doesn't like me."

She found a tiny chemist on one of the backstreets that had been crowded with tourists the night before. At two in the afternoon, it thronged with an altogether different crowd. Deliverymen unloaded bottles of butane from badly parked vans, chefs headed to work for the evening shift, tourists wandered aimlessly.

No one who looked like Rufus's PI, although the feeling of eyes watching her never went. *Paranoia,* she told herself. *Just to add to everything else.*

When Annie pushed open the door, a jingle went off and a middle-aged woman behind the counter glanced up and bowed slightly. Annie's smile was weak. *What the hell did tampon boxes look like in Japan,* she wondered.

Aisles overflowed and colorful boxes were piled higgledy-piggledy across the floor. Shampoo and toothpaste mingled with ginseng, amino drinks, and skin lightening cream. On a shelf nearby Annie found tiger balm and did a double take, realizing the neatly packaged toys next to the tiger balm were purse-sized vibrators, and the rubber bands next door were cock rings.

All she wanted was tampons. Aware of the woman's gaze, she moved to the back of the shop, finding small disposable diapers. A closer inspection revealed them as super-large sanitary towels. She hadn't worn those since she was thirteen and didn't plan to start again now.

Apart from anything else they'd never fit inside her jeans.

Eventually, she found a small pile of boxes in two sizes. Nothing about them suggested that they were tampons, except their proximity to sanitary towels and the size of the box. Without knowing if she was buying mini or superplus, Annie grabbed a box of each, wiped dust off the cellophane, and decided not to think about whether tampons had expiration dates.

Painkillers proved easier.

Annie simply used the same principle of color coding and location she'd used with the tampons. Biffren were silver and red, sounded a lot like Ibuprofen, and sat on a counter with other pharmaceutical-type products. Logic said they had to be painkillers. Since the woman only smiled and nodded to all of Annie's questions, the only way to find out was to buy them and hope.

From habit, she showed the woman Scarlett's photograph and indicated the shop around her. But the Japanese woman just kept smiling and nodding. So maybe Scarlett had used the chemist and maybe she hadn't.

A block farther on, a coffee shop, loosely modeled on Starbucks, gave Annie a chance to find a loo. Then she ordered a black Americano to wash down her pills. Which of her many aches they dealt with Annie didn't much care, as long as they removed either her headache or the cramp.

The word *Americano* was strangely comforting after the chaos of packaging in the pharmacy and, as Annie forced herself to eat a rock cake before washing down the painkillers, she found herself reading the English menu behind the counter for reassurance. Even the TV screen hanging from the ceiling boasted English subtitles to its rolling twenty-four-hour news. She was safely back in tourist town.

Ordering another Americano, Annie settled down to watch.

A silver-haired newscaster was talking to a politician about the proposed privatization of the post office. Annie wasn't much interested and knew even less, but she watched the debate anyway. Although her head still pounded, her stomachache had finally begun to fade. One more hit of coffee and she was out of there. Ready to start on the restaurants and bars, going door-to-door with her picture of Scarlett.

"How hard can it be?" Annie asked herself.

She had a good idea of Scarlett's last day in Tokyo. All she needed was to find someone who recognized Scarlett from that night. Someone must have seen her, but right now too many people were busy saying precisely nothing.

The debate finished, and the newscaster became animated as a picture of a moderately good-looking man somewhere in his forties filled the screen. Like all the men before him, this one wore a dark suit, white shirt, and tie, but Annie was yet to see a Japanese executive over the age of twenty who didn't.

A film star? A local executive? Someone from the government?

Letting her eyes drift to the subtitles, Annie read, *Yahoro Itou, an accountant from Kawaguchi, has been held for the fate of four foreign women.*

"What?"

Leaping up, Annie dashed across to the counter. "What did he say?" she demanded of a girl who was loading the dishwasher.

The girl, in her late teens, glanced up. "So sorry," she said, her English near-perfect. "I didn't listen." She stopped what she was doing and looked at the screen. "It seems," she said after a silence that seemed to last minutes, "they have the Ripper." Her accent slipped on the first part of the killer's nickname, but there was no mistaking what she said.

"What do you mean, have?"

"Arrested him."

"Charged?"

"No. Questioning. About four young women."

"It should be five," said Annie.

The girl glanced back at the screen. "Four," she said firmly.

"Anything else?"

"I'm afraid, no. Sorry."

"No, not at all . . . I mean, thank you." Back at her table, Annie ate the last mouthful of rock cake and washed it down with the dregs of her second Americano. Four girls, not five. And a man who didn't even live in Tokyo.

There was only one way for Annie to find out who this guy was and what, if anything, he'd been charged with. She'd have to call the man she'd more or less thrown out of her hotel room, Phil Townend.

His phone was answered immediately. One ring and he picked up.

"Imagine that's you," he said, before Annie could open her mouth.

Could he be any more smug? thought Annie, then realized his tone was anything but. Hurt was more like it. Another one to add to her list. Annie Anderson's never-ending revenge on the male sex for producing Tony Panton.

"We had a deal," said Annie, her voice all business, ignoring the fact that things had already gone way beyond the realms of any deal. "You were going to give me whatever you got from Ryu."

"Yes . . . ," he said. "I know."

Annie couldn't tell whether his guardedness was because of last night, or because a colleague was listening in. Or maybe Phil simply didn't do sharing. Annie could understand that; sharing wasn't her favorite thing either.

"I just got back from the damn press conference," he said. "It was a riot, in as much as any Japanese press conference is ever a riot."

"Is it him?"

"Looks that way."

"What are they saying?"

He hesitated, ready to refuse Annie the information, and then told her anyway. A deal was a deal. "Maddeningly little. Name's Yahoro Itou, forty-five, an accountant from Kawaguchi, out beyond Ueno, married, one child, and works for one of the big corporations. The usual."

"Come on, Phil. There must be more."

"Honestly. I'm not holding out, but the police are, that's for sure. All they'll say is their version of 'he's helping us with inquiries.'"

"What about the 'four girls' rather' than 'five girls' thing?"

Phil went quiet. "Where did you hear that?"

"Same place everyone else did," said Annie. "It was on the news."

"What a city," he said.

"Meaning?"

"Look," said Phil. "What I'm about to tell you didn't come from Ryu, okay?"

He had Annie chewing at her nails. *Get to the point,* she wanted to say, but had the sense not to.

"I got it from a different contact. He says Itou's confessed."

"Why haven't they charged him?"

"Are you going to let me finish?"

She put up a hand in a gesture of surrender that Phil could not see.

"He's confessed to four killings. Abduction and murder. Don't know about sexual assault, but it seems foregone to me."

"Four?" said Annie.

"Not Scarlett," he said. "The way my guy tells it, Itou insists he didn't even know Scarlett existed until he read about her in the papers. . . ."

"You believe it?"

"Of course not. I think the fucker's lying, because that's the killing which brought down the heat. What do *you* think?"

"Not sure," Annie said. It was true, she wasn't sure what to think, but why admit four murders and not the fifth? There was nothing to gain from it. Unless Phil was right . . . The others didn't count, being from average backgrounds, your average gaijin on the block?

Whereas Scarlett was Rufus Ulrich's daughter, with a public profile to match? Alternatively, someone else killed Scarlett?

Had Scarlett killed herself?

"Phil," said Annie.

"What?"

"I'm sorry about . . ."

"It's all right." His voice was hard.

Annie could hear the shutters coming down. "No," she said. "It's not. . . . It was unforgivable." *Bloody hell*, thought Annie. *Annie Anderson apologizes. Shocker. Just a shame it was to the wrong guy.* She expected him to speak, but all she got was silence. "It was wrong and I'm sorry. If I could undo the damage I would."

"You have your reasons?" he said finally.

"Yes," said Annie. "I have my reasons."

"And you're not going to tell me what they are?"

"No," Annie said. "I'm not."

"Okay then, look after yourself." It was more than he needed to say and much more than she deserved.

"And you," said Annie, and she meant it.

It wasn't until Annie had changed her tampon and washed her hands that she noticed an envelope on the carpet by her hotel door. She'd obviously stepped right over it in her haste to use the bathroom. The envelope was white, emblazoned with the hotel's logo, and obviously expensive like most things about the Akasaka Prince. Annie's name was written in a neat hand, *Miss A. Anderson.*

Tearing it open, she extracted a single sheet of hotel paper.

Miss Anderson,

A Japanese gentleman called for you this afternoon. We were not able to contact you. He did not wish to leave a name or contact details, but said he would call again.

It was signed, *The Concierge.*

A man who wouldn't leave his name and knew where she was staying. Not good.

Chris, Rebecca, Lou, and Phil. She could count on one hand the people who knew her hotel address and not need her thumb. Except, she'd forgotten Rebecca's PA, who booked the hotel. Oh, and Ken, who Annie had also told. Two hands then.

No way would either *Handbag* or *The Post* give out her address, nor would Chris without good reason. This meant she had to have been followed.

Annie glanced around the room, checking the points of entry and exit, noting the number of windows (not much use thirty-two floors up), and the doors she hadn't bothered to open since she got back. Three wardrobes and two bathrooms would now need surveying.

"Do it," she told herself.

The wardrobes were empty, of course. One of them didn't even have any floor space, because the room safe was in there. The other was hardly big enough for a child-sized burglar to hide. The bathrooms were the same, the loo cubicles in each bathroom reassuringly empty.

"See?" she said. "How hard was that?"

It was funny how you were supposed to feel safer in hotel rooms than anywhere else. Confident in the locked door that lay between you and the outside world and cocooned from reality by room service and cable TV.

Even before Milan, she'd found that hard to swallow. And Milan hadn't helped. Scarcely six months earlier, her hotel room in Milan had been burgled, her suitcase ransacked. It happened the day after Patty Lang overdosed, while staying in a wing of the Mantolini family palazzo.

Annie could have died in that hotel room. And it was there she first went to bed with . . .

Oh, God.

Burying her face in her hands, Annie wondered who she could call now with her fears. No one, but that was how she liked it, wasn't it?

Wasn't it?

Think, she told herself, hangover and stomach cramps forgotten. *Think.*

Assuming whoever it was didn't know her room number, Annie was safe for the moment, but he was still one up on her. For a start, he knew *who* and *where* she was and possibly *why* too.

Annie had yet to get the basic *who*. Even twenty minutes earlier Annie would have assumed "he" was the Ripper himself. But now Yahoro Itou was in custody, it couldn't be. There was, of course, a possibility the police had the wrong guy. And the right guy had come by her hotel that morning . . .

Alternatively, the Ripper was telling the truth. He hadn't killed Scarlett, and the man who had . . . Or it could be something to do with Rufus Ulrich's PI. But then what did she have that he might want?

Assuming Itou was the Ripper and he was not Scarlett's killer, who else might want to speak to her, but not be prepared to leave his name? The obvious answer was someone from Scarlett's agency. Annie had put in a call after getting the number from Lou. Maybe this was their way of making contact? It wouldn't be hard to find her. After all, she'd left them her . . .

Damn that made almost two hands' worth of people who knew where she was.

And there were other options, of course. The mama-san from the Blue Flamingo could have sent someone to warn Annie off. All she'd have had to do to discover where Annie was staying was have someone follow Annie back. If so, she'd have known the nice tourist couple weren't even staying in the same hotel, they weren't a couple, and chances were, they weren't tourists at all. It was a risk Annie had to take last night, when she'd showed Scarlett's picture to the American girl.

Annie ran that thought past herself again. *When she'd showed Scarlett's picture . . .*

Two thoughts were fighting in her head. One involved the photograph. The other . . . ? What did people do when they got scared, what did she want to do right now? She wanted to hide, and if that wasn't a choice, she wanted to run away from the mess she made of her life. Either of those would suit Annie just fine.

They might also have suited Scarlett.

And what did people do when they wanted to hide? They disguised themselves, obviously. And, if they were really clever, they lost themselves in a crowd. Now say it was a small crowd, in fact little more than a handful of others.

Victims of the Roppongi Ripper.

Picking up the phone, Annie called UK directory inquiries to pin down a number in Muswell Hill, one of the nicer suburbs of North London.

Handbag's art director was less than pleased to hear from her, and when she ran the time back nine hours in her head, Annie could understand why. Clearly, concisely, she explained what she wanted, apologized for waking him, and apologized again for wanting the work done now.

"Rebecca would want . . . ," she said. "Really sorry."

On the other end of the line, the man groaned.

"Don't make the files too big," Annie added. She didn't have time to waste waiting for the pictures to download.

thirty · seven

Annie's instincts said get out, go where there are as many people as possible, and stay there. But she had a new collection of Scarlett pictures on their way. All of which would need printing out in the hotel's business center. And before she did that, Annie had to call Lou, and tell her what?

A man had been arrested for murder, but claimed to have killed only four out of the five missing girls? She certainly wasn't about to pick up a phone and tell Lou that.

Then there was Chris. Had he told his friends at work? Had he told his parents, or worse, told hers? Were his possessions in boxes ready to be moved? He was as hard-line as she was, in his way. Chris would move fast. His pride would make him, just as Annie's would make her.

In the end, she e-mailed Lou to say a local man was helping police with inquiries and she'd be back in touch later that day, just as soon as she heard anything else.

One other question continued to plague Annie. . . .

Why would a model who'd made the teen top-ten rich lists both sides of the Atlantic for the best part of a decade, a girl with a trust fund to keep her in luxury for the rest of her life, chat up middle-aged Japanese men for a few hundred quid?

The fifteen thousand pounds Jess Harper said Scarlett had saved was a drop in the ocean of her childhood earnings. It was barely a month's interest, if that. Even if the trust fund was locked solid until Scarlett was twenty-one or twenty-five or even thirty, it still didn't add up. Plenty of banks would lend to trust-fund heirs, some of them made a business out of it.

She would ask Arabella who the trustees were. She spent ten minutes composing an e-mail that put the question in not too bald a way and pressed SEND. It was the first e-mail she'd sent Arabella direct. If she was lucky, Arabella might even answer.

Picking up the phone, she dialed Jess's mobile and wasn't surprised to get voice mail. She decided against leaving a message. Jess probably wouldn't return the call anyway. Annie's only chance was to catch her unawares and ask Scarlett's flatmate one last time if Scarlett had ever given the slightest clue what she was saving up for.

And then there were the new photographs, courtesy of *Handbag* magazine's overworked art director. Scarlett as someone else. A brunette, cropped and makeup free, redheaded and curly, in a black wig and dressed neatly like an OL, one of Tokyo's famous office ladies. Maybe she should start with those?

So much for being safer outside! As storm clouds gathered, the late-summer sky grew dark. A strong wind came from nowhere to turn her hotel umbrella inside out and then snapped two of its spokes completely.

The wind lashed trees lining stone steps up to a half-seen shrine on a slope above the road where Annie tried to shelter as rain drove into her face. Fat, heavy drops of rain. As if high overhead one of those strange Japanese nature gods was crying.

Annie had never seen anything like it.

Whipped by the wind, she turned to escape the worst of the rain but it was impossible. So clutching her trench coat around her, Annie shielded her face against the weather and started walking again. The legs of her jeans below the coat were already soaked, and she could feel her coat get heavier as it took in water.

Her first thought was to run back into the hotel. What then? Pick up an umbrella? Wait for whoever had been following her since she arrived in Tokyo to reappear? Because Annie was certain someone had, she'd been feeling it for days. She should have trusted her instinct earlier.

No way. She was outside and she had a coat, her hair was short enough to dry in five minutes flat. She might as well keep going.

Annie had a hunch about Scarlett. It was just that—a hunch, nothing more. She wasn't quite ready to share it with Rebecca.

As for Ken, he couldn't be trusted not to put her hunches on the front page, he'd done it before. And Lou? She'd still be furious, if that last voice mail was anything to go by.

Annie, you're a fuckwit.

Angry with Rufus, upset about Scarlett, and furious at Annie's treatment of Chris, Lou's summing up of her character had been vicious. Annie was finding it hard not to agree.

Retracing her steps, which she hoped were Scarlett's steps, to the bars and shops of Akasaka's backstreets, Annie began to trawl lanes that were just beginning to pass for familiar after five days in Tokyo.

The first place Annie reached was a 7-Eleven just off the main drag. A floppy-haired boy behind the till bowed slightly and smiled when she approached with a sticky pink amino-acid health drink in one hand, a ten-thousand yen note in the other.

"You speak English?" she asked, as he counted her change onto a small plastic tray.

"You lost?" he replied, laughing.

Annie shook her head. "I'm trying to track down a friend of mine."

The photograph in Annie's hand showed Scarlett with a mousy bob and no makeup. It was impressive what you could do with Photoshop and an art director on tap.

Taking the picture, the boy looked at it closely, his frown telling her that the face rang a bell, he just couldn't place it. "No," he said finally. "Sorry. Many gaijin women work around here."

Annie smiled. *And they all look the same to me.* She knew what he meant and he knew she knew but was too polite to put it into words.

The rain was still torrential outside and the streets deserted, so Annie picked an Italian restaurant that was setting up for dinner. Inside, obscured from Annie's view by a window display of plastic pizzas and spaghetti Bolognese, a young woman spread checkered cloths across tables, and put red candles in wine bottles that already dripped with wax. *Bella Napoli*, it looked like a caricature of what someone thought an Italian restaurant should be.

Annie tried the door. Discovering it locked, she knocked.

Frowning, the woman shook her head.

The second time Annie knocked, the waitress came to the door. "We open twelve to three, six to ten. You see?" She pointed to a sign on the door.

"Actually," said Annie, "I don't want to eat."

Another frown.

You want to watch it, Annie thought, as a force-nine gale tugged the edge of her sodden coat. *The wind might change and you'll be stuck like that.*

"You lost?" the woman asked. "You not find address?"

Foreigners who couldn't work out Tokyo's complex system of house numbering were obviously a regular fixture. Something to be tolerated with an appearance of good grace.

Shaking her head, Annie produced Scarlett's picture from her bag. This time Scarlett had a short dark crop, like Annie's own, only neater and not dripping water down her face.

"I wondered," said Annie, "if you'd seen my friend."

"She tourist?" the waitress asked, her face giving nothing away. "Or she work here?"

"Work," said Annie.

The waitress bowed slightly. "Sorry, no."

It was interesting, Annie thought, how a change of hairstyle could alter the shape of a person's face. A cut and a dye job, new clothes, a change of personal style, and only a close friend would recognize someone who didn't want to be recognized.

Drug dealers remade themselves as art collectors. Wanted criminals ran corner shops. At least they did in Glasgow. For all Annie knew, corner shop owners remade themselves as criminals. It happened the world over.

People woke up and decided to walk away from their lives. Was that what had happened to Scarlett?

Annie was beginning to wonder.

Working her way down the narrow street, Annie gave the Blue Flamingo a wide berth. She flitted damply from one doorway to the next, getting wetter as cascading gutters and awnings found her anyway.

Every few yards, Annie would enter a beauty parlor or bookshop, restaurant or chemist, even a pachinko parlor, getting out a different photo of the same woman each time.

All she got was the same answer.

Without her trademark long blond curls, even Scarlett's face, once the most recognizable on the planet, was bland and anonymous. Of course, there had been the occasional flicker of recognition; something had flashed across a porter's face and caused Annie to pause.

"No," he said. "Sorry."

Annie hadn't done proper door-stopping, the press equivalent of door-to-door inquiries, for years. Right now, she remembered why. Having exhausted Akasaka's narrow lanes, she followed signs leading her southwest. The streets became busier and less pretty. After an area of offices and a BMW garage, she hit a sign announcing the opening of a new Louis Vuitton store. And then, as quickly as it arrived, the money disappeared and she was back into narrow streets and pokey little shops.

She was tired, her feet hurt, and her clothes were wet through, but at least the rain had decided to stop. As for her hangover, it had sunk to a nagging ache behind her eyes. So maybe she wasn't ready for the forty-eight-hour variety yet.

She had almost reached Roppongi when the rain decided to reappear. *One more bar,* Annie told herself. Just one more and then she'd head for Happy Daze and see if that Australian girl was there. Show her the re-worked photos, see if her memory had improved.

Club Goodnight looked like it had been built in the eighties and never had a facelift. Annie didn't doubt, given the cyclical nature of fashion, that black and chrome would come again, sooner rather than later. The door was designed to look as if carved from onyx, but was actually Formica. A gray plastic crate held it ajar, and a delivery van stood outside, its rear doors open, the driver nowhere to be seen.

Annie stepped over the crate and found herself heading downstairs toward a basement.

A small desk and cloakroom at the bottom were unstaffed, hardly surprising since it was not yet evening. The room beyond was black and chrome with smoked glass tables. Voices drifted from a door beyond.

"Can I help?"

Annie turned to find there'd been a second door, which now stood open. The fact the questioner was English made her jump. Roughly Annie's age, the woman had fair hair pulled back in a ponytail, stray strands tucked behind her ears. She was wearing the white shirt and black knee-length skirt of a waitress.

"If you're looking for hostess work, I'm afraid we're not hiring."

Annie couldn't help but laugh. "I'm flattered," she said, running one hand through sodden hair. "But no. I'm trying to find a friend. I wondered if you'd seen her?"

Annie pulled out a picture. It was one of the least battered, not too creased and not yet curling with damp. Long dark hair framed Scarlett's cheeks, making her face look longer and thinner.

"She lived round here, worked in Tokyo for a few months," Annie explained. "Maybe longer. But she's gone missing."

The woman stared at the picture, her eyes growing wide.

"I can't say for sure," she said slowly. "We had a girl here for a while who looked a bit like this. It's not her, though. Her hair was different. Blond and curly. But she did look a lot like this. It's spooky."

"Do you still have her contact details?"

The woman shook her head. "I'm afraid not, she left several months ago. Five, maybe six, but it can't be her . . . " The voice trailed away.

"It might be, it would be really helpful if you could tell me."

"It's not Scarlett," the woman said firmly. "She's dead."

"No," said Annie. "She isn't called Scarlett. You must be thinking of someone else."

"Hmmm." The woman looked thoughtful, gazed at the picture, and then glanced again at Annie. "I certainly hope so."

Even the unfailingly polite concierge looked appalled as Annie squelched across the marble floors of the Akasaka Prince, one of Tokyo's grandest hotels. Annie had little doubt that she was leaving soggy footprints and trails of water from the sodden hem of her coat.

A girl in the lobby nudged another, and when they both giggled at Annie's bedraggled appearance, she realized the suave Japanese executives and rich tourists who made up the hotel's usual guests were outnumbered by a horde of teenage girls. All gathered, it seemed, for the hotel's famous biweekly Very Berry, all-you-can-eat cake buffet.

As they flocked around the long white tables placed to one side of the lobby, they giggled some more and piled their plates with every permutation of creamy, fruity gateaux and pastry, pie, and chocolate roll, as if calories had never been invented. Mind you, given that ninety-nine percent of the meals Annie had seen in Tokyo involved raw fish, Japanese girls probably didn't need to count calories in quite the same way as their Western counterparts.

As she waited for her elevator to arrive, Annie fumbled in her bag for her key card and eyed the Japanese girls enviously. Their slight bodies and narrow frames seemed immune to carbs as they prowled the Very Berry buffet, leaving no cake unturned.

It was late and she'd returned from Roppongi via a different route, stopping on the way to show people her retouched photographs of Scarlett at every café or bookshop that looked likely.

Exhaustion had overcome hangover when the elevator finally deposited Annie at the thirty-second floor. Up here the corridors were dimly lit and silent, scarcely touched by the winds that still howled outside, the carpets muffling Annie's tread and deadening what few sounds came from behind bedroom doors.

The overhead lights, being Japanese, turned themselves on as she approached and off again after she'd gone. So Annie was constantly walking into twilight, with her own little pool of brightness to fend off the shadows.

She should have noticed when they flickered up ahead.

Senses numbed by period pain and headache, clothes clinging wetly to her sodden skin, Annie was focused on the bath she'd take and the e-mails she needed to write before she could allow herself the luxury of sleep. She didn't notice a shadow in the corridor ahead, the shift as unexpected lights lit. At least she didn't notice until it was too late.

thirty · eight

A man's arm was around her neck. It was a slick, quick move, too fast for Annie to do anything but register the professionalism of the attack before fear came flooding in. Instinct made her struggle.

All that happened was his arm tightened, and a hand slapped across her mouth before Annie could scream.

"Shut it," the man said.

At least Annie imagined that was what he said. It was in Japanese.

She knew nothing about the Tokyo underworld, other than what she'd read, but she'd read enough to fear it. Her kidneys yelped as something smooth and hard pushed against them and Annie twisted slightly. His grip increased, the gun at her back became more obvious.

As it did so, her bag began to vibrate. Annie's rented mobile. If only she could reach down somehow. But right now, the slightest wrong move might be her last.

"You have a card key?" The voice might be young, male, and Japanese, but his English was flawless. Young and male were bad, but the good English gave Annie hope. You don't send your best if all you want to do is hurt someone.

"Card?" he repeated.

Annie tried to nod and failed, her throat tight against leather. Instead she held up one hand.

"Good," he said. "We walk."

Her room was at the far end of the corridor, which meant they stumbled the distance in an awkward three-legged race, with the lights coming on as they approached and going out behind.

A hotel phone was ringing.

In the seconds it took to reach her room, Annie searched for a way out, her eyes flicking toward each door as they passed. There was no emergency exit, no stairwell, not even a broom closet or housekeeper's room. Every door was firmly shut. A tiny CCTV camera hung from the ceiling at either end of the corridor. If luck was on Annie's side, the screens would be watched in real time and the security guard wouldn't be on his tea break.

She didn't hold out much hope.

"Open the door."

Sliding her card into the slot, Annie prayed the light would flash red, refusing them entry, just as it had a half a dozen times in the five days since she first arrived. Sod's law, the tiny diode lit green and the door clicked open.

Annie heard the man kick the door shut behind him, but he didn't release his grip, merely walked her across the room until they reached the window. It was a glass wall of nighttime Tokyo. Lights and logos rioted across a darkening sky, their luridness making the sky darker in contrast.

Advertisements flashing for everything from beer to bedding jostled with signs for clubs, bars, and restaurants, while a giant digital clock told Annie it was 20 degrees Celsius and 18:30 exactly.

Directly below, the logo of a jazz club glowed fuchsia, green, and yellow, to the beat of some unheard jazz classic. And above it all, twenty-five-story-high cranes, loomed precariously like Godzilla and MechaGodzilla, their red eyes flashing against the oncoming night, each with a red claw poised to strike.

It was strange and alien, unrecognizable as the district she'd tramped through less than an hour earlier. Annie was aware it might be her last sight of the city, of anywhere come to that. And she thanked a God she didn't believe in that the window didn't open.

"Sit," he said, releasing her throat and pushing her forward at the same time. As he pulled away, he grabbed the bag still attached to Annie's shoulder and she spun, slamming into the reinforced glass, which was all that stood between her and thirty-two floors to oblivion.

"*Shit.*" It hurt.

"Sorry . . ."

Annie turned to see a very young, very pretty Japanese boy in a suit, barely a man at all, staring at her in shock, a gun held loosely in his hand. *Blue Flamingo,* she thought. He'd been sitting at the bar.

"Are you all right?" he asked.

She put her hand to her forehead and found that her fingers were sticky. Her skin had split where she slammed against the glass. Blood was beginning to trickle down the side of her face.

"You need a Band-Aid."

Stitches, probably . . .

Only too aware that yes was usually the best answer in these sorts of situations, Annie nodded. "Er, you're right. I do." She was astonished to see him bow slightly. Astonished and relieved, because his bow was not mocking nor sneering. Whatever this was, it was not what it seemed.

"I'll get one," he said, keeping his gun on her. "Don't move. Okay?"

Annie nodded again.

The boy had obviously stayed in expensive hotels before. Either that or all Japanese hotels offered chemist's sundries in a little tray in the bathroom. "Here," he said. "Use this." He held out a paper tissue and a Band-Aid. "You sure you're all right?"

"My head hurts," said Annie. She went to the mirror, dabbed the cut, and stuck a Band-Aid in place.

"So," the boy asked gruffly, when she'd finished. "Who are you?"

"I'm Annie Anderson. . . ."

"No," said the boy. "I know that!" He pulled a familiar white card from his jacket pocket. "See?"

It was her *Handbag* business card. *How the hell had he got hold of that?*

"I'm a journalist," she said, waiting for him to nod before she continued. "I work for an English fashion magazine, I'm investigating . . . writing a story about Scarlett Ulrich's disappearance."

"Why?" he demanded, shifting the gun in his hand.

Annie had known a Glaswegian whose gun could have been grafted direct to flesh, it was so much a part of him, yet this boy held his gun as if afraid the weapon might be about to bite him.

Now her fear had begun to subside, Annie found the boy fascinating. He was young, but not as young as he looked. At university, maybe even post-grad. A late developer, by the look of things. It would probably take him about six months to grow a decent beard. He had high cheekbones, chin-length hair, dyed that strange *chapatsu* orange that Japanese men favored. It flopped around his face, framing large almond eyes.

A boy with a gun.

An impossibly beautiful boy with a gun. Annie had been in some strange situations before, but this was a new one to her.

His eyes were the most interesting thing. Insomuch as Annie could trust her own judgment, she was sure these were not eyes to be afraid of. This was not a cold-blooded killer. The only way this boy would kill was from panic, fear, or by accident.

That was what concerned Annie right now. The way he jittered from foot to foot, glancing nervously from the door to Annie and back, with a gun in his hand. Somehow, she had to get the gun off him or calm the boy down enough to ensure he didn't use it.

"Tell my why you are here," she said, relieved when he appeared to consider her question.

"No," he said. "You tell me. . . . Everyone knows Scarlett Ulrich is dead. *He* killed her."

"He?"

"The Ripper."

"I'm not sure he did."

"Of course, he did," the boy said, raising his voice. "Why are you looking for Scarlett Ulrich?"

Annie chose the truth. "Because Scarlett's sister asked me to find her."

The boy stopped jittering. "Her sister?"

"Half sister."

"Not her father?" Suspicion crowded his brows.

"No," said Annie, frowning. She'd expected to be warned off, perhaps hurt, and left fighting the urge to take the next plane out of Tokyo. Did everything always come back to Rufus Ulrich?

"No," said Annie firmly. "Not her father."

"Don't move," he said.

Crouching down, his gun wobbling slightly as he unzipped Annie's bag, the boy felt his way around the inside. A triumphant look crossed his face as he pulled the photographs from where they lay, creased and damp in an inside pocket.

"What are you doing with these?" he demanded. "I know you have been showing them around. People have told me. Why are you doing it?"

"What people?"

"It is not for you!" he shouted, then took a deep breath. "Answer my question."

"I already did," said Annie. "I'm looking for Scarlett, because her sister's my best friend and she asked me to, and because . . ." Annie paused, wondering whether to say it. She had little to lose, except her life, of course. "I don't believe she's dead."

The boy stared at her, his face a mixture of confusion and shock. "Why not?" he asked, and for a second he looked like one of Annie's nephews, who'd just been told his lie wouldn't work, the plate didn't just fall off the table by itself. About four years old.

"Why?" he repeated.

Annie shrugged.

She had some answers, but not many. The Ripper insisted he didn't kill Scarlett, and the pressure on him from the police to say he did must be enormous. She wouldn't be surprised if he confessed eventually. All the same, she believed he was telling the truth. Why deny just one murder?

Her other reason was less to do with logic and more to do with gut feeling. One of the richest teenagers in the world worked a grotty club in Tokyo, making nice with boring suits to save a few thousand pounds? It didn't make sense.

Everybody, except her immediate family, seemed too keen to bury Scarlett and move on. In the last few days Annie had begun to wonder if Scarlett herself might be one of them. Her modeling career was over, and who were the people who wouldn't let Scarlett put it behind her?

The very people who were looking for her now.

None of this was said aloud. Instead Annie just watched the boy as he stared at first one Photoshopped picture, then another.

"Where did you get these?" he asked, when he'd finished leafing through the pile. Annie would have killed to know which of the mock-ups reduced his voice to a sad flatness. There had to be one, and it wasn't of Scarlett as she used to be, looking blond and curvy.

"Which one?" said Annie.

"All of them."

"That picture I got from the paper. You must have seen it."

He scowled. "I mean the others."

"Our art director made them."

"Made them?"

"Yes, on a computer." Annie smiled, trying to reassure him. "I asked a designer to scan Scarlett's picture and put different hairstyles on her, juggle her clothes around a little, imagine her in different kinds of makeup."

"Why?" His voice was intense, his simple question hiding an anguish that had him clutching the gun.

"Because," said Annie, "if you want to vanish that's how you do it. You change your appearance. It's obvious, isn't it?"

Silence hung between them, as the boy looked mournfully from the handful of photographs in his hand to Annie's face and back.

As he did so, Annie couldn't help but wonder how she looked to him. She'd looked in a state even before she went out that morning, before the drenching rain, and before she got slammed into a window and her forehead split open.

"She is dead," he said.

Annie said nothing.

"I have to ask you to stop looking. Let her rest."

"Why? Are you a friend of Scarlett's?"

The boy scowled at Annie. "Because it is better," he said, refusing to answer the second part of her question.

"Who for?"

"For Scarlett."

Annie swallowed and then she said it anyway. "Scarlett's not dead, is she?"

The boy sighed, the gun still hanging loose from one hand, the sheaf of photos in the other. "Everybody thinks she is," he said. "And Scarlett wants to be, so please, I am here to ask, leave her alone. Go away and never come back. You are the only one who refuses to believe it."

"Rufus Ulrich has sent an investigator to find her."

The boy sneered. "He believes she's dead."

"Maybe now," said Annie. "But he might not believe it once he hears the Ripper denies killing Scarlett."

"That's not true."

The gun was up again.

"It is true," she said gently.

"It can't be. He was charged, late this afternoon, with killing all five girls."

Is the boy bluffing? wondered Annie, unable to tell. He didn't seem to have it in him. She noticed for the first time the message light on her hotel phone was flashing. Must have been her phone she'd heard ringing.

"Can I?" she asked, pointing to the bedside cabinet where it sat.

"No," he said. "You can't."

"Well, you do it," said Annie. "It might be important. It might be about Scarlett."

He considered this for a moment, and then backed across the room. Picking up the receiver, he pressed a button and listened intently, concentration etched into his face. It had to be much harder to understand a foreign language on the phone, when you were unable to see the speaker's mouth moving.

"It's a man," he said. "An Englishman. He says this too." The boy hesitated. "What I tell you, he says the same . . . You listen."

He held out the phone but didn't move when Annie took it. Instead he stood right next to her, his head near hers, with the hand holding his gun angled across his chest so its muzzle pointed toward her.

"Just listen," he said. "No calling anyone else."

The message was from Phil.

"Itou's been charged," he said. "All five, Scarlett included. Only now he's denying the lot. He's retracted his confession, says he's never been near any of them. Ryu says the guy's going down. That's all." Phil hesitated, as if he wanted to say more. . . .

Then the phone went dead.

"So now?" the boy said when she'd hung up.

"So now the Ripper's been charged with four murders he did commit and one he didn't."

"That's not what the police think."

"Maybe not, but it's the truth, isn't it?"

The boy raised his gun and put it to Annie's head. His fingers were not shaking now. "I am telling you to stop looking."

Swallowing hard, Annie stared him in the face. She didn't think he would do it. In fact, she was ninety-nine percent sure. The other one percent she would have to bluff. Although that thought made bile rise in her stomach.

It was the tears in his eyes that gave her hope.

"Take me to Scarlett," said Annie. "Let me talk to her."

He didn't answer and Annie didn't speak. She was counting backward from ten. When she reached zero, she added, "If you do, I promise I'll go and I'll never come back. And I won't tell a soul."

Except, she thought, mentally crossing her fingers, *Scarlett's big sister.*

"You promise?"

Annie nodded.

"I will think about it."

Before he let himself out of her room, the boy bowed, apologized for the cut on Annie's forehead, and asked if her head still hurt.

thirty · nine

Annie found an envelope pushed under the door when she woke the following morning. After the boy had gone, she'd double locked her room, changed the Band-Aid on her forehead, and gone straight to bed, sinking into sleep the second her half-clothed body slid under the covers. When she woke she saw that she'd slept for ten hours straight, but though rested, every muscle in her body ached.

An unavoidable outcome, she decided, of cold, damp, fear, and the added tension of keeping herself tightly wound for the best part of an hour. But when she opened the letter she knew it had been worth it.

Gone was the neat script and the niceties of hotel notepaper. This had not been delivered by any concierge, but by the boy himself, as Annie slept. It was torn from the Japanese equivalent of a ring-bound reporter's notebook. The kind Annie usually carried, more from habit now than any actual need.

Scribbled in blue biro were three words:

Meiji Jingu 10 A.M.

The shrine in the park where Jess Harper had taken her that afternoon after the knitwear casting. The place where they'd sat on a bench and eaten noodles. Well, she'd eaten noodles.

The writing didn't look neat enough to be the boy's.

Yesterday's storm had eased when Annie left her hotel. In its place was a limpid sky and cotton wool clouds that hung low over the sprawling city, almost scraping the tops of its tallest towers. Watery sunlight was finally beginning to venture through.

By 9:45, the time Annie exited the subway at Meiji Jingumae, the sun was bright enough to force her to remove her raincoat and push up the sleeves of a black turtleneck.

Weird weather, Annie thought, moving with the crowd toward the park that spread like a cloak around Japan's most famous Shinto shrine.

Weird bloody place, actually.

It wasn't just the weather, which was not that different from England, just hotter and a lot wetter, it was the vibe . . . a feeling of repression combined with a sense that just below Tokyo's surface everything ran wild. People dressed smartly. Annie had seen more navy-blue suits and sensible shoes on both men and women in a week in Tokyo than she'd seen in her entire life. Everyone was polite, everyone bowed *all the time*.

Even the Harajuku kids, already assembling on the far side of the bridge in their ball gowns, ripped jeans, and cloaks made from silver foil— even they covered their mouths when they laughed.

Of course, Annie saw only the surface, but it just wasn't natural to be so polite and mean it; and most people obviously weren't and didn't, not really. It was the gap between the private and the public. The one Phil Townend had told her she had to understand if she was to understand anything about Japan at all.

The route to the shrine was impossible to miss, thanks to a line of uniformed schoolchildren who streamed in a line up a tree-shrouded drive toward the shrine's entrance. A neatly bobbed woman, who stood little taller than her charges, shouted something, and the children stopped, instantly in line on the edge of the road, to let a coach pass.

The place was going to be packed with school kids and tourists. On getting the note, she'd assumed Scarlett had chosen the Meiji Jingu because of its tranquillity. Now Annie could see that Scarlett—assuming Annie was here to see Scarlett—had other motives. She'd come here to hide.

Built in 1920, according to her guidebook, firebombed in 1945 and rebuilt thirteen years later using Japanese cypress . . . A popular place for weddings . . . Annie tried to appear just another foreigner soaking up the culture.

Was Scarlett already here? she wondered. *Watching her?*

Gradually the tourists and school parties split off, some plowing ahead and others taking paths into a gift shop and restaurant, or venturing into an old Imperial garden that stood near the shrine.

As Annie headed for the shrine, walking through carefully formed wilderness, she realized that, while there were still several groups around her, they had all fallen silent, as if hushed in reverence.

Streams and trees, sudden views of little stone bridges, and gravel that crunched underfoot. Something about this place was beguiling. A vast torii gateway was up ahead, positioned above the wide gravel drive. It was wooden, had three bronze chrysanthemums high overhead on its crossbar, and had been painted purple, well, probably . . . The paint looked worn.

With one eye carefully on her watch, Annie strolled past the occasional elderly worshipper, letting the park's calm atmosphere soak through her as she worked out what to say when she finally met Scarlett.

If she met Scarlett.

And, more importantly, what to tell Lou.

The quietness of Meiji Jingu reminded Annie of New York's Central Park. Once you were away from its edges, the place swallowed you up, until only the tip of a skyscraper seen poking above the trees let you know you were still in the heart of a city. Straining her ears, Annie heard no traffic, not even noise from the railway she knew ran on the far side of those trees.

Only the crows broke the silence. But then, for all she knew, they counted as *kami* to the Japanese, nature spirits. They certainly behaved as if they owned the place.

Up ahead was another torii, smaller than the previous gateway but still decorated with the three chrysanthemums along the top. As she entered she noticed a stone basin to the left, in the busy courtyard beyond. Several old women were rinsing their hands and swilling out their mouths with water from bamboo ladles.

The women were cleaning themselves before entering the shrine itself. Annie watched half a dozen more men and women do the same, so that she could blend in and copy the locals . . .

Doing as they did, and following their patterns of behavior.

It was the first rule of undercover.

She'd been undercover in her own life for so long she could hardly remember how it felt not to be. But now she wasn't. Undercover here, or in her own life. And Annie wasn't sure she could handle it.

Make yourself like everyone else, if not in appearance, then in behavior. Annie wondered if Scarlett knew that. All the haircuts in the world wouldn't make you invisible if your mannerisms and outward personality remained the same.

Annie suspected Scarlett did.

She passed under the final gate and stopped, awestruck. She had never seen anything as beautiful as this shrine. Its carved wood and ornate tiles, its copper roofs weathered to a soft peppermint green. The rebuilding of the original, which had been destroyed in the Second World War, was faithful down to the tiniest detail.

New York's skyscrapers might astound you, Tokyo's midnight skyline assault your senses. But there was more to the Meiji Jingu than mere architectural miracle-working. This was . . . Searching for a word, Annie found one she rarely had much use for . . . *spiritual*.

The outer courtyard was more or less deserted, but for robed monks who sold postcards and amulets in a gift shop and a Shinto priest in full regalia who wandered sedately out one door and in through another. The sky was blue, the air was hot. The shrine itself smelled of resin and warm wood.

No one was waiting for her, not the boy from last night, not a young woman who looked like a younger and prettier Lou.

That Annie still knew nothing about the boy was just one of many frustrations about the previous evening. No name, no real idea of who he was or how he knew Scarlett.

She had to be important to him, or why would he have taken the risk? Holding a gun to the head of a foreign journalist in one of Tokyo's most famous hotels wasn't a risk you took for a casual friend. Unless he'd been paid, of course. Only it hadn't felt that way to Annie. She knew a hired gun when she saw one, and the boy didn't even begin to fit the profile.

He was too passionate, too involved. He took it all too personally.

A friend of Scarlett's ex-boyfriend? Not for the first time, Annie wondered about the deported photographer's assistant from Shinjuku. What was his part in all this, if any? Glancing at her watch, Annie realized Scarlett was late, but not that late.

There was still time.

And anyway, Annie reminded herself as she passed into the cool heart of the shrine itself, *you don't even know what Scarlett looks like these days.*

Shrouded in shadow, the inner shrine's contrast with the sunlit courtyard behind was even more extreme. All was silent but for the muffled sound of hands being clapped in prayer.

Annie stepped aside, near a wall, the better to watch without intruding on the worship of strangers. One by one, men and women, smart and scruffy, plus the occasional tourist, stepped up to a rail and tossed a few coins into a long wooden box, bowed twice, then clapped twice, their claps creating an impromptu orchestra of prayer.

All bowed again, some clapped once, others didn't. She'd never seen prayer like this. It had no preaching, no bibles or hymns, no one told anyone to stand up or sit down. She had to admit, it appealed to her.

The steady flow of people bowing and clapping had almost lulled Annie into a reverie, when a slim, dark, Western-looking girl tossed her coins into the offering box and bowed twice, her face composed and serious.

There was something about her profile that caught Annie's eye. Her nose, Annie decided. The girl had Lou's ski-slope nose.

Her hair was deep brown, cropped in a gamine cut, and though she was poised and undeniably pretty, far more poised than most young women of her age, she lacked that indefinable fame-making *something*.

Call it an aura, charisma, whatever . . . this young woman didn't have it. Staring at the young woman in her baggy jeans and loose black top, Annie wondered at what point the hunger for fame had drained out of her, at what point Scarlett had known she needed to move on.

Gone was the gaucheness Annie had seen in the autographed photo of Scarlett and Bree O'Shaughnessey with Leonardo DiCaprio, gone also was the angelic beauty of the child model. In their place was serenity, an unexpected confidence that had turned Scarlett from a girl into a woman.

This was the person Annie had traveled three-quarters of the way around the world to find. Annie was surprised to feel a degree of anger on Lou's behalf and, bizarrely enough, Arabella's. Although it would be going too far to say she felt anger for Rufus.

Whether Annie's stare caused the young woman to turn, she didn't know. Whatever, when she saw the woman straight on, Annie knew without a doubt that she was looking at Lou's half sister.

Scarlett had the same ice blue eyes as Lou. Eyes she'd seen both laugh and cry, eyes that could fix you with a stare Lou used to advantage in meetings, scaring the living daylights out of those who didn't know what a soft touch she could be. Eyes that looked altogether colder on Rufus Ulrich.

Something flickered across Scarlett's face.

Resignation, sorrow, or determination, it could have been any or all three. When she gave Annie the tiniest bow, then turned and walked out into the sunlight, Annie assumed she was meant to follow.

When Annie caught up, Scarlett was standing by a circular prayer wall, built around the trunk of an old tree. Thousands of small wooden prayer plaques, each with a message scrawled onto its bare surface, hung from metal hooks on the wall. Scarlett was writing slowly, far more carefully than she'd written the place and time on the torn sheet of paper her friend had delivered to Annie's room.

Knowing the balance of power didn't lie with her, Annie hung back to read the prayers of other worshippers. Most were in Japanese, but a few were in English or French. Those Annie could understand asked for luck or help in difficult times, or for a child to do well in his exams. One asked for a son to get a good job.

Finishing her prayer, Scarlett hung it carefully on the wall and, without so much as glancing at Annie, walked over to the gift shop.

Feeling vaguely guilty, Annie slipped around to the other side of the tree to read Scarlett's prayer. In bold black ink, between a prayer for recovery from breast cancer and a wish to pass a driving test, was written *Let me find peace.*

Maybe Annie didn't need to feel guilty about reading it after all? She couldn't help but wonder whether the message was intended for the gods or her.

forty

Annie followed Scarlett to the gift shop. She was holding a tiny bag of embroidered silk and handing over three one-hundred yen coins to a monk in exchange for it.

"What's that for?" asked Annie. It wasn't how she'd intended to open this conversation, but it would do.

Scarlett smiled, and her faced opened.

She was beautiful. Much more so than Lou. "It's an amulet," she said. "To protect against evil." Her voice surprised Annie, who'd been expecting the uptown twang of a Park Avenue princess. The accent was hard to pin down, diluted by years of living a transatlantic life. It even held an inflection of Japanese.

Annie smiled back. "And those?" she asked. Keep the conversation going; it was one of the basic rules.

"For safety in busy traffic," Scarlett said, adding, "No, really," when she saw Annie's expression.

"Traffic?"

"That's the thing about *kami no michi*," said Scarlett. "It's an extremely practical religion."

"*Kami* what?"

"Shinto," said Scarlett. "*Kami no michi*, the way of the Gods."

"Do they have an amulet for period cramps?"

Scanning a line of amulets arranged on the counter, Scarlett selected one. "Relief of pain," she said. "It's close enough. You shouldn't open it," she added. "In case it lets out the magic."

She picked up another amulet. "Good luck in exams," said Scarlett.

"And this"—she picked up a pencil—"is blessed for help passing tests. There are charms for foreign trips, air travel, family difficulties, uniting a couple, you name it."

"Which is the one for uniting a couple?" Annie asked.

Scarlett handed her one.

"Better make that two," said Annie, handing over one thousand yen. She didn't think a pouch of embroidered silk was going to make a blind bit of difference to the havoc she'd allowed Tony Panton to wreak on her own and Chris's life over the past ten days. No, on the havoc she'd allowed herself to wreak . . .

Still, anything was worth a try.

In the courtyard behind the gift shop, a wedding party was posing for photos. A Japanese girl and a blond boy were dressed for a full Shinto ceremony, the girl's father smiling through gritted teeth, the boy's mother in head-to-toe lilac, better suited to the mother of a groom in a Richard Curtis film. She looked dazed with jet lag and culture shock. Annie wanted to go across and say, *It gets better, believe me.*

She couldn't begin to imagine how her own parents would react in the same situation—with tears, probably.

"We should talk," said Scarlett.

"Yes. We should."

"Somewhere quiet."

As Scarlett passed the wedding party, she stared at the bride and something wistful crossed her face. But she said nothing, and soon the group was far behind them and Annie and Scarlett had reached the park beyond the shrine.

"First," said Scarlett, when Annie chose a bench, "I'm sorry about that." She nodded to the Band-Aid on Annie's forehead.

"And second?"

"You've found me. Now what?"

"That's up to you," Annie said, itching to turn on her tape recorder. She was sitting next to a major news story. Annie could turn this into promotion, security, three million dollars from Rufus bloody Ulrich, possibly even another Press Award. But loyalty to Lou kept the machine in her jacket pocket.

"It's not up to me, though. Is it?"

"Yes," said Annie. "It is." She'd made her decision. *Annie Anderson passes up a story, shocker.* "I'm here for Lou."

"How do you know Loulou?"

"She's my best friend," Annie said fiercely.

Scarlett flinched. "How is she?"

"All right, I guess," said Annie, making herself relax. "Scared for you. Worried . . ."

"Worried?"

The incredulity in Scarlett's voice shocked Annie. She knew Lou had resented Scarlett and blamed Arabella for replacing her own mother. It just hadn't occurred to her that Scarlett would know. God, she'd only been a child at the time.

"I wouldn't be here," said Annie, "if Lou wasn't worried sick."

"Rufus didn't send you?"

"Uh-uh." Annie shook her head. "As I already told your friend, it's the reverse. Rufus wants me off the case."

"Case?"

"*Story,*" said Annie, amending it the moment she saw Scarlett's face.

"You won't tell him?"

"I promised your friend I wouldn't."

"I know, Akio said. He doesn't believe you and didn't want me to come. I didn't think I had a choice, thought maybe I could persuade you to leave me alone."

"Persuade away," said Annie. "And you could start with Akio. He must be someone if he's prepared to try to scare me off. So tell me who he is."

Scarlett couldn't keep her face from softening.

"He's my fiancé."

My fiancé? Annie had thought she was one step ahead, but she hadn't seen that one coming. Her eyes flickered to the hands the young woman kept folded together.

"There's no ring," said Scarlett. "Don't worry, you didn't miss that. I am going to marry him, though. One way or another. That girl back there"— Scarlett nodded toward the shrine—"That's going to be me."

"So what about the other one, the photographer's assistant? Don't tell me he wasn't really your boyfriend. . . ."

"I wish," said Scarlett. "I was lonely, Mike was available. No, Mike exists all right, but it wasn't a love thing, it was a lonely-in-Tokyo thing. We split up ages ago. I guess you could say I finished it, but I'm not sure Mike even noticed. He doesn't believe in being *exclusive.* He forgot to tell me that before we started."

Been there, thought Annie. *Done that, had the tests.*

"And Akio?"

"We've been friends for a while. I already knew I was in love with Akio when I went to Mike's flat in Shinjuku and found him in bed with someone else. Not that Mike knew about Akio, he's part of a different crowd."

"What sort of crowd?"

"Oh, it's not what you think. He's not yakuza, or anything. He's a medical student in Sapporo. Mike, on the other hand, only read books with pictures, and even then his lips moved." Scarlett's laugh was more wry than bitter. "Have the police been giving Mike a hard time?"

"He was deported," said Annie. "A couple of weeks before you disappeared."

"I had no idea."

"Did Jess know? About Akio, about your plan?"

Scarlett shook her head. "No way. I wouldn't do that to Jess. She was the first person the police would question. So I thought it was better for her not to know anything. And I wasn't worried about Mike. Mainly 'cause Mike doesn't give a shit about anyone but himself. You know the type."

Annie did.

"And you," said Scarlett. "You went after Jess. And so did that investigator Rufus paid. No, as far as Jess is concerned, I'm . . . well, dead, I guess."

"How nice for Jess," said Annie. Then something else occurred to her. "If you haven't been in contact with Jess how do you know all that? About me and Rufus's private investigator?"

"Lise. She goes out with a friend of a friend of Akio's cousin."

Who the hell was Lise? It rang a bell, but . . .

"She doesn't know I'm alive, either. But she knew I was friends with friends of Akio, and when you showed up at Happy Daze with a photograph of me, she mentioned it to Akio's cousin's friend, who . . . Well, you get the picture."

Shit. Lise was the Australian girl in the damn cake shop.

Annie couldn't believe she'd come so close to an answer on her first day.

"I'm sorry, for Jess," said Scarlett. "I am. Only Akio and I couldn't see any other way. And we left her all my stuff."

Annie decided not to comment on that.

"So that's what all this is about . . . marrying your Japanese boyfriend?"

Scarlett's face clouded, as she hugged her arms around herself. She looked like Lou, hunkered down on her father's sofa on the Upper East Side, having reverted to twelve and sulky.

"You make it sound trivial," said Scarlett. "Like a game."

"And it isn't?" said Annie, regretting it the moment the words were out of her mouth.

"No!"

Annie held up a hand. "For God's sake," she said, and then bit back her anger. "Your face is all over every paper in the world. There's a three-million-dollar reward. Because you're *you*, Scarlett Ulrich. You're famous. . . ."

The girl's wince didn't pass Annie by.

"How long do you think you can get away with it?" Annie demanded. "People like you don't just disappear; it doesn't work like that anymore. Times change, you're not Lord Lucan."

Scarlett frowned and Annie realized the young woman was far too young to know who she was talking about.

"And now someone's been charged with your murder, and you're sitting next to me in the September sunshine. That can't be right."

"I know," said Scarlett. "But he killed the others." She hesitated. "Well, I imagine he did and this was the only way."

"It was Akio's idea?" said Annie.

Scarlett shook her head. "Mine," she said. "When the others went missing and the *Tokyo Herald* started talking about the Roppongi Ripper . . . I realized that everything about me fitted the target and knew this was the chance I'd been looking for."

"Looking?"

Scarlett nodded. "It was too soon and I hadn't saved as much as I wanted. I was hoping to save fifty thousand before I vanished. That's enough to start again."

"In Japan?"

"We're going to move north, near where Akio's parents live, a long way from here. Lie low for a very long time. I'm learning Japanese, even how to write it."

She sounded so young, Annie thought. Maybe blind faith was what you needed when everything else had run out.

"And then?" Annie asked.

"Change my name, my life, my nationality, if I can do it without drawing attention." She stared Annie straight in the eye, the way Lou did sometimes. Using her glare to hide the insecurity within.

Annie was spooked.

"It will be as if Scarlett Ulrich never existed." And before Annie could say anything, she added, "I've been looking for a way out for a long time, even thought about killing myself."

Annie sighed, struggling to prevent irritation from crossing her face.

Irina Krodt, the teenage prostitute Annie befriended, had wanted to kill herself too. Annie had less sympathy for poor-me little rich girls.

"I know," said Scarlett. "I know what you're thinking. Everyone thinks it. Poor spoiled little rich girl, it must be so hard having a trust fund, and going to private schools, and attending premieres, and having parents who only want the best for you. . . . I'd think that too, from outside. But it's different on the inside."

Annie nodded. It was always different on the inside.

"Anyway . . . I swallowed a whole load of pills, and then made myself throw them up again. I'm good at that, throwing up. The truth is I wasn't brave enough to kill myself, and I didn't want to die, I just wanted Scarlett to . . ."

"All this happened when?"

"After Milan. That's why I came to Tokyo. Oh, I knew I didn't have any choice, Rufus made me. He can't stand the fact my career is over. It's been dead for years, but I only worked that out a while ago. I agreed to come to get him off Arabella's case and because I can't think of anywhere farther away from Rufus than here."

Rufus again, Annie thought.

It had always fascinated her the way Lou called Nina by her first name. Lou had never called Rufus *Dad* either, but that was different. Lou hated Rufus. It was beginning to look like Scarlett's feelings weren't that different.

"Why did you want to get away from Rufus?"

The girl's eyes narrowed. "You'd want to get away from him, too," she said. "Everyone does in the end. Lou has no idea how lucky she is."

Annie couldn't help herself. *"All Lou ever wanted was her father!"*

Scarlett's smile was bleak. "She's welcome to him. Let me give you a snapshot of life with Rufus."

When Scarlett had finished, the sun was high in the sky, the gravel drive to the shrine was crowded with visitors, and the girl seated in front of Annie was close to tears. She didn't claim he beat her, she didn't claim he sexually abused her, but she made it clear that Rufus Ulrich didn't understand boundaries or other people's free will.

Scarlett had lived the life of a puppet. With Rufus pulling the strings no one else saw. She lived and died on his smile and frown, until she was exhausted from trying to live up to his expectations.

When Scarlett's story reached Milan and the Mantolini casting Annie felt like crying herself. After Italy, and the groping of middle-aged men at the endless parties Scarlett was expected to attend, having dinner with a hyper-polite Japanese executive for two hundred dollars a time didn't seem like such a bad deal.

"Now do you understand why you have to let me go?"

Annie looked at the girl. There was none of the horror she'd seen look-ing into the eyes of Irina Krodt or Patty Lang. Just tiredness, loneliness, and a fear of the known. Fear that Annie might make her return to the life she'd only recently escaped. Already Scarlett looked different and it was more than the hair. She looked thinner and . . .

"Jess told me Rufus made you have a boob job."

Scarlett looked hurt. "He did."

Unable to stop the reflex, Annie glanced at the girl's nonexistent chest, as if to say, *Where is it then?*

Shifting so her back was to the path, Scarlett began to lift her baggy T-shirt.

"No," said Annie. "It's all right. You don't have t—" She stopped, alarmed. After all, Tokyo was hardly the place for public displays of naked breasts. Es-pecially not in the outer gardens of the city's most famous and revered shrine. And then Annie realized what Scarlett was really showing her.

Row after row of tightly wound bandages.

"You've bound them flat?" she asked, horrified.

Scarlett smiled for the first time in an hour and shook her head. "I've had the implants removed," she said. "It took more than a third of my money, but I'm glad they're gone." She let her T-shirt drop. "Satisfied?"

Slowly, Annie nodded.

"You aren't going to make me go back, are you?"

Annie shook her head. "No," she said. "I'm not." Somewhere between the tales of bed-wetting and bulimia, way before Milan, cocaine, and the boob job, Annie had decided she had no right to play God with Scarlett's life. People had been doing that since the day the girl was born. But what the hell was she going to tell Lou? ·

"Your sister," she said. "I have to . . ."

"I want to show you something," said Scarlett, pulling a crumpled square of card from her back pocket and handing it to Annie.

It was a photograph, faded by the years. An image of two blondes, their heads tight together, both smiling for the camera. One, six years old and cherubic, beamed adoringly from beneath a halo of blond curls at a gawky sixteen-year-old, who smiled tightly at the camera, her hair already scrunched up into what Annie considered Lou's trademark messy bun.

The little girl had her arms clamped tight around the elder girl's neck, as if scared someone might force her to let go.

"Wait here," said Scarlett. "I'll be right back."

As Annie watched the girl vanish into the crowd around the entrance to the shrine, she turned the picture over and over in her hand. *Casa de la Torre, 1992.* Leaving the photo with her had to be intentional, decided Annie, as she rummaged for her own mobile.

It wasn't proof, not really. Annie could have found it at the flat or been given it by one of Scarlett's friends. Just because she had a photograph to show Lou didn't mean Scarlett was still alive. But Annie knew Lou would understand what it meant, so she fired up her Nokia anyway.

Annie's mobile might have been unable to get a connection her entire time in Tokyo, but its camera still worked. Holding the faded image in front of it, Annie clicked, and then clicked again, taking two or three shots for luck. Though the photo was old, there was no doubting the identity of the two girls now staring from the screen of her mobile.

When Scarlett returned she was no longer alone. Akio, not much taller than Scarlett and clad in jeans and a leather jacket, had one arm wrapped protectively around her waist. Scarlett's body was relaxed into his, and they walked in unison. Annie wondered how long he'd been waiting. She guessed he'd been there all along, hovering in the distance, in case his girl needed protecting.

"Hello, Akio," she said. "Where's the gun?"

He blushed and Annie decided she'd probably been unfair.

"It's okay," she said.

He looked at her through floppy hair. Now that Annie saw him in bright daylight and without the power of his weapon, Akio looked not much more than sixteen or seventeen, despite the fact Annie now knew he was twenty-three. He also looked besotted.

"Your head," he said. "I'm sorry about yesterday."

Annie shrugged.

"I do it for Scarlett."

"I know," said Annie, shocked to feel herself on the verge of tears. What the hell was happening to Annie Anderson, hard-bitten hack?

"This is for you," Scarlett said, holding out a pale yellow paper bag, covered in Japanese script.

"For me?"

"Well, no. Not you. I want you to give it to Loulou for me."

There was no need for Annie to look to know what was inside the bag. It contained the silk-embroidered amulet Annie had seen Scarlett buy earlier.

"Charms against evil," said Scarlett. "I thought she might need it."

"What am I supposed to tell her?"

"Nothing," Scarlett said. "She doesn't need to know where it came from. I just need to know she'll get it."

Annie didn't answer. She was going to tell Lou anyway—for so many reasons, some of them selfish—but she would make sure Lou told no one else. Lou was Annie's friend. Annie would betray Scarlett that far, but no further.

"Annie . . ."

She was staring at the photograph still lying on Annie's denim-clad knee.

"Oh," said Annie. "You'll be wanting this back."

"Please," Scarlett said. "I never go anywhere without it."

"Not even into your new life?"

Scarlett smiled an enormous face-splitting beam that briefly transformed her into the six-year-old cherub from the cover of a platinum-selling album.

"Not even there," she said.

forty · one

It took Annie about five minutes to pack. She simply bundled up her dirty clothes and stuffed them into the bottom of her suitcase, then folded her unused dress and jacket on top. She crammed what remained of her Japanese tampons into one corner and arranged her laptop charger and mobile phone wires so they didn't look too much like a bomb, should anyone scan her case at Narita Airport.

A quick skim of the nearby table to check she hadn't missed anything obvious, and a clatter of opening drawers while she confirmed they were empty, and Annie was done. A pile of carefully shredded photographs in the bin, a couple of empty mineral water bottles, and that day's edition of the *Tokyo Herald* were all the evidence left of her stay.

She debated stealing the tiny toothpastes with their cutesy graphics and kanji characters from the bathrooms for Lou, who liked that sort of thing, but decided not to. She'd buy her friend something at the airport.

One of those smiling little cat gods, with upraised paw and wide grin. A peace offering. A way of saying sorry for screwing up their friendship and being afraid to face a confrontation with Chris. He wasn't Tony and she wasn't the scared little teenager she used to be. Although now might be too late to realize that.

The elevator down was empty apart from a uniformed girl. Annie tried to remember to return her bow before exiting the elevator.

Annie wasn't sad to be leaving.

The Akasaka Prince was an amazing hotel and Tokyo an amazing city. Stranger than any city she'd ever been to. Japan was exotic and familiar, and its memory would stay with her forever.

Despite the shambles she'd made of her own life, the fact she had no story for Rebecca, and, once the news about her splitting with Chris was out, her own mother would probably never talk to her again. Despite all that, Annie was proud of herself.

Annie Anderson, the small-town girl who blew it all at seventeen and flunked out over some creep who didn't know the meaning of the word no, had survived her week in the strangest of cities. Or at least, had survived enough to do what she set out to do. Find Scarlett for Lou. Alive.

At the desk, a smartly suited man bowed as Annie handed back her key card and the little cardboard slip case in which it had come.

"Checking out, madam?"

Annie smiled.

There was more on the minibar bill than she'd imagined, mostly alcohol and chocolate, although Annie was surprised to see she'd also eaten a packet of pistachios. After trying to remember when, Annie hastily decided not to bother.

Approving the bill, Annie handed over her company Amex and returned the man's bow when he handed her back her card, holding it precisely by its edges.

"I hope you enjoyed your stay?"

"Very much."

A porter took her suitcase without being asked. Annie had only one suitcase, plus her bag and laptop.

"Limousine bus?" asked the porter.

She produced her ticket, already booked from the bell desk the night before, and he whisked away her luggage, standing guard over it outside the hotel's front door. An hour to the airport, an hour buying Lou's little china cat, and Annie would be gone, on the next flight for London, and then on to Milan.

She breathed a sigh of relief.

"Miss Anderson?"

The voice behind her was abrupt, a voice used to being obeyed. Annie loathed it, before she'd even had time to remember where she'd heard it before.

Rufus Ulrich.

Turning, she looked at the man. Forcing her stare to sweep across his clothes, from silk tie to immaculately shined shoes, as she had seen Rebecca do to an incompetent driver in New York.

"Yes?" she said.

"I didn't see you at the press conference."

"That's because I wasn't there."

His eyes narrowed. "I'd heard you were in Tokyo."

"From your pet Australian?" Annie wasn't worried about upsetting the man, not after what she'd heard from Scarlett.

"I don't know why Luella bothered," said Rufus. "It's not like there was anything you could do."

"Maybe she just wanted to help."

Rufus snorted. "That girl's never helped anyone in her life. I don't know what she's paying you, but she's not getting it from me."

"Never got much from you, has she?" said Annie. "What with you being so much more interested in Scarlett."

"You know nothing about it."

"I know enough," Annie said, "to understand why Lou hates you. And she's not paying me, she's my friend . . ."

"I'm supposed to believe that's why you're here?"

"Yes," said Annie. "I'm here because Lou's my best friend."

And because I'd rather open someone else's can of worms than deal with my own, and because I was too gutless to face a fight with Chris, so now I've blown the only relationship I ever wanted . . .

But Annie kept that to herself.

"Scarlett was probably already dead," said Rufus, but he seemed to be talking to himself. "I was too late. I should never have let her come to Tokyo."

"You mean . . . you should never have sent her."

And Annie watched a wound open inside Rufus that time could never close. Turning, he walked away. Whatever he saw as his glance swept blindly across the vast lobby, she doubted it was a Japanese hotel.

She hadn't even meant to hurt Lou's father, though there was no doubt he deserved it. She had simply spoken the truth, as told by Arabella and Jess, long before Annie had ever heard it from Scarlett herself.

forty · two

Milan's Piazza Affari was crowded with dark-blue Mercedes, parked nose to nose and bumper to bumper. Annie wondered how the hell their drivers imagined they would get out of there when the building that housed the second of that night's Versace shows emptied in a few moments' time.

She'd been hoping to identify Lou's driver and wait for Lou in the car, rather than risk being seen hanging around outside by Rebecca or the rest of the *Handbag* posse. So far, without luck, all the drivers Annie approached denied having heard of Lou McCartney or *The Post*.

It was Monday night and Rebecca knew Annie was due in from Tokyo; her PA had booked the ticket after all. She just didn't yet know Annie had already arrived, and that was the way it had to stay, until tomorrow at least.

Annie needed to see Lou first, because without Lou's agreement Annie would have to admit she'd returned empty-handed from Tokyo—and Rebecca would not consider that a good look.

Having flown for seventeen hours straight, with the briefest touchdown in London to add insult to jet-lagged injury, Annie had come straight from Linate Airport, another look Rebecca would not appreciate. And as if that wasn't bad enough, touching down at Heathrow had put her within spitting distance of her own bed and instead she'd had to fly on here.

Not that her own bed was that promising an alternative right now. What with Chris and all; except Chris was in Milan himself, handling UK press for Mariolina Mantolini's show. Annie tried not to think about that, because it was all just too complicated.

She didn't even know if Lou had received the text saying Annie needed to see her the moment Versace ended, and was standing outside, right now, in the far corner of the piazza.

As the doors of the Borsa flew open, fashionistas began to flood out. After a week in Tokyo the sight of the Milan fashion circus at full tilt hurt Annie's eyes. It was not a black season, and the kaleidoscope of outfits that burst from the sandstone building made Annie feel exactly what she was, a shabby mess in serious need of a shower, blow-dry, and clean clothes.

Still no reply from Lou.

God, thought Annie, *please let Lou find me before Rebecca does.* And then Annie's phone rang and order was restored to her world.

"Annie!" screeched Lou. "I'm outside, where are you?"

Lou's fury over Chris and the vicious voice mail were obviously forgotten. Annie sighed. It must be so much easier to have anger that simply flared and then burned itself out.

"Where are *you*?" asked Annie, and then she saw her friend, standing on the steps, waving and looking around wildly.

"For God's sake," hissed Annie. "Stop yelling my name. Rebecca might hear. I'm near the back, to your right."

She watched as Lou scanned the square, looking for a dark head in a sea of dark heads. When she thought Lou's gaze was nearing her position, Annie raised her hand as discreetly as possible.

"Got you," said Lou, hurtling down the steps, ignoring everyone who turned to speak as she passed.

Back in Lou's room at Hotel Straf, Annie unzipped her suitcase on the cold concrete floor and pulled out a large brown envelope. It had arrived at the Akasaka Prince the night before Annie left Tokyo, addressed to Ms. A. Anderson, although the envelope inside was marked *Lou McCartney*.

Annie had known who it was from but opened it anyway, which made her feel even more guilty, because dozens of tiny envelopes addressed to *Loulou* tumbled out. It was as if she'd ransacked someone's personal diary.

But she'd had no choice.

Getting on a plane from the Far East and carrying a parcel without even checking its contents was how people ended up in jail. The envelope told Annie something else. Scarlett had known Annie would break her promise and tell Lou, and so Scarlett had decided to tell Loulou herself.

"Okay," said Lou. "So what happened to your head?"

"Long story."

Her friend nodded, willing to let it go for now. "Vodka, gin, whiskey, brandy, or all four?" she asked.

"I'll have the vodka," Annie said. "Lots of ice, forget the tonic."

Lou smiled nervously. Annie and neat vodka was a bad sign, but she emptied a double-shot Smirnoff into what looked like a toothbrush mug and added ice. "Sorry," she said. "Room service took the old glasses this morning and forgot to replace them."

Annie clocked the "glasses" but didn't call Lou on it. Instead, she took a swig, choking as the vodka hit the back of her throat. She knew alcohol might finish her off and she didn't much care.

"That bad?" asked Lou.

"Yes and no," Annie said, sitting herself on Lou's bed. It wasn't much softer than the floor. "Just spent seventeen hours on a plane, give or take airport lounges, with a stopover at Heathrow. No sleep, relationship fucked, other than that . . . yeah, I'm fine."

"Let's talk about Chris in a minute, shall we?"

Annie nodded, not caring that Lou could see tears glisten in her eyes. "All right," said Annie. "We'll deal with Scarlett first."

Lou frowned. "I know she's dead," she said. "You don't have to tell me. Rufus called. You know that PI he hired? It's case closed, Itou's been charged with the five murders. It was on the news. Not that I don't appreciate you wanting to break it to me in person."

Annie felt tears well up again and clutched Scarlett's envelope to her chest. Then she thought of something.

"I want you to look at this," said Annie, pulling out her Nokia. Scrolling through the pictures she found the image she wanted and handed her phone to Lou.

Lou stared at its screen, her eyes struggling to focus. Realization dawned and as it did her vision blurred. She looked at Annie. "What does this mean?"

"It's you and Scarlett."

"I know what it is. It's the holiday from hell in Majorca, with Arabella and Rufus's bloody mother. I don't even remember this being taken. Where did you find it?"

"It's Scarlett's most treasured possession," Annie said slowly. "Lou, she worships you."

Lou's blue eyes turned glittery and she blinked rapidly. It could have been the strain of Lou focusing on the Nokia's screen in the hotel's tastefully subdued lighting, but Annie didn't think so.

Finally, Lou looked up. "She's not dead. Is she?"

Annie shook her head.

"But then why . . . ?"

"You can't tell anyone," said Annie firmly. "Not Arabella, and not Rufus."

"As if . . ."

"Not even Nina."

Lou looked doubtful.

Annie gave Lou her hard stare. "Not even Nina," she repeated, and then handed over the envelope she'd been clutching for the past ten minutes. "These are for you. Read, and then decide."

The package contained a bundle of letters, a mixture of plain envelopes and patterned. My Little Pony and Barbie notelets gave way to pink flowery paper and then sheets carelessly torn from what looked like school exercise books and stuffed in the nearest envelope available.

There were thirty-four in all, the first written in the cumbersome writing of a small girl, maybe six years old, the last in the confident hand of an eighteen-year-old who was changing her life for the better. Everyone, except the last, was signed Lettie. The last had been written only thirty-six hours earlier.

As Lou read, Annie finished first one neat vodka and then another. After that, she filled Lou's bath to soak away the plane's grime.

Hot water poured from the tap to scald Annie's feet and she'd just topped up the bubbles for a second time when Lou came in, put down the toilet lid, and sat on it. Her eyes were red, her face puffy, and she'd chewed her bottom lip.

"Scarlett wrote to me," she said unnecessarily.

Annie nodded, smiled. "I know."

"All those years, I envied her so much and she was writing to me."

"Don't blame yourself," said Annie. "You weren't to know. She didn't send them."

"Someone didn't."

It was a good point, one to which neither Lou nor Annie would ever know the answer. Had Scarlett's letters to her big sister been intercepted by Arabella, or had it been childish self-censorship?

"To think I envied her because she had him."

"Really," Annie repeated, "you weren't to know."

"Nina was right," said Lou. "We *were* better off without Rufus."

Annie smiled, tears welling in her own eyes. Tears of fatigue, sympathy, and self-pity. But mostly tears of relief, as the Lou she had grown to love over the past five years reappeared in front of her.

"I thought Scarlett had it all," said Lou, shaking her head.

"Scarlett has what she wants now," said Annie. "She's so happy, you should . . ." Annie caught herself. Lou would never see Scarlett again, no one would, the girl was turning herself into someone else.

"Trust me," Annie said. "She's happy. Her only regret is you."

"What about Arabella?"

"Hardly mentioned her. Forget Arabella. If Scarlett can, you can."

"I can't believe the boob job," said Lou, incredulous. "How could Rufus do that to her?"

"She's undone it," said Annie. "I saw the bandages. Scarlett's systematically undoing everything he did to her life."

Lou nodded, rocking back and forth.

"That's not all, is it?" said Lou. A couple of minutes had passed and Annie was nodding off in the slowly cooling bathwater. Her head hurt, her eyes ached, and Lou had insisted on replacing the Band-Aid that decorated her forehead.

"What's not all?"

Lou forced a laugh. "I know you, Annie Anderson," she said. "What about your exclusive? Without Scarlett, all you've got is me. Lou McCartney talks about her murdered sister."

Annie thought about lying and decided against it.

"It would help," she said. "I'm up shit creek otherwise. I don't know who'll be madder, Ken or Rebecca. Not that Ken's my problem these days, but I could do without getting the sack right now. That would just be shit on shit. But if you say no . . ."

She made herself say it.

". . . I'll understand."

"All right," said Lou. "I'll do it. For Scarlett. But give me time. Anyway, you have stuff to do first."

"Stuff?" Annie said.

"Unfinished business," said Lou. "And so do I."

She tossed Annie the toweling robe from the back of the door, and waited while Annie clambered into it, foam still dripping from her body.

"Look," Lou said. "I'm in a relationship that's bad for me. I guess I always knew, but now I really know, and I'm going to do something about it, for good."

Annie frowned. "Russ seemed all right to me."

"Russ?"

"Tall, blond, tanned, guitarist, six foot four, great in bed. About twenty-two?"

"He's long gone," said Lou.

"You only started seeing him six weeks ago," protested Annie. Part of her loved Lou's easy-come, easy-go approach to men. Some days she wished she could adopt it herself. "Who's biting the dust this time?"

"James."

"Bloody hell, you move fast." Annie laughed. "Do I know him?" And then she realized Lou wasn't laughing. She wasn't even smiling; her pale eyes were just sad.

"You don't know him," Lou said. "James is different. He's forty-four, married, has two children, and I've been seeing him for a year. He's not the first but I promise—I promise you and I promise me—he's going to be the last."

"Lou . . ."

"I know," said Lou. "You're my best friend and I should have told you before. About the real men in my life. I've been looking for something I was never going to find. Something I know now was never even worth looking for. Annie, I'm sorry. There's so much I've never said."

Annie wasn't one to talk.

"So . . . you can crash in my room tonight, all right? But I need you to bugger off now while I make this call."

"No problem," said Annie. "I'll go see if the bar's still open."

Lou shook her head. "There's something else you've got to do first. Chris is in the hotel across the road. You should go over there and talk to him."

Oh shit, thought Annie, realizing she'd just been ambushed.

"It's my price," said Lou. "For giving you an interview . . ." She hesitated on the edge of saying something else.

"Go on," Annie said.

"You didn't mean it, did you?"

"Mean what?"

"The things you said to him."

Shame crept up Annie's face. "Oh," she said. "Chris told you what I said in the voice mail message?"

"Of course he did. How could you?"

"I don't know. Really, I don't." All Annie wanted to do was hide, from Lou's sadness and from herself, but there was nowhere to go and wherever she ran, she always caught up with herself eventually.

"Did you mean it?"

"A little," Annie admitted. "At the time. But not now, no."

"Good," said Lou, face serious, looking more like Scarlett than ever. "I won't let you sabotage this. You have no idea how much Chris loves you."

Annie wanted to bawl.

She knew it, of course she knew it. He was nice, he was decent, he didn't go to bed with total strangers, he didn't . . . Well, he didn't do most of the cruel things Annie had believed all men did.

"He's staying at The Gray," Lou said. "Across the road. Room 301."

Annie didn't rate her chances of Lou letting her back in again if she left to let Lou make her call and didn't go to Chris. All the same, she didn't want to go right now, before she'd had time to think about it. And yet, what was there to think about? She loved him and she'd treated him like shit. She had no option but to beg.

If she was Chris, she wouldn't take her back.

But Annie had to try.

Grabbing a last pair of clean knickers from her case, Annie pulled that day's clothes back on. There was no alternative until she found a dry cleaner.

"I probably won't be that long," said Annie.

"Just talk to him," Lou said. She put out her hand, to block Annie's bolt for the door. "Look," she added. "Whatever happens, I just wanted to say . . . you know, thanks. For going to Tokyo and everything . . . For finding Scarlett."

Annie smiled.

"It's okay," she said, hugging her friend and feeling Lou's ribs like twigs beneath a fine jersey top. "I didn't find Scarlett, though. Remember?"

Lou nodded. "But I need you to do one more thing."

"Of course," said Annie. "As long as it doesn't involve Rufus!" She hadn't told Lou about running into him in Tokyo and didn't plan to.

"Fix it," Lou said. "With Chris, I mean."

The smile froze on Annie's face.

"Or don't. End it if that's what you need to do. But do it properly. He's one of my oldest friends and you're my best friend and I love you both. Please don't let it finish like this. . . ."

For a second Annie held Lou's gaze, then let her eyes drop to the floor. "I'd better leave my suitcase here," she said, when she summoned the courage to look up again.

"Yes," said Lou. "I think you had."

And somewhere inside Annie felt her heart snap.

forty · three

Shutting her mobile, Lou tossed it onto her bed and picked up Scarlett's present. Her sister had given her the courage to do that, make the break and swear to herself that she had the courage to remake her life.

Lou turned the tiny bag of embroidered silk over and over in her hands. "Don't open it," said Scarlett's last letter. "You'll let the luck escape."

By now, Lou had read each of the letters so many times she knew every word by heart. A rainbow of raw, adolescent emotion in silver, blue, and pink handwriting. It was hard to believe how much Lou and Scarlett had shared without ever speaking. Scarlett might have had the money and the dresses, the ponies and the lifestyle, but she'd also lost her father when Rufus moved on to a new wife and a new daughter, forever searching for next year's model. What she hadn't lost was Rufus's control over her life.

Lou now had little doubt which of them got the best deal.

As for Annie, she'd been gone for thirty minutes and that could only be a good sign. Lou had hoped Chris would take Annie back, she just wasn't sure how Annie would react to his new set of rules. They'd be all right, Lou was sure of it. For a start, Chris was learning how to handle Annie. Plus, he had something she wanted—him.

Strangely, finishing with James hadn't hurt as badly as Lou thought it would. As badly as it had hurt in the past, when her married lovers had done it to her. In fact, his anger at being phoned at home only made it easier.

Maybe Clem was right all those years ago. Perhaps she really had been looking for a father figure to fill the gap in her life. If so, she was well and truly over it. Lou could picture James standing in silence in his dressing gown in the sitting room of his huge house on Liverpool Road as she told him it was over.

No, she'd said, it wasn't that she wanted more commitment from him. She didn't want Friday nights or the occasional weekend. This wasn't about birthdays or Christmases or bank holiday weekends.

She was over unobtainable men.

Lou wanted a proper relationship, with someone who was available to give her the love she had finally realized she deserved. She wanted a relationship, all right. Just not with him.

And as he stood frozen in the deep dark night of his six-bedroom house, Lou heard a voice in the background. *"Who is it, love? Is everything all right?"*

It was a woman's voice, coming closer.

"I . . ." said James, his voice muffled, hand now over the receiver. And Lou hung up, never to hear herself described as a wrong number again.

Even knowing Lou would never speak to her again if she chickened out, Annie almost did a runner. *You're a coward,* she told herself, as she wandered the streets around The Gray for thirty minutes and tried to bully herself into going inside. *You think you're so tough. Really you're just pathetic.*

Then Annie realized she was talking to herself and a doorman was eyeing her suspiciously from the far side of a huge glass window. So she took a deep breath and pushed her way through the swing doors.

"Buona sera," Annie said confidently, before marching straight to the elevator. As usual, in Italian hotels, nobody stopped her and nobody asked if she belonged. Whoever said hotels were safe?

Riding the elevator all night seemed like an attractive option. But Annie stepped out when the doors slid open at the third floor and walked to the end of the corridor. She knocked without giving herself time to think or prepare her speech. Even a moment's hesitation and she would have run.

After a few seconds, there was the sound of a lock being turned, and the door opened to reveal Chris, looking sleepy.

His hair stuck up on end and tiredness dulled his eyes. An all-purpose hotel robe had been pulled around his body. It looked even worse than the crappy blue toweling job his mother had given him years ago. Annie had intended to replace it this Christmas. Now she wasn't so sure. The blue dressing gown was part of him.

He stared at Annie for a second, adjusting his eyes to the brightness of the corridor and the person standing in front of him. All she could see in his expression was caution, and a wariness, as if he imagined she might punch him.

That hurt.

"Chris . . ."

"D'you want to come in?"

Annie nodded. "Yes, please. If that's all right?"

He stepped aside, holding the door for her. It took all of Annie's will to pass without touching him.

"There's nowhere to sit, I'm afraid," he said, showing the bed. One side was rumpled, the other, the side Annie had begun to think of as hers, strewn with magazines and papers. Just as she had, he'd already started to sleep only on one side, even when alone, and he'd been alone a lot lately.

"That's fine," she said, moving a magazine. She tried not to think it mattered when he sat himself on the opposite side.

"You didn't tell me you were coming."

"It was last minute," said Annie. "The police charged someone with Scarlett's murder. I had some notes to write up, some calls to make. Then I headed out."

He nodded. "It was in the papers. So Scarlett's dead?"

Annie glanced away. "No one will see her again," she said. It was the truth.

"Poor Lou," said Chris, and Annie remembered why she loved him. "Your forehead," he said, reaching up, then hesitated.

"I slipped," said Annie. "It looks worse than it is."

Chris looked like he wanted to say something to that.

"Obviously," she said hastily, "I don't expect to stay here with you." It wasn't intended to sound the way it came out. "Sorry," she said, getting to her feet. "I'm screwing this up. I'd better go."

"Yes," he said. "You had."

"Chris."

"Don't," said Chris. "Just don't, okay?"

"*I'm sorry.*"

"It's all right, really."

"*No,* I mean it. Making that call, I don't know what . . ."

"Yes," he said. "You do." And the look he gave Annie was not anger, fury, or hatred, just sadness. It physically hurt.

"*I didn't mean it.*"

"Oh, Annie," he said sadly. "You did. I know you. That's the point."

You don't know me, she wanted to scream. Only Chris did. He knew her all too well. That was what this was all about.

"Annie . . ."

"*Wait,*" she said, surprised by the anger in her voice. If Chris knew her so well, he'd know it was aimed at herself, not him. "*Please, just wait.*"

She could say it or not. Her entire life hung in the balance and Annie wasn't sure she was that brave. "Tony Panton turned up because he's getting divorced. He wanted to make sure I didn't testify against him in court."

Chris was watching her. "Would you?"

"If necessary. I'm going to e-mail his wife and tell her so. It won't come to it, because the moment he knows that he'll settle." Annie took a deep breath. "Look," she said. "I've told you things I've never told anyone. Not even Lou. You can destroy me. All you have to do is tell me that what happened in my teens was my own fault. How do I know you won't?"

"You don't," said Chris. "You just have to trust me."

"I've . . ."

"Never trusted anyone in my life," said Chris, finishing the sentence for her. "I know," he said. "But you have to start sometime."

Do I? thought Annie. "I'm scared," she said. "I love you and it scares me."

Chris smiled. *"You* scare *me,"* he said.

He might have been smiling but he wasn't joking.

"Annie, it's meant to be scary. I want us to be together. I hope forever. That's a long time. How can something like that not scare the living daylights out of anyone? I don't want to lose you, I can't imagine not being with you, but as you said yourself, *this isn't working.*"

Fear rose like nausea from Annie's stomach to her throat. "What d' you mean?"

"What I said."

She waited, terrified of what came next.

"Come on," said Chris. "You know things have to change."

"You're not going to forgive me?" Annie burst out. *Oh no,* she thought. *For God's sake, don't pick now to cry.*

"I'll forgive you anything," he said. "But it's not working like this. So we need to rethink."

Annie stared at him. There'd been moments like this at the beginning, when she knew what came next might change everything, without knowing whether it was for good or ill.

"Rethink it how?"

"Well, I'm crowding you. Aren't I?"

"No, you're . . ."

"Annie . . ."

She shut her mouth, and kept it shut. He was crowding her, it was true.

"So," said Chris. "I'm taking you at your word. I'm moving out . . . It's not over," he added hurriedly. "Unless you want it to be."

Staring at his mattress so Chris wouldn't see the tears running down her chin, Annie shook her head and dislodged enough tears to speckle the bed.

"I've rented a place of my own," he said. "While I look for something more permanent."

"Where?"

"Greenwich."

"South of the river?" Annie was surprised; Chris didn't have a good word to say for South London.

"Greenwich Village."

"But that's . . ."

"New York," he said. "Yes. Remember the company that offered me a job six months ago? Well, I called them up and they nearly bit my hand off. I can take my clients with me and Mariolina says I can handle her U.S. press too. So I'm going. After Paris."

"But that's two weeks!"

"I know."

"You can't go."

"It's the only deal I'm offering. If we've got something worth hanging on to, it'll survive."

Annie stared at him, her heart pounding in her chest. Chris was leaving her, he really was. "You're leaving me," she said quietly.

Standing up, Chris came around the bed to sit beside her. When he slid his arm around her shoulders, Annie thought she was going to break.

"Never," he said. "I couldn't leave you if I wanted to. I'm trying to make it work . . ."

She looked at him.

"Anyway," he said. "You like planes. Look how much time you spent on them when I was trying to get you to stay home."

about the author

Sam Baker has been a writer and editor for
numerous British women's magazines including
New Woman, Chat, and *Take a Break.* After
successfully relaunching the seminal teenage
magazine *Just Seventeen* as *J-17,* she became editor
of the British young women's magazine *Company,*
and then went on to be editor in chief of
Cosmopolitan in the UK. Now editor in chief of *Red*
magazine, she is a regular broadcaster on women's
issues. She lives between Winchester, Hampshire,
and London with her partner, the author Jon
Courtenay Grimwood.